Dealt an Unfortunate Hand

It suddenly dawned on me that this man was waiting for me to say something, and the first tinges of panic tickled my neck. I had no idea what this death card was trying to say. To distract the man I laid down another card. This card was labeled THE TOWER and showed a huge medieval tower being struck by a bolt of lightning, sending its roof off to smash on the ground. People were running out of the tower as if their lives depended on it.

As I looked at this card, there was the tickle of a thought on the edge of my intuition, but it was faint and distant. I called out loudly to my crew, and demanded their presence immediately, furious that they would abandon me at the beginning of a reading. To stall for a little more time I laid down another card—this one labeled JUDGMENT, which depicted three luminescent human figures rising from the earth with outstretched arms toward an angel blowing a trumpet. In one electrifying moment I felt my crew smash back into place and I snapped my head up to look at the man in the chair as I gasped, "Oh my God! . . . You've killed someone!"

BETTER READ
THAN DEAD

A Psychic Eye Mystery

Victoria Laurie

A SIGNET BOOK

SIGNET
Published by New American Library, a division of
Penguin Group (USA) Inc., 375 Hudson Street,
New York, New York 10014, USA
Penguin Group (Canada), 10 Alcorn Avenue, Toronto,
Ontario M4V 3B2, Canada (a division of Pearson Penguin Canada Inc.)
Penguin Books Ltd., 80 Strand, London WC2R 0RL, England
Penguin Ireland, 25 St. Stephen's Green, Dublin 2,
Ireland (a division of Penguin Books Ltd.)
Penguin Group (Australia), 250 Camberwell Road, Camberwell, Victoria 3124,
Australia (a division of Pearson Australia Group Pty. Ltd.)
Penguin Books India Pvt. Ltd., 11 Community Centre, Panchsheel Park,
New Delhi - 110 017, India
Penguin Group (NZ), cnr Airborne and Rosedale Roads, Albany,
Auckland 1310, New Zealand (a division of Pearson New Zealand Ltd.)
Penguin Books (South Africa) (Pty.) Ltd., 24 Sturdee Avenue,
Rosebank, Johannesburg 2196, South Africa

Penguin Books Ltd., Registered Offices:
80 Strand, London WC2R 0RL, England

First published by Signet, an imprint of New American Library,
a division of Penguin Group (USA) Inc.

First Printing, June 2005
10 9 8 7 6 5 4 3 2 1

For my dear friend, mentor and one of the greatest psychics in North America—Kevin Allen. Thank you so much for your ideas, wisdom, gifts and encouragement.

Acknowledgments

I would like to thank the following people for all their help, support and encouragement in the development of this book. My sister, Sandy, who suffers through my jaw-clenching "creative" phases with bold and dogged enthusiasm, my amazing agent, Jim McCarthy, who is just a glass-half-full kind of guy—thank you for your constant reassurance, encouragement, and friendship; my incredible editor Martha Bushko, who has simply fantastic instincts and made so many of my dreams come true, assistant editor Serena Jones; and the rest of the editorial support staff at NAL. "Thanks" is far too simple a word to express how grateful I am to all of you. And Kevin Allen, psychic and friend extraordinaire, who once told me a story about a wedding he attended, and in that way gave me the seeds for one heck of a good tale; Detective Don Swiatkowski of the Royal Oak Police Department, who gave his time and energy to all of my crazy "hypotheticals"; Silas Hudson, who is one of the greatest human beings I have ever known, and who graciously allowed me to capture him in Milo Johnson; my handyman, Dave McKenzie, for being such a wonderful craftsman—you turned my house into a palace and gave me the character I needed to round out the Psychic Eye cast. And of course, my dear friends and supporters who have been the best cheering section a girl could ask for: Laurie Comnes, Thomas Robinson, Kimmie Whelchel, Brian Gorzynski, Joy Austin, Kelly Hale, Drue Rowean, Sheila Doherty, Susan DeLorenzo, and Jon and Naoko Upham. My greatest thanks to you all.

Chapter One

The three cardinal sins to be avoided by *legitimate* professional psychics are:

1. Never make up or alter a psychic message
2. Never betray the trust of a client by revealing details of a reading to others
3. Above all, never, *ever* use your intuitive gift to cause harm to another person

As I stood in the thickening pool of blood leaking from the man I had effectively killed, I couldn't care less that I had flagrantly committed not one, but all three of these cardinal sins. Instead, as my karmic debt for such crimes mounted to new and overwhelming heights, my only thought was the sick satisfaction of finally getting my eye for an eye.

I wasn't always like this, you know. A mere three weeks earlier I could have been the poster child for ethical intuitives. I believed in my work as a professional psychic, giving helpful advice, lending my talent wherever it was needed and using my "gift" for good. All that changed one rainy, autumn afternoon the day before Halloween—don'tcha just love irony?

"Kendal, you *cannot* do this to me!" I complained into my cell phone as I navigated the rainy-day traffic of downtown Royal Oak, Michigan.

"Abby, I've called everybody else. You are the only person left who can pull this off—and besides, you owe me," Kendal answered unsympathetically.

"Oh come on Kendal! Of all the crappy times to call in *that* favor, you had to pick tomorrow night?"

"Not my wedding, sugar. I didn't pick the date; the bride and groom did."

My breathing was coming in short, irregular bursts of frustration. I didn't want to say yes. In fact, I had a very strong feeling I should say no, but Kendal, another professional psychic, was in a jam, and he had helped me out a few months ago when I'd had to take a few weeks off from my own business to recuperate from a tango I'd danced with a psychopath. He was right: I did owe him, big-time, and owing people was not something I was particularly comfortable with.

The hard part of Kendal's request was that my boyfriend was due back from his training with the FBI at Quantico, and tomorrow night was supposed to be *our* night—if you get my drift.

My boyfriend, Dutch, used to be a detective for the Royal Oak PD, until he'd been recruited by the FBI. We hadn't dated very long; in fact, we had yet to consummate our relationship—hence why the following evening was such a big deal.

"Kendal, I'm *begging* you, isn't there *anyone* else? Another psychic-in-training? Some guy off the street who could fake it?"

"There's no one else, I swear. And this gig is really important to me. It's for Ophelia Kapordelis, and her father, Andros is a very wealthy man. I could use the *considerable* cash they're willing to pay us, and besides, you owe me."

I pulled the cell phone away from my ear and stuck

my tongue out at it. If he said that one more time I was going to crawl through the thing and tie his nose in a knot. I sighed audibly and gave it one more valiant try. "Can't you just do it alone?"

"An entire wedding party? Abby, are you nuts? Even with the two of us, we'll still be lucky to make it through thirty people. I promised the bride two psychics, she's already paid for two psychics and she is going to get two psychics because *you owe me!*"

My eyebrows lowered to dangerous levels; damn it, he'd said it again. "But I don't even know how to read tarot cards!" I shouted.

Kendal had informed me at the start of our conversation that the bride had insisted on using tarot card readers. Kendal had originally booked the event with a friend of his who also used tarot. Unfortunately, his friend had been wheeled into the OR for an emergency appendectomy an hour earlier, hence Kendal's frantic phone call to me.

"I can teach you. Just meet me at my house an hour before the reception and we'll go over it when we get to the reception hall. It's pretty easy; you'll probably pick it up right away. Besides, if you get stuck, you can just put down a card and say whatever comes to mind. You're pretty much free-form as it is, aren't you?"

I had pulled into my assigned parking space in the parking garage across the street from my office by now, and, sensing defeat, I let my head bang forward onto the steering wheel. I wasn't going to get out of this.

I left his last question hanging, as my mind continued to look for possible ways out. My intuition was buzzing loudly in my head, and I knew that my "crew"—the spirit guides and assorted angels I typically consulted with on such matters—would totally back me up.

But the truth was that I did owe Kendal; he was in a jam and he needed me, and the job paid extremely well. He'd highballed his typical rate, and the purse was a grand apiece. My bank account could really use the cash. "Fine," I said, closing my eyes.

"Terrific! Okay, the reception is downtown at the

Plaza Casino. Why don't you come over around six and I'll drive us over there. Do you remember how to get to my house?"

"I'll find it."

"Good. Remember to dress up a little; this is a wealthy family, from what I understand."

"Kendal?" I asked, my eyes still shut, and my mouth turned down into a hard frown.

"Yeah?"

"After this our little debt is paid in full, okay?"

"No problemo, sugar. See you tomorrow."

I flipped the lid of my cell phone closed without wishing him good-bye. I was pissed at myself and didn't trust that I wouldn't take it out on him. I didn't want to do the party, and I was mad at myself for caving.

Sitting up straight I flipped off the engine and grabbed my purse off the passenger seat. If only Kendal had gotten my voice mail, I probably could have dodged him until after the freaking wedding. But when my phone rang I'd been hoping it was Dutch, so I didn't check the number on the caller ID before picking up. I got out of my car and walked grudgingly out of the parking structure and across the street toward my office building.

I live and work in a suburb of Detroit called Royal Oak. I love the town for its rather eclectic nature and the fact that it welcomes the odd, strange, bizarre, boring, common and obscure with equal portions of measured warmth. It is a unique town for that: No one is disenfranchised, from the homeless who seek shelter in the doorways of downtown, to the pierced, "fashion-rebellious" youth who crowd the various clubs and music stores, all the way up to those double-income, minivan-driving, two-kids-and-a-Labrador-named-Buddy couples that I tend to look at while stifling a yawn. Everyone is welcome. It's the perfect climate for a little freak like me.

Now, don't get me wrong. Even though my profession smacks of surrealism, my life is sadly bland. I live in a small two-bedroom bungalow that's been undergoing renovations for as long as I've owned it, I have a small miniature Dachshund named Eggy and a car with eighty thousand on the odometer, and a wild evening for me consists of watching the ball game with my boyfriend.

At least in the man department I've hit a ten on the wowser meter. My boyfriend—the FBI agent, or as I like to refer to him, "Mr. Sexy."

The title fits Dutch perfectly. He's tall, about six-two, with light blond hair and incredible midnight-blue eyes. His body would put Greek gods to shame, and his baritone voice has some sort of Pavlovian effect on me—I tend to salivate just talking to him.

He and I first met through one of those online dating services, and the fact that I'd struck a home run with him was apparent to me right away. He took a little longer to come around, although it had helped a bit that at the time I was being pursued by a serial killer—it brought out his protective side. His major obstacle had been warming to my profession—I mean, how many professional psychics have *you* dated?

Luckily he got over it, and we were on our way to advancing our relationship when a phone call came eight weeks ago informing Dutch that he had been accepted into the FBI, where he's been training in Virginia ever since. He's due back tomorrow morning, and I've been about as patient as a five-year-old on Christmas Eve.

Tomorrow night—Halloween—was our planned reunion, and we had intended to pass out candy to the kids in the neighborhood, then share a romantic candlelight dinner, and the rest of the evening get reacquainted. The French-maid outfit I'd purchased was just one of the colorful ideas I'd come up with for the reacquainting part.

Now I'd have to reschedule. Son of a bitch.

I crossed the street and walked quickly through the rain into the front lobby of my office building. I work in a large, tan brick office plaza, which is a magnificent example of architectural indecision. The building hogs one square block of downtown, squatting its bulky and irregular frame like a giant water buffalo. The structure houses boxy sections, spiked towers and sharply angled corners. It's an architectural acid trip if ever there was one.

I took the stairs this morning to my second-floor suite. I'm over thirty now, and the prospect of being seen naked again for the first time in three years had been doing wonders to inspire me to take a little Jell-O out of my J-Lo.

Panting, I reached the second-floor landing and walked down the corridor to my office suite, number 222. It's the one down the hallway and to the right, sandwiched between an accountant and a computer graphics firm. If you have a nose, you can just follow the aroma of the incense I burn on a regular basis. Nothing too frou frou . . . I prefer musky scents. So far no one's complained, and I've taken that as silent acquiescence from my neighbors to continue the practice.

As I rounded the corner to my doorway I noticed a tall figure pacing in front of my door. The thundercloud over my head evaporated the moment I placed his face. "Milo!" I shouted, and ran toward him.

"Umph," he said as I crashed into him with a big bear hug, squeezing him tightly. "Hey, Abby, I see you've gotten your strength back," he said, laughing.

I backed away and beamed up at him. Milo Johnson used to be a detective with the Royal Oak Police Department, and partners with Dutch until last August, when he'd played the lottery and won big-time. Of course, he'd had a little help from yours truly. He'd played the numbers I'd given him, a notion I was quick to point out. "Here to give me my cut?" I asked with a mischievous grin and an outstretched palm.

Milo's a gorgeous man. Tall, black and elegant, he has fine facial bones and sumptuous lips that part into a fantastic smile when he's amused. I was graced with the full grille as he looked at my outstretched palm and wheezed his contagious laugh, while reaching into the pocket of an expensive overcoat. "Actually, yes. After all, it wouldn't be fair for me to keep all the money when your numbers did the winning."

In my palm he placed a personal check colored with more zeros than I'd ever seen in my life. My humor faded immediately as I looked from him to the check with a mixture of excitement and shock. "Milo," I said, a little breathless, "I was just kidding. I didn't *actually* expect you to give me half."

"Abby, are you for real? Take the money, girl—and run."

I stood for a moment bouncing on the balls of my feet. There was close to two million dollars in my outstretched hand, and I noticed how my palms were suddenly sweating with the thought of all I could buy, and how much fun I could have. I wondered if my wealthy sister ever felt this way when she checked her bank balance. The experience was too surreal for me to take in, and I was just about to pocket the check when my intuitive phone began to vibrate on high.

For most people intuition is nothing more than a random thought making its way from the unconscious to the conscious, a commercial break during regular programming; but for me the experience is completely different. My intuition is more like a surround-sound infomercial—and I'm usually a captive audience. Having used it every day of my life for the past four years, I'm now ultrasensitive to the messages, tickling sensations, random thoughts, humming sounds, disconnectedness and physical pressures that affect my body.

In that moment before pocketing the check I got a "buzz," if you will, like a telephone ringing in the background letting me know there was a message to be picked up. I turned my head for a moment and listened with my mind. My left side felt thick and heavy—my sign for no. I checked the indication by sending out a question in my mind: *Should I take the check?* My left side again felt thick and heavy.

Often I get messages that, at the time, seem off. This one was pure bull. *Why the hell not?* I asked in my head as I looked longingly at the check. Immediately in my mind's eye I saw an image of a baseball field and a playground. I looked at Milo and asked, "Were you considering donating some money to a baseball field or a playground or something?"

Milo had been watching me intently as my head cocked to one side and I searched out the meaning of the messages coming to me. He now looked a little astonished when I asked this question, and said, "Actually, I was. The Boys and Girls Club in my neighborhood has been struggling financially, and when I was a little kid they were the ones who kept me out of trouble and pointed me in the right direction. A lot of kids in my old neighborhood ended up dealing drugs or dead, and I was lucky enough to steer clear of all that because of the club. I've already sent them some cash, but every little bit helps."

I hungrily looked at the check for another beat, my left side feeling thicker and heavier by the second. Finally I took a deep breath and tore it down the center, then again lengthwise and handed the pieces back to Milo with a chagrined look. "Milo, let's not give just a little; let's give 'em a lot and make a damn difference."

He took the bits of paper from me and asked, "All of it? I mean . . . that's a lot of money. You could quit doing this and retire to someplace tropical if you wanted to."

I held my hand up in a "stop" motion. "Please don't tempt me. Besides, this is what I'm supposed to be doing. I'm meant to be in this line of work, and winning the lottery isn't going to change that purpose. Trust me, this money will be of better use in your old neighborhood."

Milo patted me on the back good-naturedly and said, "I always knew you were a sucker for a good cause."

"I'll agree with you on the sucker part. You want to come in?" I asked, turning to unlock my office door.

"Wish I could, but I've got a meeting with the captain in a little while, and I don't want to be late."

"The captain? I thought you quit your job."

"I did, but losing me and Dutch at once has really hit the department hard. They've asked me to consider coming back part-time for a while."

"Are you gonna do it?" I asked, already subconsciously scanning his energy.

"You think I should?" he asked me seriously.

Automatically I said, "Yes. There's something they really want your help with, Milo. Something big, and you're the guy for the job. I really feel like you're the one who will help solve the crime. But be careful. You're playing with fire." At that moment a cold prickle tickled my spine. I didn't know why, but I shivered involuntarily.

Milo looked at me quizzically for a minute, then soberly nodded his head. "The truth is that retirement is pretty boring, and I could use something to focus on. Thanks, I appreciate the advice," he said, leaning in and giving me a quick hug.

"Anytime. By the way, Dutch will be back tomorrow. Why don't we all get together for lunch soon?" I asked as he stepped back.

"That'd be great. Have him give me a call when he gets in, and we'll set it up. Happy Halloween, Abby."

I waved good-bye, then let myself into my office. I glanced at the clock and noticed that I'd better get a move on if I wanted to be ready for my one-o'clock appointment. I hurried through the tiny lobby into the back office and put my coat and purse away.

My office suite is set up in a T formation. As you walk through the doorway you enter a tiny lobby with two chairs and a side table laid out with magazines. Straight ahead is my inner office, where I have a computer, phone, filing cabinets and fax machine. To the right of my lobby sits an empty space that at one point was occupied by my best friend, Theresa—a medium who moved to California a few months before—then by a massage therapist who was scared off by the same serial killer who'd put me out of commission for several weeks. I was currently interviewing possible replacements for the space, but as yet no one had seemed like a good fit.

To the left of the lobby was my reading area, a quaint ten-by-eleven-foot space painted a beautiful azure blue with cream trim and wood floors. The room housed two overstuffed plush chairs that faced each other and a small table that held a tape recorder dividing the space between. A large credenza butted up against three enormous windows on the room's east wall, and the daylight through the windows played nicely over the various crystals I had arranged on top of the credenza. Candles dotted surfaces here and there, a mosaic mirror hung on one wall, and a large waterfall sat in one corner, giving rhythm to the room.

My reading area had always been a source of comfort for me. It was the room where I fully became myself. A place where I wasn't someone's neighbor, sister, friend or girl-next-door; but me, Abigail Cooper, professional psychic. Only in this little nook had I never been self-conscious of my gifts. Only here were there never any worries about being accepted or rejected. I could be completely myself, and for that reason it was the most precious space in the world to me.

I paused for a moment in the doorway, letting the serenity of the room wash over me like a cool shower on a hot day. With a sigh I quickly began lighting candles and incense, then picked up a brand-new cassette from the credenza and put it into the recorder. After that I sat in one of the white plush chairs and closed my eyes, getting my mind ready for my first reading.

Now, I've read a lot of books by other psychics who say they spend hours meditating before beginning their sessions. I'm a Capricorn, and we just don't have that kind of patience. For me it's literally a two-minute routine in my head, where I clear my mind as best I can and focus on the task at hand. Think of it as what you might do before taking a test. You've studied, crammed, memorized and prepared, but in those final moments before you're allowed to turn your paper over, mentally you're telling yourself, "You can do this . . . piece of cake . . . you know the answers!" It's a bit like holding a mini pep rally in my head.

At exactly one o'clock there was a small knock on my door, and I hurried out to the lobby to greet my appointment. My one-o'clock was a new client named Cathy Schultz, a pretty girl I'd guess to be in her late twenties with shoulder-length blond hair and bright pink lipstick. We shook hands and I led her into my reading room. After taking our seats I got comfortable, turned on the tape recorder, closed my eyes, focused on her energy and began.

"Cathy, the first thing I want to say is congratulations. Did you just graduate from college or something?"

"Yes, this past August," she said.

"Cool. Now, this wasn't undergrad but graduate, like you got your master's, right?"

Cathy chuckled and said, "Yes, that's correct."

"And did you also just get hired, or find a new job?"

"I'm going for my third interview at an advertising agency today at three."

"Great! I have the feeling that you'll get the job, or they'll want you, but you may ask for time off before you start or something."

"Uh . . . I hadn't planned on it."

I opened my eyes at that point and looked quizzically at her. "Really? Because my feeling is that you'll need some time to tend to something before you can start."

"Uh, no, honest, I can start right away."

I get this all the time. Sometimes how I phrase something won't fit a situation exactly at the time I say it, but connects perfectly a little later. I figured this was one of those times, so I didn't push. "Okay, then just in case you need to attend to something before you start, it's all right to do that. Also, what's going on with your headaches?"

"What headaches?" she asked.

I put my hands up to my head as if it hurt and said, "You know, your headaches. Have you gone to the doctor yet about them?"

"I don't have headaches," she said, looking at me like I was from Mars.

I checked in with my crew, who were insisting that my information was correct, so I said again, "Well, this is really weird, because the feeling that I get is that you're going to see the doctor about your headaches, and not to worry; you'll be fine."

Cathy just shook her head at me, clearly not understanding. I dropped that subject and asked my crew for something else. "So who's the skier?" I said.

"The skier?"

"Yeah, the skier. Is there a guy who likes to ski who's been hitting on you? He's got dark hair I think?"

"My boyfriend has brown hair," she said by way of explanation.

"Does he like to ski?"

"Not that I know of."

I focused a little harder and said, "Is your boyfriend mean to you?"

"No, he's really sweet."

"Did you just start dating?"

"No, we met in undergrad three years ago." Cathy's tone was beginning to turn from cooperative to impatient.

"Okay, the feeling that I have is that there's this guy with dark hair and he likes to ski. He's a real jerk, though. He may hit on you or try to flirt with you, but you shouldn't have anything to do with him. He's totally bad news."

"Is this someone I know?"

"I'm not sure. I mean, he feels new to me, and if you don't recognize who this guy is by my description then obviously he hasn't made himself known to you yet. He may come off as being really nice, but he's a wolf in sheep's clothing, so be very careful around him."

Cathy was just staring at me with a confused look, so I moved on. Now I'm getting something about procrastination. Do you always put stuff off? Like errands or something?"

Finally I got a chuckle out of Cathy and a nod. "Yeah, that would be me."

"My crew is telling me that you need to spend a little time breaking this habit. They're specifically saying don't wait until the last minute to go grocery shopping. You need to take care of business when you should, not put things off."

"Ugh, I absolutely hate grocery shopping. In fact, I've been meaning to go for a couple of days and I haven't made it there yet."

"They're saying take care of business, because if you don't, it could cause problems—like you could get to the store and it's closed or you could be late for something else."

"All right," she said.

For some reason, though, I couldn't let this topic go, and the thought kept spinning in my head. "Cathy, I'm not sure what they're getting at, but this is really important. You can't put your errands off; they keep repeating it."

"I get it, tell them message heard."

Still, the thought persisted to whirl in my mind. I tried for another topic and got nothing but the same message. I closed my eyes and concentrated, but all I could hear in my head was the message about the grocery store. For the first time in four and a half years of being a professional psychic I was stumped. I couldn't get past this message about Cathy's errands. After a very long pause I opened my eyes and looked with a pained expression at Cathy. I knew what my guides wanted me to do. "Cathy, you're going to think I'm crazy, but that's all I'm getting for you. I can't move beyond this message about you procrastinating, so I'm just going to stop. I won't charge you for the session, because we've only been at it fifteen minutes. Also I think you should get your errands done before your big interview."

Cathy looked at me with a rather shocked expression, and finally said, "Uh, okay. That was weird."

"Tell me about it," I said, a touch of pink hitting my cheeks. "Listen, if you want to reschedule for another date I'd be more than happy to try again. This has never happened to me before. I don't understand what's so important about you going to the grocery store right now, but that's the only message I can come up with."

"I see," she said, looking very disappointed. "How about I call you if I get this job and we can set up another appointment then?"

"Sure," I said, fully aware that Cathy was giving me the big blow-off. I handed her the cassette tape and walked her to the door. She smiled sheepishly as she took the tape and asked, "Are you sure I don't owe you anything? I mean, I'm willing to pay you for the time you did spend with me."

For the second time that day I turned away money I could have used. "No, really, it's okay. I'm sorry; this has never happened to me before," I repeated.

"It's okay, Abby," she said kindly. "I'll call you if I get the job and we can try again." *Liar, liar, pants on fire . . .*

One of the pains about having an inboard lie detector is that sometimes courtesy demands you pretend not to know when people are lying. "That'd be great," I said, smiling politely. "Good luck on your interview."

She waved at me as she walked through the door, and I rested my head against the doorjamb. So far today I'd nixed a guaranteed night of hot monkey love, a $2 million addition to my bank account, and any potential future business with Cathy and any of her acquaintances. Of all the days I should have stayed in bed, this one had to be a topper.

I sighed and dragged myself back into my office and sat down at the desk, looking for something to interest me before my next appointment. I glanced at the phone and was wondering who I could call to pass the time when it rang, making me jump a foot. Grabbing it, I said, "Abigail Cooper speaking," in my most business-like tone.

"Hello, sweethot," smoldered a deep baritone doing a great Humphrey Bogart impression through the receiver.

My slumped shoulders immediately perked up, and a smile plastered itself onto my face. "Hey, there, good-looking. This is a pleasant midafternoon surprise."

"Yeah, I had a couple of minutes before they partner us up and hand out our assignments, so I thought I'd call and leave something inappropriate on your voice mail."

"Oh, and instead I get to hear it firsthand. I'm *so* lucky!" I said playfully.

"Or I could just show you tomorrow night—"

My shoulders slumped again. Crap. I'd almost forgotten. "Uh, Dutch? About tomorrow night—"

"I thought I'd pick up some Chinese; you like Chinese?"

"Well, see, the thing of it is—"

"You don't like Chinese?"

"No. I mean yes, I like Chinese, but there's a problem with tomorrow night . . ."

"What kind of problem?"

"Uh, do you remember Kendal Adams? He's that psychic friend of mine who helped cover for me when I was in the hospital. And, um, unfortunately because of that I kind of owe him a favor, and he decided to sort of call in that favor for tomorrow night."

Silence.

I laughed nervously and continued. "See, he was scheduled to be the entertainment at this wedding reception with another psychic, but that guy had to have an emergency appendectomy. Kendal tried everyone else, but no one but me was available, and so since I sort of owe Kendal, I agreed to do the reception with him. . . ."

Silence.

"It's not like I *want* to do the party. I mean, I fought really hard to get out of it, and I told him I had other plans, but he was just *relentless,* and he kept saying how I owed him, and, well, I caved. I'm really, really sorry. Can we possibly get together on Saturday instead of Friday?"

The air hung heavy between us for a very long time before finally Dutch said, "I'll be home tomorrow afternoon. We'll talk then," and with that he hung up. I held the phone to my ear long enough for the dial tone to come on; then, as tears brushed my lashes, I hung up the phone. Now I could add "boyfriend" to my list of today's nixes.

Several hours later I crawled home, wanting to wave a white flag. My afternoon hadn't improved, as I'd had three more difficult readings to cap off the day. I opened my front door and was greeted by Eggy, my twelve-pound Dachshund, who slobbered wiggly kisses all over my face as soon as I picked him up. The best part about owning a dog is the wild, wet frenzy they perform when greeting you. It's enough to make any kind of day just a little bit better.

Eggy wriggled and licked and kissed and squirmed, his tail beating a frantic rhythm against my chest, and, soon enough I found myself smirking. After a minute I heard, "Abby? That you?" coming from upstairs, accompanied by the sound of heavy footsteps descending my staircase.

"Hey, Dave," I answered as I set Eggy down.

Dave McKenzie is my handyman. He's like a freeze frame from the movie *Easy Rider,* tall with broad shoulders and long blond hair braided down his back into a fine point, thick beard and mustache, abused shirts, ripped jeans and a chain connecting his wallet to his belt loop. Up close, however, are the telltale signs of decades passing, with hints of gray in his beard and sideburns, permanent crow's-feet lining his eyes and the slightly rounded belly of a man in his mid-fifties.

In early March I'd purchased a home that had "lots of potential," only to discover I was in way over my head. A client who knew someone who knew someone gave me Dave's number, and I'd called him in desperation. He'd been a complete godsend, turning my dilapidated little bungalow into a cozy home sweet home.

My home had once been a ranch until the former owner added a staircase and converted half of the attic into a bedroom. Because the bedroom was small, and I really didn't need the extra storage I was having Dave extend my bedroom by tearing down the wall that separated the attic from the bedroom. Of late he'd been busy ripping out the old insulation in the attic.

"How's it going?" I asked.

"Getting there," he said noncommittally. Squinting his eyes my way, he added, "You look like hell."

"Gee," I said flatly, "try not to bowl me over with so much flattery."

"No, really, you look like crap. What happened?"

"The shorter answer would be to tell you what *didn't* happen," I said, turning toward the kitchen to get Eggy his supper.

"That bad, huh?"

"Let's just say I've renamed today 'Black Thursday,' " I said as I got down a can of dog food.

"So I guess I should wait till tomorrow to fill you in on the attic?"

I stopped fussing with Eggy's dinner and glanced sharply at Dave. "What about the attic?"

"It's nothing I can't fix. . . ."

Eggy barked, reminding me that I was holding up his

dinner, so I got out the can opener and said casually, "I'm assuming that's the good news. Care to share the bad news with me now?"

Shuffling his feet, Dave said, "Fine, I'll give it to you straight. When I took the old insulation down I noticed quite a bit of water damage to the rafters. It looks like the old owner waited about twenty years too long to redo the roof, so I'm probably going to have to take down about three-quarters of the rafters and replace them."

I groaned as I set Eggy's food down on the floor, then stood back up and closed my eyes as I asked, "How much?"

"Good question. The short answer is, I'm not really sure. It might not be as bad as I think, and it could be only the one small section I've uncovered so far. . . ."

My radar buzzed in and I said, "No, it's bad. Trust me, it's bad."

Dave looked at me with compassion and sighed. "Why don't I go to Home Depot in the morning and see if I can't work out some deal on the wood? I'll try to cut you a break on the labor too."

I forced myself to smile then; Dave worked for fifteen paltry dollars an hour, and was always trying to shave time off the clock. He was a generous, good-natured man who had also become a close friend, so for his sake I put on my acting face. "Don't be ridiculous. It's no problem, really. Besides, I'm working a big party tomorrow night, and that should go a long way toward helping out with the repairs. Really, it's fine. I was just curious."

"All right, then, I'll get started on that tomorrow. I'll have to take down all the insulation in the attic, so your bedroom could get pretty cold until I'm finished."

"No problem. I've got plenty of comforters and blankets. I'll be fine."

"Okay, then," Dave said, rocking on his heels and looking for a way to drop the topic. "I should be shoving off. Don't want the old lady to throw a fit if I'm late for dinner." His casual remark about his common-law wife didn't phase me. I knew Dave was completely devoted to her.

"I'll see you tomorrow," I said as I walked him out.

After he'd gone I went back to the kitchen and opened up the fridge, checking the contents for something edible. I had a carton of eggs, soy milk, ketchup, half a jar of sweet pickles and bagels. Cathy wasn't the only one who put off grocery shopping. Sighing, I got out the frying pan and scrambled some eggs. Eggy stood at attention by my feet while I cooked. His love for eggs had been the inspiration for his name, so after I'd shoveled some eggs onto a plate for me, I gave him a small portion, and we ate in companionable silence.

Later that night I checked in with my sister, Catherine, who called me from her swanky hotel room in New York City. Cat is the female alternative to Donald Trump. She's a savvy businesswoman who started her own company and is now worth a gazillion dollars, lives fast and furious, and has no patience for stupid people. She typically plays the role of surrogate mother to me, often worrying over her little sister like a frantic hen. She lives in an affluent suburb of Boston but was in New York on a business deal that seemed to be going well, given her excitement and rapid rate of speech. I didn't have the heart to bring her down, so I declined to inform her about Black Thursday.

Finally she paused and asked, "So are you excited about your dinner tomorrow night with Dutch?"

There was way to avoid it now. "Actually I had to cancel."

"Cancel? Why would you cancel?"

"Do you remember Kendal Adams, my friend who took some of the overflow off my hands when I was in the hospital?"

"Vaguely . . ."

"Turns out he's calling in his favor. He needs a fellow psychic to help him with a wedding reception tomorrow."

"I don't understand," she said.

"Apparently the bride wants Kendal and another psychic to read tarot cards as part of the entertainment for her wedding reception."

"But you don't read tarot cards," Cat said.

"Try telling Kendal that."

"So does that mean you're going to fake it?" she asked.

"No. Kendal's going to give me a lesson tomorrow an hour before the reception."

"You can learn to read tarot cards in an hour?"

"According to Kendal it's really easy; anyone can do it."

There was a very pregnant pause on my sister's end of the line before she said, "Where would one get tarot cards if one wanted to experiment with them?"

"I'm not sure. I think most bookstores sell them. Why? You thinking of getting a deck?"

Cat laughed and said, "You know I love this stuff. Who knows, maybe your gifts are hereditary, and perhaps they've just been lying dormant inside me, waiting for some tool to access them."

I laughed heartily for the first time all day. I didn't mean to; it was just that the thought of my very all-business, highly polished sister sitting at a table in her three-thousand-dollar Hermès silk suit pouring over a deck of tarot cards struck me as hilarious. "What's so funny?" she asked, taking offense.

"Nothing," I said quickly. "It just struck me as funny. I can see you at a board meeting with all those old curmudgeons sitting around the table and you reading their fortunes . . . it's just *funny!*" I couldn't help it; I dissolved into a fit of giggles.

"Frankly I don't see how *that's* funny. In fact, I think that you just may be a little bit nervous that perhaps you're not the only one in the family who's gifted."

"What?" I asked, quickly stifling the giggles. "That's absurd."

"Is it? Is it *really?*"

"Oh, for God's sake, Cat, I didn't mean to offend you. I just had this image in my head, and . . ."

"Oh, look at the time; I have to go," my sister said abruptly.

"Cat, wait—"

"Good night." And with that she hung up the phone.

Ah, the perfect end to the perfect day. I decided to throw in the towel and so headed for bed. As I turned out the light and curled myself around Eggy, I thanked God the day was over.

At ten to midnight, my phone jolted me out of a sound sleep. "Hello?" I said groggily into the receiver as I flipped on the light and sat up in bed.

"Abby? It's Milo Johnson. I need you to come down to the police station right away."

"Wha . . . ?" I said, shaking my head vigorously, working to make sense of what Milo had just said.

"I need you to come down to the police station immediately," he repeated. "I sent a car to pick you up. It should be at your door in two minutes."

"What's happened?" I asked, my heart beating rapidly.

"It's one of your clients; she's been attacked."

"One of my clients?"

"Yes, Cathy Schultz. She was attacked and raped this evening."

"Oh, my God! Where?" I asked, now fully awake.

"At the Farmer's Market grocery store on Twelve Mile. We need to talk."

"Sit tight, Milo," I said, jumping out of bed. "I'm on my way."

Chapter Two

Ten minutes after hanging up the phone with Milo I was at the Royal Oak police Station being escorted up a flight of stairs to the Detectives' Unit. As I passed through the doorway into the unit I saw Milo sitting on the corner of his desk, looking through a police file.

"Hey," I said to get Milo's attention as I walked over to him.

Milo looked up at the sound of my voice, his face a mixture of concern and anger—quite different from this afternoon. His jacket hung wrapped around his desk chair, and the sleeves of his white shirt were rolled up, revealing corded mocha-colored forearms. His tie had also been removed, giving him a disheveled appearance, and I had an awkward thought that I liked this Milo better. My encounters with him were always with an impeccably dressed man with elegant taste in clothes, but seeing him in a rumpled state made him appear more accessible. "Thanks for coming so quickly," he said. "I'm sorry to get you out of bed," he added, noting my appearance.

I quickly looked down at myself; I was dressed in sweat bottoms and a flannel pajama top, with a zip-up hoodie thrown on haphazardly. Sheepishly I replied, "I guess I was so worried about getting here quickly that I didn't even think about changing. How's Cathy?"

Milo closed the file he'd been reading and placed it, without looking, behind him on the desk. He folded his arms and regarded me. "She's in rough shape."

"What happened?" I asked, taking a seat in one of the folding chairs in front of Milo's desk.

"As far as we can tell, Cathy met with her boyfriend at a restaurant to celebrate a job offer, and she left the restaurant around eight thirty. She told her boyfriend she had to stop at the grocery store to pick up some items, and she would meet him back home. They live together in a house on Glennwood. By ten o'clock she still hadn't come home, so her boyfriend drove over to the Farmer's Market to look for her. He found her car in the parking lot, but no sign of her. The store closes at nine, and her car was the only one in the lot. The boyfriend called nine-one-one. The police came to the scene and found her half-naked and unconscious behind the store, lying near one of the Dumpsters."

For the first time I noticed how fast my heart was beating, and how dry my throat felt. I started to feel a little light-headed, and Milo got up off his desk and came to squat by my chair. "Hey, you okay?" he asked gently.

"I think I need some water," I said, my voice no louder than a whisper.

Milo quickly got up and retrieved some water for me from the nearby watercooler. I took the paper cup and downed it in two gulps. Milo retraced his steps to the cooler, this time bringing two full cups to me. I emptied one of them again but set the last one on his desk. After a moment I felt better. Finally I asked, "How did you know she was my client?"

Milo picked up a familiar cassette tape from his desk. "We found this in her coat pocket."

"Déjà vu," I said, smiling ironically. This past summer similar cassette tape of mine had been found on another woman. Unfortunately she hadn't survived her attacker.

"Kinda freaky, don't you think?"

"Milo, I don't think there's anything 'kinda' about it," I said seriously. "Have you listened to it?"

"Yep. Right before I called you."

"So that's why I'm here?"

"Yep."

"Okay," I said searching his face. "How can I help?"

"Here's the thing—unlike like my former partner, Dutch the cynic," he said, grinning, "I'm an absolute believer. I mean, it's hard for me not to believe you're a real psychic after winning the lottery. I've got to work this case alone because unfortunately the department's really stretched these days. I could use your skills to help me get a line on this bastard. That is, if you're willing?"

My heart began beating rapidly again. The last time I'd lent my skills to solve a major crime I'd come very close to becoming a victim. I didn't want to go through that again, but on the other hand, if I walked away, how could I still look myself in the mirror every morning?

After all, Cathy was my client. She'd been put in front of me for a reason; didn't that obligate me somehow? I played seesaw with myself for a minute, when my crew tickled my conscience. Fine, they wanted to weigh in? *Go for it. Should I get involved in solving this case?* Immediately my right side felt light and airy—my sign for yes. "Okay, Milo," I said more firmly than I felt. "What do you want me to do?"

Milo beamed his beautiful smile at me and sat down at his desk. After pulling out a pad and pen he looked at me and said, "That's great, Abby. I appreciate it. Now, is there any way you can tune in on this guy's name?"

I sighed audibly. Names had never been one of my fortes. "Sorry, Milo, names just don't translate well for me. I'd hate to guess and risk pointing you in the wrong direction. Maybe we can try another angle?"

Milo nodded and glanced at the cassette tape. "Okay, maybe it would be good to talk it through first. You told Cathy that she had to go to the grocery store before her interview. We know she blew that off, because we also found a receipt for a manicure in her pocket, and the time indicates that she paid for it about an hour after she left your office. So tonight she ended up at the wrong place at the wrong time. I think that all the parts that didn't make sense to her during your reading with her were actually a warning.

"Like you mentioned headaches, and you said that she would have to see a doctor about her headaches. Her attacker hit her over the head with some sort of blunt instrument. She's currently unconscious and in the hospital, so she is seeing a doctor about her headache."

I nodded, a little taken aback by the accuracy of a message that just a few hours earlier had made no sense at all. Milo continued: "The problem, however, is that with this kind of trauma, when the vic wakes up they often can't remember anything about the attack. Cathy's doctor just called, and luckily we got to her in time. She's unconscious, but not comatose, and at this point they don't feel that surgery is necessary. He said her other wounds should heal quickly and that he was guardedly optimistic about her condition. She should be fine in a few weeks. When she's conscious we'll certainly check to see if she remembers anything. If you can't hit on a name, how about trying for something simple, like what this guy might have used for a weapon?"

I squirmed uncomfortably in my chair. Even though I was willing to help Milo out, the truth was that I hated this stuff. Tuning in to something violent is a little like sifting through garbage, it's smelly, full of yucky things, and while you're doing it, all you want to do is stop and take a shower. I scowled in distaste, bracing myself, then closed my eyes to concentrate, telling myself this was all for the greater good. I focused first on the weapon. "Okay, they're showing me a tire, like a flat tire or something. I don't think he hit her with a tire. . . ."

"No, but you need a tire iron to change a flat," said Milo, putting two and two together.

I popped my eyes open and smiled. "Yeah, that's kind of obvious, huh? So a tire iron seems to be the most likely weapon. Nothing was found at the scene?"

"Forensics is still examining the area, but I don't think we're going to find anything."

I nodded, then closed my eyes again. "Okay, ask me something else."

"What can you tell me about the attacker?"

I concentrated, and after a moment I said, "I get the feeling that this guy is a real scumbucket. I also feel like he's done this before. . . ." I paused and followed that thought. "Yes, he's absolutely done this before. Have you guys heard about any other attacks that were similar?"

I could hear Milo scribbling furiously; he paused only briefly to remark, "Yes," then waited for me to continue.

"Then I'm on the right track," I said. "I get the feeling he's a repeat offender. Like he thinks he can get away with this. There's also a connection to Vegas here."

"Las Vegas, Nevada?"

"Yes, they keep showing me Vegas. I think he may have a tie to Las Vegas, like he may go there a lot, or he may have done this there. He might be a compulsive gambler. I keep seeing the slot machines and the bright lights of Las Vegas, so I think it has something to do with either gambling or the city.

"You should check with the Vegas police to see if maybe he's been attacking women there. There could be a connection. Also he's very conscious of time. Like he sticks to a schedule. Like he's very routine . . ."

"Uh-huh." More furious scribbling.

"I also get the feeling that he has dark hair, and dark eyes. No, it's more than that. This guy is ethnic-looking. I'd say he was maybe Latino or something. He's got dark skin. . . ."

"Black?" Milo asked.

"No, not black," I said checking with my intuition. "More . . . Italian or Latino or something. He's also tall, and I wouldn't be surprised if he was very good-looking. I feel he's clean-shaven, and takes very good care of himself. There's also this connection to money. Like he may win a lot of money when he gambles."

"Got it."

"And there's a reference to skiing. I don't know what this is about, but there's a huge reference to skiing."

"He's a skier?"

"Yeah . . . or something to do with skiing. I can't

quite get the meaning behind this, but they're saying something about skiing. It's a clue that's close, but I'm off somehow."

"Can you tell me where he likes to ski?"

I focused all of my energy on the clue in my head. I kept seeing a pair of snow skis, but there was something about the connection to skiing that was off. I was close to what my crew was trying to show me, but I hadn't figured it out yet. "I'm sorry, Milo, I don't understand it. They're not telling me, or I've misinterpreted."

"That's okay. What can you tell me about where he likes to hang out?"

"Vegas."

"Only in Vegas? What about a local place?"

"I'm not getting anything local, just the strip in Vegas. And I keep seeing slot machines—which is my symbol for gambling. My guess is that he's either from Vegas, or maybe he goes there a lot."

"Anything else you can tell me?"

"There's something about the women he attacks, like they represent an image. There are similarities between all of the women—they may look alike—and something about where he puts them. You said you found Cathy by the Dumpster. This has significance because he thinks that women are trash. He thinks of them like taking out the garbage. . . ." In that moment I was very close to touching this man's energy, and physically I was repelled. I snapped my eyes open and shuddered.

"You okay?" Milo asked.

I nodded and reached for more water. I hated this, and wanted to stop. Milo gave me an apprising look and put his pen down. "Had enough?"

"More than enough," I said quietly.

"Okay, we'll stop. I will tell you, however, that you're right on the money here. There have been two other rapes in the Royal Oak area, each occurring on a Thursday night at roughly the same time. The other two victims looked enough like Cathy to be sisters, and all were beaten unconscious and found right next to or behind a Dumpster. I'll check with the Vegas PD and see if they can give us any insights."

"Have the other two victims been able to tell you anything?" I asked.

"No. One is still in a coma, and we're not sure if she'll come out anytime soon. She wasn't found for quite some time after she was attacked, and she almost died. The other woman was unconscious for three days and doesn't remember a thing about her attacker. She's still pretty traumatized by the whole event, so we're waiting to see if she remembers something on her own that can help us."

"You should take this to the media, Milo," I said seriously. "Women in the area need to be warned."

Milo nodded and sighed heavily. "The tough part about taking it to the press is that it's a double-edged sword. You're right in that we do need to alert the public, but you know how the news stations can be. They're going to blow this whole thing out of proportion, and with the exposure comes every kind of suspicious behavior being called in as the rapist. Our department will be flooded with information that will take up all our resources and lead us nowhere. So before I play that card, I want to make sure we've done everything we can on our end to find this guy."

"And what does that include?" I asked, curious about how the police would proceed.

"We've been canvassing the neighborhoods to see if anyone's seen anything, and maybe we'll get lucky. If we don't catch a break by next Wednesday I'll call the media myself and put the public on notice."

I nodded tiredly; my earlier adrenaline rush had completely worn off and been replaced with a sluggish exhaustion. Milo must have noticed, because he reached for the phone and paged the officer who had picked me up. Then he came over from around his desk and offered a hand to help me up. "Come on, girl; let's get you back home to bed. You look whipped."

"I'm beyond whipped," I said, taking his hand. "Say, do you think I could visit Cathy tomorrow? You know, maybe I could pick up something intuitively from her energy."

"I doubt her doctor's going to let anyone but family

around her for a couple of days, but I'll check with him and let you know." Just then my chauffeur arrived and Milo nodded to him as he walked me to the door. "Thanks again for all your help. I appreciate it."

"Absolutely. I don't know how helpful I was, but call on me anytime," I said, and I gave his arm a quick squeeze before exiting through the double doors.

"I'll be in touch," Milo called after me as the officer and I descended the staircase.

A little while later I was back home and curling back up in bed as I noticed with a groan that the clock now read almost two a.m. I was asleep within seconds.

The next morning the phone again woke me up. I snatched up the receiver and growled, "This had better be good."

"Hey, Abby. Milo here. Sorry about waking you up again, but I just came from the hospital. Cathy's awake and she's asking to talk to you."

"What time is it?"

"Six thirty."

I groaned audibly.

"I've got a piping-hot cup of coffee waiting for you . . ." Milo sang into the phone, static buzzing at the end of his sentence.

"Are you on your cell?" I asked, sitting up a little and peeling my eyelids open slightly.

"Yes, I'm in the car."

"Where's your car?" I asked, wondering how long I had before he arrived.

"In your driveway."

Milo had always struck me as the enthusiastic half of the partnership between him and Dutch. I suddenly had a whole new appreciation for Dutch's patience. "So there's no way I can ask for another hour of sleep before we go see her?"

"Mmmm," Milo said by way of answering me, "this coffee sure is good, and oh! What's this? A delicious blueberry muffin! It's warm too. Yummy, and it's got your name written all over it. Better hurry though; I'm starting to get really hungry."

Milo's good humor only provoked my irritation. What can I say? I'm definitely *not* a morning person. "Knock yourself out. I'll call you when I wake up." And with that I hung up the phone and burrowed back under the covers.

Mere moments later there was a barrage of hard knocks on my front door. Eggy, asleep through most of my late-night comings and goings, bolted out of bed at the sound, running down the stairs and over to the front door, barking like a banshee all the way.

I groaned and pulled a pillow over my head, squeezing my eyes shut, but the pounding on the front door only grew louder, and Eggy's frantic barking was teetering on the verge of howls, so finally I got up and stomped down the staircase. Pushing Eggy gently to the side with my foot I opened the front door and bellowed, *"What are you, some kind of sadist?!"*

Milo responded by pushing a small bag in my face and brushing past me into my living room. "Wow!" he said, noting my living room, "I love what you've done with the place. Great improvement." The last time Milo had seen my home was before it had flooring and furniture and it had looked far less appealing.

I scowled moodily at him; I wasn't going to be so easily appeased, "Milo! This is nuts. If she's awake now, then one more hour won't hurt! I'm freaking exhausted here, no thanks to you, and I've got a big day today!"

For the first time since I'd met him, Milo turned to look at me with a face that very clearly put me in my place. "I get it," he said with dead calm. "You're tired. But you know what? There's a young woman lying in a hospital bed who's just discovered she's been beaten, raped and traumatized, and the only person she's asking for is you. So I'm really sorry this is such an *inconvenience,* but to be honest, Scarlett, frankly, my dear, I don't give a damn!"

I sucked in a breath at the force of his words, my cheeks turning red in shame. Then, turning toward the stairs, I said, "I'll be just a moment."

As promised I was back downstairs four minutes later, and without a word we walked out to Milo's waiting car.

I came up short as I spotted the auto in the driveway—
a brand-new black BMW 745i sedan waited in shiny
magnificence for us.

"You like?" Milo beamed as he rounded to the driver's door.

"Are you kidding?" I gushed. "This is gorgeous!"

"Get in; the seats are heated and I've already warmed
up your side."

As we drove to the hospital I swished back and forth
in the leather seat, reveling in the feeling of my bum
getting warm as I carefully ate my muffin and sipped at
the coffee, conscious of not spreading crumbs all over
the immaculate interior.

We arrived at Royal Oak's Beaumont Hospital a short
time later and found a good parking space, then walked
briskly in the cold morning air to the visitors' entrance.
Visiting hours weren't officially open for another two
hours, but Milo simply flashed his badge at the security
camera and we were allowed to enter.

I followed behind him through the lobby to the eleva-
tors, then up to the sixth floor, down two corridors, and
inside a small, darkened room that smelled like antiseptic.

A thin curtain divided the room, and we quietly crept
past a figure lying prone in the first bed, around the
curtain to the second bed. There I came up short and
caught my breath, my hand quickly moving to cover my
heart as I laid eyes on the same woman I'd made casual
conversation with only the day before.

Cathy was propped up on several pillows, an IV snaking its way over the rails of the bed and up her forearm.
There was a thick bandage on her head, her hair matted
and disheveled. Her face was puffy and bruised, and one
of her eyes was swollen shut. Around her throat was a
large scratch; her lip sported a deep red cut that still
oozed a little, while a trickle of water leaked a steady
stream out of her good eye, and a wad of used tissue
lay twisted and torn in her right hand. She looked up
as we rounded the curtain, and seeing me seemed to
undo her.

She looked at me for the briefest moment, her eyes

pleading with an unspoken request; then a great sob escaped her and she lowered her face into her hands. I don't know that I've ever felt so ashamed in all my life, and I swore I would never be so insensitive about getting out of bed when I was needed again. I went to her side, barred from hugging her by the IV pole, the bed railing and my own fear of hurting her. Instead, I pulled up a chair and sat next to her, stroking the side of her head that wasn't bandaged and making *shhhh* sounds.

After a few minutes she seemed to collect herself and, gulping a little, she looked up at Milo and said, "Thank you for bringing her."

"The least I could do, Cathy." I realized by their familiarity that Milo had already been here, and that he'd probably had a chance to talk to her. I wondered for a brief moment if he'd ever gone to bed last night.

Cathy turned to me and said, "Thank you for coming, Abby. I really needed to see you."

"Of course," I said, whispering, not wanting to jar her with the full volume of my voice.

"I wanted to ask you if you knew?" she said to me.

"If I knew?" I repeated, perplexed by the question.

"Yeah, I mean yesterday, when I came to see you. I wanted to know if you knew I was going to be attacked, but just didn't tell me."

As preposterous as that sounds, you can't do my work professionally without understanding the motivation behind asking such a question. One of the main reasons people are afraid of psychics is that they're scared to death we will tell them something bad. The truth is that very few of my clientele ever hear bad news but still the perception prevails. The flip side to this coin is the belief that we won't tell a client about something awful when we see it. Instead we'll filter it out and tell our clients only the good news. This, I reasoned, was where Cathy was coming from. She must have believed that I'd seen her imminent attack, and that I'd simply chosen to edit it out.

I was quick to reassure her. "Absolutely not, Cathy. I swear to you, my guides didn't tell me you were in danger of being harmed."

Cathy looked at me for a moment, assessing the sincerity of my face; then, with eyes full of accusation, she asked, "But why not? I mean, if you're such a good psychic and all, why didn't you pick up on this and warn me?"

I took a moment to tramp down the defensive feelings burbling beneath my surface. It irked me to no end when people blamed me for the bad things that happened to them. It wasn't my fault, and it truly wasn't my responsibility to make sure that all my clients lived happily ever after.

My personal feeling is that information comes to me only in a way that the client can handle. Like, if I'd told Cathy, "Don't go to the grocery store because a psycho is going to rape you," she probably would never go grocery shopping again for the rest of her life. How would that serve her?

I went over in my mind what I had told her in the reading the day before. In hindsight, the message had been there, but she hadn't taken the responsibility of listening and getting her shopping done before her job interview, when it was still light out. Instead she'd blown off the message and done the opposite of what I'd advised and was now paying the price.

I couldn't very well point that out to her in her present condition, however; she'd been through enough, and I guess if she wanted to transfer blame to me then I had big shoulders and I could carry it for a while.

I finally looked at her and said, "Cathy, I think information comes to me so that it's easy for me to interpret and pass on to my clients in a way that won't shock them. It's no good to live your life in fear of something terrible happening, so I think that most of my messages are given to me in a way that makes them palpable to the client. I think we had some of the clues yesterday, but without the context to put them all together. I'm so sorry you went through this, and I'm working with Detective Johnson here to help find the guy who did this to you as soon as possible."

Cathy dissolved into tears again, and I really felt for her. I couldn't imagine what she was going through, and felt more powerless than I ever had in my life. After a few moments she nodded at me and struggled to regain some control, while carefully wiping her good eye with her crumpled tissue. Then she glanced up at Milo and said, "I remembered something else, Detective."

Milo quickly reached into his coat pocket and extracted a small spiral notebook. Flipping quickly to a blank page he nodded at her, and she said, "The last thing I can remember after he grabbed me from behind, right before he pulled me around the back of the building, was that he was wearing a mask."

"A mask?" Milo repeated.

"Yeah, I had a really brief glance at it from the corner of my eye."

"Like a Halloween mask?" Milo asked.

"No, not a Halloween mask. It was a ski mask, one of those Gore-Tex ones."

"The skier . . ." I said breathlessly, a little startled by the revelation.

Cathy looked sharply at me, her mouth dropping open at the connection. "Oh, my God . . . yesterday you told me to be careful of the skier. After I left your office I remember thinking that you must have been talking about my next-door neighbor. I think he skis, and he's always trying to hit on me."

"Could he have been your attacker?" Milo asked.

"I . . . I don't know. Maybe? I have no idea; that's just who came to mind when I was wondering who Abby was talking about."

"He's your next-door neighbor?"

"Yeah, he lives in the redbrick ranch right next to ours. He's always trying to talk to me when Kenny isn't home. He's creepy too. Last summer I caught him spying through the fence between our properties when I was sunbathing."

"You know his name?"

"I think it's Jeff, or John . . . something with a *J* . . ."

"It's Jeff. Jeff Zimmer," said a voice from behind us. We all looked up quickly, and around the curtain stepped a young man with sandy-blond hair and eyes full of pain. Cathy's boyfriend, no doubt.

"Hi, sweetheart," Cathy said with longing in her voice. Quickly the young man moved to the opposite side of the bed from me and took his girlfriend's hand protectively. Cathy began to melt again with emotion, and I sent Milo a look as I got up and stepped away. These two people needed some alone time. Milo nodded at me and closed his notebook after jotting down the name Cathy's boyfriend had given him. "Thanks, Ken," he said. "We'll check it out. Cathy, why don't you rest, and if you remember anything more just call my cell phone. You have the card, right?"

Cathy nodded as tears made tracks down her face. Milo and I waved a small good-bye, exiting the room.

On the way back to my house, Milo filled me in on what else Cathy had remembered, which was very little. She'd gotten to the market just before closing, and the staff was already locking up as she left. She was halfway to her car when she was grabbed from behind, dragged backward behind the building, beaten and hit over the head into unconsciousness. Luckily she had no recollection of her rape—a small blessing, in my opinion.

Milo pulled his car into my driveway, and after shifting into park he reached over and squeezed my hand. "Thanks for coming. I'm sorry I was a little hard on you this morning."

"No, you were absolutely right," I said, looking at him, still feeling chagrined. "Mornings have never been good for my personality, and I'm sorry I was so insensitive."

"I won't tell if you don't," Milo replied with a mischievous grin.

"Deal." I laughed as I got out of the car. Right before closing the door I asked, "Call me if anything new develops, okay?"

"You got it," Milo answered, giving me a small salute.

I walked up my walkway and into the house, where an impatient Eggy pestered me until I'd cooked his morning egg. Then, glancing at the clock, which now read eight, I ran upstairs for a quick shower. While I was shampooing I heard the phone ring, and being one of those impulsive types who can't let a phone ring without answering it, I got out of the shower and grabbed the cordless before the call went to voice mail.

"Morning," came my favorite baritone.

"Hey, there, Dutch," I said, feeling relieved that he seemed to be in a better mood this morning. "Listen, I'm in the shower. Can I call you back in a couple of minutes?"

"Need someone to scrub your back?"

The flirtatiousness of the question caught me off guard, and I dissolved into a fit of nervous giggles. Sometimes I'm *so* sophisticated. "Uh, ha-ha, no, actually, I'm just rinsing off . . . I mean I'm almost done . . . I mean, hee-hee, not that I would normally turn down your offer . . . ha-ha, I'm just running late this morning and—"

"Just call me when you're through, okay, babe? I'm at home," Dutch said, obviously recognizing that I needed help putting an end to my embarrassment.

"Deal," I said hanging up the phone and rushing back into the shower. Quickly I rinsed off and folded myself into my favorite flannel robe; then, with my hair bound up into a giant turban I called Dutch back. "Morning, sailor," I sang when he picked up.

"Hey, there. I wanted to catch you before you headed off to work and see if you were still intent on working tonight."

My shoulders slumped; I'd almost forgotten about my obligation for this evening. "Yeah, I'm sorry, but Kendal did me a huge favor last summer and I really owe him. Besides, you and I have all weekend, or parts of it anyway. I'm working Saturday and Sunday, but we still have the evenings. Honest, I can make it up to you, I promise."

There was a long pause on Dutch's end, then, "Could you at least have lunch with me this afternoon?"

"Absolutely!" I said perking up immediately. "I have a break from noon to one. How's that grab you?"

"Sounds like a winner. I'll pick you up right at twelve."

"Sailor, you can pick me up anytime, anywhere . . . I won't complain," I said, doing my best Mae West.

Dutch doesn't share my love of impressions, so he simply replied, "See you then, babe," and hung up.

With a quick glance at the clock I rushed back into the bathroom to get to work on hair and makeup.

My looks have always been the one thing about me that I've been pretty comfortable with. Having a sixth sense took years to come to grips with, but not my appearance. I know people who stare at themselves in the mirror and long to be different. Not me.

Now, don't get me wrong: I'm by no means a supermodel, but neither am I plain-Jane, either. I'm somewhere in between, sort of a girl-next-door type with long, waist-length hair the color a mixture of auburn, brunette and a few recently added blond highlights. My face is an inverted triangle, with a broad forehead, high cheekbones, a regular nose and an angular chin. My eyes are steel blue, my complexion fair and—usually—blemish free. I do have freckles, though, which I remember in my youth not being so fond of, but over the years I've gotten used to them.

My shoulders are broad for a girl, my hips are curvy and my butt has just a hint of J-Lo. I'm small in the chest, but since the invention of the Wonderbra, it's been less of an issue.

I stand five-foot six, and due to a busy schedule of late, I weigh a little less these days than I did a few months back; I'm down to 120 pounds.

My one weakness is that I'm a clotheshorse. My closet is bursting to overfull, and my fashion sense leans toward Darth Vader.

When I was a little girl, most of the other little girls in my neighborhood wanted to be Princess Leia. And although I liked Leia, and cheered for her, Luke and the gang . . . it was Darth Vader who captivated me.

Here was a guy who was different. He could do stuff with his mind that others couldn't. He could tap into the future and see things that were about to happen. He'd had some sort of freak accident that prevented him from mixing with polite company, so he too was on the outskirts of the "in" crowd.

To this day I remember the power emanating from

Lord Vader as he strode down hallways, his black cape billowing dramatically behind him as the music trumpeted his footsteps and the eerie sound of a ventilator sounded a warning call to one and all.

Everyone in his path shrank from his presence as, even masked, he still dominated the screen. Darth Vader stole every scene, he commanded absolute respect, and nobody messed with him. As a lonely little kid known to have rather "odd" talents, which provoked a slew of verbal and even physical attacks, sometimes I longed for that kind of presence.

Now, in the real world I can't very well parade around in a cape, no matter how much I'd like to, so given my dramatic flair, you can imagine how happy I was the day sweater coats came into vogue. I must have fifteen of them, most in shades of gray, black or charcoal.

My typical wardrobe for a day at the office is a sweater coat, jeans and spiky boots that, of course, *must* match the sweater coat, so I have ten or fifteen pairs of those too. Gee, and I wonder why my savings account remains so low.

This morning I chose faded blues, black silk blouse, black sweater coat and black boots. Look out, Dutch; here comes Darth Vadora.

After half an hour of primping in the bathroom I was done, and I rushed down the steps trying not to trip in my heels. After letting Eggy out one last time I locked up and headed to my office.

The morning passed normally, although I found myself having to work hard to concentrate as the time to meet Dutch came closer. I hadn't seen him in eight weeks, and I wondered, insecurely, if we'd still have that same spark between us.

At exactly twelve noon there was a knock on my outer door, and with a quick breath I rushed to open it. As the door swung open there stood Dutch Rivers, leaning against the doorjamb in cool magnificence. I tell you, ladies, *no* man should look that good.

He was wearing a tan suede jacket, brown cashmere sweater and faded blue jeans. He'd obviously just show-ered, as his light blond hair still looked slightly damp, and the subtle scent of a spice-laden aftershave tickled my nose. "Hey, there, Edgar," he said, using the nickname he'd coined for me months ago, after the famous psychic Edgar Cayce. The way it came out of his mouth, all throaty and masculine, made me want to jump him right there and then.

"Hey, yourself," I said, my voice cracking and a smile erupting on my face. I saw him straighten, looking intently at me, and it froze me in place. I don't know what I imagined this moment would be like, especially after not seeing each other for so long, but I do know I didn't think it would be this intense. This charged. This . . . *hot*.

I waited for him to do something, and for several seconds all we did was look at each other. Then I heard him inhale deeply and move forward, grabbing me around the waist with one hand and lifting my chin with the other. I allowed myself to be pulled forward as he kissed me long and deep. I couldn't help it; I moaned. This of course gave him added encouragement, and his kiss deepened, his embrace tightened and I began to swoon.

My senses were filled with him. His smell. His warmth. His kiss. His touch. We pawed at each other, breathing heavily and consuming each other like ravaging animals. At some point, however, I heard someone pass by and cough loudly, saying, "Get a room."

I didn't care, but Dutch was probably a little more self-conscious, and he pulled back slightly and looked behind him to the departing figure, then back at me, and grinned. "That's a great suggestion. Shall we take him up on that?"

Just as I was nodding my stomach gave a very loud, rebellious growl. It had been hours since I'd eaten. We both looked down at my midsection in surprise, and Dutch let out his throaty, seductive laugh. "Guess we'd better feed you first, huh?"

My stomach answered with another growl. I giggled myself this time and said, "Yeah, might be a good idea."

"I've made reservations anyway," Dutch said, releasing his firm grip on me.

I smiled shyly as I smoothed back my hair and read-justed my clothing. How had my blouse come unbuttoned? When I'd put myself back together, I grabbed my purse and smiled as I brushed past Mr. Sexy while he held the door. After locking up we headed companionably down the hallway, his arm tossed casually across my shoulders. "So, gorgeous, how ya been?" he asked while taking up a small lock of my hair to examine my new highlights more closely.

One of my favorite things about Dutch is how quick he is with a compliment.

"I'm good," I answered. "Busy, but good. You like?" I asked, indicating the highlights.

"Yeah, it's nice," he said, smiling, "but you could be bald as a billiard and still look good to me."

God help me, I'd found the perfect man. "So where we going for lunch?" I asked as we stepped into the elevator, heading toward the lobby.

"Well, I made reservations at Maverick and Moon's, but about that . . ."

"Yes?" I asked as we reached the front lobby.

"I wanted to introduce you to my new partner, so . . ."

"You extended an invitation," I said, letting the disappointment hang in my voice.

"Uh, yeah. Technically I'm still a trainee, and I'm sort of under Joe's command for the first six months."

There was an unspoken apology in Dutch's voice, and I really wasn't up to picking a petty argument over something so small. We'd have time to get reacquainted later anyway, so I shrugged off my initial annoyance. "Dutch, it's okay. I'd love to meet your new partner. Speaking of which, have you talked to Milo lately?"

Dutch and I had reached his car at this point, and my question hung in the air as I saw him bolt around to the front of his car—parked illegally, as usual—and snatch a small white piece of paper from under the wipers. "Son of a bitch!" he exclaimed.

"What's the matter?" I asked, alarmed.

"That son of a bitch Bennington!"

Immediately I knew whom he was referring to. Shawn Bennington was an archrival of Dutch's. Passed over for detective half a dozen times, Bennington was most recently reprimanded due to his lack of professionalism in a murder case Dutch and I had solved. Dutch had made a lot of noise about Bennington's sloppiness, and as a result Bennington had been demoted to meter maid. The ticket wadded up in Dutch's hand was evidence that Bennington was taking his revenge any way he could. "I'm gonna kill that asshole!" Dutch said, looking around for any sign of the patrolman. Not seeing him, he mashed up the ticket and stuffed it into his coat pocket, his brow furrowed and his mouth set in a firm line.

"Hey," I said, trying to sound reasonable, "it's okay, really. So you make a quick call and the ticket goes bye-bye. What's the big deal?"

"The big deal is that this guy is a menace, and he's not fit to be wearing a uniform. He got off easy with the meter-maid assignment, and it sticks in my craw that the man's still employed by the Royal Oak PD," Dutch snapped testily.

I got in the car not knowing what else to say. I didn't want to argue about it, and I was beginning to feel really disappointed that our lunch reunion was quickly filling up with so many pitfalls.

We drove to the restaurant in silence, Dutch still simmering over his ticket and me trying not to provoke a long-winded dissertation on Bennington's ineptness. After all, I'd heard it all before.

By the time we'd reached Maverick and Moon's, Dutch seemed to be cooling off. He pulled into the parking lot and stepped around to my side, holding the door open. When I got out he hugged me and whispered, "Sorry about that." He then kissed my forehead and said, "That guy gets under my skin, and I shouldn't take it out on you."

I beamed up at him and took his arm as we strolled into the restaurant.

Maverick and Moon's is a popular, swanky haunt on the outskirts of Royal Oak. The exterior is white stucco with a shingled roof and mosaic patterns bordering the windows. The interior is eclectic, booths are round and cozy, tabletops are marble and no two chairs are alike.

The lighting is soft and romantic, and the fare adventurous and bold. It was one of my favorite restaurants, and I smiled to myself as I thought about how Dutch had remembered that I'd raved about it the last time we'd had dinner here.

In the lobby we were greeted by a petite hostess who took Dutch's name and looked at her seating chart. "Yes, Mr. Rivers, the other half of your party is already seated. John, will you take these two back to table number twenty-four?"

A young man stepped forward, and we followed him in a fishtail path through other tables to a four-top, where a gorgeous brunette stood up to greet us. "Hello!" she said as we approached. *Oh, how nice,* I thought, *Dutch's partner brought a date too.*

"Abby, this is Joe La Bond. My new partner."

My mouth fell open as if my brain had suddenly leaked out of my ear. The woman claiming to be Dutch's new partner was at least five-ten with shoulder-length dark brown hair and full, seductive lips set prominently on her gorgeous face. Her eyes were huge brown orbs that gave her an innocent baby-doll appearance. She had olive skin, long limbs and narrow hips—oh, and her boobs were enormous.

Now, I know what you're thinking—and yes, I *am* still comfortable with my looks, but *anyone* can feel intimidated when they stand next to Catherine Zeta-Jones.

The air hung around us as Dutch and Joe waited for some kind of reaction on my part other than, "Duh." Finally I shook my head a few times and tentatively extended my hand. "Nice to meet you, Joe. Sorry, but I thought you were a guy."

Joe chuckled, a smoky, seductive sound. "I get that a lot. 'Joe' is actually short for 'Josephine,' but you can't be taken seriously in the Bureau carting a name like that around."

Dutch and I laughed politely, although mine was a little more forced than his, and we all took our seats. Out of the corner of my eye I could see Dutch looking slightly flustered. I had a feeling he'd been so distracted by his parking ticket that it'd completely slipped his mind to fill me in on his partner's gender and appearance. To set his mind at ease, I shot daggers at him and mouthed, *You are so dead . . .* as I snapped my menu open.

"So!" Dutch said into the tension-filled silence, "what's good here?"

Joe answered abruptly, "Everything, but the pumpkin tortellini is a favorite of mine." Turning to me she added, "Dutch asked me where he should bring you for lunch, and I recommended this place to him. You'll love the food."

I fought back the venom I wanted to spit at my boyfriend, and instead said icily to Joe, "Yes, I know. He and I actually came here last summer the night before he left for Quantico."

Dutch looked at me in surprise, then glanced around the room quickly. "Oh, yeah. I *thought* this place looked familiar." So much for giving him points for sentimentality.

Joe mouthed *Uh-oh* and averted her eyes back to the menu while I glared at my boyfriend. "What?" he asked defensively.

Could men *be* more stupid?

"*Nothing,*" I snapped. "Nothing at all."

There was a long period of uncomfortable silence as we all pretended to look at our menus; and after a minute or two our waiter, Bob, came by to take our drink orders. I ordered a glass of red wine; Joe and Dutch both ordered iced tea. I felt awkward being the only one at the table to order alcohol, so I tried to retract my order when Joe said, "No, no, Abby, you go ahead. Dutch and I are on duty."

"On duty?" I asked, surprised as I glanced at Dutch, who began to cough loudly.

"Yeah, we're on assignment right after lunch. We've got to catch a plane later on tonight, and we'll need to stay focused," Joe said smartly.

I looked at the her with my mouth hanging open. I could not believe the deluge of crap being spoon-fed to me in the course of the last ten minutes, so I kept the wine, sent the waiter scurrying to the bar and rounded on Dutch. "You're going on assignment and you have a plane to catch?"

"Uh, you see, the thing of it is . . . ." he tried to explain as he leaned over to lay a reassuring hand on my wrist.

I looked at his hand as if a turd had landed on my skin, and Dutch quickly pulled it away. Again Joe decided to get in the middle of it and make things worse. "It's not his fault, really. We got our assignments yesterday, and you can't really put off the Bureau just because you miss your girlfriend."

At that moment the waiter came back with our drinks and asked if we were ready to order. Joe took charge and ordered the pumpkin tortellini, Dutch dittoed that and I rebelliously picked the most expensive item on the menu, the roasted duck with a side salad. Truth be told I didn't even like duck and I had no real intention of eating Daffy, but I was hungry, so I'd have to make do with the salad.

When the waiter left I took a tremendous swig of my glass of wine and looked anywhere but at either Joe or Dutch. I was fuming and trying valiantly to tramp down my feelings. I pictured all sorts of scenarios that began with me thumping Dutch on the head and him pleading for mercy. Trying for small talk, Joe asked sweetly, "So, Abby, Dutch has told me so little about you. What is it that you do?"

So little about me? "I'm a psychic," I said icily.

Joe sputtered the iced tea she was sipping, "You're joking."

I shot a question mark at Dutch and found him picking at the lint on his napkin, avoiding my gaze. Feeling hurt at his obvious discomfort with the topic of conversation, I shifted my gaze back to Joe and said, "No, not joking at all. I'm a psychic. I look into a crystal ball and wear lots of scarves and dance under the full moon bucknaked while I howl like a coyote. Didn't Dutch tell you?"

Joe tilted her head back and laughed heartily. She thought I was kidding. Dutch squirmed in his chair and

I continued to take large sips of my wine. "No, really. What line of work are you in?" Joe persisted after she'd had her laugh.

I sighed and turned my cool stare directly on her as I said, very deliberately, "I *am* a psychic. I tell people their futures . . . for real."

Joe smirked and cocked her head slightly as she looked at me, waiting to see if I'd crack a smile. Finally she said, "Okay, so what am I thinking?"

Oh, brother. Here we go. "I said I was psychic, not a mind reader."

"Is there a difference?"

"A big one," I said dismissively as I downed the last of the wine.

"Like what?" she persisted.

I didn't like this woman. Not one bit. Her attempts to be helpful were just a bit too over-the-top for me, and this whole warm and fuzzy routine was getting on my last nerve. I sighed heavily. "Psychics are able to see glimpses of events, opportunities and obstacles that may happen, or have already happened. Mind readers, who are sometimes referred to as mentalists, use extrasensory perception to get a sense of what you're thinking or feeling."

"Huh," Joe said, looking at me with narrowed eyes. Then she smiled and said, "Personally I think the whole thing's a bunch of baloney, but there are a lot of gullible people out there, so I'm sure you're doing quite the business."

The wine had hit my empty stomach and drained the restraint right out of me. I couldn't believe what she had just said to me. I half stood out of my chair in a shaky motion; I was going to hit this bitch but good.

Dutch bolted up and caught my shoulders; pressing me back down in the chair he said, "Abby, easy there. What Joe means is that until she sees proof, she's going to remain a confirmed skeptic. Right, Joe?"

Joe cocked her index finger and her thumb in a gun motion and winked at Dutch, "You got it, partner."

I glowered at Dutch, my cheeks flushed with anger that he would so quickly take her side, but sat back down anyway. I rolled my eyes, crossed my arms and glared at the tabletop. *Screw them. Bring on Daffy . . . and another glass of wine!*

While I pouted sullenly, Dutch and Joe talked softly between them mostly about some paperwork they needed to do before checking in.

"Checking in?" I asked, butting into the conversation.

Dutch coughed loudly again and made a small "no" motion to Joe as he stood up and excused himself to the restroom.

One thing I'd learned about my boyfriend was that he had the bladder of a hamster. As he departed the table I caught Joe visibly watching his derriere, and my anger, jealousy and now-empty glass of wine got the best of me. "Listen here," I said with a deadly voice, leaning in, "I don't know what you think you're up to, but Dutch is spoken for. Got it?"

Joe swiveled her head in my direction and regarded me with narrowed eyes. "Relax, Miss Cleo," she said. "I'm not interested in your boyfriend." *Liar, liar, pants on fire . . .* "Dutch is my subordinate, and it's against Bureau policy to date a subordinate. Although, if I *were* interested in him I'd have plenty of opportunity, given that we're about to go undercover as a couple, and we'll be spending pretty much every moment together. In fact, we're headed out of town this very evening, and we'll be rooming together—you know, so we can become better *acquainted.* . . ." She said this with a grin and a wink that I wanted badly to slap off her face.

"Oh! I get it," I announced thickly, waving an unsteady hand at her in a flaring motion, the wine freeing up my tongue. "You're *easy*. Well, allow me to divine your future, honey," I said, bringing my hand up to my head in mock concentration. "It's not very long, and it's absolutely bound to be painful if you even think about—"

"Whoa!" came a deep baritone right behind me. "Abby, what the . . . ?" Dutch said as I swiveled my head to look back at him. He was wearing a look of shock that was quickly turning to anger.

"She—" I began, pointing an accusing finger at Joe, but he cut me off.

"Please excuse us for a minute, Agent La Bond," he said, and grabbed my hand, practically pulling me out of my chair and escorting me to the front of the restaurant.

When he found a spot near the coat check that offered a small amount of privacy, he hissed, "Just what the hell do you think you're doing?!"

"*Me?!* What about her?" I hissed back.

"*What* about her?" he asked, but his tone suggested he wasn't the least bit interested in my answer.

"I've got breaking news for you, buddy," I said, wobbling slightly as the wine wrecked havoc with my balance. "You may not realize it, but you're partnered up with Miss F-B-I'm-a-whore over there, and you have the *nerve* to try to make me feel guilty about having to work tonight when you're about to go off on some assignment with that . . . that . . . *that? !*" I couldn't think of a good pejorative, so I just kept stuttering.

"Oh, for Christ's sake, Abby!" Dutch hissed again, "She's my *superior!* There's nothing going on between us—"

"Try telling *her* that," I spat.

"Come on!" Dutch whispered impatiently. "Cut me some slack, will ya? For your information it's against Bureau policy to date a subordinate. She could lose her job if she even—"

"Yeah, yeah, yeah!" I said loudly, no longer keeping my voice down. "I've heard that line before. The point is that you allowed me to feel terrible about not making our dinner tonight when you're the one about to jet-set off with Miss Silicone Valley."

"Listen," he said, squeezing my arm, his body language pleading with me to lower my voice, "my plane wasn't leaving until after ten, and if you had been available we still could have had an early dinner and gotten *reacquainted* before I had to leave."

"Wham bam thank you, ma'am. Gee, Agent Rivers, how romantic of you," I deadpanned, giving him a flinty glare.

"And why did you have to tell her you were a psychic?" he asked, changing the subject completely.

"*Excuse me?*" I screeched, now utterly offended.

"I mean, come on! This is the first time you meet my partner and you have to open with the fortune-teller bit? How do you think I'm gonna live that one down?"

"What I do is not a 'bit,' " I growled, my face feeling flushed with anger. "And she asked me what I did for a living. What would you have had me tell her?"

"Hell, I don't know," he said, sighing heavily and running a hand through his blond hair. "Anything, I guess—"

I didn't even wait for him to finish the full sentence. I was completely fed up. I turned on my heel and exited the restaurant, stomping my way over to Dutch's car.

He caught up to me ten yards from his sedan. "Abby," he said, grabbing for my arm and stopping me, "what's got you so fired up?"

I glared up at him as all the insecurities about our relationship and his new beautiful partner welled up inside me, "Did you suddenly forget, Agent Rivers, that my psychic abilities practically *led* you to a certain serial killer last summer?"

"No," he snapped, clearly growing tired of our argument, "I didn't forget. But this is different."

"*How* exactly is this different?" I demanded.

"Because people in my line of work aren't that open-minded. And you knew I was the new guy on the block at the Bureau, and you still had to go on and on about baying at the moon buck-naked." I bit my lip nervously, suddenly ashamed of the colorful description I'd painted for Joe. "Jesus!" he continued, his voice rising in anger. "Do you know what's going to happen when we get back to headquarters? I'm going to be the laughingstock! You could have said you were a stripper and I'd probably get razzed less than telling my boss that you're psychic."

I sucked in a huge breath, feeling as if he'd struck me. That was it; he'd crossed the line. *"You are an utter asshole!"* I yelled, and turned on my heel.

"Okay, maybe that was a little harsh—"

I ignored him and continued to stomp away.

"I'm sorry!" he called from behind me. "That was a stupid thing to say. I didn't mean it."

I arrived at his car and stood next to the passenger-side door, waiting with balled fists and a temper on sizzle. "Take me back to my office *immediately*," I said through gritted teeth when he caught up to me.

"Abby—"

"Did I stutter? Did you not understand me?" I snarled over my shoulder as he stood behind me. "You will take me back to my office right now, or I *swear to God* I will cause a scene like you have never imagined!"

Sighing, he unlocked the doors and I got in with a huff. He stood outside the sedan for a moment and made a call on his cell phone. I could hear snatches of the conversation from inside the car: ". . . just have them put it in a to-go bag and I'll meet you back at headquarters in an hour . . ."

Finally he got in and began to drive steadily back to my office. After several minutes of stony silence he said, "Can we talk about this?"

I ignored him, looking stoically out the window.

"Hey, come on, Edgar," he tried in a soothing tone. "I'm headed out of town for at least a couple of weeks on an undercover assignment, and I won't have a chance to call or talk to you for a while. I'd really rather not have this hanging over us until I get back."

"You don't have to worry about it," I finally said, breaking my silence. "There is no more 'us.' "

"Excuse me?"

"You want a girlfriend who won't embarrass you? Then feel free to go mine a strip club, Dutch, 'cause we are over. Done. *Finito.* End of story."

"Abby, come on. You don't mean that. . . ."

Just then we pulled up in front of my office, and for the first time I felt the full sting of the disastrous afternoon as tears welled up and blurred my vision, threatening to spill over. The car had barely come to a stop and I was already opening the door. Dutch grabbed my arm as I was getting out. "Hey, wait, Abby. Come on, let's talk about this," he pleaded.

"Go to hell, you son of a bitch!" I said viciously, yanking my arm away as I got out and slammed the door behind me. I ran inside and up the stairs, keeping my head down as the tears came. When I reached my floor I rushed down the hallway to my suite and quickly unlocked the door. Bolting into my reading room I curled up into a ball on my chair and cried my eyes out.

Chapter Three

Sometimes, at least, I'm actually able to catch a break. After my disasterous lunch date with Dutch I was a sniveling, sobbing mess, and in no shape to see clients. Luckily, my last two appointments for the day—booked together—were no-shows. After waiting fifteen minutes longer than their appointment time, I closed up shop and headed home.

I drove through my neighborhood in a stupor, replaying the scene at the restaurant over and over. I had been under the impression that Dutch had come to respect my occupation. After all, only a few months ago it had helped him nab a serial killer. How was it possible that now he was embarrassed by what I did?

As I drove I tried to take my mind off things by making an effort to absorb the beauty of the crisp fall day. Autumn in Michigan is a breathtaking event.

Sometime toward the end of September, summer abruptly ends and there is a rather sudden natural reversal of color, sight and smell. Overnight the sky turns gray, the clouds turn blue, the flowers turn brown and the leaves turn orange, red, yellow and pink. The sweet smell of summer flowers gives way to the hickory scent of burning leaves, crisp mornings and a flurry of activity as the cold entices people out of their hammocks and into chores of leaf raking, garage cleaning, and preparing for winter.

By the time we get to Halloween, most of the leaves have fallen and the chill has settled in for the duration. While I combed my way through my subdivision, I smiled a little as I took in the lavish display of Halloween decorations: plastic spiders dangling from trees, white ghosts poking out of windows, witches' brooms leaning in doorways, and headstones on nearly every lawn.

As I pulled into my driveway, I sighed as I realized time had gotten away from me this year, and the grocery bag full of decorations I'd planned on hanging up would have to remain in their packaging for one more year.

The only thing I'd managed to do to promote the spirit of Halloween was carve two pumpkins, and I'd done that only to get to the seeds.

I loved pumpkin seeds, and as it happened so did Dutch. I pouted as I thought about how I'd made a special batch for him with extra salt, just like he'd told me he liked them. They were sitting on the counter in my kitchen in a large Tupperware container with his name on it, and as I got out of my car I was already having second thoughts about ending our relationship so abruptly.

The problem was that even though I adored him, I couldn't possibly date someone who didn't completely accept me for who I was. Still, the man *was* beautiful. My mind drifted back to my office that afternoon, when we'd been *this* close to public indecency.

So in essence, my libido was having a huge quarrel with my ethics. I sighed heavily once more and got out of the car, walking toward my house. As I got close my front door opened unexpectedly, causing me to jump, which was a good thing because I was almost knocked over by several large two-by-fours making their way out of the doorway on Dave's shoulder.

"Hey, Abby," Dave said, grinning under the strain of the wood.

"Hi, Dave. Those the old rafters?"

"Some of 'em. There's still more to take down, but I got ya a great deal on the replacement lumber. Oh, and I broke that window in your attic with one of the rafters, but I'll take care of it when I'm through with the job."

I moved aside as Dave hefted the wood in the direction of his truck. "So how much damage to my bank account are we talking?" I asked.

"I'm doing my best to keep it under a grand, honey."

My mouth fell open. At the moment I was a little short on cash. I'd done some very grown-up things recently, like opening up an IRA where I'd sunk in the maximum for the year, as well as buying up a bunch of stock my sister had recommended to me. The grand was going to hurt, but I refused to flinch, remembering I was working a party this evening that would, in essence, pay for the repairs. "No sweat," I said. "I can swing it."

Dave had thrown the old lumber into his truck and was now walking back by me to get another load from inside. As he passed me he said, "Fifteen hundred at the very most."

I gulped, feeling a tightening sensation in the middle of my chest. The past two days had taken all the fight out of me. "Whatever," I said moodily, and walked in behind him.

Dave caught my inflection and paused to look at me critically before gathering up the next load of wood littering my living room. "You okay?"

I lowered my gaze and bent low to greet an anxious Eggy, then scooped him up and quickly turned toward the stairs, not wanting Dave to make a closer inspection of my tearstained face. "Nothing that a bubble bath and cup of hot soup won't cure. I'll be upstairs if you need me," I said, and with that I bolted to my bedroom. I headed straight to my bed and fell backward, Lipton-tea style, holding on to Eggy as he kissed away my tears. Finally, when I'd regained a little composure, I left the pooch' on the bed and walked into the bathroom to inspect my reflection.

Hollywood is filled with starlets who look even more attractive when they're bawling their eyes out. I don't know how they do it, because when I cry my nose gets red and runny, my eyes swell up and my cheeks get puffy. In other words, I look like I've gone a few rounds with Evander Holyfield—hardly glamorous. Sighing, I turned on the faucet and swept cool water over my face until my makeup was good and runny, then reached for the soap and cleaned off the rest. Next I wound my hair up into a high ponytail, pinning it to the top of my head as I ran a bath.

While the tub filled with hot water I trundled back downstairs and fixed an instant cup of soup, and a peanut butter-and-jelly sandwich. Toting these back upstairs, I set them on the side of the tub and, after disrobing, got in. For a few minutes I just let the warmth of the water soothe me like a down comforter.

Finally I reached for my soup, sipping at it and eating my sandwich without pause, noticing for the first time since my meltdown that I was famished. After polishing off my late lunch I sank back down into the warmth of the tub until I was pruny, then got out and wrapped myself in my flannel robe.

Making my way back to my bedroom, I noticed it was getting close to five, and I hurried my pace a little. I had to meet Kendal at six. After looking through a few choices in my closet for suitable wedding-guest attire, I selected a charcoal cocktail dress, black heels, and a pearl necklace with matching earrings. Next, I went back to the bathroom and wound my hair up in a French twist, securing it with several dozen bobby pins, then brushed my cheeks with blush, my lashes with mascara, and my lips with burgundy lipstick.

When I was finished I perused my reflection in the mirror. Satisfied that I could pass for an attendee at a funeral, wedding, or breakfast at Tiffany's, I left the bathroom and headed for the stairs.

Once I got to the living room I noticed that Dave had long since gone home, and had kindly fed Eggy before leaving. I went back into the kitchen, got down a huge wooden bowl from my cabinet and filled it to overflowing with Halloween candy. I really hoped that the kids in my neighborhood would be conscientious enough to take only a handful of Snickers bars and move on—but most likely the bowl would be empty after the third trick-or-treater.

I let Eggy out one last time, then grabbed my coat, purse and keys, flipped on the porch light put the wooden bowl in the center of my welcome mat and with a deep sigh headed toward my car.

Kendal lives just a few minutes away from me, a little closer to the neighboring town of Ferndale. His clientele is mostly based in the distant town of Mount Clemens, where he grew up, but recently he and his partner, Rick, had purchased an adorable Tudor just a few miles from me. When I pulled into his driveway I noticed he was already coming out of his house to greet me.

I've known Kendal for years; he was something of a mentor to me when I first got started in the business. He's a gorgeous man, tall, with broad shoulders, wavy brown hair and deep-set blue eyes rimmed smartly with wire glasses that only accentuate his good looks. He has an infectious smile, a machine-gun laugh, and most of his clientele are madly in love with him. In fact, were he not gay, I might have made a bid for him myself once upon a time.

As psychics go he's one of the best I've ever known. His readings are freakishly detailed, peppered with humor, and always full of hope. No matter how desperate the situation, Kendal will give you the silver lining. I respected him immensely for his talent, his wisdom, and his positive attitude. Plus, even though he played for another team, he was still nice to look at.

We met in the driveway, and he gathered me up in a tremendous hug that, I'll admit, I badly needed. Setting me down he stepped away and immediately said, "What's happened?"

"Nothing I want to talk about," I said dismissively. I didn't want to be read tonight; I just wanted to get this stupid reception out of the way and go back home to bed, which I might never leave.

Kendal looked at me for a long moment. I was familiar with the look; it's the faraway stare most psychics have when we're gathering intuitive information. "Kendal, really, just leave it alone," I pleaded.

"It's not over, sugar, even though you think it is. . . ."

Against my will my eyes welled up and I turned quickly away and walked over to his car, where I waited to be let in. After a long pause I sneaked a look at Kendal, who smiled apologetically at me, shrugged his shoulders and hit a button on his key chain, unlocking the door. I climbed in without a word and Kendal joined me a moment later. Without further delay we backed out of the driveway and headed downtown toward Detroit.

"Did you bring two sets of tarot cards?" I asked as he drove, remembering our little tutoring session before the reception.

Kendal tapped his left pocket and said, "I've got it all covered."

"You sure I'm going to be able to pull this off?" I asked apprehensively.

"Sugar, if anyone can pull this off, you can. Really, it's a piece of cake. Trust me."

Anytime someone says the words "trust me," it's a pretty good indication that you'd be wiser to head for the hills. I squirmed as we got off at the exit for downtown, and took calming breaths as we drove into the parking structure across from the casino.

"So what's the scoop on the bride and groom?" I asked as we walked toward the casino. "I mean, it's a little odd to have a couple of psychics entertaining at your wedding reception."

"They're getting married on Halloween, so I doubt having us attend is odd for them."

"Good point."

We headed into the Plaza Casino and through a brilliantly lit foyer. We found the concierge desk, and Kendal asked about the wedding reception. We were directed down a corridor to the left of the foyer and made our way briskly to the appointed ballroom. As we walked through the double doors my eyes got large looking at the lavish decorations and opulence of the place.

I don't know what I imagined—something like little pumpkins for centerpieces, and orange and black streamers in a cacophony of bad taste—but the room had no trace of that kind of thing anywhere.

The tables were dressed in brilliant white tablecloths with ornate floral designs and votive candles demurely providing much of the lighting. The chairs were wrapped in huge chiffon bows of autumn rose, and soft pink Christmas-tree lights wrapped every pylon, and hung in a drapelike fashion from the ceiling.

The bridal party was to be seated at a long table on a large dais, raised slightly so that even those in the back sections could see the bride and groom clearly.

Over to one side was an extravagant table with a large ice carving of a mermaid and tray upon tray of crab claws, jumbo shrimp and oysters. The opposite side of the room held the dessert table, literally strewn with small confections of chocolate, and in the center sat an enormous three-tiered wedding cake with a basket-weave pattern, and sugared leaves in various fall colors spilling down each tier.

There was a flurry of activity as banquet workers hurried to set each table with sterling silver and gilded china and fold each napkin into a swan. There was enough room to seat 350 attendees, and I had a brief moment of insecurity as I thought about how many guests we'd have to read to even make a dent.

Just then a short, round woman with a bad case of helmet hair waddled over to us. She wore an earpiece and a small microphone over one ear, with a cord connecting it to a phone clipped to her skirt. She carried a clipboard and a permanent scowl, which was so stern it made me move behind Kendal and avoid eye contact. "May I help you?" she asked crisply.

"Yes, hello. You must be Constance, the wedding planner?" Kendal asked.

"Correct," the woman answered impatiently.

"I'm Kendal Adams, and this is my associate, Abigail Cooper. We're the psychics hired for the party."

"Oh, yes," she said as she read from the clipboard, "you're very early."

"We just wanted to get set up and be prepared by the time the guests arrived," Kendal explained smoothly.

Constance's scowl transformed itself into a snarl, which was quite possibly her version of a smile. "Very good. We've got you two set up over there in the back corner by the dessert table," she said as she pointed to a small section curtained off and nearly invisible from where we stood. Kendal nodded and motioned with his head to me as we took our leave of the wedding planner and moseyed over to the far end of the reception hall.

We reached our assigned area, rounding the curtain, and as we had a chance to survey the scene we quickly smiled at each other. The section behind the curtain had been subdivided, separated by yet another curtain. Each small section held a tiny table, two cushioned chairs and two votive candles for light and ambience. We would have to speak softly so as not to drown each other out, but other than that it was a good setup.

"This is perfect," Kendal said.

"It'll do," I said as I took off my coat, wrapping it around one of the chairs. Kendal did the same and sat down across from me at the first table. "Are you ready for your tarot lesson?"

"Should I take notes?" I asked, reaching for my purse. I had included a small pad of paper and pen in my purse before leaving the house.

"No, it's really not that complicated. You should pick it up right away," Kendal said as he retrieved two tarot decks of large cards from his jacket pocket. "I teach intuitive tarot, and being that you're already a very developed clairvoyant, this should be an elementary exercise for you."

I looked at the decks he had placed in front of him. They were oversized, about one and a half times the size of regular playing cards. Their backs were black save for a silver pentagram painted squarely in the middle. I reached forward and picked up one of the decks curiously, turning it over and surveying the faces.

They were richly decorated with strange and detailed scenes on every face. Some held snapshots of events caught in midmotion: a man chasing a woman around a banquet table, two swordsmen in the heat of battle, two people climbing up a cliff. The tarot deck was much thicker than a regular set of playing cards, however, and I wondered how Kendal could possibly teach me the meaning of each card in so little time.

"The secret to reading tarot is not memorizing a bunch of traditional meanings and then regurgitating that for your client," Kendal said. "I mean, *anyone* can do that. What sets you and I apart is our ability to interpret the metaphor displayed on the card."

I screwed up my face, giving him a "huh?" expression, and Kendal smiled patiently at me. "Let's start at the beginning. Tarot is an art form with roots that date as far back as ancient Egypt. The cards were developed to be used as tools to assist in triggering your subconscious thoughts—and not, as some people believe, a literal translation of the picture on the card itself. In other words, the magic is in you, not in the deck. The card is only the catalyst for the thought, a thread leading to a much richer fabric, so to speak."

I nodded, even though what Kendal was saying was about as clear as mud, and I began to worry that I wouldn't be able to catch on in time for the first wedding guest. "Uh-huh," I said uncertainly.

Kendal smiled patiently and tried a different tack. "Okay, let's take an example, shall we?" After I nodded he laid down his deck in front of me. "Let's say we want to know what's coming up in my life, so we'll set the intention and think about what we want to know, then flip over a card."

I nodded again, and he said, "Now focus on my energy and ask in your mind what's about to happen in my life." After a moment in which I set my concentration and focused on his energy, he flipped over a card, revealing a picture of a large sun. "Can you tell me, just by looking at this picture and seeing what it reminds you of, what's coming up in my future?" Kendal asked.

Without hesitation I said, "You're going someplace warm and sunny—south, like Florida or the tropics."

Kendal laughed and replied, "See? See how easy this is? Now, the truth is that I don't have anything like that planned, but you never know—my mother lives in Tampa, so maybe I'm going to visit her soon."

"Cool," I said, encouraged. If that was all I had to do then this wasn't going to be so hard after all.

"Let's try another, shall we?" And Kendal flipped over another card. This one was a picture of a woman walking through an archway of three swords. I couldn't see her face but there was an instant feeling of betrayal. I stared at the card for a brief moment, letting my mind go where it wanted, and said, "There's a triangle here. Are you cheating on Rick?"

Kendal looked at me, his brows lowering slightly as he said defensively, "Absolutely not." Then he looked closer at the card and said, "Ah, the three of swords. I think this card is probably meant for you. . . ." He let the rest of his sentence hang and I averted my eyes. I'd almost forgotten the earlier part of my day.

Kendal grabbed up the two cards in front of me and said quickly, "Don't worry about it; you're a pro. If you get stumped just lay down a spread and use your own method. No one's going to be paying attention to the cards; they're only going to want to hear what you have to say."

I nodded, swallowed hard and after a moment looked up again. I seriously needed to get a grip on my emotions here. "So how do I lay them out? I mean . . . I know there's a pattern to how the cards are laid down, right?"

Kendal nodded and said, "Yes, most definitely. I'll teach you the simple Celtic cross method; it's the easiest to remember." I watched as he shuffled the deck briskly, then laid out two cards in a perpendicular fashion, then four more in a circle surrounding the first two. He then set down four additional ones in a column alongside the circle, for a total of ten cards. Tapping the first he said, "Position number one represents the client, and describes him or her as a person while position number two indicates what is helping or hurting that client presently, like if the client were worried about their job, this card could be a coworker who was undermining their efforts at work."

"Got it," I said.

Kendal smiled and said, "Positions three, four and five are the past, present and near future, respectively, and cards six through ten talk about specifics of that future. For instance, number six indicates the client's attitude toward that future, number seven is about their hopes and fears, number eight represents friends and family, nine is for environmental or general surroundings . . ."

"Huh?" I interrupted pointing to the eighth position. I had no idea what he meant by that.

"Ummm . . ." Kendal said, thinking of a good example, "What I mean is that this card could represent the client's surroundings, the environment where he lives, what his home is like, what his work is like etc."

"Okay, I got it," I said waving for him to move on.

"And last but not least, number ten talks about the final outcome, like if your client stays on the path that you've laid out for them, this will be the end result."

My brow furrowed as I struggled to take it all in. There was a lot to remember so I pointed to each card and recited, "Client, helping or hurting, past, present, near future, hopes and fears, friends and family, environment, and final outcome."

"Good job!" Kendal said proudly, "See? You catch on fast. Now, let's talk about the suits. Just like a regular deck the tarot has four suits, pentacles, wands, swords and cups. These four represent the four elements: wands are air, swords are fire, cups are water, and pentacles are earth. They also represent the four directions and the four seasons."

"Oay," I said trying to force my memory to retain all this information.

Kendal continued, "For example, pentacles are north and winter, swords are east and spring, wands are south and summer and cups are west and autumn."

"North-winter, east-spring, south-summer, west-autumn . . . got it," I said pointing to each suit.

"Good! Okay, last and most important, the suits represent the four facets of man; wands for creativity, cups for emotion, swords for intellect and pentacles for work or money like income."

"Okay, I think I'm catching on," I said as my brain swam with information. Easy as it seemed, it was still a lot to take in.

Kendal chuckled and patted me on the arm reassuringly. "Hey, don't sweat it. If a card stumps you, you have two choices: You can lay down another card or two until you get the whole picture, or you can just close your eyes and use your own method to get there. I'm confident you'll be just fine."

I nodded as my throat tightened up and little butterflies fluttered in my stomach. The last time I'd felt this way was nearly five years earlier, when I'd done my very first reading.

Kendal got up and picked up his jacket. "Listen, I'm going to go next door to the other table and get squared away. If you need me, just holler."

I got up too. "That's fine. I think I'll head over to the bar and see if I can't find a bottled water. You want anything?"

"Bottled water sounds good, thanks."

"Back in a flash," I said, and rounded the curtain.

The very first wedding guests were just now arriving, and I walked briskly to the bar, not wanting to get stuck in a line that was sure to fill up fast. I caught the eye of a young bartender, who winked at me and said, "What'll it be?"

"Two bottled waters, please," I said putting a dollar in his tip jar. I took the waters he gave me and was making my way back toward our area when I noticed two huge baskets set to one side that I hadn't seen before. Taking a quick detour I trotted over to investigate, and saw they were filled with dozens and dozens of masquerade masks. There were black masks for the men, and white masks for the ladies, each one beautifully decorated with intricate beading and silver or gold lace ribbon.

Ah, so this was the Halloween theme coming into play, only instead of wearing tacky rubber in the shape of ghouls and goblins, this bride had chosen a masquerade theme. Nice.

I trotted back to our tables, and handed Kendal his

water. He was already getting into mode, doing some deep breathing and sitting straight in his chair with his eyes closed. I figured I'd better join him, so I took my seat and closed my own eyes. In the background I could hear the energy of wedding guests burbling with excitement and laughter as they tried on their masks and got their first drinks and made their way to the crab claws. I tuned them out and focused on calling out to my crew, where I had a one-way mental conversation that went something like this: *Gang, I need your help tonight. Please assist me in any way you can, and if I get stuck reading the cards, please fill in the blanks. Don't let me fall on my face, okay?* My right side felt light and airy; my crew would assist all they could. Feeling more confident I opened my eyes and was surprised to see a masked woman already seated in the chair across from me.

"Oh!" I exclaimed.

"Sorry," she said quickly. "I didn't know if you were ready, so I just thought I'd wait until you opened your eyes."

I giggled at being caught so unaware, and said, "No problem, I'm ready." I very nearly forgot the tarot cards at that point, but remembered suddenly and began to shuffle nervously. Stalling long enough I inhaled deeply and asked the woman her name and birth date, then turned over the first card.

The picture on the card was of a man holding a painting palate in one hand, a paintbrush in the other, and sitting before an easel that had several wands already painted there. Immediately I said, "This says you're very creative, but it's more than that. Like you're big on decorating, or even that you're an expert at decorating or painting or something."

The woman giggled and said, "I'm an interior decorator."

I heaved a huge sigh of relief. Okay, this was going to work. I continued with the cards and laid down another. The picture held a queenly-looking woman with dark hair, holding a pentacle in one outstretched arm. "I get the feeling you're very good at what you do, but you have a client right now who's holding out on you. A woman with dark hair hasn't paid her bill yet, and you have a cash-flow problem until this account is settled."

"Oh, my God! That is so true! One of my biggest clients is a woman with dark hair, and she's been ducking my calls to pay up!"

I relaxed and let myself sink back in the chair, realizing I'd been holding myself very tightly until now. I'd been so worried I would have trouble doing the conversion from free-form to interpreting the cards, but this was like child's play. I continued on with the woman for ten more minutes and then ended the session. She beamed at me and got up excitedly. "Do you have a business card?" she asked.

"Certainly," I said, reaching into my purse and pulling out a pile of them. I laid all but one on the table, and handed it to her. I felt confident now about advertising.

"You were wonderful," she gushed.

"Thank you. Thank you very much," I said humbly.

The woman trotted off, and no sooner had she gone than a young, very good-looking man with jet-black hair, dark brown eyes and olive skin stepped around the corner. Unlike the woman who had just left me, he was maskless. He sat down and we shook hands. "Hi, I'm Jimmy," he said.

I shook his hand and noted, "Not one for the masquerade theme, eh, Jimmy?"

He chuckled and explained, "No, it's not that. I'm the groom. The rules are that everyone wears a mask but the bride and groom."

"Oh! Congratulations! I didn't know the bride and groom were going to get a reading."

"Yeah, my wife's idea. She's in with your partner right now. We wanted to get in before the party started rocking so we'd have a chance to see you two. Ophelia loves psychics. She's always going to see them. That's how we met, you know."

"Really?"

"Yeah, the woman she used to go to told her she was about to meet a man at the grocery store, and I guess she described me to a T. Well, Ophelia goes to the store every night for two weeks, but no one looks like the psychic describes. Then one night she's over at her aunt's house, helping with dinner, and her aunt needs some goat cheese or something. Ophelia doesn't want to go to the store to get it because she said she didn't look good, she'd been lounging around all day. So her aunt insisted that she go, and wouldn't you know it? I got in line right behind her."

"That is a great story," I said, smiling. I wondered if Ophelia knew how lucky she was. This young man had wonderful energy. "Okay, Jimmy, you ready?"

"Sure," he said, and moved his seat closer.

I asked his full name and birth date, shuffled the deck and began. The first card I turned over was a picture of a man scribing on a parchment in deep concentration. There was an abacus on a shelf near him, and several pentacles lined the bottom of the card. "You're an accountant," I said matter-of-factly.

"Whoa! You're good," he said, sitting up in surprise.

I gave him a big toothy grin and continued: "I get the feeling that you're new to your company. Like this is a pretty big firm, and they don't take just anyone, so the fact that you even got hired is a big accomplishment."

"That's all true," Jimmy confirmed.

I drew another card and laid it down across the first. This one held a kingly-looking man holding a sword. He looked quite menacing to me. "I get the feeling that your boss is a taskmaster, and you're having to burn the midnight oil at this new job, where nothing is ever quite good enough."

"You're right on the money," Jimmy confirmed.

I drew again. This one was upside down and depicted a pregnant woman sewing on a tapestry. "There's also an issue of debt here. You owe a lot in student loans?"

"A bundle," Jimmy said, squirming at the mention of debt, but still giving me his full attention.

We kept on like that for another ten minutes or so. I talked about how the money he and his new bride would receive from the wedding would be a considerable help, but the thing that would help him the most was a promotion he was about to receive.

"A promotion?"

"Yup, and it's a big one. Luck is on your side this year, Jimmy. Very soon you're going to come into a position of power and influence. Trust me: You're doing good work at your firm, and even though you think you're not appreciated, you are. You're going to get a raise that will allow you a lot of freedom in the future."

"Cool. Does it say anything about our honeymoon?"

I laid down another card that depicted eight cups on a fountain catching water from the top of the fountain. In the background there was a large mountain covered in snow. My eye went to the mountain and focused on the snow. "You guys going to Aspen?"

Jimmy barked out a laugh and said, "Vail. Ophelia's father gave us the use of the family condo in Vail for two weeks."

"You're going to have a ball," I said. "Although I'm not sure how much of the outside world you guys will see. This says you could be spending most of your time indoors in the hot tub."

Jimmy laughed again. "Yeah, the condo's got a huge hot tub, and we'd already planned on putting it to good use. Say, what can you tell me about kids?" he asked.

I laid down a card, the two of wands. "I see two. Both boys, but not for a couple of years yet. You and Ophelia should enjoy some time together before you jump into parenthood."

"That's what we'd planned on. Listen, this was awesome, thank you so much!"

"Anytime," I said as he got up, taking several business cards with him as he left. I reached down for my bottled water then, which I'd tucked under my chair, and as I sat up another figure dressed in a black tuxedo, a rose cummerbund and a black mask walked in. I held up a finger as I took a swig from the water, then tucked the bottle back underneath my chair. I smiled gamely at my newest guest and said, "Good evening."

The man simply nodded and sat down. I shuffled the cards several times, then swished them briefly around on the tabletop. I didn't want to get the same sequence, so I made sure to shuffle them fully. Finally I looked at the man sitting in the chair and asked, "Okay, so that I can focus on your energy, may I have your full name and date of birth?"

"Bob Smith. June sixth, nineteen sixty." *Liar, liar, pants on fire . . .*

I had already closed my eyes when "Bob" gave me his name and birth date. Surprisingly, it's not all that uncommon for people to want to hide their personal information. They don't trust psychics, and want to give us as little to go on as possible. I repeated his information in my head anyway; mentally tripping when I realized the birth date he'd given me was 6/6/60. Usually this would make me chuckle and roll my eyes, but tonight I shuddered involuntarily.

I opened my eyes and turned over the first from the deck. The death card stared up at me. Kendal had once told me that the death card didn't usually mean death. It was really about old endings and new beginnings. Still, the hooded skeleton smiling up at me from the face of the card wasn't very reassuring, and mentally I reached out for the comfort of my guides. In an instant I realized they were gone.

Now, believe it or not, I have a physical sensation when my crew is around. Think of it like feeling static electricity on one side of your body. I'm so used to this feeling that it doesn't faze me when they show up, but having them exit stage left in the middle of a reading gave me a moment of panic. Why would they leave?

About then it dawned on me that this man was waiting for me to say something, and the first tinges of panic tickled my neck. I had no idea what this death card was trying to say, nor why my guides would suddenly leave. To distract him I laid down another card. This one was labeled, THE TOWER, and showed a huge medieval tower being struck by a bolt of lightning, sending its roof off to smash on the ground. Even more disturbing was a depiction of people being tossed out of the tower by the force of the lightning bolt, captured midfall as they plummeted to their deaths on the rocky ground below.

As I looked at the graphic images there was the tickle of a thought on the edge of my intuition, but it was faint and distant. As the seconds ticked by, I could feel the mounting pressure of this man's expectations as I continued to stare at the two cards on the tabletop and got no clear message to deliver to him. In a panic now, I mentally called out loudly to my crew and demanded their presence immediately, furious that they would abandon me at the beginning of a reading. Not knowing what to do, and to stall for a little more time, I laid down yet another card labeled, JUDGMENT, which depicted three luminescent human figures rising from the earth with outstretched arms toward an angel blowing a trumpet. In one electrifying second I felt my crew smash back into place as a message tumbled into my mind with the force of a physical blow. I snapped my head up to look at the man in the chair as I gasped, "Oh my God . . . ! You've killed someone!"

For a moment the man only sat there, neither moving nor speaking. I could see his mouth form a grim, set line, and then slowly he nodded exactly once. I sat there petrified of what I had said out loud. My heart was racing, and my palms were sweating, and I didn't know what else to do, so I pulled my head back down to the cards. I looked at the judgment card, and my eyes focused on the many figures rising up to meet the angel; then I looked back at the tower card and saw the people falling to their deaths, and another thought bulleted through my head: "No, not just one person . . ." I said breathlessly. "You've killed many people."

The man's reaction was even more chilling as he actually chuckled and replied, "Hey, you're pretty good."

I stared at him for a long moment, my mouth working open and closed and my eyes wide. It suddenly occurred to me that if I showed him how much fear I felt, he might worry that I knew a little too much, and take care of me as well. I needed to continue with the reading if I had any hope of saving my own skin. With a gulp and a shaking hand I drew another card, forcing myself to get a grip already. "Uh, this says that you do this for a living," I said before I could stop myself. Where the hell was my filtering mechanism today?

"You could say that," he shrugged.

I turned over another card, "This indicates that your family is very supportive of you; in fact you may even work for your family."

"In a way," he replied.

I tentatively turned over another card, and with a quaking voice I said, "Uh, well, there's plenty of work out there for you. I mean, you're in demand. I mean—"

"I get your meaning," he said quietly.

With unsteady fingers I turned over another card, thinking that if he hadn't killed me yet maybe I could talk my way out of this. "This says that there's some sort of rift, like there are members of your family that have gone down a separate path, and that you no longer speak to one another, and there's some really bad blood forming here, like people are turning on each other. . . ." I paused, not really understanding what I had just said.

The man leaned in, suddenly interested. "Go on," he insisted.

"Uh, well, I get this feeling that there's a member of your family who has betrayed you somehow, and that you're right to keep him at a distance, but . . ." Something kept playing in the background of my head, and I paused to pay attention to it.

"What is it?" the man demanded.

"Well . . ." I hesitated.

"Tell me," he said in a voice that wasn't kidding.

"I keep hearing, 'He who lives by the sword shall die by the sword.'"

The man sat back and regarded me for a long moment before standing up abruptly and reaching into his jacket pocket, I assumed for a gun. Reflexively I pulled back in my seat and squeezed my eyes shut. He was going to kill me! I'd said too much!

There was a pause, and then I felt something flutter lightly in front of my face. Squinting one eye open I looked down to see a twenty-dollar bill on the table in front of me.

"Thanks," he said, reaching down to pick up one of my business cards. "You're good." And with that he walked out of my area.

No sooner had he gone than I bolted up and scurried

around the curtain, where Kendal was just finishing up with one of the bridesmaids. As she squeezed past me Kendal looked alarmed and asked, "Abby? What's the matter? You look white as a ghost."

"Shhhh!" I hissed at him, and jumped forward, grabbing his arm and yanking him out of his chair. "Come with me *immediately*!"

Kendal didn't argue, and we made our way out of the curtained area and quick-stepped across the large ballroom through the double doors and down the hallway to a small cubby, where I was sure we had minimal privacy. Still, I kept my voice at a hiss level. "How could you book us for a *mob* wedding?" I said, accusation in my eyes.

"What?" he asked me, taken aback by my statement.

"Mob, Kendal! As in M-O-B, mob! *This is a mob wedding!*"

"What are you talking about?"

"I just read a hit man for the freaking mob!"

"You *what? !*"

"Am I going to have to keep repeating myself, or will you eventually listen to what I'm saying!" I said, hissing vehemently in my state of panic.

"I heard what you said; I just don't understand how you know you were reading a hit man for the Mafia," Kendal said calmly.

"This is how it went," I said, taking a breath to gather my thoughts. "I laid down a couple of cards—"

"Which ones?" Kendal asked, interrupting me.

I sighed impatiently. "The death card, the tower, and judgment."

Kendal's eyes got large. "All together?"

"Yep. Bam, bam, bam," I said, slapping my palm with the back of my other hand. "In a row, one, two, three. So I get that he's killed someone, and before I can stop myself I'm saying this out loud—"

"You told him what you *saw*?" Kendal asked, his eyes growing even bigger.

"I told you, I couldn't stop myself, and he says, 'Yeah, I've killed someone,' like it's no big deal."

"He *admitted* it?"

"Oh, for Christ's sake, Kendal! Will you catch up?" I squealed, not bothering to whisper.

"Sorry, sorry, please continue," he said.

"So then I looked back at the cards, and it dawns on me that he's killed more than one person; in fact, he's killed a *lot* of people, and again before I can stop myself I tell him what I'm getting." Kendal's hand abruptly moved to his brow, where lines of sweat were forming, as I continued, "And he admits that too! So next I start telling him that this is a family business, and there's some kind of feud, and he who lives by the sword dies by the sword. . . ."

"Wait, wait, wait!" he said, holding up his palm in a stopping motion. "How do you know that this guy isn't just some guest? I mean, maybe he's just here as a wedding guest, like a friend of the family . . . a *distant* friend of the family?"

"Well," I said, shaking my head, "I mean I *don't* know . . . but I *know* . . . you know? He's related, and this *is* a mob wedding!"

Kendal's brow furrowed in thought as I waited for him to do something. Exactly what I expected him to do, I wasn't sure, but I wanted him to do *something*—anything. "Let me ask you this," he said after some thought. "Would you recognize this man if you saw him across the room?"

"No," I said, exasperated. "He was wearing a mask."

"I know, I know, but maybe you'd recall his tuxedo or something."

"He was wearing a tux with a rose cummerbund."

Kendal's face fell. "He was wearing a tux with a rose cummerbund?"

"Yes, why?"

"Well, the first person I read tonight was one of the guests, who owns a tailor shop, and he said that he supplied all the tuxes for the bride's family. Her side are all wearing tuxes with the rose-colored cummerbunds. This guy must be a relation."

"Mob wedding, Kendal."

There was a beat as we both looked at each other, then said simultaneously, "We're outta here!"

Together we ran back down the hallway, and stopped abruptly in front of the double doors. I looked at Kendal and asked in a panic, "Wait! What's our story? What's the reason we give for leaving early?"

"I'll tell the wedding planner that you have some sort of food poisoning or something, and that I have to get you to a doctor right away. You look pale enough to fit that bill anyway. We'll both go in, and you just do your best to lean on me and look sick, okay?"

"Got it," I said, taking his arm and leaning on him.

We pushed through the doors together and spotted the wedding planner immediately. Kendal waved his hands frantically to get her attention, and, spotting us she came quickly over. The look on her face was not friendly. "Where have you two been? We've got a whole line of people waiting for you!"

"Constance, I'm so sorry; however, my partner here has fallen very ill," Kendal explained. I groaned convincingly, and let my head bob onto Kendal's shoulder, playing it up for all I was worth. "I've got to get her to a doctor right away!"

The wedding planner backed up a few paces, probably afraid I would spew at any moment. "But what about the guests?" she demanded.

"I know, I know," Kendal said soothingly. "They'll be disappointed, but I really must get her to a doctor. Tell the bride that I will mail her a full refund tomorrow, first thing. . . ." At that moment I groaned again, this time more loudly, and grabbed my stomach. The wedding planner backed away a little farther and said, "Fine, Mr. Adams, go then. I'll explain it to the guests, but be sure to mail that check in."

"Of course, of course," Kendal said with a wave of his hand. Sitting me in a nearby chair close to the door, where I continued to bob my head and moan for effect, he dashed behind the curtain, grabbed our belongings and rushed back to me. I got up as quickly as a "sick" person would and leaned on him as we exited.

Once we were safely out of the hallway and back into the foyer we bolted out of the casino and ran to Kendal's car. Ten yards away he popped the locks, and we jumped in, breathing hard. He started the engine and peeled out of the parking lot, adjusting his rearview mirror to see if anyone was following.

Within moments we were back on the highway and blazing a path toward home, both of us continually checking over our shoulders.

"I cannot believe you conned me into doing a mob wedding!" I said moodily.

"Oh, please. Like I knew the family was *family*!" Kendal snapped defensively.

"Well, what the hell are we supposed to do now?" I asked, fear gripping my insides like a vise.

"We could go to the police," Kendal said, looking confident that he'd found the solution.

"And tell them what? 'Hi, Mr. Policeman?'" I said in my Little Bo Peep voice. "Yeah, I'm a psychic and I just read a hit man for the mob. Oh, what's that you say? What's he look like? Well, I have no idea; he was masked, you know. . . .' Great idea, there, Sherlock."

"Don't take this out on me!" Kendal snapped. "Just because you had a tough day is no reason to get snippy."

I crossed my arms and sank low in my seat. Kendal was right—it wasn't his fault. After a moment I asked again, "Okay, so what do we do?"

"I don't know. Why don't we go back to my house and talk to Rick? He's pretty levelheaded. Maybe he'll have a good idea."

I nodded and said nothing more until we reached Kendal's house. We pulled up in the driveway and noticed that all the lights were out and a strange car was parked out front. "He's not home?" I asked about his partner.

"Hmm. No, his car's here. Maybe he's taking a nap. Come on; we'll wake him up." We got out of the car and walked up to the house. He fumbled with his keys for a moment in the dark, then unlocked the door, and we stepped inside. The scent of musk oil hit my nostrils something fierce. I also noticed muffled music coming from the bedroom. "Rick?" Kendal called. "Rick, honey?"

Kendal stepped past me as I waited in the living room,

switching on a light as he went to find his partner. I heard him call to Rick one more time as he opened the bedroom door; then the muffled sounds of something a little more primal caught my ears, followed quickly by Kendal's scream.

I rushed forward to Kendal's aid, certain he was being attacked, when he bolted past me, his hands over his eyes and shrieks coming out of his mouth. Following quickly behind him was a naked and very greasy Rick, slipping on the wood floors chasing after Kendal, trying to talk above the noise. "Kendal! I'm sorry! It was just an experiment, I swear!"

As I stood back and watched the scene unfold I wondered if tonight could get any worse.

"Rick?" came a female voice from the bedroom. "Rick, what's going on?"

Hmm, apparently it could.

A moment later the owner of the voice appeared when a naked and equally greasy woman came running out of the bedroom past me. "Rick? Who is this guy?"

"How *could* you?!" Kendal screeched in a voice so shrill my mother would have envied it.

"It was just an experiment! A onetime thing, I swear! It doesn't mean anything! I still love you!" Rick pleaded.

"Hold on here!" the naked woman yelled stepping between the two men and pointing an accusing finger at Rick. "You mean you're *gay*?"

Oh, boy. Time for me to leave. As unobtrusively as possible I edged out of the room and through the door. I walked to my car as the argument continued from inside the small house, and without a backward glance I got in and pulled out of the driveway.

As I drove home I felt numb from head to toe. The past two days had been horrible, and I wondered when the pattern was going to break. I felt melancholy and sad, and without realizing it I pointed my car toward Dutch's house. Suddenly I didn't want to break up with him. I wanted to tell him I was sorry for being so jealous and petty. I wanted to curl up next to him and hold on for a long, long time. And I figured I could tell him about the mob hit man while I was at it, and he would have the perfect solution. I stepped on the gas and hurried my pace.

When I got to his house, however, the place was completely dark, and Dutch's car was gone. I parked in the street and walked up his driveway anyway, needing to double-check. I rang his doorbell twice, but no one answered. He must have left early for his assignment. "Crap," I said, summing up the night.

With a tired sigh I got back into my car and went home. After I let myself in I scooped up Eggy and climbed the stairs two at a time. I got ready for bed, exhausted and spent, deciding to worry about the hit man in the morning. With another heavy sigh I turned out the light and went quickly to sleep.

Chapter Four

My alarm went off at seven, but I'd already been up for a couple of hours. I'd had a rough night's sleep. I kept waking up and picturing a masked man shooting me with a gun, and where the bullet hit me a rose cummerbund appeared to squeeze me until I couldn't breathe. With a heavy hand I shut off the alarm, but continued to lie there. I didn't need to be at work until after lunch, because weeks ago I'd anticipated that this morning would involve lounging in bed with Dutch, munching on croissants and coffee, and I'd rearranged several of my appointments to accommodate the expected postcoital breakfast.

As I lay there in a well of self-pity, feeling extremely sorry for the fact that I'd bungled yet another relationship, my phone rang.

I almost let it go to voice mail, but the idea that someone was calling so early made me rethink that decision. Nothing mundane ever happens before nine a.m. "Hello?" I asked tiredly.

"Abby?" came a voice I didn't recognize.

"Yes?"

"Hi, I'm really sorry to call you so early, but have you by any chance seen Kendal?"

I shook my head, trying very hard to place the voice, wondering who could be asking me about Kendal. "Uh, no. I'm sorry; who's this?"

There was an embarrassed laugh, then: "My apologies; this is Rick . . . uh . . . Kendal's partner. I'm really sorry that you had to witness our little spat last night. I had no idea you guys were coming home so early."

"Obviously," I said flatly, annoyed that Rick was trying to butter me up.

"Yeah, well, Kendal and I talked most of the night, and I thought we were going to try to work things out this morning. He slept in the other bedroom, but when I got up this morning to make breakfast he was gone."

I sat up in bed and scratched my head. "Gone?"

"Yeah. His car's missing too. I'm not sure if he just went somewhere to cool down, or if he's taken off somewhere. . . ."

I didn't know what Rick was fishing for, so I remained silent, waiting him out.

"Anyway, I was just wondering if maybe you could tune in for me and possibly tell me where he's gone?"

One of my eyebrows lifted as my mouth thinned into a flat line. There was no way in hell I was going to help this guy. The arrogance of the question! Assuming I would betray my friend's confidence by giving Rick an indication where Kendal had gone was absurd. I remembered the night before, when he had been tutoring me, that I'd mentioned he would be traveling down south, to Florida, but there was no way I was going to tell Rick that. "Sorry, Rick, can't help you."

There was a pause, then: "Can't or won't?"

"Won't," I said, my voice hard.

"Okay, sorry to have disturbed you. Good-bye," he said, then hung up the phone.

I replaced the receiver and went back to staring at the ceiling. My feeling was that Kendal had left town to get some distance from Rick and think about their relationship before committing to working things out. From what I knew of Rick, that was a very wise move. I'd met him a total of three times, including last night's streak fest, and I'd never really liked him much.

Kendal made a good living, working longer hours than I did. In fact, he'd worked six days a week steadily for years, building up his clientele, traveling long distances to perform at psychic parties, sacrificing sleep, personal time, and much of his social life to build a career.

On the other hand, from what I knew about Rick, he didn't do much of anything. He'd had stints as a golf caddy, a waiter and a shampoo tech for a hair salon, but mostly he sponged off of Kendal.

Also puzzling was that, compared to Kendal, Rick wasn't all that much to look at. He was overweight, stocky and going bald. Kendal was a definite "shazam!" so personally I couldn't understand the attraction. I reminded myself that this was Kendal's relationship, not mine, so he'd have to figure it out. If he wanted to get away and think about things for a while, then more power to him.

I lay back down and scooted further under my down comforter. My room was freezing now that most of the insulation had been pulled out of the attic. I was just closing my eyes when my phone rang again. Now what?

"Hello?" I asked, letting annoyance creep into my greeting.

"Abby?"

"Milo?" I asked, recognizing the voice and sitting up again.

"Yes. Listen, there's been a development in the rape case. Can you come down to the station this morning?"

"Sure. Give me half an hour," I said, already swinging my legs off the bed. The thing I realized I needed most right now was a distraction, and Milo's case was perfect for that. I also figured I could ask his advice about the hit man I'd read the night before. I'd have to be subtle; I didn't want him to grill me for details and then force me into some kind of witness protection program or anything.

I threw on some jeans and a thick sweatshirt, pulled my hair back into a ponytail, quickly slapped on some mascara and blush, then headed downstairs to feed Eggy and scarf down a pumpernickel bagel with peanut butter. Exactly thirty minutes later I was at the Royal Oak police station sitting at Milo's desk waiting for him to come out of his captain's office. My knee bounced up and down as I metered out the minutes. To kill time, I looked around the Detectives' Unit, watching the other investigators as they typed on their computers and made phone calls. Being the nosy-Nelly type, I listened in on a few conversations I probably shouldn't have, getting the scoop on a local anchorman who'd been picked up for being drunk and disorderly the night before.

Finally Milo came out and flashed me his famous smile, adding a wink for my patience. "Thanks for hanging out. I'm sorry to keep you waiting."

"Not a problem; I have a light morning ahead. So whatcha got for me?"

"We arrested Jeffrey Zimmer this morning, and we're holding him on suspicion of rape in the Schultz case."

"Jeffrey Zimmer," I said, trying to recall the name. "Oh, yeah! He's the neighbor guy. The one that Cathy caught peeking through her fence."

Milo nodded. "Yep. We got a search warrant yesterday and found his computer full of hidden-camera shots of Cathy. He had nearly a hundred of them, all taken through her window when she wasn't looking. He's been doing this peeping-Tom thing for a year or so, judging by the photos. Plus he's got no alibi for the night of her rape, or those of any of the other victims. He claims he was sitting home alone watching television, but when we talked to him this morning he can't remember what he was watching."

"Hmmm," I said, nodding my head in a "By Jove, Watson, I think you're on to something" way.

Milo rearranged some files on his desk as he added, "Oh, and we also found a bunch of ski equipment in his basement."

"Did you find the mask?"

"No, not yet, but we're still looking."

I checked in with my crew, tossing the name "Jeffrey Zimmer" around in my head, waiting for something to feel "on" about it. Nothing was forthcoming so I asked, "So why am I here?"

"I'd like you to take a look at him and see if you can

get a read on him. Maybe pick up another clue as to where we can find the tire iron he used, or the mask he wore."

"Don't you have some kind of physical evidence, Milo? I mean, I'd be more than happy to give it a go, but weren't there any fibers, or body fluid, or something left at the scene that you can go on without having me get more involved?"

Milo cocked his head a little, probably curious about why I was apprehensive. "That's just the thing—the rapist used gloves and a condom, so all we've been able to collect so far are a couple of pubic hairs, but it's going to take several weeks before the forensic lab can make a positive ID on the DNA."

I sighed heavily. I didn't want to see this guy, and I was stalling for a way out. Brutality against women, children and animals is particularly abhorrent to me. I hate violence in all forms, and the methods of this rapist seemed to me to be incredibly cruel. I had a feeling that honing in on this guy's energy was going to leave me feeling unclean, rather like walking through a smoke-filled room and having the scent of cigarette smoke cling to your clothing long after you've left the building.

Then I reminded myself that I had agreed to assist Milo any way I could. "Fine," I said, getting up and squaring my shoulders.

"Great," Milo said as he stood up and motioned for me to follow him. "Come with me. He's just down the hall in one of our interrogation rooms."

Milo took me down a short hallway and in through a door to an observation room just on the other side of where Jeffrey Zimmer was being held. We walked quietly into the dimly lit room, and through a large window we could observe the young man as he sat with large eyes and one arm handcuffed to a table.

He was alone in the room, his gaze fixed firmly to the scarred tabletop in front of him. As we watched he barely moved, his thoughts seemingly far away and frightened. He was a young man—I'd say mid-twenties—with wavy dark hair and a prominent nose. His lips were thin, and his chin receded into his neck. He had a severe overbite, and his mouth never quite closed over his protruding teeth. He seemed ruffled, as if he had been startled out of bed, wearing only a dark blue T-shirt with the Detroit Tigers emblem on one sleeve and old raggedy jeans. His brown hair was tousled, and it appeared he hadn't shaved in a couple of days. His breathing was heavy, his face very pale, and I suspected his heart rate was rapid. He didn't appear like what I'd imagined a rapist would look like: There was no expression of malice about him, no hatred in his eyes, no arrogance for the system. Instead he seemed scared and pathetic, and I wondered whether Milo had indeed found the right man.

Milo looked at me expectantly. I nodded; then I closed my eyes and prepared myself.

One of the biggest misconceptions about psychics is that proximity equals accuracy. In other words, people believe that a psychic must be in the same room as a subject in order to obtain information about that person. The truth is that the client could be in outer space and we'd still be able to give just as good a reading.

For instance, I have clients all over the United States, and two others in London, and when I do readings for them it's never in my office, but through a phone line. The dimensions of space and time rarely act as interference for us. It's merely about the connection itself. So I probably could have gotten the same reading back at Milo's desk as I could standing within view of him but I understood why Milo thought I needed to be near him to read his energy.

As I stood in front of the one-way mirror I cleared my head of all other thoughts except Jeffrey Zimmer. I gathered my energy much the way a pitcher winds up before a pitch, then beamed my intuitive arrow directly at him. I felt an almost immediate connection and began my assessment. I was finished in under a minute, and pulled my energy back as I opened my eyes. Milo stood in front of me with a small notebook in his hands and a pen poised to take notes. "Well?" he asked.

"He's not your man," I said bluntly.

"What do you mean?" Milo asked, his face completely taken aback.

"He's not the rapist," I said, pointing to Jeffrey.

"How do you know?"

"Well, for one thing he's about as bold as a hermit crab. The guy's afraid of his own shadow. He would no more attack a woman than jump off a building. His energy isn't lying, Milo. He's scared to death that he's going to get blamed for something he didn't do. I've scanned his energy twice, and trust me, if he were a violent rapist I'd pick it up."

Milo blinked at me for several moments, weighing his belief in me against what he'd seen at Zimmer's house.

In the silence I looked back at Jeffrey and let my eyes go unfocused; within seconds I could see his aura. It had gone bright white, and there were beams of brilliant white energy shooting straight up through his energy field toward the ceiling, and I now understood what was whirling around inside his mind: The young man was praying.

By the look of it, he was probably praying like he'd never prayed before in his life. I blinked and shook my head a little, then turned back to Milo. "I'm telling you, this is not your guy. He's just some nerdy neighbor who's a little too obsessed with Cathy and likes to take her picture. He doesn't have a mean bone in his body, and right now he's praying to God and every saint he can think of to get him out of this."

"Abby, his hard drive was filled with photos of Cathy," Milo insisted.

"Which is the only connection to her you have for him," I pointed out. "If he's the rapist, then why did he rape the other two women first?"

"Practice," Milo said too quickly. Obviously he'd asked himself the very same question.

"Okay," I said, thinking fast. "Then why the violence? Why did he beat her?"

"Because she ignored him. She blows him off and he wants to teach her a lesson."

"So why go to the grocery store? If he is the rapist, why not rape her in her own house? I mean, he could have waited until her boyfriend went to work, then attacked her in the privacy of her own home. Raping her at a grocery store involves a lot more risk. He could have been seen by another shopper or an employee. She could have screamed before he had a chance to knock her out. Plus, it's cold out. Not to be graphic, but who whips out their dipstick when it's thirty-five degrees out? Wouldn't it make a lot more sense to get her where he knows the patterns of both Cathy and her boyfriend? Where he's assured of some privacy and warmth?"

Milo muttered a curse under his breath at my barrage of questions, then shook his head and said defiantly, "Abby, this *is* the guy."

I threw up my hands and rolled my eyes at him. "Fine, Milo, think what you want. But while you guys are trying to make this case stick another man is out there targeting women, and you've only got five more days until he does it again."

There was a cold prickle that went up my spine just then, and I shivered in spite of myself. Milo's brow had darkened, and I could see he was very close to getting snippy with me. With a tightly controlled voice he said, "Okay, thanks for your help. I'll take that under advisement. Come on; I'll walk you out."

I wanted to yell at him. I hate getting the brush-off. The same thing had happened the last time I'd been asked to assist with an investigation, and the pattern was starting to tick me off.

We walked in silence back down the hallway and through the second-floor investigative department before stopping at the double doors. Remembering my encounter with the hit man from the night before, I decided, in the interest of gathering information, to play nice. "Sorry I couldn't help," I offered.

Milo looked at me and responded with a tiny grin. "It's okay. I know you're trying to be honest with me, and I appreciate that you want to help."

I nodded and, seemingly out of the blue, said, "You know, I worked this wedding reception downtown last night. It was really spectacular."

Milo looked at me, curious about the sudden change of subject, and said, "Uh-huh?"

"Yeah. The father of the bride must have blown a wad of money for this thing. It was incredible, no expense spared. . . ."

Milo was looking at his watch, giving me a not-so-subtle hint that I needed to wrap it up, so I quickly got to the point. "I'll bet you've heard of the family the Kapordelises?"

Milo snapped his head up and asked, "Kapordelis? As in Andros Kapordelis?"

"Yeah." I nodded, smiling my relief that he'd heard of them. "He's the father of the bride. The wedding was held downtown at the Plaza Casino, in Greek Town. I think Andros owns it or something. . . ." My voice trailed off as I watched Milo's instant reaction. He was looking at me like I'd just said I was a space alien from the planet Zorvox. Defensively I asked, "What? What did I say?"

"Are you insane, or do you just have a death wish?" we snapped, his voice rising in anger.

"What are you talking about?" I asked, taken aback. I had no idea why Milo had gotten so angry so fast.

Grabbing me by the elbow, he pulled me away from the double doors, across the room and into a small kitchen area. As he shoved me roughly into a corner by the microwave his face invaded my personal space and he hissed, "Why in the *hell* would you agree to perform for the Kapordelis family?"

"Why?" I whined. "What's wrong with the Kapordelis family?" I didn't want Milo to know I knew about the family's rather checkered connections.

He was breathing hard, trying to control himself. I had never seen him get so angry before. He always played the good cop to Dutch's bad, so this sudden switch was a tough one for me to swallow. Finally he said in a hushed voice, "Listen to me, and listen good. The Kapordelis family is not one you want to get too friendly with. When they invite you to a family function you politely decline, and then you *change your number.*"

Oh, God, it was worse than I thought. "Why?" I whispered again, my eyes large with fright. I wanted Milo to say it, to confirm that I'd absently blundered into the lion's den, so that I could ask his help in figuring out what to do with what I'd intuitively picked up at the reception.

He straightened and looked around the kitchen area, his eyes suspicious and his jaw grinding. Finally he looked back at me and said in a hushed voice, "Let's just say that even this police department isn't immune to the influence of that family. If they invite you back for an encore, take a vacation. A very *long,* extended vacation. Got that?"

I gulped and nodded my head. Thank God I hadn't opened my big mouth and told him about the hit man. What if someone had overheard us? I was pretty convinced by Milo's reaction that he thought the topic of conversation was not a safe one to discuss in public.

Milo released the grip he'd had on my arm and dipped his head in the direction of the double doors again. "Come on. I'll see you out."

This time I made it through the doors and double-timed it down the granite staircase. I wanted out of there bad. He had shaken me up, and I was scared. I'd seen a tinge of real fear in his eyes when he'd mentioned Andros Kapordelis. I wondered if he was the man I'd actually read. I didn't think so, because the connection to the bride hadn't seemed to me to be very strong, but who really knew?

As I reached my car I fumbled with my keys, my hands shaking. I closed my eyes for a brief moment and concentrated, taking deep breaths and trying to calm myself. I got into my car and sat behind the wheel for a moment, thinking about what to do next. I was close to my office, so I decided to head there and think things through. Absently I turned the ignition and headed out of the police parking lot, thinking that I was probably overreacting anyway. So I read a hit man? So what? It wasn't like I'd seen his face and could ID him; I mean, it wasn't like I could pick him out of a lineup or anything. After all, I reasoned, hadn't he tipped me? If the man wanted to kill me because I knew he murdered people for a living, why would he waste twenty dollars?

It had been an arrogant gesture, not the kind of thing you'd do if you wanted to off someone later. Right?

Besides, hadn't Kendal and I gotten home without incident? No one tried to stop us from leaving the wedding, and no one followed us on the way home. I was blowing this all out of proportion. In fact, it was actually kind of funny when I thought about it.

I had parked in my assigned parking space by the time I'd reached this conclusion, and I actually chuckled to myself as I reached over to grab my purse and got out of the car. I locked the door and turned around to walk to my office, still chuckling, when I banged smack-dab into a massive chest.

Startled, I backed up against my car and looked up—and up and up—into the face of one of the biggest men I have ever seen in my life.

"What's so funny?" the massive man asked me, his speech thickened by what I assumed was his gigantic tongue.

A chill had spread up my spine as I reclined backward against my car, unable to say anything and waiting for whatever would happen next.

"I asked you a question," the man said as his massive pronounced brow lowered over his dark eyes.

"I . . . I . . . I . . ." was all I could stammer out.

The man was suddenly in motion, grabbing me by the scruff of the neck and shoving my head forward as he practically lifted me off the ground. My breath caught as I was propelled forward; there was no chance to scream or fight. I'd been completely taken off guard. Before I knew it I was violently shoved headfirst into a car, where my brow hit the opposite window with terrific force. I barely managed to stop myself before falling forward onto the car floor, when I heard the other door close behind me. I scrambled up onto the seat and grabbed for the door handle, pulling at it frantically, but it wouldn't open. There was only the sound of menacing laughter behind me.

My head was pounding fiercely from its blow against the door, but my mounting panic overrode any attention

I might have paid to it. I began to pound on the window as we peeled out of the parking garage, and I screamed for help through the tinted glass at pedestrians on the streets.

I was still screaming when I was yanked by the shoulder and slapped so hard across the face I saw stars. I cowered in the corner after that, nursing my bleeding lip and swollen cheek, staring at my kidnapper as he instructed the driver in a language I didn't know. I did catch one word, however, and that sent a fresh wave of fear along my spine. The word I heard was "Andros," and it was then that, just like Jeffrey Zimmer, I began to pray for my life.

Chapter Five

It occurred to me several miles into the jaunt with my kidnappers that I didn't know where the hell we were. I'd been too busy watching the giant goon who'd thrown me into the car, waiting for him to try to hit me again. He, on the other hand, seemed to be in some sort of trance, sitting calmly facing forward, ignoring me and not moving much. I supposed that to move that amount of mass must take a lot of energy, so this posture had to be a recuperative technique.

After about fifteen steady minutes of watching him, I decided to risk peeking out the window, looking for any telltale signs of where we might be headed. My first observation told me that we were on I-75 headed south.

As the tall columns of the Detroit Renaissance Center came into view, they confirmed the suspicion. Shortly after spotting the Ren Cen we exited the highway and entered a neighborhood that made me want to lock the doors, even with a seven-foot-tall goon in the car.

Soon we were heading down several side streets, and the topography changed. As near as I could tell we were somewhere in the warehouse district, over by the Eastern Market. There were large dilapidated buildings closed off by fifteen-foot fences crowned by razor wire. Not much traffic cruised up and down these streets, and I knew that if these guys didn't kill me, but let me go in any one of these neighborhoods, I was probably in for a day of trying to get my lily-white ass out of the heart of racially divided Detroit. Any way you sliced it, I was in trouble.

Finally the car turned a sharp corner and pulled up to a small driveway with a call box. The driver, whose eyes I'd seen in the rearview mirror, lowered the window and pushed a button on the call box. A garbled voice responded, and the driver said something I couldn't understand. A moment later the huge gate in front of the car began to creep open, rust making it screech in protest.

When the opening was wide enough the car pulled forward and circled around the large warehouse. I could see men on the property; they were rough-looking types, mostly in jeans and light coats. None of them looked up at the car when it approached.

We came to a stop in front of a side door, and my heart began to pound again. If they killed me here, no one would ever find me. I kept thinking about Cat, and how upset she'd be, holding out hope that I was still alive and wondering what had happened to me. I wondered too who would take care of Eggy.

The driver clicked a button on his control panel, and I watched as the lock on my side flipped up. Tentatively I tried the door handle—it worked. Without being told I opened my door and got out, staring up at the building and wondering what I was in for.

Goon came around to my side and grabbed me by the collar, lifting me slightly as he propelled me forward. I walked quickly ahead on my tippy-toes, becoming more and more irritated as we moved up a few steps and into the building.

Goon trotted me down a long dimly lit hallway, around a corner and into an office. There was a trashy-looking woman with overbleached hair sitting at a desk, filing her nails and popping her gum when we came in.

Goon released my collar and stood in front of her. She smiled winningly up at him and picked up the receiver on her telephone, hitting a button and popping her gum a few more times before she said something into the receiver that I couldn't catch. She then hung up the phone and pointed to the door behind her, smiling as we shuffled past.

We walked through the door and into a large interior office, luxuriously decorated with thick shag carpeting, crepe-colored walls, black leather couches and a gigantic oil painting covering almost an entire wall.

At the opposite end of the office sat a massive creature squeezed into his leather chair and puffing on a smelly cigar. Andros Kapordelis was huge, but not in the same way that Goon was huge. He was probably close to six feet tall, with a thick salt-and-pepper beard and mustache, a receding hairline and squinty dark eyes. His chins numbered in the double digits, and his massive belly made his breathing audible from way back here.

He wore a tweed overcoat and a red silk shirt, open several buttons to reveal tufts of black hair poking out as a large gold medallion was nearly swallowed by his chins. His arms rested on his belly, but kept slipping downward, and even from here I could smell his BO above the cigar. It was a struggle not to gag at the sight and smell of him.

"Ah, Miss Cooper, thank you for joining us on such short notice. I see you've made a complete recovery from your sickness?"

My brow furrowed for a moment in confusion. What the hell was he talking about? Then it dawned on me; I'd left the reception last night pretending to be sick. Looking at Andros I knew he was on to Kendal and me, and no amount of playacting was going to get me out of this, so I simply nodded.

"Yes," Andros continued. "I suspected as much. Come, come, now. Join me for a discussion, won't you?" he said, waving one fat pudgy hand toward a chair in front of his desk.

I hesitated, not wanting to get any closer to the smelly,

unctuous man; then Goon had me up by the shirt collar again, wielding me forward and depositing me in a seat that faced Andros.

This whole thing was really starting to tick me off, and I couldn't understand what point these guys wanted to make before killing me. If they wanted to see me beg for my life first they were going to be sorely disappointed. I wasn't afraid to die, just sad that I still had so much to do, and there was no way I was going to give these assholes the satisfaction of watching me squirm.

"That's better," Andros said when I'd been shoved into the seat facing him. "Now we need to take care of some business, you and I."

Here it comes, I thought.

"You see, you and your partner, Mr. Adams, greatly disappointed my daughter last night," Andros explained while taking a puff of his smelly cigar. "Ophelia was embarrassed that the entertainment she herself had arranged for on the most important night of her life was ruined so abruptly."

Andros paused and regarded me, waiting perhaps to see what I might say. I continued to stare at him in stony, stubborn silence. I'd be damned if he thought there was any way I was going to apologize to him. After a moment he continued: "Not only that, but these two 'professionals' seem to have kept the money my Ophelia paid them to entertain her guests. What do you think about that, Miss Cooper?"

That last statement caught me slightly off guard. I had forgotten that Kendal had promised to mail in a check to reimburse the bride for paying us in advance. I hadn't seen any of the money, and I didn't understand how all this was suddenly my problem. "Listen, Mr. Kapordelis, I had nothing to do with the money. Kendal was in charge of mailing you back your check, which I have no doubt he'll do. If you'll just try to contact him, I'm sure he can cut you a check for a full refund—"

"Yes, well, that is part of the problem, Miss Cooper," Andros said, cutting me off. "You see, we have discovered that Mr. Adams flew to Tampa early this morning, taking our money with him."

I looked at Andros with a mixture of shock and embarrassment. I was going to kill Kendal the next time I saw him. Quickly I said, "I see. Well, Mr. Kapordelis, the only resolution I can offer you is a personal check," I said, reaching for my purse, which had dropped to the floor. Goon grabbed my hand before I could reach it and lifted the purse away from me. He dug around in it for a minute as I watched him with a flinty stare, then handed it back to me without a word. I glared at him, then fished around in my purse and extracted my checkbook. Flipping it open to the first available check, I began to scribble in the date. "Okay, so Kendal said that you had paid two thousand dollars for the evening?"

Andros laughed and answered, "Yes, but you see, getting back only what I paid for is hardly adequate compensation."

"Excuse me?" I said, my hand pausing while I looked up at him.

"Yes, I think it only fair if some punitive damages are applied. After all, my Ophelia was quite distraught on her wedding day. You and your partner were the one blemish to an otherwise perfect evening. I think that double your original fee is more than adequate, don't you, Miss Cooper?"

What little blood was left in my face drained right out. His question was less "question" and more "demand," and I knew it. I also knew that by handing over four thousand dollars to this man, I'd be left with less than five hundred dollars in my bank account. It had been a very long time since I'd had so little liquid cash on me, but what choice did I have? I inhaled a huge breath and wrote out the check to "Cash," for four thousand dollars, ripping it off angrily and handing it to Andros, who inspected it for errors, then tucked it away into his pocket. He regarded me for a long moment as I wondered what the next move between us would be.

"There is one more thing that you will need to do for me to square up your debt."

"Of course there is." I sighed as I glared at him.

"My associate tells me you are quite a remarkable psychic."

Shit, I was in trouble.

"I would like a reading, please, before you go."

He had to be kidding. He wanted a reading . . . *now*? This SOB had kidnapped me, roughed me up, dragged me down to an old warehouse, extorted four thousand dollars from me and now wanted a reading? No fucking way. "Sorry, Mr. Kapordelis, but I'm afraid that Goon here," I said thumbing toward the giant behind me, "has given my third eye a black eye, so I will be unable to comply with your request."

"I see," Andros said, pulling the fat cigar out of his mouth and eyeing it with amusement. "Leave us for now," he said, looking at Goon and waving him toward the door. On lumbering footsteps I heard Goon leave, the door closing quietly behind him. Andros turned his attention back to me and sized me up for a long time before saying, "Miss Cooper, you may not understand the powers of persuasion that I am capable of invoking when it comes to getting my way."

"And you may not understand how the pressures of duress conflict with my ability to intuit information," I said smartly, making a point to caress my swollen cheek.

"Ah, yes," Andros said, "I am sorry we had to include a degree of force with our invitation, but it was imperative that I see you."

"What the hell for?"

"That is what I'd like you to tell me," Andros said, and waited while I pondered that.

Just for the sake of curiosity I took a tiny measure of his energy and knew right away what he was getting at. Impulsively I said, "So how long have the doctors given you?"

I had passed the first test; Andros smiled broadly at me. I noticed distastefully how yellowed and uneven his teeth were. "Not long. They want me to undergo some experimental procedures. I don't think they will work."

I scanned his energy a little deeper now, sucked into the question, and said, "You're right. I'm surprised you're still standing."

About a year ago I'd spent a little time working with

a medical intuitive, who had taught me how to scan the body for disease. I had practiced on several of her clients, and had come to understand what several common diseases "felt" like, including cancer, which to my sixth sense "felt" like gray sludge. The more intense the cancer, the thicker the sludge.

Andros's body was riddled with thick, dark gray goo—cancer. Most of it was concentrated in his lap, so my guess was that his prostate and lower intestines were engorged with it.

"What else?" he encouraged when I said nothing more.

Moodily I obliged. Hell, I was already in the middle of it anyway; why not finish it? "Well, there's also something about a huge family conflict. Like a crisis connected with your death. The feeling I get is that there is some kind of family rift going on here, and neither side trusts the other, and you're trying to repair this rift before you go. Am I on the right track?"

Andros was nodding his head at me, puffing away on his cigar, "Yes. Please continue."

"Okay, so I get the feeling your half of the family and the other half of the family are about to have a meeting of some kind, like one side wants to offer the other an olive branch, and it's an opportunity to heal this huge rift, am I right?"

"Yes."

"And there have been several missteps in this process, like no one wants to swallow their pride, and you can see an opportunity to make peace, but you're not sure if the other side will come to the table, right?"

"Correct," Andros said, his beady eyes watching me closely.

"There is some sort of business deal that is coming up that could solve this matter and bring the two sides together again. But it takes a lot of trust on your part, and you're not sure if they're telling the truth."

I paused, trying to assess something that was like a tangle of weeds. There were conflicting messages here, like both parties were full of lies and deceit, and trying

to navigate through to the truth was like being blind-
folded and walking through a jungle. "Please continue,"
Andros said as I concentrated.

"Well," I began, trying to figure it out, "I'm not really
sure what to tell you, Mr. Kapordelis. You're stuck between a rock and a hard place, so I'm just going to tell
you to trust your own instincts on this. I'm not really
sure how it will all turn out."

Andros tugged on his beard for a moment, thinking;
then he asked, "I want to hear your thoughts on which
of my sons should take over for me when I pass on."

Great. I was going to pick the next don for the Kapordelis family. How the hell did I get myself into this
mess? I hesitated before answering and asked, "I want
your solemn vow that if I tune in on this question for
you that you will take me safely back to my office."

Andros smirked benignly at me. "You have my word,
Miss Cooper."

I waited for my lie detector to go off, and when it
didn't I closed my eyes and focused. "The first thing
I get is that you haven't told anyone you're sick yet,
have you?"

"No, that is a secret between you and me." His tone
indicated it would remain a secret.

"Of course, of course," I said, waving my hand dismissively and hiding an urge to gulp. "Well, the thing
of it is, your oldest has issues, and he's up to something
that could get him in a lot of trouble." I had concentrated on the first of Andros's sons, and I didn't like his
energy at all. There was something off about this guy's
brain chemistry; he was sick in some way, and I wondered if Andros knew. "Has your son ever been in
therapy?"

Andros barked a laugh at my question. He thought I
was kidding.

"No, I'm serious," I insisted. "Your son makes choices
that are not good choices, and no offense, but there's
something not quite right up here," I said, pointing to
my head and making circular motions for crazy. "Plus if
you put this man in a position of power, I promise you,
he will betray your trust."

Andros didn't care for my assessment, and his eyebrows darkened over his beady little eyes. "You are wrong," Andros said. "My son Demetrius loves his father and would never betray me."

Left side, heavy feeling. "Mr. Kapordelis, I'm not wrong on this, seriously," I insisted, my intuition screaming the message at me. "Your oldest son cannot be trusted, especially where your family is concerned. . . ."

Andros slammed his fist on the desk in front of him angrily, and I jumped a foot. Wisely, I decided to drop the subject and go on to the next son. "Anyway, maybe your firstborn isn't such a good choice. Now your second son, he's the artist, correct?"

Andros nodded. "Yes, Darius is very talented."

"He's in school, right?"

"Yes, he's on the last year of his master's at the University of Chicago right now."

"He's really, really gifted, Mr. Kapordelis. I see this work . . ." I paused, focusing on the sculpture that had just appeared in my mind's eye. "He sculpts, right?"

"Yes."

"With metal, right? Not clay, but metal, correct?"

"That is correct, Miss Cooper."

"I see this work making him famous someday. I see him being sought after, especially on the West Coast. Has he been thinking of moving to California?"

Andros chuckled. "It's all he talks about. He wants to move there when he's finished with school, but I want him to come here and be with his family."

"Good luck with that," I scoffed. There was no way this young man was going to give up his dreams of becoming an accomplished sculptor, but sometimes you just had to let parents arrive at their own conclusions. I moved on to the next son. "Okay, your third son. . . ." I paused and focused, sensing a familiar bitter taste in my mouth and wanting to roll my eyes. Great, I'd have to be delicate. "Mr. Kapordelis, do you know your third son has a substance-abuse problem?" I asked tentatively.

Andros nodded gravely. "Yes, I'm aware of Dorian's experimentations."

Oh, brother. How naive could you get? "Sorry to be

the bearer of bad news, but I'm getting that Dorian is way past the experimentation phase, and well into the addiction phase. This kid's got major problems." In my head I saw a small bird sitting in a cage swinging back and forth on a little swing. "If he's not careful he's headed to prison. I'm telling you he'll get caught, and quite frankly it's not a bad place for him, considering how much of a problem he's already got. Going up river might save his life, unless someone gets him into rehab, pronto."

Andros's eyebrows furrowed again down into the danger zone. This guy didn't like hearing about his sons' shortcomings, which were considerable. I moved on to the next in line. "Okay, so your fourth son is the one who should inherit the business. He's the one who's got a great head on his shoulders, and a nose for numbers. He's really lucky with money, like he has the Midas touch. My guides are saying that everything he touches turns to gold. He's someone you can trust, and he's a man of his word, like he keeps his promises. I'm surprised you hadn't automatically considered him; he's absolutely the natural choice," I finished triumphantly. That was a piece of cake.

Andros, however, didn't look happy. In fact, he looked downright confused. "I hadn't considered whom, Miss Cooper?" he asked me.

"Your fourth son. You have four boys, right?"

Andros looked at me pointedly for a long moment and answered slowly, "No, I have three sons and a daughter."

That caught me totally by surprise. I'm really good with numbers, and it's a very rare instance when I'm off on an offspring or sibling. I blinked at him a couple of times, asking my crew to confirm the number four. They did. What was I missing?

Then an idea occurred to me. "Okay, so do you have a nephew or someone who's like a son? Someone in your family, or a really close friend of the family who is like a son?"

Andros lost himself deep in thought for a moment, saying, "Perhaps . . ."

I offered, "Sometimes the answer isn't so obvious, and it takes thinking about it for a minute to figure it out. Like maybe it's a stepson. Do you have a stepson?"

Andros looked at me sharply, "No, my wife had no other children," he said, turning to a small bookshelf behind him to look at a black-and-white photograph on the shelf of a beautiful woman with soft blond hair in a style that was dated some thirty years past.

"Is that your wife?" I asked curiously. There was something about the photo, something intriguing; like it was a clue to something—I wasn't sure to what.

"Yes, this was Dora," Andros said, picking up the photo and wiping the dust off with his sleeve.

I peered over the desk at the photo. The way he said "was" made me believe that his wife had died, so I expected to see the picture appear flat and one-dimensional. I have a knack for being able to look at a photo and know if someone is alive or dead. It's hard to explain, but if the person in the photo appears one-dimensional to me, sort of flat and pancakelike, then they have crossed over. If they look more two-dimensional then they're probably still alive. Dora didn't look flat, and curiously, I had a feeling she was still alive, so I couldn't understand why Andros looked so distraught over the photo.

I got my answer when he began to speak in a soft voice filled with the emotion of a painful memory. "Years ago, when my daughter was only two, my wife disappeared without a trace."

"She left you?" I asked, stunned. Who would have the guts to try to walk out on *this* guy? He seemed like the type who would not rest until he'd found you and made you pay for every moment you'd been away from him.

"Perhaps she left me," he said, still caught somewhere far away. "Perhaps not." He set the photo down and turned back to tell me the story. "I was here at work one afternoon—it was a day very much like today, in fact—and a call came in from our nanny. My wife had gone out to run some errands one afternoon, and never came home. My son, Demetrius, had been with her. He was . . . what?" Andros paused, thinking. "Seven or eight at the time, and he had wandered away from her, and when he went back to find her, he couldn't. A Good Samaritan finally stopped and asked him what was wrong. The police were called and they contacted the house and my nanny.

"We lived in a very safe neighborhood back then, so it was impossible to think that Dora had been kidnapped, but her car was still in the parking lot, and the credit cards she had on her person were never used. Over the years I've put my considerable resources to work trying to locate her, but we never found any trace. To this day I have only my suspicions, but no real answers."

Something lit in my brain as he said the word "suspicions," and I blurted out, "That's what caused the rift!"

"What?" he asked, startled by my statement.

"The rift in your family. You think another family member had something to do with your wife's disappearance!"

Andros nodded, seeming a little awed at my accuracy, and said, "Yes, that's correct. Dora and my cousin Nico's wife, Sophia, were best friends. Sophia denied knowing anything about Dora's disappearance, but I knew she was lying. Nico refused to force Sophia to tell me where Dora was, and that caused a war between us. He and I used to be partners, but I wanted nothing more to do with him after Dora vanished. He went his way and I went mine, and we haven't spoken a word since."

"But recently that's changed, right?" I asked.

"Perhaps," Andros said elusively. I was prying a little too deep, and it suddenly dawned on me that the less I knew about these people, the better it probably was for my own continued health and longevity.

"Well, then," I said, leaning forward in the chair, changing the subject and ending the session, "if you'll excuse me, I have clients this afternoon, and I'd like to get back to my office."

Andros nodded, continuing to look at me thoughtfully. After a moment he said, "I'd like to see you again, Miss

Cooper. I could use someone of your talents for a few business dealings I'm wrapping up."

He had to be kidding. "Well, I'd really love to help, Mr. Kapordelis; however, I'm afraid I'm completely booked for the next several months. But good luck with that . . ." I said, getting up from the chair.

"You know, I had a woman of your abilities work for me several years ago," he continued, as if I hadn't already made my intentions clear.

I stopped midstep around the chair and looked back at him. "Then why not ask her to help you?"

"Madame Jarosolov. She was Russian," he said with a faraway look. "Have you heard of her?"

"No."

"Yes, she was very good. Ophelia loved her."

"Uh-huh." Gooseflesh had suddenly appeared on my arm. I didn't know the point of this story, but I knew I wasn't going to like how it ended.

"Yes, she was a great help to me," Andros said, again toying with his cigar.

"What happened to her?" I had to know.

Andros looked at me for a long, pointed minute. Finally he said, "She betrayed my trust and my family. I dismissed her."

The way he said "dismissed" left little doubt as to what he actually meant by that. Obviously, Madame Jarosolov had been fitted with a comfortable pair of cement sandals, and shortly thereafter had gone swimming in the Detroit River. I gulped but stood my ground. "Well, Mr. Kapordelis, as I said, I'm quite busy."

"This is a very good offer I am making you, Miss Cooper," Andros replied. I understood from the note of arrogance in his voice that *very* few people turned him down.

Still, I stuck to my guns. "No, thank you. I'm really not interested."

Andros squinted at me, snakelike, his reptilian features making me shiver. "I think, Miss Cooper, that you will need some time to warm to the idea, so I will give you a week or so to think it over, and then you will tell me your answer." Andros lifted his phone abruptly and barked a single Greek word into it. The door opened immediately, and Goon stepped through the doorway.

My heart began to pound again as I wondered whether or not Andros would keep his word about taking me back to my office unharmed. I walked by Goon out the door and past the secretary, thankful to be under my own stewardship and not with the assistance of the not-so-gentle giant behind me.

I led the way, remembering the way out, and once outside walked purposefully straight to the car. I opened the door and got in. Goon got in on the other side and we were off.

The next twenty minutes were probably the longest of my life. I watched the road pass by as I stared out the window, willing the miles to pass more quickly. I wanted to go home and take a long, hot shower and forget this day ever happened. Mostly, however, I really, really wanted to talk to Dutch.

I had a sinking feeling that this wasn't the last I would see of Andros; his cryptic message about persuading me to work for him left a haunting feeling in my bones. I didn't know how the hell I was going to get myself out of this mess, but Dutch might.

The problem was that he was unreachable. All I knew was that he was somewhere out of town on assignment, undercover and unavailable. Oh, and with a woman who was more than ready to comfort him on a lonely night if he needed it. I sighed heavily, suddenly wanting to cry, but straightened up abruptly as Goon looked over at me, a question mark on his face. I ignored him and continued to stare out the window, concentrating on willing the car to hurry.

Finally we pulled into the parking garage and up the ramp to my car. The driver flipped a switch again, and before anyone had a chance to change their minds I was out of the car and bolting to my Mazda. I already had my key out and quickly inserted it into the door, shoving myself into place and slamming the door closed with one hand while I hammered down the lock with the other. I had the key in the ignition and the car in reverse before you could say "Yankee Doodle," and I peeled out of the garage much faster than the posted speed limit allowed. I had only one brief glimpse of the Kapordelis car behind me, as I turned right out of the parking structure, noting with a fragment of satisfaction that my kidnappers wisely turned left.

I took side streets home, vigilantly checking my rearview mirror for any signs of a tail. I made it home and pulled my car quickly into the garage, then bolted inside, slamming the front door closed behind me.

Dave was upstairs in my attic, and I walked tiredly up to greet him.

"Hey, there, how's it—" He stopped midsentence and scrutinized my face, nearly dropping the hammer he was holding and stepping over several beams to get to me quickly. "What happened to your face?" he demanded.

Belatedly I remembered my split lip and swollen cheek, and my hand went up to cover the area. "It's nothing," I said dismissively. There was no way I was going to involve Dave in this.

"Horse hockey," Dave said, setting down the hammer and taking me by the arm. He led me downstairs and into the kitchen, where he sat me on a chair and walked over to the freezer. He extracted a package of frozen peas, closed the door and handed them to me.

I gave him a muffled, "Thanks," and put the cool package against my cheek. It felt wonderful.

"So you want to tell me about it?" Dave asked, reclining against the sink crossing his arms and looking at me like an errant child.

"No," I said flatly, staring at the ground.

Dave looked at me for a long moment, anger brimming behind his eyes. Finally I watched him straighten and walk over to stand tall above me. In the sternest voice I have ever heard him use, he said, "I'll kill that son of a bitch Dutch if I ever see him again."

I couldn't help it; I had to smile.

"What?" Dave asked, offense creeping into his voice.

"Dutch didn't do this to me, Dave, so please don't kill him," I said gently.

Dave cocked his head, assessing whether or not I was telling the truth, then demanded, "Well, then who the hell did?"

"It's embarrassing," I said, stalling for time to think up a story.

"Then I promise not to repeat it," he said stubbornly.

"Well, the truth of it is that I got into a fight in the parking structure by my building. See, I have an assigned parking spot, and I saw this woman pull into it before I had a chance to, and I boxed her in with my car and we got into it. . . ." *Liar, liar, pants on fire . . .*

Dave looked at me for a long moment; then a grin spread across his face, and a chuckle escaped him before he had a chance to muffle it. "Road rage?"

I nodded and tried my best to look chagrined. "Guilty as charged," I said, holding up my palm.

"Does she look better or worse than you?" Dave asked.

" 'Bout the same," I said.

Dave chuckled again and patted my hair. "You've had a tough couple of days, haven't you?"

"You wouldn't believe the half of it," I said.

"Well, sorry to add more bad news to your plate, but I'm gonna need a check for the replacement lumber today."

Son of a bitch. I looked at the kitchen floor as I said, "Yeah, about that . . ."

"What's up?"

"Well, remember that party I was supposed to work last night to pay for the repairs?"

"Yeah?"

"Well, it turns out the party got canceled, so I'm afraid we're going to have to hold off for a couple of weeks."

"You know, if you're in a money crunch I can spot you for it."

I smiled up at him. He was such a good guy. "No, no, Dave. I'd really rather not. Why don't we just stop where we are and give me a couple of weeks to get the money together, and then we can pick it back up then?"

Dave nodded but avoided my eyes. "Sure, whatever you say."

Dave had worked for me solidly since March, and it was going to feel really strange coming home to a quiet house. "Besides, don't you have a job for your cousin that you've been putting off?"

Dave nodded again. This time he met my eyes and said, "Yeah, I've been brushing him off for a while. Listen, this is no sweat for me, but I've pulled all of the insulation and most of the rafters in the attic section down. It's pretty cold in your bedroom. You definitely want me to finish this job before it gets much colder, and if we have to work out a payment plan then that's fine with me. Really."

I smiled at him and stood up, squeezing his arm playfully. "I can't imagine that it will take me any longer than two weeks to get back on track."

"Okay, I'll get my things then and be on my way. Call me when you want me to come back okay, Rocky?" he said, and phantom-boxed with me on his way out of the kitchen.

I saw him off and closed the door, then looked quickly at the clock, which read eleven thirty. I had only an hour and a half before my first appointment, so I raced upstairs and got underneath the showerhead, letting the hot water console my anxious heart. Still, it was a long time before the cloying scent of cigar smoke and malice snaked their way down the drain.

Chapter Six

Sunday night found me chatting happily away to my sister, who had completely forgiven me and was back home from her trip to New York. The excitement in her voice wasn't from her success in the Big Apple, but more about the book she'd read on the plane ride home, *Fifteen Minutes to Tarot Magic!*

"Abby, this book makes it really simple. I've already memorized all of the meanings for the major arcana."

"The major what?" I asked. Even with my lesson from Kendal—the expert—I still had no clue.

"You know, the *major arcana*," she insisted in a tone that meant I should know this. "The face cards like the fool, the magician, the high priestess . . ."

"Oh, okay, I get it. And the other suit cards are called what?" I asked, suddenly curious.

"Those are the *minor* arcana, silly. You can't have a major without a minor."

"Uh huh," I said, losing interest again.

"So anyway, I think I may try to put together a party of my own next week."

"A party of your own?" I asked.

"Sure! Why not? My book club meets on Tuesdays,

and I thought it would be fun if instead of talking about some boring book we could have a little psychic party."

My eyes had grown large. Cat was so successful at everything she tried that she tended to try everything, but this . . . well, *this* was different.

As her sister, however, it was impossible for me to try to insert a word of caution without coming across as a doubting Thomas. I'd have to tread carefully. "Are you sure that's a good idea?" I asked tentatively.

Cat's voice immediately grew defensive. "What do you mean, do I think it's a good idea?"

Oh, crap. I'd blown it. "Well, it's not that I think you wouldn't be good at this. . . ." *Danger! Danger, Will Robinson! Danger!* "It's just that it really takes a lot of practice to become proficient enough to offer your skills to an audience."

"So you're saying my party isn't a good idea?"

Warning, minefield ahead! "No, it's not that. It's just that intuition is a tricky thing to master. It's harder than it looks, and maybe you'd be better off giving individual readings to one or two close friends first, then working your way up to a group setting."

"You don't think I can do this, do you?"

Duck and cover! "Uh, well the thing of it is, Cat, that reading an entire group of people puts a lot of pressure on you. It sets a level of expectation, so to speak. You know what I mean?"

"You think I'm going to fall flat on my face, don't you?" Indignation and hurt were clearly evident in Cat's voice.

Arrroooga . . . ! Abort! Abort . . . ! Arrroooga! "Of course not. I know if you put your mind to doing something you absolutely will do it. You know what, honey? Go for it! Do the party!"

"Really?" she asked me, nearly pleading for me to believe in her.

"Of course. You'll be fantastic!" *Left side, heavy feeling.* "Really, I think you'll do great!" *Liar, liar, pants on fire . . .* "You should absolutely go for it. I mean, if you can't practice on a few friends, how will you ever learn. Right?" *Brruck, bruck, bruck . . . Chicken Little!!*

"Exactly," she said, relief in her voice. "So I'm thinking that I'll give everyone a written survey after each reading so I can get some honest feedback; what do you think?"

"Great idea." *Liar, liar . . . pants on fire . . .* My sister couldn't help but insert her business sense into everything she did.

"I know! It is, isn't it? Well, listen, on that note I need to go; I've still got mountains of memorizing to do, and Tommy will be home with the twins soon. I'll talk to you later, okay?"

"Sure, sure. Have a great night, Cat," I said, thankful to have gotten away with it, and I hung up the phone, easing backward into the comfort of the overstuffed chair and ottoman my sister had purchased for me the previous summer. Eggy was curled up on my lap, and a down throw was spread over us as the television played across the room.

Normally at this hour I would be upstairs curled up in bed, watching the telly in my bedroom, but it was freezing up there, even with the heat on high, so I'd given up going up to bed until the last possible moment.

I could, of course, pull the hideaway out from the settee in my study and sleep on that, but it wasn't nearly as comfortable as my own bed, and I sighed again at the bleak financial picture I'd painted for myself.

With the readings from this weekend added to the abysmally low balance in my checking account, I'd just barely be able to make my office rent and mortgage payment, which, by the way, was being automatically withdrawn from my bank account on Monday.

As it was I'd even resorted to calling ten clients on my waiting list and booking them on my two days off, tomorrow and Tuesday, just so I'd have a little something higher than a goose egg in my bank account for the next few days.

If I kept adding a few clients here and there I figured I'd be back on my feet in a couple of weeks, and then I'd be able to call Dave and get him back to work.

I could, of course, ask my sister for a loan, but that was an absolute last resort. Cat wouldn't hesitate to "loan" me the money—she was famous for her generosity—but that was just it; she wasn't the type who allowed you to pay her back, and even though, in her mind, I would never be indebted to her, in my mind I always would.

Take my furnishings. While I was unconscious in a hospital bed, Cat had worked some major magic and refurnished my entire home. It was always in the back of my mind when I sat down on a chair, or made my bed, or did a load of laundry that it was my sister's doing that allowed me these small luxuries. I wish I was the type of person who could receive a generous gift like that and think nothing of it, but I wasn't. Privately, it bugged the hell out of me.

I sighed again as I thought about the other opportunity that I'd completely blown off. If I'd accepted Milo's check, or even a small tiny fragment of it, I wouldn't be in this predicament. It was too late to call him and tell him I'd changed my mind too. I'd already gotten a large gift basket filled with homemade chocolate-chip cookies, a ceramic ashtray, and a large card with the signatures of everyone at the Boys and Girls Club thanking me for my generous donation. A plaque with my name would be permanently displayed at the park once renovation was complete.

In a state of depression I'd eaten every cookie, and was now feeling a little sick to my stomach. My eyelids were feeling droopy when the phone rang unexpectedly, startling me out of my stupor. Quickly I picked up the receiver and whispered, "Hello?"

"Why are you whispering?" came a familiar baritone.

"Dutch?" I asked, sitting up, blinking my eyes awake.

"Yeah, babe, I just wanted to call. . . ."

My heart flip-flopped in my chest. A peace offering! "I'm really glad you did," I said, squeezing the receiver.

"I don't know what happened the other day. . . ."

"I know, I know. Me either."

"I'm sorry."

"Me too."

Silence, as we both searched for something else to say.

"You sound tired," he said after a bit.

"I am. It's been a bitch of a week. Where are you?"

"South, babe," he said evasively.

"How's it going?"

"It's going." Dutch was never a man of many words. "So I have a small favor to ask you."

"How small?"

Dutch chuckled. "Teensy-weensy."

I smiled in spite of myself. "I'm listening."

"Virgil's being looked after by my neighbor's kid while I'm away, but I was hoping you could stop by my house and check on him to make sure he's getting enough food. I think he'd really like to see a familiar face." Virgil was Dutch's pet cat, and although I've never been big on felines, I had to admit that I had a particular soft spot for Virgil.

"I'd be happy to. Where's the key?"

"Under the flowerpot on the back porch. You remember the alarm code?"

"Is that a hint that your birthday is a mere seven months away?"

Dutch chuckled. "Yeah, I'm subtle like that. Say, how'd your party go the other night?"

I suddenly remembered the weekend like a splash of cold water, and was so thankful that I could finally talk to someone about it that my eyes welled up with tears. "I am so glad you asked, Dutch, because there's something I have to tell you. . . ."

"Shoot," he said in a voice that said he could handle it.

"Well, the thing is, the reception was actually downtown, and when Kendal and I arrived we had no idea who the bride's family really was, and as it turned out—"

"Dutch? Dutch, are you in here?" I heard a female voice say in the background of the phone call.

"Yeah, I'm on the phone," Dutch said, pulling his voice away from the receiver.

"Oh? Okay, well, we still have some things to go over yet, so can you please wrap it up?"

"I'll be there in a minute, Joe."

"Kinda late for you two to be having a meeting, don't

you think?" I snapped, suddenly overcome by a certain green-eyed monster.

"I'm on assignment. There are no time frames to follow. It's what we do," he answered defensively.

"I see. How convenient," I said tersely. My eyes had become slits, my foot had begun to snap back and forth and my fingers were drumming in irritation against the arm of the chair.

"Abby, *please* don't start this again," Dutch said, exasperation in his voice, which only fueled my anger.

"Start? *Start?!* I didn't *start* this the last time! Your overly amorous partner started this, pal! So don't pin this on me!"

"I'm not trying to pin this on you," Dutch said, his voice tensing further. "I'm just trying to . . . Oh, for Christ's sake! Why the hell are we even *having* this conversation?"

"You don't want to converse? Fine, let's not converse!" I said, and slammed down the receiver.

Screw him!

Screw her!

Screw everyone else!

I gathered up Eggy, who had slept through my entire tirade, and turned off the television and the living room lights. I marched up the stairs and into my bitter-cold bedroom, where I quickly got undressed and piled on a few extra blankets. I hurried into bed and wrapped myself around Eggy as I struggled to relax my breathing. It was hard, but around one a.m. exhaustion finally won out and I drifted off to a fitful sleep.

I was cold.

I remember that the most. I was really, really cold . . . and severely underdressed. I was standing in a large parking lot, in a T-shirt and shorts, hugging myself with my arms, and trying to remember how I got there. "Hello?" I called into the darkness. No one answered. I looked around the dimly lit parking lot. There were a few cars scattered about, but I couldn't see a sign of anyone anywhere. I turned in a circle, surveying the scene, and noticed at the edge of the lot was a large store. I decided to go there and see if I could find help. I walked on the cold pavement, shivering and hearing my teeth rattle, when a man came out of the darkness and began walking toward me. I felt relief as I recognized the blue jacket and red-white-and-blue patch sewn onto the upper right shoulder of his jacket. He was a mailman. I couldn't see his face, but as I watched him approach I noticed that he reached into his mailbag and extracted a mask, which he then slipped over his head. This alarmed me for reasons I couldn't understand, and I hesitated in my progress toward him, pausing for a moment as he neared me. Something flickered on the edge of my thoughts, and I knew I shouldn't be walking to him. I needed to run away, but I couldn't remember why.

The mailman grew closer, walking intently straight for me now. He was only a few yards away, in fact, when he reached into his mailbag once again and came up with a tire iron. Now I remembered why I was afraid, and why I needed to run. I turned to bolt but my feet were stuck. I couldn't get them to move. I felt drugged, sluggish and like I couldn't quite open my eyes all the way. I tried to scream, seeing how close he was to me, but no sound would come out.

The postman was ten feet away now. Nine. Eight. Seven . . . With all of my might I pulled up with my right leg and kicked forward, jumping into motion and straight out of bed onto my hardwood floor. My eyes snapped open, and my breathing came in great, frantic breaths. "It was a dream," I said into the darkness. "It was just a dream."

After a moment I collected myself and got up from the floor. I stood on shaky legs and grabbed my flannel robe from the hook by the door; then I walked out of my bedroom and down the stairs, through the living room, which was significantly warmer than upstairs, and into the kitchen, where I flipped on the light, squinting until my eyes adjusted, and I sat down at the kitchen table to collect myself.

I sat there with my head in my hands, thinking about the dream and how terrified I'd been, while trying to rationalize that my subconscious was just trying to work through some of the inputs that I'd picked up during the day. There was something different, however, that I couldn't quite shake. Something I needed to pay attention to.

I got up and fished through the cupboards for a minute, reaching for the instant hot chocolate I always keep on hand and a large coffee mug. I filled the mug with water and set it in the microwave for a minute, waiting for the water to heat.

Next I grabbed a notepad and a pen off the counter and set those down at my place at the table, then, when the timer dinged, I got the mug from the microwave and mixed in the hot chocolate. I walked back to the table and took a seat, staring blankly ahead, trying to ponder things for a moment. Obviously the dream was about the rapist, and I felt that there were several clues within the nightmare that I needed to make note of.

After a few warm sips of hot cocoa I picked up the pen and began to write down everything I remembered from the dream: the dark parking lot, the cars, the postman, the ski mask and the tire iron. After I finished I looked at my notes, my intuition buzzing.

Eggy came down while I was staring at the words I'd tossed onto the page, and I reached down to pick him up. He was sleepy, so I folded him into my lap and spread the sides of my robe around him.

I looked back at my notes again and asked myself, *What does the mailman represent?* Mail could be news, or messages, or information. Because it came from the mailman it probably meant that it came from a distance. I wondered if Milo had had any luck with the Vegas PD, remembering that I'd connected the rapist to Vegas.

For some reason, though, that didn't feel like it fit. There was something more significant about the postman that I wasn't connecting. There had been no mail in the mailbag, just the mask and the tire iron. So what did the postman represent?

Then it hit me, and I sucked in a breath. I got up and carried Eggy to the living room, where I laid him gently on the couch, then darted to my purse. It took a moment, but I found the card I was looking for and quickly dialed the number. After the tone I punched in my home number and added a 911, then hung up and paced the floor.

Within two minutes my phone was ringing and a groggy voice answered my anxious greeting with, "Abby? What's up?"

"Thank you so much for calling me back, and I'm sorry to get you up at"—I hesitated as I looked up at the clock on the wall—"uh . . . wow, four in the morning, but I have to ask you something. Does Jeffrey Zimmer work for the post office?"

"What?"

"Jeff Zimmer, your suspect in the rape case!" I was practically shouting into the phone with excitement. "Does he work for the post office?"

There was a slight hesitation as Milo seemed to struggle with my question; then he said, "No. He's a computer tech at Verizon."

I knew it. "He's not your rapist," I said firmly.

"Do you want to tell me what this is about?"

"Okay, you're going to think I'm nuts, but I had a dream tonight, and in it I was in this big parking lot and I was cold and lost and the only person in the lot was a postman, but I couldn't see his face, and he reached into his mailbag and pulled out a ski mask and a tire iron and put them on!" I was so excited I was dancing on the balls of my feet.

"You're kidding me, right?" Milo said in a tone that let me know he wasn't amused.

I was irritated that he didn't get where I was going, so I said, "Well, Milo, *funny* as that story is, I'm actually *not* kidding you. So as I was saying—"

"Abby?" Milo interrupted.

"What?" I said, getting impatient.

"Call me in three hours," he said, and hung up the phone.

"Hello?" I said several times into the receiver, not believing he had actually disconnected.

With a scowl I hung up my end and paced back and forth in the room like a caged animal. I was totally onto something here, and it frustrated the crap out of me that Milo was refusing to listen. I thought about calling him again just to tell him what he could do with his "Call me in three hours" baloney, but decided against it.

Instead I went into the kitchen and opened the refrigerator door, peering inside with interest. I'd gone shopping on my lunch break, looking around the grocery store at every suspicious-looking person, ready to fire my antennae at anyone who seemed to be lurking in the shadows. Mostly the store was filled with old men and frayed mothers toting screaming children in their shopping carts—not exactly a suspicious group of characters.

Still, my fridge was full, so I set about making a huge omelet, with a side of home fries.

I'm not a good cook, but I know my way around breakfast. Eggy came loping tiredly into the kitchen the moment he heard the crack of the first egg, so I made him a miniomelet too.

He's less into table manners than I am, and he scarfed his meal down in about two gulps. I ate mine in a dainty three.

By the time I'd washed the dishes and put the ingredients away it was only five a.m. Two more hours to go.

I sighed and trotted into the living room again, wired for no apparent reason. I picked up Eggy, who had claimed my favorite chair, and set him in my lap as I plopped down to watch infomercials.

At exactly six fifty-nine I paged Milo again. I waited five impatient minutes before sending another page to his cell phone. Then another five minutes after that, then every minute for the next ten minutes until finally at seven-twenty, just as I was listening to the instructions for leaving a page, my call waiting beeped. Flashing over, I answered, "Hello?"

"What the *hell* has gotten into you?" Milo shouted into the phone.

"You wouldn't return my call!" I shouted back.

"I was in the shower!"

"Then *why* did you ask me to call you at seven a.m.?" I snapped.

There was a very long, irritated sigh on the other end

of the phone, then, "Okay, you win. What's this all about?"

Finally I had his attention! "Listen, I don't always get prophetic information in dreams, but I just have to tell you about this one, okay? There's definitely a clue in it, and I just know it's important. I think the rapist is connected to the post office somehow. I mean, I remember distinctly that the villain in my dream was a mailman, and mailmen usually know all sorts of important information about the people on their routes. They know their names, how many people live in the household, what kinds of hours they keep, and what their habits are. I think this guy might be a postal worker or a postal carrier."

"You're sure it wasn't just a nightmare?"

"Yes! I'm sure. My guides are trying to tell me there's a clue at the post office. I'm sure of it."

"So what do you want me to do?"

"Well," I said, growing impatient again, "how about checking to see if the three women who have been raped so far were on the same postal route? I also know that there's usually a person who floats between several routes covering for the main carrier's day off, so you might want to check that out too."

"Anything else?" Milo asked, still not convinced.

"Yes, and this is nonnegotiable," I said, my voice taking on a flinty tone.

"Here we go," Milo said, more to himself than to me.

"You absolutely *must* warn the public before this Thursday. Your guy didn't do it, Milo, and if you don't warn women then it's going to happen again."

"We've already got a contingency plan for Thursday. I've got all the local food markets covered by plain-clothed police. There's no way this guy's going to attack another woman this week."

Left side, heavy feeling. "Milo, *please,* don't be a fool. If by some chance another woman gets raped and it comes out that you didn't warn people, it's going to be your ass—"

"I'm well aware of the possible fallout, but there are also consequences for starting a public panic. Think about the owners of these grocery stores, what kind of financial loss this could bring to them. Not to mention the tidal wave of overzealous tipsters who will flood our severely understaffed unit with a lot of false leads. I'm confident we have the right guy in custody—"

"Milo, you need to listen to reason!" I shouted, growing more and more anxious.

"Will you let me finish?" Milo barked. When I was silent he continued, "As I was saying, I'm confident we have the right man in custody, but *because* I believe in you I will follow up on this postal carrier connection, and contact the media about a news story where we think we have the right man in custody, but that women should think twice about any late-night shopping they need to run."

I sighed in relief and said, "Thank you."

"Now, may I please go back to getting ready for work?"

I made a face at the phone and said, "Yes, and get a cup of coffee as soon as you can. You're awfully cranky this morning."

"Yes, that tends to happen when I get woken up in the middle of the night."

I rolled my eyes and said, "Oh, get over it, Milo. I *so* owed you anyway."

There was the smallest of chuckles as Milo relented and said, "I guess you did. Thanks for trying to help, and if I get any leads on this postal carrier thing I'll call you, okay?"

"Deal," I said, and said my good-byes. I hung up the phone and let out an exasperated sigh. Now that I'd gotten my way I was completely drained, and feeling the effects of only three hours' sleep. I turned to the clock and groaned.

Mondays and Tuesdays are my usual days off, but with the whole bank account fiasco I'd moved up ten appointments over the next two days so that I could put a few dollars back into my kitty. My next day off wouldn't be until the following week, promising that come Sunday I'd be in one mighty grouchy mood.

The clock read seven forty-five, which left me just

enough time for a quick shower before I would have to bolt downtown for my first reading at nine. *Ugh.*

While I was in the shower, the dream from earlier kept swirling in my head. I couldn't shake the feeling that I'd missed something obvious, but what it was I couldn't be sure. My head felt full of cobwebs anyway, from lack of sleep, and I decided to push it out of my mind and think about it later, when I wasn't so exhausted.

I went to work, did my five readings, came home, and collapsed into bed, where I slept straight through to the next morning without pausing to ponder the dream further.

Tuesday, I woke up anxious but late for work, so I didn't analyze why I felt anxious until later on that night. I felt restless and on edge, but couldn't place the feeling.

To distract myself, I called Cat to see how the preparations for her psychic party were going, but she said that three of the members of her book club had come down with colds, so the group had decided to postpone until the following Sunday. I could hear a hint of relief in her voice as we talked, thinking she was probably glad to have a little more time to prepare.

I didn't tell her anything about the rape case I was working on, or the Mafia wedding I'd attended, and especially not about my little jaunt downtown with the gorilla escort.

Cat worried about me enough as it was, and if she suspected I was in harm's way she wouldn't hesitate to call a few friends of hers, who also just happened to be merchant marines, and send them here to "persuade" me to move to Boston, where I could be better supervised. I loved my sister, but I also loved my independence, so I typically selected the topics of our conversations very carefully.

After I hung up with Cat I flipped on the television just in time to catch the six-o'clock news. One of the lead stories was about Jeff Zimmer, and how the police suspected he'd been responsible for three rapes in the Royal Oak area. The news anchorwoman said, "Police believe they have enough evidence to link Zimmer with at least one of those rapes, and he is currently being held without bond. We have more on this story from Action News reporter Cindy Minsford." The TV screen flashed to a perky-looking blonde standing next to Milo just outside the Royal Oak police station.

"Yes, thank you, Janice. I'm here with Royal Oak Police Detective Milo Johnson, who is the lead investigator on this case. Detective Johnson, what led you to believe that Mr. Zimmer was responsible for the horrific attacks against these local women?"

Milo was dressed in a three-piece ebony suit, crisp-starched white shirt and silver-banded tie. His face was set in a serious expression, and he appeared very comfortable in front of the camera. "Our major break came from one of the victims, who was the neighbor of our suspect."

"And isn't it true, Detective, that you found evidence in the home of the suspect linking him to these crimes?"

"Well, Cindy, I'm not at liberty to go into specifics here, but let's just say I'm confident this man is our prime suspect and is, at this moment, safely behind bars."

My left side felt thick and heavy, causing a frown to shadow my features.

"I'm sure the women in the Royal Oak area will breathe a sigh of relief tonight knowing that a serial rapist is safely behind bars, right, Detective?"

"Perhaps, but it's always a good idea to be extra cautious, Cindy, especially when walking to and from your car, in places like grocery stores and shopping malls."

"Can you tell us a little bit more about how to avoid being a rapist's next victim?" Cindy asked.

I scowled. This was how Milo intended to "warn" the public?

"Glad to, Cindy," Milo said, smiling charmingly at her. "Now, the thing to remember is that rapists tend to look for easy targets, like women who are walking alone, seem lost in thought, like talking on a cell phone, or are not paying attention to their surroundings. Women who have long hair make it easy for a rapist to grab onto something, so if you have long hair or a ponytail you may want to consider tucking it into your clothing. If you are attacked, the best thing you can do is fight for your life. Scream, kick, bite, claw and make as much noise as possible. Try not to yell for help, but shout, 'Fire!' instead. This is sure to get some notice. Also, never, ever get into a van or vehicle with an attacker if you can possibly avoid it. Chances are your attacker will take you to a remote location where no one will hear you if you yell for help.

"Taking time to do your errands in broad daylight is also a good idea. The later in the year we get, the earlier it gets dark, so if you can, save your shopping for the weekends or your days off, and go when it's light out, never at night."

I was nodding my head to every one of Milo's helpful hints. Even though it wasn't the warning I was hoping for, at least the advice was good.

Cindy was also nodding, and when Milo had finished she said, "Excellent advice, Detective Johnson, thank you." She then turned back to the camera and said, "Reporting live from Royal Oak, this is Cindy Minsford. Back to you, Janice."

I sighed and clicked off the TV. I'd gotten basically what I'd asked from Milo, but I still felt uneasy. I got up and paced the floor, but couldn't shake the feeling. I headed into the kitchen and made dinner to distract myself, but as I ate my tuna melt on rye I couldn't stop thinking that there was something on the edge of my intuition that I wasn't getting.

After eating, I decided to call Milo and ask him if he'd found out anything about the postal connection I'd come up with. He answered on the second ring.

"Johnson," he announced.

"Hey, Milo, nice tie," I said.

"You saw the broadcast," he stated.

"Yeah. I guess that was the best you could do, huh?"

"Abby, we got the right guy. I can feel it. It's him."

Left side, heavy feeling. I shook my head, but decided not to argue. Instead I asked lightly, "So did you have a chance to run the lead on the postal carrier?"

"I did."

"And . . . ?"

" 'And,' we didn't find a connection. Three different sections of town, three different postal carriers."

"What about the floater?"

There was an exasperated sigh, then, "No, I'm sorry. It's a dead end."

Damn it. "Milo, there's something there. Something obvious—"

"Abby, listen to me. You're starting to obsess about this stuff, and I want you to relax and let us do our job down here, okay?"

"Now, wait just one minute. If memory serves me, and I believe it does, *you* were the one who asked for *my* help, and if I seem a little 'obsessive,' " I said in a snide, high-pitched voice, "then it's only because I am in fact, *trying to help you!*"

"You sure it's not because you're trying to distract yourself from something else?"

My eyes grew large. I had a foreboding about where he was going with this, and I couldn't believe he would play that dirty. "What do you mean, 'distract' myself?"

"Well, maybe if you focus all your energy on this case, you won't have to work things out with a certain FBI agent who recently made a jackass of himself?"

My voice dropped to a whisper as I asked, "He called you?"

"This morning."

"What did he say . . . exactly?"

"He said that he tried to introduce you to his new partner and that backfired, and then he insulted your intelligence and your profession and topped it off by getting defensive when you called him on it the other night."

"That his summation, or yours?"

"Mostly his." Milo laughed.

I sighed heavily and said, "Milo, I like that idiot so much it's pathetic, but he frustrates the hell out of me."

"Now you know why he's been playing it single for so long. The guy has no idea how to relate to women."

"So what do I do?"

"Well, he told me he may be headed back into town

soon, and that he'd try contacting you. My suggestion would be for both of you to listen to each other before passing judgment and see if you can work this out."

"Do you think it will be worth it in the end?" I knew I was reaching for something to hold on to, and I was hoping that Milo could give it to me.

"All I can tell you is that I've known Dutch Rivers for ten years, and in all that time I have never seen him so crazy about a woman as he is about you. Hang in there a little longer, girl; he's worth it."

My eyes welled up, and I was nodding my head in a yes motion. I found I couldn't talk without risking more tears, so I said quickly, "Thanks. Gotta go."

"I'll talk to you later," Milo said; he obviously understood.

I hung up the phone and curled up in my favorite chair with Eggy, crying softly and wishing I weren't such a girl.

Thursday morning I didn't need the alarm to wake me. I'd been up for an hour already. I'd had the dream again. This time I'd been able to run away, so it hadn't been quite as scary, but the other elements were exactly the same. I knew my guides were trying hard to get a message through to me, but what it was I couldn't put my finger on.

Finally I got up and took my shower, throwing my hair into a ponytail, and not fussing too much with my reflection. I was too tired to care.

In my line of work it is really easy to overdo. I've learned that if you take on too many clients in one day, or work too many consecutive days in a row, it can feel like you've run a marathon. No amount of sleep will help. Only a day or two off work will do the trick.

In extreme cases, when I'd really overdone it, I'd experienced what can only be described as a psychic headache. It's hard to explain what this feels like, but essentially the area above my head from my right ear to my right eye will hurt with a very sharp intensity. The weird part is that this isn't a pain *in* my head as much as it is a pain *around* my head—and no amount of aspirin can cure it.

I had one of these this morning, and I still had four days to go before I could take a small breather. To add insult to injury, even through my exhaustion and worn-out antennae there was the oppressing fact that today was Thursday, the day the rapist—if he was still at large—was likely to attack, and I was convinced he would.

I dressed for work sluggishly, choosing a gray sweater coat and jeans. I dragged myself downstairs and fed Eggy, then fixed a bagel and ate only half.

My jeans felt looser than usual, and I concluded that I'd been so worn-out lately that I really hadn't had a lot of time to take care of myself. Tonight I'd make sure to eat something hearty for dinner.

I drove to work in a stupor, and once there I dutifully played my voice mail and took down all the client information. The last call came as a surprise, and sent a ripple of goose pimples across my arms. "Abigail Cooper, this is Andros Kapordelis calling. I wonder if perhaps you have considered my offer. There is a project I would like you to work on for me; in fact, I can't believe I didn't think of it sooner. You may call me at 313-555-6978 at your earliest convenience."

I didn't bother to jot down the number; there was no way I was calling him back. I erased the message and got ready for my first client.

The day dragged on, and my headache grew worse. There was now a high-pitched whine humming just inside my energy field, annoying me no end. At five o'clock I dragged myself home and came through the door, greeted by a fervent Eggy. I fed him but was too tired to cook, so I called my favorite Thai food restaurant, Pi's, and ordered a delivery of pad thai.

They promised to have it to me within forty-five minutes, so I sat in my big chair and waited, but I couldn't shake a mounting sense that something was wrong. Finally I called Milo, if for nothing else than to hear that no one had been attacked yet.

"Johnson," he said, as he answered on the second ring.

"Hey, Milo. It's Abby."

"Hey, there. I was just about to call you."

"Really? Why? Has something happened?" I asked in rapid-fire succession.

Milo laughed and said, "Whoa, hold on, there, girl; nothing's happened. I was just going to tell you that they broke ground today over at the Boys and Girls Club. They're going to put up one big, beautiful facility."

I sank back into my chair and gave a small smile. "That's great! Really, I'm so happy the money's going to good use."

"Hell of a thing you did, girl. I wish you'd let me tell the press about it."

I laughed at that. "No way! People will think I still have a lot of money, and they'll be hitting me up right and left. You can continue to keep my name out of it, okay?"

"As promised."

"So?" I asked, rounding to the point of my call, "it's been quiet, huh?"

Milo chuckled. "Very. Listen, I know you're worried, but I've got an army of plainclothed police out at every local grocery store in town. I've even called the neighboring cities and put them on notice. If something goes down we'll be the first to hear about it."

My feelings of disquiet refused to subside, even through Milo's reassurances. "Uh-huh," I said.

"Listen, if it makes you feel any better, why don't you come on down to the station and hang out with us tonight? That way you'll be the second person to know if something happens—which it won't—and that way I won't jump the fifteen times you call me tonight to see if anything's happened."

I smiled, relieved. Milo had actually read my mind. "You like Thai food?"

"Only from Pi's," he said, humoring me. I'd once gone on and on about my favorite Thai restaurant, and how I was convinced that once you tried Pi's you never went anywhere else.

"An order of pad thai coming right up," I said, and

hung up, then immediately redialed Pi's and doubled my order, changing the delivery to pickup.

I was at the station a half hour later, two steaming portions of sweet rice noodles topped with chicken, peanuts and bean sprouts in hand. I found Milo sitting at his desk with his feet up and the receiver pressed to his ear.

"Uh-huh," he said into the phone. "Okay, well, if you come across anything you can reach me at that number day or night. We got the suspect in custody, but there was a lead I was tracking down that may connect this guy to your area."

What? I mouthed when I caught his eye while I set out his dinner.

Milo shook his head and held up a finger as he finished his call with an, "Okay, thanks again, Jack. I hope I hear from you." He hung up the phone and clapped his hands together over the scent of peanuts and lime curling up from the Styrofoam container. "This looks awesome!" he said, beaming me a smile.

"That's because it *is* awesome." I said, taking my seat and folding the paper napkin onto my lap. "Was that about your suspect?" I asked, pointing to the phone with my plastic fork.

"Yeah, that was Detective Jack Stevens out in Vegas. I was double-checking on your advice to see if they had any rapes in the area with a similar MO."

"And . . . ?" I said through a mouthful of noodles.

" 'And' we don't know yet. Stevens is going to check through their database, but nothing comes to his mind right off the bat. I did a little background search on our guy Zimmer, and it turns out he goes to Vegas at least twice a year, so there's your connection."

Left side, heavy feeling. Even though my intuition was saying no, I was quiet, letting Milo continue.

"We still haven't found the mask or the tire iron, but this guy could have thrown them away somewhere after the last rape."

I pondered that awhile, my brow furrowed. It didn't

make sense that Zimmer would use the same tools for three successive rapes and then all of a sudden get spooked on the last one and toss them someplace no one could find them. To change the subject I asked, "So how's Cathy?"

"I talked to her this morning. She's doing better. She's going to start her new job in a couple of weeks, which is good because it gives her something to look forward to. She's feeling better, and she's been seeing the hospital shrink. And, like so many other women before her, she will find a way to deal with it."

That last sentence made me sad. It sucked that we lived in a world where so many centuries after man had become "civilized," women still had to learn to deal with rape.

Milo and I continued to eat our dinner in companionable silence, each pretending to ignore the other's frequent glances at the phone. After we'd finished eating, Milo gathered up the Styrofoam containers and threw them away, then opened his desk drawer, pulled out a deck of cards and began to shuffle them on his desk. Briefly they reminded me of the tarot deck I'd used at the wedding the week before, but I quickly shoved that thought aside. I had enough on my plate at the moment.

"Penny poker?" Milo asked with a sly grin in my direction.

I smiled knowingly; my inboard lie detector was going to make mincemeat out of him. "I'm game," I said easily, flashing him a Bo-Peep smile.

Milo and I played penny poker with five other detectives in the unit until about ten thirty, when it was clear we could all probably relax. Only two calls had come in on Milo's line, and both were from his wife, Noelle, checking to see when he'd be home. Otherwise there had been nothing unusual going on in the local neighborhoods, as the presence of so much police power out on the streets had settled the community down early for the night.

Around that time the atmosphere in the Detective's Unit switched noticeably from tense to celebratory; we'd done it. We had the right man in custody, and Royal Oak could rest easily—its serial rapist, Jeffrey Zimmer, was behind bars. Then somebody in the group suggested switching from penny poker to strip poker. Everyone looked expectantly at me to see if I'd agree, and since I'd thumped them all well and good at penny poker, I felt pretty cocky going for the gusto.

Within a short period of time I had every detective in the department stripped down to his skivvies, and a load of laundry littered the floor around my chair. I hadn't lost a single hand.

Technically Milo should have been buck-naked twice over, but for the sake of modesty I'd counted his cuff links, watch and gold necklace as separate pieces of clothing. All that was left between his showing us his "hello, Dolly" were his underwear and his wedding ring . . . which I'd spotted him twisting nervously.

I'd love to be a fly on the wall when he got home and had to explain to his wife either why he was naked, or why he was in his underwear with no wedding ring.

The clock on the wall now read close to midnight, and I leaned back tiredly in my chair, stretching and yawning as the latest poker victim gave up his undershirt. If we played one more hand someone at this table was going home in his birthday suit, and as I looked around at all the out-of-shape bodies on display, I decided that wasn't an image I particularly wanted to carry home with me to bed.

Thinking this game wasn't going to end until I ended it, I stood up and said, "Well, fellas, it's been swell, but I'm afraid I'm going to have to call this a night."

Closely guarded relief swept through the five detectives gathered around Milo's desk, and they all gave halfhearted calls for one more game. I laughed as I gathered up my winnings, fully intending to carry every article of clothing home and teach these men a valuable lesson about trying to outsmart a psychic.

As I bent over to retrieve someone's pants Milo's phone rang, and we all looked sharply at it in surprise. Milo hesitated only a moment, then answered it in one smooth motion. "Johnson."

We watched Milo's face closely, looking for clues as he listened to the caller. In my heart I knew even before I saw his face grow taut and heard him utter, "Goddamned son of a bitch," that it was terrible news. "I'll be there in five," he said, and hung up the phone. Then he looked at me with an odd mixture of intense anger and regret.

"Someone else has been raped," I said breathlessly.

"Yes," was all Milo could muster at the moment, his furious breathing taking all other effort.

"But how?" I protested, my mind trying to make sense of it. "I mean, you had all those men staking out the grocery stores. . . ." The caller had gotten it wrong somehow; this couldn't have happened. We'd taken precautions; we'd done our homework.

Milo shook his head, staring at the ground for a moment, then looked up and met my wide, horrified eyes as he said, "She wasn't attacked at the grocery store. One of the patrolmen coming off duty just found her."

"Where?" I asked.

"Behind the post office."

I sank heavily down in my chair, the clothes still heaped in my arms. "Oh, God . . ." I said. "Oh, my God . . ."

As the news sank in the men were all moved to action. One of the detectives next to me gently eased his shirt from across my shoulders, and taking the hint I quickly set the large pile of clothing in the middle of Milo's desk as each man began to sift through, looking for his belongings. Our festive mood had instantly evaporated with the news, and everyone but me was moving about quickly. I sat there mutely in the chair as the group rushed to get dressed, wondering how, with all the patrolmen we had out there, this could still happen.

I watched Milo as he snapped his pants out of the pile of clothing and furiously pulled them on. He was shaking with rage. I continued to stare at him as he shrugged into his shirt, not bothering with his cuff links, and noticed there was something tragic about the way his face was set. Something he was holding back made me ask, "Milo? She'll be okay, right?"

Everyone stopped dressing suddenly and fixed their attention on Milo, waiting for his reply. Perhaps it was lingering in the air. Perhaps it was the way he was so angry. Perhaps it was because I knew the answer even before I asked the question that made everyone stop and look at Milo, forcing him to face me, which was hard for him to do, I could tell.

"No, Abby," he said softly as he cinched his belt more tightly than he should have. "She'll never be okay again, because she's dead. This time that fuck killed her."

Chapter Seven

It was Sunday evening and I was sitting in my favorite chair, Eggy curled in my lap and a glass of red wine perched on the small table to my right.

Somehow I had made it through the week, and if I'd had the energy I would have patted myself on the shoulder, but as it was I was nearly too tired to lift the glass of wine.

I hadn't slept well in days; between the persistent nightmare of the postman and thoughts of remorse over the latest victim, I'd been unable to get a restful night's sleep; hence the vino on my right to coax me into a relaxed state of mind.

I'd gone home the night of the murder haunted by Milo's words: "She'll never be okay again, because she's dead. This time that fuck killed her." And I'd been haunted by them ever since.

I couldn't reconcile it, the nagging questions that wouldn't leave my mind alone. How had I not seen the obvious? How had I been so obtuse as to lead Milo down the wrong path, having him check out mailmen instead of the post office itself? It was so obvious when I thought about it, such a gigantic clue from my intuition, and I'd misdirected it. The guilt of it was pounding me like a sledgehammer.

Milo had called and left several messages for me on Friday, Saturday and this morning, but I had yet to return any of them. From the moment I'd heard the news that a woman had been killed, I was out. Done. Finito. I wanted no part in this scenario anymore—because the culpability of getting it wrong was killing me.

Oh, sure, it had been fun and exciting to get involved in solving a real criminal mystery; that was until someone was murdered. It had dawned on me like a bucket of cold water that this wasn't a game, or my next big adventure. This was for keeps, and people were dying.

The news had carried the story of the thirty-year-old mother of three who was brutally attacked, raped and bludgeoned to death, then left partially naked behind a Dumpster at the Royal Oak Post Office. Karen Millstone had been young, talented, pretty, and had everything to live for. Now she was dead, and I'd decided to shoulder the blame.

The television drummed on as I drank my wine and felt my mind slowly wind down after a day of spinning. This morning I'd woken with an idea that I couldn't shake. It had been like a little fly in my head, buzzing around and interrupting all other thoughts, and the fact that I was even considering it scared the stuffing right out of me. I was thinking about quitting.

Before becoming a psychic I'd been an assistant manager at a local bank, and I was thinking, with melancholy, that I could return to that life if I wanted to. I even had a degree in finance to back up a career change. I could go back to school and get a master's, or I could apply to a few banks and see what happened. I'd make far less money, but the house was almost finished, so I didn't need as much income to support myself now as I did when I'd first bought my home.

More important, a career change would put an end to the misfires. No more ambiguous clues that I tried to make sense of and couldn't. No more clients who were attacked or murdered. No more responsibility for the health and well-being of all my clientele, which was really what was bothering me here. As a professional psychic I'm supposed to keep my patrons out of mischief. That's why they come to me in the first place, and so far I didn't have a very good track record.

That, coupled with my recent disaster on the Royal Oak serial rapist, I reasoned, was enough to put me on the bench . . . permanently.

I reached for the glass of wine again and sipped the smoky liquid. I had a nice buzz going now, and the trick was to keep the buzz, but not let it get more intense to invite a night with one foot planted on the floor to stop the world from spinning. I'm a real lightweight, so this scenario was probably going to happen anyway.

Just then there was a soft knock on my front door. I looked at the clock on the wall—nine fifteen.

Eggy jumped into action at the sound and raced to the front foyer, barking and digging at the hardwood floor. Lazily, I got up and went to check the peephole. Milo stood with one hand on his hip and his head slightly cocked, listening for movement behind the door.

"Shit," I whispered as Eggy looked anxiously from me to the door and offered one more loud bark.

"Abby?" Milo called from my front porch. "You in there?"

"It's late, Milo; can we do this another time?" I asked, leaning my head against the wood frame.

"Abby," Milo said sternly, "come on; let me in. I need to talk to you. . . ."

I hesitated. I didn't want to let him in. I didn't want to see him, or talk to him, or work with him . . . I just wanted to be left alone.

"Hey," he called, and knocked again. "You might as well open the door because I'm not going away."

Son of a bitch.

"Fine!" I sighed, and undid the lock, letting him in.

Milo stepped into my living room without a word, and waited for me to close the door and retake my seat before talking to me. I could feel his eyes moving from me to the glass of wine to the flat expression of my face. I braced for the reprimand I knew was about to follow.

But Milo surprised me. Instead of a lecture he took a

seat on the couch next to my chair, his eyes drifting to the muted TV. After a moment he asked, "Whatcha watchin'?"

"Alias."

"Great show."

"The greatest."

"Jennifer Garner can sure kick some ass, huh?"

I nodded dully. "And take names while she's at it . . ."

"Yeah . . ."

Silence.

Irritated by Milo's presence, I purposely sipped a little more wine; my buzz was intensifying but I didn't give a hooey. Milo looked at me pointedly, but I ignored him. I wasn't going to stop drinking on his account.

Finally he asked, "Abby?"

"Yeah?"

"You got any beer? Or are you just a red wine kind of gal?"

His question stunned me. I had expected something completely different to come out of his mouth, a lecture of some type, for my drinking alone, or for not returning his calls. Being asked to be a polite hostess never even dawned on me. "In the fridge," I said. "Dutch still has some Bud in there from August."

Milo smiled kindly and got up. "Thanks," he said as he moved into the kitchen.

My eyebrows shrugged as I heard him open my fridge and extract a beer. He came back into the living room and grabbed the remote from the table.

Here it comes, I thought regretfully, *the lecture.* Instead Milo unmuted the TV and we watched the rest of *Alias* together in companionable silence. It was the first time in weeks I'd felt myself completely relax, like I was finally able to exhale after holding my breath for so long.

At ten o'clock the credits rolled, and Milo muted the TV again. The room grew heavy with silence, and then as I looked at him he said to me in a voice barely above a whisper, "I just wanted to tell you that I'm sorry."

I nearly dropped my glass of wine. "What?" I asked, giving him my full attention, "What are you sorry about?"

"I should have listened to you. If I had just listened

to you that woman would still be alive, and we'd probably have that bastard in custody."

"What are you talking about?" It was probably the wine, but I honestly could not compute what Milo was trying to tell me.

"The clue you gave me about the post office. It was so obvious, and I completely ignored it. Instead I had all my men wasting their time at the local grocery stores. We weren't patrolling anywhere else, and that basically laid out the red carpet for this guy to make his move somewhere else."

My mouth fell open. I could not believe Milo was taking the blame. "Milo . . . it wasn't *your* fault. *I* was the one who told you to look at mailmen, not specifically the post office. If I'd just said *watch the post office* you would have, and *I* could have prevented this. It's not your fault; it's mine."

Now it was Milo's turn to look astonished. "You're kidding me, right?"

"No, I'm dead serious. I mean, what good is it to have me work on this case with you if all I do is point you in the wrong direction? I should have figured it out. I should have covered all the bases, and I fell short. Here you were counting on me to help you, and I blew it, and now this woman is dead." Tears had welled up in my eyes, and try as I might I couldn't prevent them from pooling over to make tracks down my face.

Milo looked at me with such compassion that it only made me feel worse, and I swallowed hard to hold down the sob that wanted to burst from my throat. Finally he said gently, "Abby, *you* were the one who told me I had the wrong guy in custody. *You* were the one who mentioned a connection with the post office. *You* were the one who came up with a tire iron and a ski mask, and thanks to you, Abigail Cooper, we now have a lot more to go on. There is no way you hindered this investigation, and the truth is quite the contrary: You've been a true help from day one."

His words were my undoing. I was fragile enough, exhausted, stressed out, and vulnerable, not to mention shit-faced, and I couldn't help it: I buried my head in my hands and sobbed like a little girl. I felt Milo sit down on the edge of my chair and wrap an arm across my shoulders as he patted me on the back and whispered in my ear that everything was going to be okay.

Finally I'd collected myself enough to sit back, and Milo handed me a tissue from the Kleenex box on my coffee table. "Here," he said gently.

I took the tissue and wiped my eyes, sniffing loudly, and mouthed *Thanks* to him.

"So that's why you didn't return my calls? All this time you felt guilty?"

I nodded as I blew my nose and reached for another tissue.

Milo chuckled and said, "And I thought you were angry at me, and that's why you didn't call me back."

"Why would I be angry at you?" I asked, surprised by that declaration.

"Because I didn't listen to you. Because I was so sure we had the right guy in custody."

"You still holding him?" I asked, curious about what they would do with Jeff Zimmer.

"No, we reduced the charges and let him go on bond."

"Reduced the charges?"

"Peeping Tom is an illegal activity."

"Oh . . . the photos," I said, remembering the pictures he'd taken of Cathy without her knowledge.

"Yeah. Cathy's boyfriend has already moved all of their belongings to another side of town, so Cathy won't have to live next door to Zimmer when she gets out of the hospital."

"Good for them."

"We also found Karen Millstone's car—remember I asked if you could tune in on that for us in one of the messages I left you?"

"Yeah," I said ducking my head. Milo had pleaded with me to come into the station and help find Karen's car. The police suspected the rapist might have stolen it, and if I could get a bead on its location, then maybe they'd have an idea where this guy lived.

"It wasn't stolen after all, but was parked in your parking structure, about four floors up."

"You mean the one across the street from my office?"

I asked, a little alarmed that death had come so close to where I worked.

"Yeah. We found some shopping bags in the car from a couple of the boutiques down the street, and we think she parked her car in the structure because it's centrally located between the local shops and the post office."

I thought about that for a minute. The post office was right next door to the parking garage, but it had a parking lot of its own, which explained why, when detectives first searched the post office's parking lot, her car wasn't found. Still, it creeped me out that the killer had been less than a block away. Had I seen him? Had I walked right past him on the street as he went on his way to kill Karen Millstone? I shivered involuntarily as the thought gave me goose bumps.

"We think she was attacked shortly after she came out of the post office. We found a few letters from her PO box in her purse, so we know she was killed after she left the building. Surveillance cameras in the lobby of the post office show her entering at around eight thirty, and leaving about three minutes later."

"Wasn't the post office closed at that time of night?"

"Yes, but if you have a post office box you can access it anytime; there's a small section of the lobby that's always open."

"Oh," I said, thinking as my radar began buzzing, but at the moment I was in no mood to answer the call.

"So you going to come back and help me solve this case?" Milo asked after a moment.

I stared at the tissue wadded up in my hand. Tonight I just couldn't say yes. "I don't know, Milo. I think I just need a little time to come to grips with all this, and maybe in a few days I'll feel okay enough to help, but right now I'm just tired and I need a break, you know?"

There was a mixture of disappointment and compassion on Milo's face as he squeezed my shoulder. "Sure thing. That's fine," he said as he got up and carried his empty beer bottle and my nearly empty glass of wine to the sink. He came back and extended his hand, helping me up out of the chair. "It's time for me to head on home. I haven't seen much of my wife lately, and I'm starting to miss her, if you catch my drift. . . ."

I smiled at the way he made his eyebrows dance at the "catch my drift" part and I walked him to the door. "Thanks for coming over."

He paused before opening the door and said, "You know, it's not up to you to always get it right. Sometimes you're supposed to understand it only so far, and because the message comes to you doesn't mean that it's your sole responsibility to figure it out. Okay?"

His words were like a balm on an open and ugly wound, and I squeezed his arm as he walked through the door, thanking my guides for sending him here tonight.

After locking up I went upstairs to bed with Eggy in tow and slept straight through for the first time in days.

The next day was spent mostly in bed. I'd purchased a space heater for my bedroom, which helped considerably with the temperature, and Eggy and I did nothing all day but lounge. I snacked on potato chips and homemade guacamole, watched three movies back-to-back, ordered a delivery of my usual from Pi's and never got out of my jammies.

At six I called my sister, whom I hadn't heard from since just before her party on Sunday, to see how the grand event had gone. I got her voice mail and left a message, expecting to get a call back within an hour.

By nine o'clock, however, I still hadn't heard from her, so I dialed again and got voice mail a second time. This was odd, because even if Cat wasn't home there was usually a nanny or housekeeper who picked up the phone. Weird.

At ten, exhausted by a full day of doing nothing, I turned out the light and went to sleep, thinking that I'd track Cat down at her office when I woke up the next morning.

The phone rang at eight thirty. I'd been awake for about half an hour, but it still pissed me off that someone would call that early. "Hello," I said into the receiver with all the warmth of an Antarctic winter.

"Miss Cooper?" a gravelly voice said, my last name obscured by a thick accent.

It took me a moment to find my voice. I was surprised that Andros Kapordelis would have the nerve to call me at home, and wondered how he'd come across my unlisted number. "How did you get this number?"

"I have my ways," he answered elusively. "I have something that I require your talents for. I will send a car this afternoon to get you and bring you to my office. . . ."

"Absolutely not!" I spat, my voice hard as steel. "Listen, Kapordelis, there is no way in hell I'm going to work for you. See, that's the great thing about being self-employed; I can pick and choose who I will read for and who I won't, and just so you know, for future reference, clients who kidnap me and have their goons assault me are not among the privileged who are allowed reentry onto my client list! We clear?" My heart was hammering in my chest, and I had to admit my palms had gone sweaty. Would this guy take no for an answer?

There was a pause on the other end of the line, and for some reason this only made my heart beat faster. Finally Kapordelis spoke, but his voice was considerably softer, more menacing and definitely more frightening. "It is not good to turn me down, Miss Cooper. You should reconsider."

I gulped, but somehow managed to stick to my guns "Listen, Mr. Kapordelis, I've refunded your money—with *considerable* interest—and I have humored you by not filing criminal charges for the kidnapping-and-assault thing, and now all I want from you is to be left alone. I will not willingly cooperate with you because you strike me as a violent man. I abhor violence, and I abhor men who condone it. My gift is not a plaything to be used and abused by you at your whim; it is mine to administer to people I willingly choose. There is no way you're going to talk me into working for you, no amount of money you could offer me. Now you may send your goon after me again, but I swear to you, Mr. Kapordelis, if you do you will still not get what you want from me. Pain blocks my intuition, and the more you exert, the more I shut down, so that won't work either."

"There are other ways of persuasion, Miss Cooper. I can see that you have not considered them yet. Perhaps I will demonstrate a few of them for you and see if you change your mind in a few days."

Before I could say anything more Kapordelis hung up with an ominous click. What other ways of persuasion was he talking about? There were goose bumps all up and down my arms as I set the cordless back in its cradle. I stared at the phone for several minutes as I pondered his cryptic last words. I was really going to have to watch my step for the next few days. It dawned on me just how precarious my situation was as I went into the kitchen to toast my bagel. This guy could hurt me, or even kill me. But there was no way in hell I was going to willingly work for him. It just went against everything I'd become.

When I was in the fourth grade I hung out with a bunch of older kids—mostly fifth-grade troublemakers, who allowed me to hang with them because I always took the blame when we got caught doing some nefarious act. After pulling one particularly nasty prank involving a classmate on crutches and my teacher's pet hamster, I was sent to the principal's office. My principal, Mr. Trombly, was a big bear of a man with bushy salt-and-pepper hair, shaggy eyebrows and a soft spot for malcontents like me.

I remember walking into his office and stoically taking my seat, setting my face defiantly and meeting his stare. We looked at each other across his large wooden desk for a long time, each refusing to blink. Finally with a heavy sigh he leaned back in his chair and picked up the report from my teacher with the laundry list of my latest transgressions. He shook his head in a tsk-tsk motion, and eyed me wisely.

What he said next had a profound effect on me, mostly because it was the first metaphor I ever really got. In his husky voice he said, "Abigail, if you walk in the mud all the time, pretty soon people are going to think your shoes are dirty."

I'd been on the straight and narrow ever since.

As I smeared peanut butter onto my bagel, I worried that I could be facing a broken leg or arm, or something my imagination had yet to conjure. I didn't think Andros would resort to killing me—I'd leave town if I thought that. But someone had to be the first to say no. Someone had to stand up to this guy, and I guess today I was that someone.

As I trotted back into the living room, Eggy in tow, there was a soft knock on the door. Eggy immediately abandoned me and started barking at the closed door. I had no idea who could be dropping by so early, and I paused, wondering if Andros had dispatched Goon to come over and do me in.

After a moment I walked to the front door on tiptoe and peeked through the peephole, my jaw dropping at the sight of the visitor on my front porch. Quickly I undid the lock and yanked it open as my sister threw herself forward into my arms, "Oh, Abby!" she wailed.

I pulled her into the living room, visually checking her over for injuries, assuming by the sight of her so distraught that she must be in pain. "Cat! What's happened? Why are you here? What's wrong?" I said anxiously.

"It's terrible!" she cried, covering her face with both hands. "I can never go back! *Never!*"

"Where? Who? What . . . ? Cat, for God's sake, *talk* to me!"

At this point I'd sat Cat on the sofa and was squatting down about a foot away, still trying to figure out where she was injured. Cat continued to wail uncontrollably, and I eyed the phone anxiously as I debated calling 911. Finally she sniffled and said, "They *hate* me!"

"Who? Who hates you?" I said gently, stroking her hair and trying to coax the information out of her.

"*Everyone!*" The announcement of this brought a fresh wave of tears as she buried her face into her hands again.

"Oh, honey," I tried, taking a seat next to her and patting her gently on the back, "that just can't be. Now take a deep breath, because I don't understand. What are you doing here, and who, *specifically,* hates you?"

Cat moaned something incoherent, and waved a hand toward the purse she'd cast on the floor when she sat down on the couch. "What?" I asked, not understanding.

Cat pointed to the purse more vehemently this time, her voice a warbled, water-clogged sound. "In there!"

I reached down and picked up her purse; opening it, I looked inside. Nothing out of the ordinary struck me, except for a folded wad of papers. I looked a question mark at her and she pointed to them. Taking them out I unfolded them and began to read:

Catherine Cooper-Masters; Psychic Reading Survey

1. How would you rate the accuracy of your psychic reading?
If accuracy were dollars, you'd be in debt up to your ass!
2. What was the most astonishing thing you remember from your psychic reading?
Probably when you accused me of bestiality—you need professional help, lady!
3. Even though this reading was free, how much would you be willing to pay for a reading of similar value?
You would owe me money!

My eyes widened as I flipped to the next page and read another survey, but the second was even worse than the first. "Cat!" I gasped as I glanced through each successively horrible review. "What did you *say* to these people?"

Cat sobbed even harder at my question, and I got up to fetch the Kleenex. I offered her the box and she snatched several tissues as she sniffled and wiped her nose, then honked into a Kleenex and regarded me with slanted, puffy eyes. "I just read their fortunes! I can't help it if the cards came up that way!"

"But, sweetie . . ." I said, glancing at another survey,

"you told this woman she was going to *die* by this weekend!"

Cat nodded, looking distressed, "Yes, I remember that one . . . Nancy Cartwright. Awful thing, that. I'll miss her when she's gone." She whimpered, squinting fresh tears into her Kleenex.

"And you told this woman her husband was leaving her for the nanny?"

"Marissa Carmichael." Cat nodded. "She's blaming *me* for telling her, when she should be calling her plastic surgeon for a fanny lift and firing the nanny."

I read on and my jaw kept dropping. My sister had apparently read a dozen women, and all the readings were outlandishly horrible. The common themes were death, adultery, impoverishment and loss of mind, although the last one seemed more a reflection of my sister.

"Catherine Cooper-Masters," I said as I read the last survey, adding a low whistle, truly amazed that she had caused such uproar.

"Actually, I'm changing my name back to just Catherine Cooper." Cat sniffled, fresh tears sliding down her cheeks.

"What do you mean? Why are you dropping the 'Masters'?"

"Well, I did a reading for Tommy, that lying, cheating, soon-to-be-*ex*bastard husband of mine! I've already called the attorney. I'm filing for divorce!"

I stood up and threw the surveys on the floor. "You *what*? Cat, are you *out of your mind*?"

"The cards don't lie, Abby," she said tightly, looking at me with a pained, convinced look.

I was speechless. I just stood above her for the longest time, my mouth agape and my hand cradling my forehead, willing my mind to process my sister's ridiculous conclusions. Finally I collected myself and sat down next to her. I began to speak several times, but had a hard time deciding where to start. After three attempts I finally said, "Cat . . . listen to me. I do this stuff for a living, so believe me when I tell you, sometimes what you take for fact is actually just a metaphor."

"What do you mean?"

I sighed heavily and tried again. "Well, let's take this example, okay? This woman . . ." I said, showing her the survey of the doomed Nancy Cartwright. "Now what made you believe that Nancy here was going to die?"

"Well, I remember pulling the death card, and it landed smack-dab on the 'present' position."

"Okay," I probed, "so what was next after the death card?"

"The chariot—and according to my book on tarot, that means Nancy will be in a fatal car crash and die before the week is through," Cat explained as if I were five.

"I see," I said, turning my intuition on and focusing on the name Nancy Cartwright. "See, what I'm getting is that Nancy just got a brand-new car, and she traded in her old one for the new—do you know if that's correct?"

Cat looked at me with a shocked expression and said, "Oh, my God, Abby, you're right! She pulled up to my house in a brand-new Lexus, and we were all wondering how she could afford such an expensive new car now that her husband's company is in the toilet."

I smirked at my sister—Cat, so aptly nicknamed. "You see?" I said. "Sometimes taking the literal translation isn't the way to go. You have to trust what your gut tells you when you do this kind of interpretation and allow that there are many possible interpretations for every card. You have to rely on your intuition to tell you which one is the most accurate. Like with the death card—I think it was really talking about the death of her old car—the chariot, and the bringing in of her new one, the Lexus."

"So I was wrong about everyone?" she asked, her voice growing sensitive.

There was just no way to sugarcoat it. "Definitely," I said. "*Most* definitely with Tommy. He's not cheating on you, Cat—*that* I know. So will you please contact your attorney and call off this divorce nonsense?"

I was worried for my brother-in-law; he took such good care of my sister, and basically worshiped the ground she walked on. I was afraid she'd done some real damage to her marriage by accusing him of things I knew he hadn't done.

Cat had started to tremble a little. Looking at her it was obvious she'd been up all night. "Oh, what have I done?" she wailed, and went back to burying her face in her hands.

"Nothing we can't fix, sugar," I said softly as I folded her into my arms and rocked her small frame while she cried. When her tears turned to hiccups I gently asked her, "So how did you get here?"

"I flew. Tommy and I got into this horrible fight last night, and I just left. The boys are at Disney with Tommy's parents, so luckily they weren't around to witness our shouting match. It was awful! I was so angry I just took myself to the airport and waited there for the first available flight, which wasn't until six this morning. I was even forced to fly *coach*, if you can believe it!"

I smiled; my sister hadn't known the discomfort of anything less than first class in at least a decade. "How did you get from the airport to here?"

"Cab."

"I tried to call you last night, but no one answered, not even your housekeeper."

"I had to let her go—her reading suggested she was a thief."

I rolled my eyes. "Who else did you give a reading to?"

"Just the gardener."

"And his fate?"

"He's going to have an awful tractor accident. I'm considering letting him go; I mean, who wants *that* on their insurance?"

I sighed heavily, stifling the urge to laugh. Cat gave a huge yawn and sighed with me. The dark circles under her puffy eyes and her slumped shoulders all indicated she was fading fast.

"All right, how about this?" I offered. "Why don't you go upstairs and take a nap in my bed? You look like you haven't slept in a couple of days. Later on we can go out for some lunch, okay?"

"And shopping?" she asked, perking up a teeny bit.

I chuckled. "Of course. I'll call Tommy and let him know where you are. He's probably worried sick."

Cat nodded against my shoulder. "Will you tell him I'm sorry?" she whispered.

"Of course, honey. Now come on; let's get you to bed." I pulled my sister up from the couch and walked her up the stairs to my bedroom. She was swaying on her feet from exhaustion, and I quickly set out a clean nightshirt for her and closed all the blinds, making the room nice and dark. Cat gave me a shy smile as I closed the door, then headed back downstairs to call Tommy.

"Hello?" he answered immediately.

"Hey, there, brother-in-law," I said easily.

"Abby? Oh, my God, I was just about to call you! Your sister's missing, and I can't find her anywhere. . . . Have you heard from her?" Tommy's voice had the mounting panic of someone truly worried. I was quick to set him at ease.

"She showed up on my doorstep this morning. She's here, safe and sound. How about I keep her for a day or two, then send her back to you?"

"Does she even *want* to come back?"

Oh, yeah, the argument. "She told me about your reading," I said.

"Abby, I swear to you, I have never—"

"Relax, Tommy. I'd know if you were cheating. I set Cat straight, and I think she feels like an idiot, but you know how proud she is."

"Those stupid tarot cards. I knew they were trouble the minute she showed up from New York with them. . . . What the hell was she thinking?"

"That's Cat for you. She's got to try everything once; you know how she is."

Tommy chuckled, probably for the first time in two days. "Let's just hope she leaves all this psychic stuff to the expert in the family from now on, huh?"

"That'd be my preference. Listen, I'll have her give you a call as soon as she wakes up. You going to be home?"

"Yeah, I canceled my tournament this morning because I had no idea where she'd gone, so now I'm stuck here for the next two weeks." Tommy was a golf pro.

"Sorry about that," I said. "I'll have her call you as soon as she wakes up."

"Thanks, Abby," he said, and we disconnected.

After hanging up with Tommy I headed downstairs to the basement to see about some laundry—I hadn't done any in a while. I loaded the darks and headed back upstairs, where I did housework and paid some slightly overdue bills until a little before noon.

Next I got dressed in my now-clean clothes and, after leaving Cat a note, headed out to pick up some groceries. I hadn't checked my messages from work yet, or gotten the mail, so I headed over to my office to take care of business. On the way I passed the post office, which sat just catercorner to my office building, and I voluntarily shivered. To think that some poor, unsuspecting woman had been murdered there gave me the willies. She had been someone simply out running an errand, some innocuous thing, and it had led her to her death. The injustice of it pissed me the hell off, and I made up my mind to give Milo a call later and get back to work on the case.

After checking messages and getting the office mail, I headed back toward home, but thinking of something I made a quick detour and pulled up in front of a familiar Cape house. I sat inside my car for a minute or two, looking up at Dutch's tidy lawn and well-manicured shrubs and sighed heavily. Even though I was still a little angry at him, I missed him terribly.

Unbuckling my seat belt I got out of the car and moseyed around back to the flowerpot that hid his house key. I found it right away and let myself in, punching in his birthday into the alarm and flipping on some lights while I called, "Virgil!" into the silence of the house. I was rewarded a few moments later by the appearance of Dutch's silver-gray tomcat as he rounded the corner with an excited meow. I bent low and scratched his ears as he rubbed against my legs and hand, his purr vibrating loudly from his throat. I then got up and went to check on his food dish, water bowl and kitty-litter box. All were being well maintained by Dutch's neighbor.

Feeling melancholy, I walked into the living room and looked around, remembering fonder moments of Dutch and me curled on his sofa watching a ball game. I smiled in spite of myself, and felt a tug of regret as I thought about how our last conversation had ended. I was about to leave when something caught my eye from across the living room, and being the curious type I walked over for a better look.

On the far end table next to the couch was a beautiful silver picture frame, and inside the frame was a five-by-seven photo of me taken when Dutch and I had gone to the state fair. I'd forgotten all about the roll of film Dutch had shot that day, and as I picked up the picture a new wave of guilt knotted in my stomach.

How could I doubt a guy who had a photo of me encased in a silver frame on his end table? To reinforce that idea, I felt my intuition weigh in, and I knew that Dutch was serious about us, and that I didn't need to doubt him anymore. My insecurities were more about past relationships than present ones, and I knew I needed to reel in the green-eyed monster and learn to trust again. With a smile I put the picture back down on the tabletop and gave Virgil one more good scratch before setting the alarm and heading home, feeling much better than when I'd arrived.

When I got back to my place I found Cat in my robe and a towel wrapped turban style around her head, sitting in my kitchen having a cup of tea. "Hey, there," she said as she gave me a small, sheepish smile.

"Hey, there," I said, playfully bumping her with my hip as I set the groceries on the table.

"Sorry I borrowed your robe; I didn't bring any extra clothes with me."

I regarded my sister ensconced in my bathrobe as it puddled around her feet. I've got six inches on Cat, and about twenty pounds. She's a natural blond to my artificially enhanced color, and her eyes are vividly bluer. She wears her hair short, spiky and messy—Sharon Stone style, and her preferred color of wardrobe is white, right down to her shoes. I haven't seen her in anything that wasn't a designer label since the nineties, and her favorite mode of transport is chauffeured. Cat believes in the finer things, and, lucky for her, she's made enough money to be able to afford most of them.

Seeing her in my beat-up flannel robe with a turban on her head took a minute to get used to. "Comfy?"

"As a matter of fact I am. What is this material?" she asked, picking at the sleeve of my robe.

"Flannel," I said, rolling my eyes. I only half believed she was pulling my leg.

"Ah. Yes, I remember. Well, are we still on for lunch and shopping?"

"Absolutely. Why don't you go get ready while I put the groceries away?"

"Meet you back here in fifteen minutes," she said, getting up from the table and picking up the bottom of my robe so as not to trip over the hem. "By the way," she called over her shoulder, "your room is a refrigerator!"

"Yeah, yeah," I said, avoiding an explanation. If my sister knew why my room was so cold she would want to fix it, and pay for it too.

Exactly fifteen minutes later Cat met me back in the kitchen wearing the same white suit I'd seen her in that morning. "Would you mind if we stopped off at Neiman's before lunch? I have *got* to get out of this suit!"

"Sure, and don't tell me you've already called ahead."

"Of course I have. We're meeting Crystal in the couture department in twenty minutes."

"My sister, ever the efficient shopper," I said, grabbing my purse and giving Eggy a kiss as we headed out the door.

Cat purchased four outfits that varied in color from pearl to off-white to two separate shades of cream. She then bought several pairs of underclothes and a silk nightgown, along with various toiletries. We also stopped in the luggage department, where she picked up a small carry-on bag so that she could lug all of her new belongings home. We left the store with Cat wearing one of the new cream outfits, and headed to PF Chang's for a gourmet Chinese lunch.

We sat in a corner booth and gossiped, laughed and caught up for nearly two hours. I could tell our waitress was losing her patience, but had no doubt she'd be grateful when she discovered the fifty-dollar tip my sister left her.

Finally at four o'clock we got back in the car, and I looked at Cat expectantly. "So, where to?"

"What do you mean?" she asked innocently.

"Come on, Cat, I know you. Which hotel have you booked?"

Sheepishly my sister confessed with a sigh, "The Troy Hilton. I believe it's just down the road." Cat would have booked the presidential suite and probably ordered a massage and pedicure for later. She considered my modest accommodations the equivalent of camping outside without a tent or sleeping bag, and she and I had a long-standing agreement that when she came to town she would stay at a nearby luxury hotel, and I wouldn't have to wait on her hand and foot. Trust me, the arrangement worked for both of us.

I smiled at her and asked, "And when are you catching a plane back home?"

"Well, I know you have to work tomorrow, but I feel like I've barely seen you at all. How about if I get some rest tonight and tomorrow we can have lunch together, then catch a movie and hang out tomorrow night? I'd also like to pop in on my friend Danielle—you remember her from high school?"

Danielle was my sister's best friend in high school. The two were inseparable their senior year, but Cat had opted for Harvard, and Danielle had chosen a small local university here in Michigan. The two now led very different lives, but still kept in touch and remained close. They had children the same age, and I knew Cat would enjoy spending some time with her.

"Sounds like a plan. Tomorrow can be our night, and you can see Danielle on Thursday and catch a plane ride back Thursday night."

"Perfect," Cat sighed, leaning back in the seat. She

looked exhausted, and I knew that an evening of being pampered at the hotel would probably be very good for her.

Half an hour later, after dropping Cat off, I pulled back into my driveway and stopped at the mailbox to retrieve the mail. I let myself inside and greeted Eggy, who was dancing on his hind legs, happy to see me. I gave him a quick kiss and walked through the kitchen to the back door, letting him out. *Poor guy,* I thought. He'd been cooped up all day.

I went back to sifting through the mail when a thought buzzed through my mind: *Go find Eggy!*

I blinked and hesitated, sorting through the mail for a moment, unsure what the message meant. Suddenly it came again, even more urgently this time.

Go find Eggy!

I dropped the mail and bolted out the back door, shouting, "Eggy!" as I came into the backyard. I looked frantically in the fading light for my chocolate-colored pooch and finally located him halfway across the yard. I breathed a sigh of relief; he was fine, just sniffing at something across the yard.

I was half turning back toward the house when I suddenly got the thought, *Go to Eggy!*

Something was very, very wrong. Without hesitation I bolted across the yard, calling to him, but Eggy was too interested in what he was sniffing. I reached him quickly and snatched him up in my arms, panic coursing through my veins, and I couldn't figure out why. That was when I saw what Eggy was sniffing at, and my blood ran cold.

A large doggy dish lay surrounded by leaves, obscuring it from the view of the house. Inside the dish was a thick steak, soaked in flourescent liquid. Next to the dish was a discarded small container of antifreeze. "Oh, my God!" I gasped, and bolted with Eggy into the house. In the light of my kitchen I looked closely at his muzzle, but couldn't tell if he'd licked up any of the liquid. In a panic I grabbed my purse and the pet carrier from the closet and ran out the door to my car. Peeling out of the driveway I flew at outrageous speeds to my vet. If

Eggy had consumed any of the antifreeze there would be very little the vet could do.

Tears slid down my cheeks as I squealed into the parking lot of the Royal Oak Animal Hospital, and I muttered, "Oh, God, please, *please* let him be okay!" I picked up the carrier with a trembling hand and ran full-tilt into the building. There was a receptionist who was startled as I came up to the counter and begged for assistance. "It's my dog!" I nearly shouted. "I think he's ingested some antifreeze! Please, *please,* you have to help him!"

The receptionist quickly came around the counter and grabbed the carrier from me, then ran into the back room. I stood there gulping my terror as I watched the door close behind her, and I tried to collect myself and stem the panic flooding my heart with adrenaline.

Seeing my distress, a kind, elderly woman approached me and gently led me over to a row of chairs. I sat down numbly and cried great painful sobs as she patted my hand and said, "There, there. He's in capable hands. They'll take good care of him. You'll see."

I wanted desperately to believe her, but terror was gripping my heart in a vise. Eggy was like my child. I had nurtured him from a tiny puppy as if he were my own baby, and I had no idea how I would ever cope without him. I rocked back and forth in the chair, anxiously watching for the reappearance of the receptionist.

She came back a few minutes later, and I stood up as she approached me. "The doctor is with him now. Can you come to the counter and fill out some information?" she asked gently.

Numbly I nodded and moved to the counter with her. There I gave her my information, then quickly took my seat again. I gave a small smile to the old woman, who offered me a tissue and held my hand as my foot tapped and unbidden tears dropped from my eyes. At this hour the waiting room was packed with pets and their owners, but no one in the lobby spoke, and as I looked around trying to distract myself I could see them all avoiding my eyes, hugging their pets a little closer.

Finally, after half an hour, my veterinarian, Dr. Markland, came out and called to me. I jumped up and nearly ran to her. "Is he okay? Is he all right? Please tell me he's okay!" I pleaded.

She put a gentle hand on my shoulder and said, "I think he's fine. There was no trace of antifreeze in his mouth, but we induced vomiting just to be safe. I didn't see any of it in his bile either, so I think we're safe. Still, I want to keep him overnight, if that's all right with you."

I let out a sob of relief, and it was a moment before I could respond. "That's fine . . . yes, anything as long as he's okay," I burbled.

"I really think he will be. How about we call you in the morning and see if he's well enough to go home then?"

I nodded emotionally, trying to get a grip. I was just so relieved that he wasn't going to die it was hard to keep it together. Dr. Markland stroked my arm and smiled kindly at me. "Did you want to see him before you go home?"

I nodded again, and she walked me to the back. We went to a large room where several dogs and cats were being boarded or treated for illness. Eggy was lying down in a wire crate on the bottom shelf, sandwiched between a miniature poodle and a Pekingese. I squatted down and poked my fingers through the bars, Eggy looked dazed and out of it, and didn't respond to my touch. I was alarmed at his nonreaction, and Dr. Markland explained, "He's been sedated. The best thing for him right now is to be calm and get some rest. We'll see how he's doing in the morning, and I'll be able to assess whether or not there was any nerve damage."

"Nerve damage?" I asked sharply. "He could have nerve damage?"

Dr. Markland's eyes became pinched. "It happens sometimes. Antifreeze is incredibly poisonous to animals. My feeling is that if he had ingested any he would have shown symptoms within two to three minutes—it's hard to miss. I really think he'll be fine, but we just want to be cautious until tomorrow, okay?"

I nodded and stroked the soft part of his muzzle one last time. I got up with my head bent and followed her back out to the lobby. Dr. Markland asked me before I left, "So how did Eggy come into contact with antifreeze?"

The question hung there for a second as my mind whirred with what to tell her. I knew in an instant who had put the poison in my backyard, and the fury of it formed a fist of hatred in the pit of my stomach. I couldn't very well tell Dr. Markland, however, that the Mafia had tried to kill my dog, so I said, "I had a jug of it in the basement, and I didn't know the cap was loose. Eggy must have knocked it over, and I found him sniffing at it when I went downstairs. I wasn't sure if he drank any or not, but I thought it was best to rush him here and make sure."

Dr. Markland nodded, accepting my explanation, and said, "Lucky you found him so quickly. Once a dog drinks more than a capful there's very little we can do."

I swallowed hard and nodded. "Thanks for your help, Dr. Markland."

She squeezed my arm and turned to go back to her next patient.

I checked out with the receptionist, leaving the carrier behind so that I didn't have to lug it there when I went to pick Eggy up in the morning. I walked out to my Mazda with a heavy heart and inserted the key. Just before I got behind the wheel I noticed a familiar sedan with smoked windows drive by, and the moment it passed me, my cell phone rang. As I watched the sedan ease down the street I flipped open the phone and said, "Hello?"

A thick voice impeded by an oversize tongue said, "Sorry about your dog," and then the line went dead.

Chapter Eight

"Really, Abby, Eggy is fine. You can pick him up anytime this morning," Dr. Markland reassured me.

I let go of the tightly held breath keeping me suspended in anxious worry. I'd been so concerned about Eggy that I hadn't slept all night, and as I sank into the cushion of relief I could feel my brain dumb down a little, the fog of exhaustion and worry making my thoughts less coherent. "Thank you, Dr. Markland; I'll be right over."

As I hung up the phone, however, my gaze strayed out to the backyard, and apprehension began to buzz around inside my chest. I'd removed the dog dish and the surrounding leaves the night before, but that didn't mean that Andros's men couldn't be successful next time. If Andros wanted to kill Eggy, I had no doubt he would find a way.

No, I thought. *Eggy is too vulnerable here.*

I could board him at the veterinary, but the problem was that I was in a cash crunch at the moment, and it would be expensive to keep him there. Plus I doubted Eggy would put up with that for long—he didn't like being confined.

Thinking of an idea I quickly picked up the phone again and dialed. "Hello?" welcomed me on the second ring.

"Good morning, Dave; hope this isn't too early to call?"

"Hey, there, Abby!" he said jovially. "No, this is fine. You need me to come back and finish your rafters?"

"Uh . . ." Oops—I'd forgotten I'd put Dave on hold. "No . . . I mean . . . not yet. I mean, yes, but probably not until next week. What I really need is a favor."

"Sure. Whatcha need?"

"Well, I'm heading out of town for a couple of days—you know, to go visit my sister—and I was wondering if you could possibly take Eggy for me."

There was a soft chuckle, then; "Sure, honey, no sweat. I don't know how my old lady's going to like it, but I really miss that little mutt. Did you want to bring him over?"

Left side, heavy feeling. Hmmm. My intuition was weighing in, and I didn't know why that would be a problem. I hesitated for a moment, drifting over to my front window. "Uh, yeah . . ." I said stalling, but as I pulled back one of the blinds I saw a strange car just down the street. There were two men in the car, and both of them kept looking toward my house. *Damn.* Andros's men were watching me. If I picked Eggy up from the vet and drove him over to Dave's house, these guys would know not only how to get to Eggy, but also how to get to Dave. "Actually, Dave, my plane leaves right away. I had to take Eggy to the vet yesterday; do you think you could possibly do me a huge favor and pick him up from the Royal Oak Animal Hospital? It's on Main and Lincoln."

"Uh . . . sure . . . I guess. Is Eggy okay?"

I stepped away from the window and went back to my chair in the kitchen, pacing the floor in agitation as I tried to keep my voice light. "Yes, thank God. He gave me a little scare last night, but it was only a scare. Listen, this is really great of you. It shouldn't be longer than a week or so. Is that okay?"

"Sure, that's fine. Hey is everything okay with you?"

"Yeah, of course," I said, concentrating on making my voice sound reassuring. "I guess I'm just a little tired. I'll give you a call next week and let you know when I'm coming back, cool?"

I hung up with Dave and quickly headed back upstairs. I had to be at the office by nine for my first appointment, and I also had to stop by the vet, pay the bill and leave instructions with them about who was picking Eggy up later. I'd have to hustle and get ready if I wanted to make it on time.

I quickly got dressed, slapped on some makeup and packed a small bag of food, toys and a baby blanket for Eggy. A lump formed in my throat as I gathered his things. I was really going to miss him while he was at Dave's, but at least this way he'd be safe.

I walked outside and surveyed the street. The suspicious car I'd noticed earlier was gone. Curious.

I got in my Mazda and drove over to the vet. Once inside I paid my bill, left my instructions and visited with Eggy for all of two minutes. It was hard to leave him behind, but I was pushing the clock this morning.

I headed back out to my car, got in and pulled forward to the edge of the driveway, waiting for an opening in traffic. A white car eased into the middle lane and put on its turn signal, indicating that it wanted to turn into the vet. It also blocked my path north, so I waited for it to find an opening in traffic. When the traffic was clear, instead of turning the driver waved me forward first with a smile. I smiled at him and pulled forward and left, when all of the sudden he stepped on the gas which caused me to ram the side of his car.

I was so shocked by the impact that it took me a full minute to regain my senses. By the time I'd recovered, I noticed that the man in the white car now stood outside my door, screaming at me and waving his fist. "You crazy driver!" he yelled. "You drove right into me!"

Traffic was now limping around our jackknifed position, and belatedly I realized I needed to get out of the road. I backed up a little, away from the man shouting at me, and pulled into the driveway of a gas station right next to the vet. The driver of the white car followed me, still waving his fist and yelling obscenities. I had the thought of using my cell phone to call 911, but by that time a police officer was already on the scene.

The driver in the white car immediately pounced on the officer, waving his hands and yelling that I was a crazy woman who had rammed right into him. It was then that it struck me that his words carried a thick Greek accent. "I was minding my own business, waiting to turn into the vet, when this crazy lady rammed into my beautiful car! I think I got whiplash; I think I may be bleeding internally!"

I got out of my car, shaken and upset. Waiting until the officer was finished with the man in the white car, I walked around to my front bumper. It sat crumpled half on my car and half off. All I could think about was my five-hundred-dollar deductible.

After taking the other man's statement, the officer looked at me with all the charm of a rodeo bull. I didn't recognize him, but thought it might be prudent to drop a few names of some friends of mine at the Royal Oak PD. "So what happened here today?" The officer asked me.

I smiled winningly at him, beaming the full grille as I looked at his name tag and said, "Good morning, Officer Paddington; thank you so much for coming to the scene so quickly. You see, there's been a simple misunderstanding between this gentleman and me. . . ."

"There's no misunderstanding! You're crazy! You're a hazard! Your license should be revoked!" the man from the white car shouted.

Officer Paddington turned back to him and said, "Sir, I have already taken your statement. You will need to step over there by your car until I'm finished with this young lady. Is that clear?"

The man shuffled off, and the officer turned back to me. "May I see your license, registration and proof of insurance, please?"

I quickly dug through my purse and handed him the items, trying to wait patiently as I noticed my watch already read nine o'clock.

Damn. I'd missed my first appointment.

After writing down all of my information in the police report, Paddington turned back to me and asked, "So you were saying something about a misunderstanding?"

"Yes, that's correct. You see, I would have gladly waited for that gentleman to pull forward into the parking lot, but he waved me forward ahead of him, then he punched the gas and hit my car. . . ."

"*He* hit *you*?" the officer asked, clearly not believing me for a second.

"Yes. Yes, he did." I nodded affirmatively. "Officer, I assure you I'm an upstanding member of the community who has no reason to lie about such things; you can even ask my friend Detective Milo Johnson about my reputation—"

The officer snorted derisively. "Yeah, everybody knows somebody at the station who can vouch for them. You're still getting the ticket, Miss Cooper."

"But—" I started to protest.

"Please get back in your car while I finish this paperwork," he said dismissively, and turned his back on me.

I had no choice but to go back to my car and wait inside. Meanwhile the man in the white car made a huge production of rubbing his hand across the back of his neck and turning his head from side to side grimacing with every movement. He had also developed a pronounced limp as he paced in front of his car. This guy was going to sue me for as much insurance money as he could get. I was totally screwed.

The officer came back to my car and waited as I lowered my window. "Here's a copy of the police report," he said, tearing off a sheet and handing it to me. "And here's your ticket. I wrote you up for failure to yield, but I could've gone for reckless driving. You need to be more careful, Miss Cooper." Did he expect me to *thank* him? I nodded wordlessly as I took the paperwork, scanning the back of the ticket for the dollar amount of the fine. The 150-dollar price tag made me grind my teeth. I started my car as I watched the officer go over to the man in the white car and hand him a copy of the police report, and swore under my breath as the two men turned to look at me and shake their heads together. *Bastards.*

Lifting my chin in a last attempt to leave the scene with dignity, I waited until I had a tremendous hole in traffic and turned left onto Main, heading toward my office. Andros Kapordelis was such a son of a bitch.

I got only two blocks when I noticed my oil light come on. "Oh, for Christ's sake!" I complained. "What now?" I made it to a corner gas station, where I purchased a couple quarts of oil and filled the tank back up. I noticed the time now read ten minutes to ten, and I groaned at all the morning delays. I needed to get to my office in a hurry so that I could call my first appointment, apologize profusely, and get ready for my second appointment.

Two more blocks into my commute my oil light came on again. "Shit!" I swore, banging the steering wheel. I went one more block and pulled into yet another gas station. This one had an on-site repair shop, and I parked in front of one of the large garage doors, waiting for someone inside to notice me. Quickly I got out my cell phone and dialed my office building's management suite.

"Conrad Management, how may I help you?"

"Yvonne?" I said anxiously.

"Speaking," my building manager answered.

"Good morning, it's Abby Cooper calling."

"Hi, Abby! How's it going?"

"Terrible. Listen, I need a favor. I've had some car trouble this morning, and I've got clients showing up even as we speak. Could you possibly put a note on my door until I get to the office?"

"Sure. How long do you think you'll be?"

Just then the bay doors in front of me began to roll upward, and a man in a greasy jumpsuit waved me forward. "I have no idea. Just make the sign say that I had an emergency, and that I will call each appointment to reschedule before the end of the day."

"I'll take care of it. See you in a little while."

Two hours later I was getting yet another round of bad news. "Yeah," said the greasy mechanic, "this is major damage." He indicated what was once my oil pan in his hand. "See, the weird thing is this hole," he said as he shoved his pinkie through a sizable hole in the bottom of the oil pan. "It's too clean to have come from scarping the bottom of your car on something. There's also this stuff," he said, pointing to a chalky-looking substance on the edge of the hole. "This stuff looks a whole lot like wax to me, and if I didn't know better I'd say that someone punctured your oil pan, then used wax to fill in the hole so that when your engine got warm the wax would melt and all your oil would leak out. . . ."

The longer he talked, the more I felt a chill creep along my spine. I couldn't take my eyes off the oil pan.

"You got any enemies out there, ma'am?"

I forced my mouth into a smile and said, "Just a crazy ex-boyfriend." *Liar, liar, pants on fire . . .*

"Well, he could easily have cost you an engine, or worse, a whole new car."

I nodded gravely as I handed over my debit card. The total cost would eat up the last 250 dollars I had to my name. The anxiety over my financial situation was wearing its own hole in the lining of my stomach.

The mechanic had also been kind enough to remove my bumper, which, he claimed, was hanging on only by a thread. My poor car now resembled something out of a demolition derby.

By twelve thirty I had finally made it to my office building. I parked in my usual space on the second floor and hurried across the street to the large brick building that was like a second home. I opted for the elevator today, completely wiped out by all the emotion, lack of sleep, and anxiety over the past several days. I had approximately half an hour to pull myself together for the next three readings scheduled for the afternoon, plus three additional phone calls to make to what I anticipated would be some pretty pissed-off clients.

After stepping off the elevator I hurried down the hall and around the corner, pulling my office keys out of my purse I came up short in front of my suite. I had expected to see a sign taped to the front of the door, as

I'd instructed Yvonne on the subject. But there was no sign anywhere. *"Shit!"* I said under my breath.

I let myself into my office and stomped over to my desk. I yanked up the phone and dialed my landlord, concentrating on keeping my voice level until I found out why Yvonne hadn't done what she said she'd do.

"Concord Management," she sang.

"Yvonne?"

"Speaking."

"Hey, it's Abby. Listen, I just got in, and I thought you said you were going to help me out by hanging up a sign on my door. . . ."

"I did," she said, a bit taken aback.

"Where did you hang it?" I asked, now confused.

"I taped a big white sign to your door indicating that you'd had a family emergency and at the last minute had to cancel your readings, but that you would call to apologize and reschedule everyone later in the day."

"And you taped this to my door?" I asked, still accusing.

"Yes, not even five minutes after you called."

My lie detector remained noticeably quiet. "Huh . . ." I said, reeling in my horns. "Well, I got here and it wasn't up, so for a minute there I thought you'd forgotten."

"Maybe one of your clients took it with them."

Left side, heavy feeling. "Yeah, maybe. Listen, I'm sorry . . . I've just had a really bad morning. Yvonne, thanks so much for trying to help."

"Anything I can do for you?" she asked kindly.

"No, thank you. Really, I've got it all under control." *Liar, liar, pants on fire . . .* "I'll talk to you later. Thanks again."

I hung up with Yvonne and sat at my desk for a minute. What'd happened to the sign? It didn't take long to figure out. Like everything else that had happened in the past two days, I had no doubt Andros and his goons were imposing their own version of persuasion. I sat down heavily and had to admit I was beginning to feel persuaded.

What I needed was a way out. Either I was going to work for Andros or I wasn't, and if I wasn't it was probably only a matter of time before I either moved to a distant state and changed my name, or something really, really bad happened.

I considered going to the police, but quickly dismissed that option. I had a sneaking suspicion that Andros had a pretty long reach, and that a complaint from me would be met with a whole lot of nonaction. Besides, what could do? I couldn't prove that Andros had been responsible for any of the things that had happened to me, and even the accident from the morning had already been written up as my fault. No, I'd lose my credibility, as most conspiracy theorists do, and then where would I be?

The best option I had was to try to talk to Dutch about it. But even then I risked a lot; Dutch, after all, worked for the FBI, and if I wanted to go the distance and do something about Andros then I'd probably have to join some witness relocation program or something. And what about Cat? She was very much an Achilles' heel for me. Luckily Andros hadn't picked her up on his radar yet, but that was probably only a matter of time.

I shook my head and got up from my desk, walking into my reading room and setting out fresh candles and incense. I worked hard at pushing away all thoughts of Andros and the events of the day as I got the room ready. I figured I'd call my missed appointments later, at the end of the day.

At one o'clock I was as ready as I could be, given the fact that I was stressed out and now very hungry—as I'd skipped both breakfast and lunch. As my stomach growled I watched the clock on my credenza tick its way up to one o'clock, then move minute by minute past until it reached one fifteen. Great, a no-show. I waited an extra five minutes without my client showing up and sighed heavily. When it rained it poured.

Trying to turn a lemon into lemonade I ordered some soup and salad from D'ammato's restaurant downstairs, and asked if someone could deliver it. I had twelve whole dollars in my purse, and was so hungry and so tired that it seemed like a good trade at the time. Ten minutes later there was a knock on my door, and a young waiter held out my food as I gave up the cash and hurriedly went back to my office to eat.

While I was nibbling on the salad I called my sister on her cell. "Hey, there!" she said brightly. "How's the car?"

"It'll be fine. The accident just damaged the oil pan, and they fixed it, no problem. Sorry about having to cancel lunch." I'd called my sister from the gas station and told her I'd had a teeny-weeny little fender bender, which was going to require some attention and the scratching of our lunch date.

"It's no problem, honey, really. I had some phone calls to make anyway. You still up for a movie tonight?"

No.

I held back a tired sigh and said, "Sure, that sounds wonderful." *Liar, liar, pants on fire . . .* "How about I pick you up at the hotel at five thirty and we'll grab a quick bite before a seven-thirty show?"

"Perfect. I'll see you then."

At two o'clock I had finished lunch and was pacing the small waiting area that is my front lobby as I anxiously waited for my next appointment. At two-oh-five I sat down and began to tap my foot. Two ten had me back to pacing, and by two fifteen I was considering choking someone. Two no-shows in one day. I'd never had such a run of bad luck in my life.

Moodily I went back to my office and began dialing the first of my skipped appointments from the morning. My nine-o'clock was really mad. I apologized profusely, but she kept ranting, so finally I simply hung up on her. I wasn't feeling particularly customer friendly today.

I waited several minutes to calm down before I dialed the next client. She was far more reasonable, and only demanded a free reading at her convenience for the *significant* inconvenience of driving all the way across town to meet with me with not even a note to indicate what had happened. Apparently I had some nerve.

The third appointment could not have been more

understanding . . . okay, she could have if she'd actually allowed me to reschedule her, but instead she stated that she was simply unwilling to commit to another date and time.

My last appointment for the day was to arrive at three, and this time I left my office door open and stood out in the hallway waiting for her arrival. The clock on my wall ticked its metronome rhythm, and my tapping foot kept pace as the minutes just before and just after three o'clock crept by. Growling my frustration I closed my door and headed down the stairs, intent on finding my client.

I reached the lobby and swiveled my head from side to side, searching the area for any signs of her. I couldn't believe that all three of my afternoon appointments simply hadn't shown up. It was too much of a coincidence.

Still, there was no one in the lobby, and as I looked through the glass doors to the street outside, it was obvious no one was about to enter the building. Squeezing my palms into frustrated fists, I stomped back over to the elevator and came up short. There, taped securely to the metal door, was Yvonne's sign, which read:

Attention Clients of Abigail Cooper, Suite 222:

Abigail regrets to inform you that she has had a sudden and unexpected family emergency that prevents her from taking clients today. She wishes to extend her sincerest apologies for any inconvenience, and will be calling all of her appointments later today to reschedule.

Thank you for your attention to this matter,

Yvonne Mitchell
Concord Management

I reached up and yanked the sign off the elevator door and angrily ripped it into several pieces. The sign hadn't been there when I'd come in this afternoon; I was sure of it because I'd taken the elevator and I would have seen it.

Wanting to scream I punched the up arrow hard enough to hurt my finger, and waited for the double doors to part and take me back upstairs. As the doors opened I marched forward, nearly bumping right into Yvonne. "Oh!" she exclaimed, startled, as we nearly collided. "Abby, I didn't see you there."

I stopped myself and quickly apologized. "No, I'm sorry. I wasn't watching where I was going. Say, I'm glad I ran into you. I just found your note," I said, and held out the torn pieces of the letter crumpled in my hand. "It was taped to the elevator door."

Yvonne looked puzzled, cocking her head to one side. "That's odd. I taped it directly to your office door. I wonder how it got down here?"

My suspicions were confirmed: Yvonne hadn't done it. "I'm not sure, maybe one of my earlier clients."

"Weird that you didn't see it when you went up to your office this afternoon, huh?" she said quickly, noting the oddity of my explanation.

"Yeah," I said simply as I got into the elevator. "Anyway, thanks again for trying to help me out. I'll catch you later."

I left her standing in the lobby looking quizzically back at me, probably thinking it was odd that I didn't seem more upset about losing a whole day's worth of income. Truth be told I was too tired to get any more upset over it. I just wanted to go home and take a nap before I had to entertain my sister.

I packed up and locked the office, heading out of the building to the parking garage with lead in my feet. Just as I got to my car my intuition began humming. I jerked my head up, looking intently around, suddenly completely alert. Something was off.

I looked all around the garage and finally noticed what was wrong: There was a silver sedan parked illegally just off to the right of my car. Its motor was running and there was a man inside watching me.

As quickly as my now-shaking hands would allow I unlocked my door and got into the car, turning on the ignition. I then reached into my purse and pulled out my cell phone, punching in 911 but waiting to send the number. With my eye locked on the rearview mirror I checked behind me; the sedan hadn't moved. Punching the accelerator I shot backward and pivoted out of my space, spinning the wheel, and shifting nearly all at the same time. I raced out of the garage and nearly missed getting into another accident as I turned onto Washington. The silver sedan had followed me out of the garage and was trailing two cars behind. I turned onto a side street, punching the gas again, and the silver sedan followed.

My heart was racing, keeping pace with my engine as I turned down several side streets, twisting and winding my way home. This was dangerous; the posted speed limit was only twenty-five, but the sedan and I added an additional twenty to the speedometer.

Finally I reached my house and zoomed up the driveway, hitting the button on my visor for the garage door. When the door was just high enough I slid my car forward into the cramped space of my garage, knocking my mountain bike out of the way. I hit the button again and counted the seconds as the garage door closed, noting that the sedan had come to rest at the foot of my driveway.

After the garage door had closed I sat breathing heavily in the car, trying to get a grip. I had no idea what terrible thing Andros's men intended to inflict on me next, so I just waited for something to happen. After about twenty minutes I decided it might be safe to get out of the car and take a peek. I headed over to the side door and peeked through the curtains. The sedan was parked directly across the street from my house, sitting there, apparently in idle.

I retrieved my cell phone and called directory assistance. When I got the operator I asked to be connected to the nonemergency number of the Royal Oak PD.

"Royal Oak PD, Sergeant Staffer speaking. How can I help you?"

"Yes, hello, this is Abigail Cooper of two-ninety-four Crown Street. I've noticed a suspicious-looking car sitting outside my house. If there's an officer in the area would you please have him check it out?"

"It might be a while; we're a little busy today, ma'am."

"No problem, it's just that I've noticed this car taking inventory of the houses in the neighborhood all day, and it strikes me as suspicious."

"Can you see the license plate number?"

I squinted my eyes, but at this angle I didn't have a clear view of the tag. "No, unfortunately I can't tell. It looks to be a silver Cadillac, and there are . . . uh . . . two passengers in the car."

"Okay, we'll send someone over." And the sergeant clicked off.

I waited ten minutes, when suddenly the silver sedan pulled away from my curb. Not ten seconds later a black-and-white patrol car cruised slowly down my street. As the police car rolled past, I came out of my garage and bolted for my front door, quickly letting myself inside.

By sheer habit I set my keys and purse down quickly, then squatted to pet Eggy, but realized midsquat that he wasn't here. Crestfallen, I walked over to my big chair and collapsed into the soft cushion, pulling an afghan around me. For the next hour, even though I tried to sleep, all I could do was feel sorry for myself.

Chapter Nine

By five o'clock I'd managed to get ready to go pick up Cat and grab a bite to eat. I felt sluggish and wiped out, as if I were traveling in slow motion. I was having a hard time thinking, and wanted only to go upstairs and crawl under the covers.

Cat, however, would never let me get away with something like that. Pouting, I grabbed my purse, coat and keys and opened up the front door, but came up short. The silver sedan was parked directly in front of my house, its motor still running. Quickly I slammed the door and threw the bolt. "Damn it!" I yelled in frustration, and I thumped my fist against the door.

Scooting over to the window I carefully peeled back one small blind and peered out. Being early November, it was already quite dark out, and I couldn't see the occupants of the car at all.

I looked at the clock on the wall. I had to leave now if I was going to be on time for Cat. Past history had taught me to *always* be on time for Cat—she ruled her life by her second hand. There was no way I was going to make it past the sedan without being seen. My car was in the garage, and I had no other mode of transport.

I looked at the phone and thought about calling the police again, but thinking through that option I realized there were just so many times I could cry wolf. Besides, the sedan had somehow been alerted to the police before they'd show up—so a call about the sedan to my local police department was probably not a good deterrent.

I could call Milo and have him come to my rescue, but therein lay another problem—explaining why the sedan kept showing up at my home.

Milo was a smart cookie—there was no way of skimping on the details around him. He'd start pelting me with questions that, if I truthfully answered them, would end with me on a one-way ticket to some Iowa cornfield and a permanent change of name.

I looked at the clock again. "Son of a . . . !" I said, and picked up the phone. I called Cat's hotel, but she wasn't in her room. I was reconnected to the front desk and asked if I wanted to leave a message. I begged the clerk to search the lobby and find my sister, and fortunately after a few minutes was rewarded with her most professional tone.

"Catherine Cooper-Masters speaking."

"Hey, Cat, it's me."

"Hi, me!" she said playfully. "Are you calling me from the car?"

I scowled. She knew damn well our connection was too good for me to be calling from the car. This was just her way of suggesting that if I wasn't calling from the car, I'd better have a damn good reason.

"Yeah, about that . . ." I stalled.

"Yes?"

"Well, the thing of it is . . . actually . . . I'm afraid I really, really, really don't feel well tonight." Not quite a lie, not quite the truth.

"You don't?" Cat's tone turned immediately to concern.

"Uh, no, see, I've had this horrible headache all day, and my stomach's upset, and I think I may have the flu . . ." *Liar, liar, pants on fire . . .*

"Oh, you poor baby. Stay right there; I'll catch a cab over—"

"No!" I shouted. I couldn't risk Andros's goons knowing about my sister. I knew the man was ruthless enough not to think twice about leveraging her safety against me.

"There was a pause before Cat spoke again. I pictured her rubbing her ear after my outburst. "What do you mean, 'no'?"

"Well, I don't want you to catch what I've got, Cat. I mean, I have a fever and the chills, and I'm sick. Sick, sick, sick!" *Liar, liar, pants on fire . . .*

"Oh, you poor thing! All the more reason you will need me to take care of you. I'll have the cabbie stop off at the drugstore and pick you up some—"

"Cat! Do *not* come over here!" I shouted into the phone.

There was a very pregnant pause; then in her most offended voice she said, "Well, *fine,* Abby, be that way. I'm just trying to spend a little time with you this week, but if you're too busy being sick and hiding away inside your house then I guess I'll just see you at Thanksgiving!" And she hung up the phone.

I put the receiver back in its cradle and walked over to the wall, where I pounded my head three times, producing the headache I'd complained to Cat about. Then I went around the house, checking all the windows and doors and making sure the alarm was set. I went upstairs to my bedroom and crawled under the sheets fully clothed. Sometimes pretending to be sick can make you feel like going to bed.

At three a.m. I bolted upright, my heart racing and panic coursing through my veins. My burglar alarm was blaring a noise so obnoxious I had to shove my fingers halfway to my eardrums. On tiptoe I stepped out into my upstairs hallway and peered down the stairwell at the darkened living room. If someone was inside, I wouldn't be able to hear them above the noise, but by turning off the alarm I'd give the intruder free rein to hang out for a while.

I looked around for a weapon, but nothing upstairs came to mind. Feeling all the hairs stand up along my arms and the back of my neck, I gave up being brave and headed back into my bedroom, shutting the door and locking it. Quickly I grabbed the phone and carried it into my walk-in closet, and shut that door too.

I dialed 911 and shouted above the blaring from downstairs that my home alarm was going off, and I suspected that someone might be in my house. Five minutes later I heard a pounding on my front door, and someone called out, "Royal Oak Police!"

Nearly crying with relief I ran as fast as I could down the stairs and threw open the door, then quickly turned to the control panel of the still-blaring alarm and shut it off. Turning back to the officer at the door I sucked in a breath of surprise in recognition, "Good evening, Officer," I said to Shawn Bennington.

"I hear you got an intruder," Bennington answered, not seeming to recognize me.

"Uh, yeah. My alarm just started going off, and I don't know why."

Bennington looked at the control panel on the wall. "What kind of an alarm system you call that?" he asked me. Apparently he was used to the kind that cost tons of money and came equipped with whole teams of people devoted to ensuring you never took a dangerous breath.

"It's the cheap kind," I answered, put off by his casual demeanor.

"Well, there you go then. The thing's probably unreliable. Probably had a short circuit or something."

"Still . . ." I insisted, extending my arm out in a welcoming arc. "As long as you're here I'm sure it wouldn't hurt to take a look for me, now, would it?"

Bennington sighed audibly, then clasped his hands onto his belt buckle and pulled upward, securing his pants over his extended belly. "Yeah, okay," he said, and came into my living room. I shut the door and turned to guide him through my house, but he was already in my kitchen with the fridge open. "Say, would you mind if I had one of these sodas?" he asked.

Of course I minded! "Help yourself," I called while thinking, *Asshole . . .*

"Thanks," Bennington said, taking a soda. As he

opened the top he pivoted in a three-sixty, looking around my kitchen, and nodding his head. "Nice place," he commented.

"Thanks. Now about looking around?" I said, my hands finding their way to an impatient stance on my hips.

"Okay, okay," he replied, and came out of my kitchen, walking through the living room and around to my study. He flipped on the light, blinked, and turned it off again. Then he came back around the corner and lifted his chin up the stairs. "You want me to look up there too?"

My face contorted itself into a deep scowl. "Yes," I said through gritted teeth, "I would like you to look in *every* room, if it's not too much trouble." In about three seconds I'd be going to jail for whomping a police officer on the head.

Bennington sighed audibly again, then climbed the staircase, his footfalls heavy on my carpet. He was up there for quite a while, so finally I called up to him, and he came out of my bedroom.

"Everything looks fine," he said, and hurried down the stairs. "No sign of forced entry, and no bogeymen in your closet."

"You were up there awhile; did you check everything?"

Bennington looked at me with a sly smile that turned my stomach. "Oh, yeah, I checked everything." He gave a small chuckle as he opened my front door, pausing to say, "My advice is to spend some cash on a better alarm system, ma'am; the one you've got's a piece of crap." And with that he was gone.

I stood in the living room with every light in the house blazing, feeling extremely vulnerable. I reset the alarm and left all the lights on as I trudged up the stairs.

Something about how quickly Bennington left bothered me, the same way it bothered me how long he'd been in my bedroom. When I got to the top of the stairs and looked into my room, I knew why. The top drawer of my dresser was pulled slightly open, and my underwear had been tossed around like a salad. Outrage coursed through my veins as I stomped forward and pulled the drawer open further, sorting my undergarments and swearing under my breath, "Sick son of a bitch!"

A few minutes later I'd discovered that Bennington had absconded with two pairs of lace panties, and the violation of that brought tears to my eyes. Milo and Dutch were definitely going to hear about this.

Shivering now because my room was very cold, I headed back over to my bedroom door, shutting and locking it. I left the light on and crawled back under the covers, but never made it back to sleep.

The next morning the silver sedan was nowhere to be found. I breathed a huge sigh of relief and quickly got ready for work. I noticed my reflection looked haggard, but through the magic of concealer I was able to hide most of the dark circles lining my eyes.

I got to work early and quickly began calling the day's clients. Luckily I got through to most of them; the others I simply left detailed instructions for. I told everyone to come in the side door around the back of the building, and to use the back elevator, and under no circumstances should they assume I wasn't here, even if they found notifications in the building suggesting otherwise.

The ruse worked brilliantly, as all three of my morning appointments appeared without incident. I ate lunch at my desk, and called the rest of my missed appointments from the day before. Luckily they understood, and I rebooked every one.

I was feeling pretty good around mid-afternoon, just as I was showing my fifth appointment into my reading room, when an earsplitting noise pierced the quiet office building.

"Oh, my God, what *is* that?" shouted Sarah, my two-o'clock.

"The fire alarm!" I shouted back. Already we could see people moving into the hallway as offices began to empty out. "Come on; we'd better go outside just in case it's not a drill."

Sarah and I, along with about a hundred other of the

building's occupants, descended onto the street via the back stairwell. I'd had sense enough to grab my coat, as the day had turned bitterly cold. We all stood around, periodically looking up at the building for any signs of smoke, and within moments the fire department showed up.

I watched as several firemen raced into the building, and Yvonne talked to someone in charge holding a walkie-talkie. I worried about my office suite, and thought anxiously about all my belongings left behind that might be consumed by a fire. For some reason this sent a disturbing chill up my spine, and I shivered violently.

Just then I noticed something out of place, and I turned slightly to look to my left. There in the back of the crowd stood Goon, his eyes pinned on me and a sly smile on his face. I now understood why the fire alarm had been pulled, and frustration welled up inside me and gave me courage. Excusing myself from Sarah's company I marched over to Goon and lifted my chin as I snarled, "Listen, pal, this stunt you've pulled? It's not going to work. There are a dozen ways around your little intimidation tactics, and I for one will not be bullied, cajoled, pushed, or *persuaded* into working for a slime-ball like Kapordelis!"

Goon was hardly swayed by my no-bullshit attitude. "Mr. Kapordelis has a message for you. He says you have until the end of the day to make up your mind, or else . . ." He let the sentence trail off ominously, but I was way beyond reason at this point.

"You can tell that ugly, cancerous tumor to go *fuck* himself!" And I stomped away.

"Abby?" Sarah said when I got back. "You look pale as a ghost; are you all right?"

My mouth had suddenly gone dry, and I'd begun to shake slightly. "Yes, I'm fine," I reassured her, "just a little cold."

At that moment we were given the all-clear to head back to our offices, and I shuffled along with the rest of the crowd. When Sarah and I got back to my suite we had only a half hour left, so I did what I could and charged her half price. Kindly she tipped me some extra and left.

My next appointment was a no-show. I waited with my office door open until three fifteen, but Kelly, one of my regulars, never came. I walked around to my desk and put my head in my hands, tears of frustration and exhaustion welling in the corners of my eyes, when the phone rang. I picked it up reflexively. "Hello?"

"Abby?"

"Speaking."

"Hey, there, it's Kelly Holms. Listen, I just wanted to tell you that there's this really scary guy standing at the end of your hallway who wouldn't let me through to your door."

"What?" How far was this going to go?

"I even think he's still there. You should call security on him—the guy really freaked me out."

"Kelly, I'm so sorry. I've been having some trouble with a former client lately, and I think he's probably the one causing the problem. Would you like to reschedule your appointment?"

"Well, how about a phone reading; do you have time now?"

I breathed a huge sigh of relief. I'd been so tired and anxious lately that I'd completely forgotten about offering phone readings. It was the perfect solution, and I mentally vowed to call all my appointments for the next day and let them know that their readings would be over the phone. I'd have to make up a plausible excuse about why I couldn't have them in my office—maybe that there were electrical problems in the building or something—but at least this way I could still keep my business afloat.

I did Kelly's reading over the phone and hung up forty minutes later feeling like a balloon after all the air had been let out. I just sat at my desk for a long moment, my mind numb and my body exhausted.

It was growing dark, so I switched on a light and began to shuffle some paperwork around, preparing to leave for the day, when I heard a scuffle outside in the hallway. Quickly I went to my door and pulled it open, and as I looked down the corridor my jaw dropped.

My sister Cat was shoving her five-foot-nothing frame against Goon's seven-foot-plus body as she struggled with her luggage and a large shopping bag to get past him. "Get out of my way, you big, dumb ox!" she shouted.

"I told you," he said, standing in front of her and blocking her progress, "Miss Cooper don't want no clients today."

"I am not her client, asshole; I'm her sister. Now move or I'll call the police!" And with that my sister pulled her cell phone open and let her finger hover over the buttons.

"Hey!" I yelled, and came running down the hallway to Cat's rescue. "Leave her alone!"

Upon hearing my voice Goon turned and looked back at me, allowing Cat to push her way past him. She reached me and latched onto my arm, her eyes large and a little frightened. "Abby, who the hell is this guy?"

Goon stood there glaring at us as I pulled my sister into my office and slammed the door. "What are you doing here?" I demanded, not answering her question. I was furious at her for coming uninvited and unwittingly putting herself in danger. Now Kapordelis knew I had a sister, and that made both her and me very vulnerable.

"I *came* here because I didn't like how we left things last night, and I *thought* we could talk about it on the way to the airport!" she snapped back, irked, no doubt, by the tone I'd taken with her.

"Oh, okay," I said, backing down. I was only going to make a tense situation worse by sniping at her. "I'm sorry. It's just that that jerk has been causing real problems for me lately, and I was afraid he might get pushy with you."

"*Who*, exactly, is he?" she demanded.

I shrugged lightly and said, "Just some client I had earlier who wasn't happy with his reading, so now he's trying to cause trouble."

"Have you called security?" she said, tapping her toe as she grilled me.

"I was thinking about it, but I hate to bring it to

Yvonne's attention. My lease is up in December, and I don't want them to think that maybe I'm too much trouble as a tenant—especially after last summer," I explained, thinking back to the time I'd been viciously attacked in my office.

"Well, you have to do *something;* that guy could be dangerous!"

"Yeah, okay, I will, but let's get you to the airport first," I said, picking up my coat and moving to the door.

"Wait a second," she said as she sorted through the bags and luggage she'd hauled to my office. "Here. I bought you something." Cat shoved a very large shopping bag at me.

"What's this?" I asked.

"Danielle and I went shopping today, and I didn't want to carry too many bags home, so I bought you a few things to add to your wardrobe."

I looked at the shopping bag Cat held out to me, and in spite of all the tension of the day I smiled. "Thanks, honey, that was really sweet of you."

"You're going to return everything in that bag, aren't you?" she asked, looking hard at me.

"Probably." I grinned. If I knew my sister, I knew that she'd put all the purchases on her credit card, and if I returned all the items her card would be reimbursed.

Cat sighed heavily and said, "Will you please consider just taking these gifts for a change?"

"No."

"Why not?"

"Because you buy me stuff all the time, and I'm not in a position right now to return the favor, so it makes me feel a little weird when you're so generous. . . ."

"Oh, for God's sake! Get over it already, will you?"

"Can we talk about this in the car? I don't want you to be late," I said as I put the shopping bag in the other office, out of sight, and turned out the lights.

Cat threw up her hands, recognizing my dodge tactic for what it was, but followed me out the door anyway. I was sure there was more grilling to come on the way to the airport, but at least she was talking to me again.

We stepped out into the hallway, and as I turned to lock the door Cat sucked in a breath and whispered, "He's still here."

I turned and looked to where she'd indicated, and sure enough Goon was standing at the far end of the hall as if waiting for us to come out. My intuition began buzzing, and for some reason I felt very fearful for Cat's safety. I turned to her and said, "Cat, listen carefully to me; take my keys and go to my car. If you go down that hallway"—I indicated behind us—"it will take you down a back staircase and out the north side of the building. You can circle around and get to the parking structure from there."

"Are you nuts? I'm not leaving you!" she hissed at me.

My intuition buzzed even louder, and hairs began standing up along my arms; Cat was in danger. "This is not open for negotiation!" I insisted, getting right in her face. "You will go to my car immediately, and if I'm not there in five minutes call nine-one-one, but you need to go *now*!" Even though I was keeping my voice quiet, my tone suggested I meant business.

Cat looked at me with surprise—it was very rare that I stood up to her—but she was still waffling about leaving me. "What are you going to do?"

I blinked a few times, thinking fast. I had no idea what I'd actually do, but after a moment I said, "I'm going to talk reasonably with the guy and give him another reading on the house. If he's still dissatisfied, then I'll refund his money."

"He looks mean," she said, sneaking a look to the end of the hall.

"Him? Nah, really, he's all bark. Trust me; I'll take care of it. Now go to the car quickly!" I insisted as my intuition gave me another buzz about Cat's safety.

I shoved Cat behind me and pointed my finger hard in the direction of the back elevator. She gave me one last look of apprehension, but walked away. When she was far enough down the hallway I approached Goon with fisted palms and major attitude.

"Cute sister," he said with a snort when I got close.

"She's not my sister," I said, narrowing my eyes.

"She said she was your sister."

"That was just to get by you."

"She sure looks like your sister . . ." Goon pressed; he wasn't about to let go.

"Dude, she's like six inches shorter than me and naturally blond. We are *so* not related. Besides," I said, going for a change of subject, "it's none of your business who's related to me and who's not. You need to back off, because I've been patient with you people and now I'm ready to go to the police. . . ."

Goon laughed heartily. It was an ugly, guttural sound. "That's a good one, Cooper. I'd like to listen in on that conversation."

"You think I'm kidding? You think I'm pulling your leg? Well, let's just see how funny it is when I talk to my good friends down at the department. . . ." I reached into my purse and pulled out my phone, flipping it open and pressing the on button. I sneered at Goon as I prepared to dial the number, when my phone unexpectedly went off and I nearly dropped it.

Goon was startled too, and he abruptly stopped laughing. I looked at him for a moment, and he looked at me; then I answered the phone with a tentative "Hello?"

"Abby? Are you all right?"

I let out the breath I was holding and said, "Yeah, Cat, no problem; we're just negotiating the terms. I should be there in a minute or two."

"Well, perhaps you can direct me to your car; I can't seem to remember where your parking space is—oh, thank you!" She giggled.

I was confused for a moment, but heard a man in the background say, "No sweat, cutie."

"Cat? You there?" I asked, confused as to whom she was talking to.

"Yes, I'm here. The most gorgeous man just held the door open for me; I swear, you have the best-looking guys in this town. So where is your car?"

"On the second floor, northwest side in the reserved parking area. Where are you?"

"Oh, that's right. It's down one flight. Okay, well, don't take—*Gulp!*"

"Cat?" I said, not understanding what she'd said. "Cat? What did you say?"

"Mmmglmph!"

"Cat! Cat? Are you there?" My ear was firmly pressed against the earpiece of the phone as I strained to hear what was happening. It sounded like my sister had just put her hand over her mouth. Then I heard a clatter, and I knew Cat had dropped the phone. Reflexively I looked to my left out the window that faced the parking structure. Two things hit me immediately: Karen Millstone had parked her car in the parking structure the night she was murdered, and that had happened exactly one week ago tonight—Thursday—the night of the rapist.

"Cat!" I shouted at the top of my lungs into the phone as I started running down the hallway. *"Cat! Talk to me! Cat!"* Mounting panic raced through my veins, *"Move!"* I said to two people who were coming up the stairs and blocking my panicked flight down. *"My sister is being attacked!"* I shouted as I shoved past them. *"Catherine! Catherine! Answer me!"* I wailed into the phone as my feet shuffled down the staircase. I couldn't seem to make it down the stairs fast enough; I was trying to hold the phone, listening to an awful struggle in the background as my sister fought for her life. She was gurgling and trying to catch her breath, and the sounds were coming more and more faintly.

As I reached the lobby and turned toward the front door an arm grabbed my elbow, and Goon whirled me to face him. "What floor is she on?" he asked forcefully.

I looked at him, not comprehending, tears streaming down my cheeks and total terror filling my heart as I frantically tried to push past him to get to Cat.

"What floor of the garage is she on?" he shouted, and shook me by the shoulders, forcing me to cooperate.

"The third floor! She's on the third floor!" I screamed.

The next few moments happened as if in a dream. Goon bolted through the doors and ran faster than any man I'd ever seen. He dodged through traffic and charged up the stairs of the parking structure. I ran after him but couldn't keep up. "Cat!" I continued to scream, my voice clogged with emotion, *"Catherine, please, God, answer me!"*

I reached the parking structure and bolted to the staircase, screaming my sister's name and sobbing my terror as my legs pushed up the stairs as fast as I could make them go. As I rounded the last flight and pushed through the door of the third floor, I saw Cat some twenty yards away, bleeding badly from her head, and held in Goon's arms. I ran full-tilt to her, pleading with God that she was still alive. Goon placed her gently in my arms as I furiously looked for signs of life. She was breathing, and I sank with her to my knees, sobbing into her hair and rocking back and forth as I held her, my terror making me oblivious to almost everything else.

I became aware of sirens screaming up the parking structure, and out of the corner of my eye I saw Goon looking shaken as he tucked something blue into his overcoat. Then I watched helplessly as he got up with one last look at me, then darted around a pylon and was gone.

A moment later a patrol car arrived and an officer hurried out and crouched next to me. He tried to take Cat from my arms, but in my terror I fought him and wailed my agony. Finally Cat was coaxed from my grip and I was helped to my feet, but I sank down again, as I didn't have the strength to stand.

Then Milo was there, and he was helping me up, lifting me into his car and securing me in place. I couldn't stop crying as I sat puddled there, shaking uncontrollably and praying to everyone I could think of to help my sister.

We arrived at the ER mere minutes later. As I leaned on Milo I was ushered down a short hallway and placed on a gurney. A doctor came over and wiped the blood from my hands and face, checking for injuries, as he asked me questions, but all I could do was plead with him to help my sister.

Someone handed me a pill and a small paper cup of water. It took a moment to understand that they wanted me to take the medicine. I finally obliged my caregivers, and within a couple of minutes I was able to stop crying, and even though the world seemed slightly disconnected, it was still better than feeling like I was coming apart at the seams.

A little while later Milo reappeared around the curtain sectioning off my gurney and smiled kindly at me. "Hey, there," he said.

"Is she okay?" I asked no louder than a whisper. My voice had gone hoarse.

"They're still checking her over. Do you want to wait out here with me?"

I nodded and got up off the gurney, shuffling over to him. Milo wrapped a protective arm around me and guided me to the waiting room just down the hall.

We sat down in the cushioned chairs and I looked dully at my feet, I couldn't seem to form a coherent thought, and although this should have troubled me, it didn't.

"Can I get you anything?" Milo asked me after a while.

I shook my head no.

"Mind if I grab something?"

"Go for it," I whispered.

Milo got up and disappeared down the hall, and I closed my eyes against the world. A few minutes later I felt something nudge my hand, and I opened my eyes to see Milo pushing a cup of hot cocoa at me. I smiled weakly up at him and took the cup. The warmth of the liquid felt good against my cold hands.

"Not now," Milo began, "but later we'll need you to give a statement."

I nodded dully, grateful that he wasn't pressing me for details tonight.

I had no idea how many minutes ticked by—my sense of time was all confused—but finally a tall, good-looking doctor approached us. He squatted down in front of me, and right away I liked him. "Miss Cooper?"

I nodded.

"I'm Dr. Burton. I've been tending to your sister."

Dr. Burton had a pleasant face, and large brown eyes behind wire-rimmed glasses. He smelled of aftershave, and his smile was full of gorgeous white teeth. "Is she okay?" I asked.

"Well, she got a pretty good knock on the head, and her throat's a little bruised, but overall I think she'll make a full recovery."

I exhaled the breath I'd been holding and reached a hand out to Dr. Burton's arm. "Thank you," was all my beleaguered voice could manage.

"Would you like to see her?"

I nodded vigorously and Dr. Burton led me down the hallway to another curtained bed. He pulled the sheet slightly away and stepped back, saying, "I'll give you a couple of minutes with her; then she'll need to get her sleep. We've given her a pretty aggressive sedative, so she might not make a lot of sense right now."

I nodded and shuffled past him but stopped just short of the bed.

I've never thought of my sister as fragile. Even though Cat's small, she's feisty. But with her lying there in her hospital gown, with her hair matted, a large gash pulled together by ugly stitches over her right temple, and horrible bruises ringing her neck, I was taken aback by her sudden delicateness. Carefully I moved forward and took her hand, lifting it gently into mine. Her hand was warm, and this gave me more reassurance than any doctor could.

Slowly she opened her eyes and looked at me, a slow, painful smile spreading along her lips, but never reaching her eyes. "Hey," she said weakly.

"Shhhh." I scolded. "Don't talk. Rest, and we'll talk later, okay?"

Cat grunted and closed her eyes. Within moments she was asleep again.

A few minutes later a nurse came in and subtly told me that it would be better to let Cat rest quietly. I shuffled back out to the waiting room, and over to Milo.

"Let's get you home," he said, getting up and wrapping his protective arm around me again.

We walked over to his car and he drove me to my house, neither of us saying a word. He parked in front, and as I reached over to grab the door handle Milo stopped me and asked, "Is there anyone you want me to call?"

I stopped and looked back thoughtfully at him. There were two phone calls that only I could make. One was to my brother-in-law, Tommy. "No, just my brother-in-law, but I think it's better if I call him. Thanks, though . . ."

"Sure. You going to be okay by yourself tonight?"

"Yeah, I'm just really tired. I'll call Tommy and then catch some sleep. When do you want me to give a statement?"

"I'll pick you up tomorrow at seven thirty and we'll drop by the station before I take you to your office. Sound okay?"

"Sure," I said, and got out of the car. My limbs felt like lead. "See you then," I said, closing the car door and trudging up the driveway. Once inside I waited until Milo pulled away, then walked over to my phone and began sifting through the numbers on my caller ID. Finding the number I wanted I dialed it quickly, my heart rate picking up as the phone began to ring.

"Kapordelis residence," answered a woman's voice.

"Andros Kapordelis, please," I said into the phone, marveling at how calm I sounded.

"May I ask who's calling?"

"Abigail Cooper."

"One moment please."

I waited for about thirty seconds; then the line was picked up, "Good evening, Miss Cooper. How is your sister?"

"I want to make a deal," I said, ignoring his question.

There was a low chuckle, and what I imagined a satisfied smirk as Andros answered, "What sort of 'deal' did you have in mind?"

"We do a trade, you and I."

"What do you want to trade?"

"I help you with this project you were talking about, and you make Goon help me identify the motherfucker who tried to kill my sister."

There was a pause on the other end as Andros considered my offer. "And what makes you think that my associate can help you identify this man? After all, he was wearing a mask, wasn't he?"

"Yes. Yes, he was—that is, until Goon pulled it off him."

"How do you know this?" Andros asked, surprise in his voice.

"By the time I got there the psycho who attacked my sister was gone, but I saw Goon tuck the mask into his coat, and then the police arrived, so there wasn't time to ask him about it. Goon saw the guy's face, Mr. Kapordelis; I'm sure of it."

There was an even longer pause, followed only by, "I see. . . ."

While Kapordelis pondered that, I had a chance to think about something that was bothering me and the valium allowed me to ask the burning question. "You know, Mr. Kapordelis, what I can't really figure out is why Goon would help us at all? I mean I'm grateful, to a point of course, but why would he come to our rescue when not two minutes earlier he was threatening me with great bodily harm?"

Kapordelis's tone grew annoyed and his answer sent a shiver up my spine. "My associate suffers one great weakness. His mother was raped and murdered when he was a small child and he witnessed the event. I can see I have indulged this weakness too much, and I will have to take appropriate measures to ensure it does not happen again. Consider yourself very lucky, Miss Cooper— if I'd sent any of my other associates to deal with you, we would be having a very different conversation right now."

"Do we have a deal?" I asked anxiously, wanting to change the subject.

"Yes, we have a deal. My associate will not make a statement to the police, but I will allow him to describe your sister's attacker, and it goes without saying that you will not mention my name to anyone at the police department."

I didn't respond to Andros's demand, mostly because he was only stating the obvious, plus I was listening for my lie detector, but the valium I'd taken had dulled all my senses, and I wasn't sure if my intuition was able to work under the influence.

My silence, however, was read as hesitation, so Andros felt it necessary to pound on me a little more. "I'm warning you, Miss Cooper, any leak to the police about myself or my associates will be met with immediate action. Are we clear?"

"Perfectly," I snarled.

"Fine, it is settled. I will send a car to get you on Sunday evening at seven o'clock and bring you here so that we may discuss my project."

"Fine, but know this, Kapordelis—I help you, you help me, then we're done with each other—understand?"

Andros chuckled ominously and answered me by hanging up.

Chapter Ten

"So then what happened?" Milo asked me. It was Friday morning, and I was parked across from him at his desk, giving him my version of what happened to Cat the night before.

"Well, I was wrapping up with a client, and I sent Cat on ahead to the car, you know, so that I could take her to the airport."

Milo nodded as he scribbled my comments on a legal pad. "Uh-huh," he said.

"And I was talking to my client in the hallway—"

"What's the name of your client?" he asked, interrupting me.

"What does it matter?" I snapped back.

Milo looked up at me in surprise, not understanding why I was so defensive. He explained: "Well, your client may be another possible witness. I'd like to follow up with them, if that's okay?"

"They didn't see anything. I got the phone call from Cat right as I was finishing with them—"

"So they didn't overhear your conversation?"

My face was turning red, and my palms were beginning to sweat. There was no way I could tell Milo the full story and live to tell about it. I wanted to cooperate with him, but only so much. My plan was to get a physical description from Goon, and then bring that to Milo later. I hadn't worked out how I would introduce this little tidbit, but I still had time to sort through the details. "No, they didn't. In fact, I think they had already walked away when I got Cat's call."

Milo was studying me curiously. He knew I was lying. He just didn't know why. Finally he said, "Okay, so this client of yours is out of the picture; then what?"

"Well, Cat said she couldn't find my car, and she said she was on the third floor, so I'm telling her that she's up one floor too high when all of the sudden I hear her being grabbed—"

"How did you know she was being grabbed?"

"Uhhh . . ." I thought for a moment. "I heard this like gulping sound and then I heard her phone drop to the pavement, and I heard sounds of a struggle—"

"Did she scream?"

"No . . . I think her mouth was covered or something. I could only hear this muffled struggle through the phone, and I just knew she was being attacked."

"Uh-huh."

"And so I just started running to the parking garage screaming at the top of my lungs, and I guess when I got to the third floor the rapist must have gotten spooked by all my screaming, 'cause all I saw was Cat, lying unconscious on the pavement."

"I see. . . ."

"So I went over to her and picked her up and started screaming for help, and a few seconds later I heard the sirens in the parking garage, and you guys showed up."

"So no one else was with you?" Milo asked.

The way he said this made me think he knew more than he let on, but I had to stick to my story for now. "Nope, no one. I just came up to the third floor and there she was. . . ." My voice wobbled a little as I recalled the image of Cat beaten and bloody, lying limp in Goon's arms.

"Anything else you want to tell me?" Milo's voice, normally soft and coaxing, had a hard edge to it. He knew I was full of crap, and it pissed him off that I was unwilling to trust him.

"Nope . . . that about covers it," I said, not meeting his eyes.

"Okay," he said, and closed the file in front of him. "We'll look at the videotape from the garage's security cameras and maybe we'll get lucky."

My head snapped up. "Videotape?"

"Yeah. Our first really good break in this case. The garage has a couple of security cameras posted around the structure. With any luck we'll be able to see the attack on your sister, and maybe help identify this guy."

Uh-oh! "That's great Milo. Really . . . that's great!" I was totally screwed. "How soon before you analyze the videotape?"

"Well, unfortunately the owner of the garage is in Morocco or something, and the management company can't release the tape without either his permission or a search warrant. We're working on both right now."

"So it could be a day or two . . ." I said.

Milo nodded, watching me closely. "You worried about something on the tape, Abby?"

"Me?" I said, forcing a chuckle. "No, not at all. I think it's great! Wow, good job! Maybe we'll catch this guy," I said with a fake smile. And then it hit me: If Goon had pulled off the rapist's mask, maybe there would be a good image of the rapist. I'd have some explaining to do, but at least we could possibly have a face to identify. I brightened at that thought and said, "Good job, Milo, really. And thanks so much for taking care of me last night; I was kind of a basket case."

Milo was thoroughly confused at my sudden change in temperament. I'd gone from dodging his twenty questions and avoiding his eyes to sincere appreciation. The switch had to be a little bizarre. "That's what I'm here for. You need a lift to your office?"

"Please. I want to get my car and head back over to the hospital to visit with Cat before I start work."

"Did your brother-in-law fly in last night?" he said, getting up and grabbing his coat.

"Yeah, he flew in on the red-eye and went straight to

the hospital. I was totally out of it by the time he landed—
that pill they gave me really knocked me on my butt."

"Valium will do that. You feeling all right today?"

We had reached the downstairs lobby, and Milo held
open the door for me as I walked through the door
leading to the parking lot. "You mean for nearly having
my sister killed right before my eyes? Yeah, I guess I'm
okay. I just want her to recover quickly and go home as
soon as possible—" *Crap!* I hadn't meant to say that!

"Go home? Why're you in such a hurry to have her
go home?"

I got into Milo's car and waited until he'd gotten in
as well before I answered, my mind working furiously
to come up with something. "Oh, trust me, it's not me
who wants her to go home; she'll be all over that idea.
If I know Cat she'll want to get back to work as soon
as possible; you know, she has an *empire* to run." I inserted a small forced laugh as I said this.

"Uh-huh," Milo said, again watching me closely.

"So!" I said quickly changing the topic. "Are you
going to talk to Cat today?"

"Yes, just as soon as her doctor gives me the go-
ahead. Probably later on this morning."

Whew! I still had time to tell Cat not to mention Goon
to the police. All I needed was for Milo to ask a lot of
questions and start sniffing around Andros Kapordelis.
That would bring a boatload of trouble down on me, as
I was sure Andros would know immediately who had
fingered him. My sister was too vulnerable. I had to get
her out of town, and then I'd help Andros out with whatever project he needed me for, get my description from
Goon, identify the rapist and finally take a nice long
vacation somewhere. I still wasn't convinced that Andros
recognized that, after this, there would be no continua-
tion of our "partnership."

The moment Milo dropped me off at my car, I sped
over to the hospital to visit with Cat. Tommy met me in
the hall; he looked pale and shaken. I hugged him hard
and asked, "You okay?"

"I'm fine," he answered in a hushed tone. "It's your sister I'm worried about. She looks like hell."

"I know, but she'll heal. She's strong, and the doctor said she's just got a bad gash and a concussion. The bruises will fade, and she'll get better quickly. Before you know it this will just be an ugly memory."

Tommy nodded and shuffled his feet uncomfortably. My brother-in-law was a gentle man. It was unfathomable to him that someone could have been so violent to his wife. "She's up if you want to see her. I was just on my way downstairs to get her something to eat. She's refusing to eat the slop they served her for breakfast."

"See?" I said with a winning smile. "Now *that* sounds like Cat, doesn't it?"

Tommy gave me a small smile and said, "Yeah, I guess. She's already got all the nurses jumping. I have a feeling they may want to discharge her early just to get her out of here."

I smiled and squeezed Tommy's arm as I moved past him and into the room with my sister. "Hey, there," I said when I saw her.

She still looked awful. The right side of her face was swollen slightly, there were scratch marks and bruises over most of her neck, and her lower lip had a cut on it, but at least she was sitting up in bed, awake and alert. "Abby!" she said warmly. "Oh, I was wondering when you'd get here."

I moved quickly over to the bed and pulled up a chair. "How're you feeling?" I asked, taking her hand.

"All things considered I think I'm doing okay. Oh, and before I forget, can I please have the address of that client of yours?"

The blood drained out of my face, and I asked, "Which client?"

Cat looked at me as if I were daft, and said, "Uh, the one who saved my life?"

I gulped down my anxiety as I looked at her, trying to come up with an answer. I thought for sure Cat had lost consciousness before Goon showed up, but maybe she hadn't. Maybe she'd seen him rescue her and then blacked out. "How do you know he saved your life?" I asked carefully.

"Because I was the one being attacked, remember? I saw him come out of the stairwell and charge toward us. My assailant let go of me and tried to run, but your client chased him down, and the last thing I remember was that they were wrestling with each other. Then I must have lost consciousness, because I don't remember much else until this morning."

My heart was racing. How the hell was I going to explain everything to Cat and get her to cooperate? If the word "mob" even remotely entered the conversation, my sister wouldn't waste a second whisking me off to some hideaway to make sure I was safe. She'd never let me set foot in this town again. She would also insist on a career change and probably a change of name. She'd be as tough to deal with as the frigging FBI. "Cat," I began, "listen, about my client . . ."

"What was his name?"

"I can't tell you."

"Why not?"

"It's complicated, but trust me, I can't tell you."

"I don't understand. He's your client; why can't you tell me his name?"

I took in a big breath, racking my brain for a plausible explanation. Finally a thought occurred to me. "Because he's hiding from the Russian Mafia." *Liar, liar, pants on fire . . .*

"I'm sorry?" she said, her eyes growing huge.

"Yeah, you remember he had an accent?"

"Yes, but he sounded more Greek than Russian."

"That's because he's been working to change his accent," I said quickly. "See, he came to this country to avoid persecution, and now he wants to go back. That's why he came to me, so that he could see if it was safe. But I told him it wasn't, and that he couldn't leave yet. In fact, I thought it might be unsafe for him here too. . . ." *Liar, liar . . . pants on fire . . .*

"You're kidding," Cat said, getting caught up in the tall tale I was spinning.

I nodded convincingly. "No, it's true." *Liar, liar . . .*

pants on fire . . . "If anyone knew he was here he'd be targeted for sure. That's why you can't mention a word of it to the police."

For the first time since I started telling her the story, Cat looked at me skeptically. "But the man's a hero, and he may be able to help track down the guy who attacked me."

I nodded and said, "Yes, of course. But I've already spoken to him, and he's willing to cooperate as long as the police don't get involved. He's promised to give me as many details as he can remember, but he must remain totally anonymous. After all, his life is at stake."

Cat's brow furrowed as she weighed the validity of my story. "So . . . what should I tell the police happened?"

"Well, instead of telling them that my client saved you, just tell them that you heard my screams getting closer, then the killer let go of you and took off running. They'll believe that, and this way my client can remain safe."

Cat pondered that a while and said, "Okay. I'm going to trust you on this but I am not comfortable committing perjury, just so you know."

"I know, I know, and I wouldn't ask if it weren't a matter of life or death for this guy. But I think after saving your skin, maybe this is the least you can do for him?"

That cinched it; Cat nodded and said, "Okay, fine. Since you put it like that, what choice do I have?"

I beamed a broad smile at her and squeezed her hand. "Thanks, honey; that's really great of you. I'll pass along your appreciation to him too, okay?"

Cat looked sharply at me, thinking of something. "Abby? *You're* not in any danger, are you?"

"What? Uh, no. Of course not . . . ha-ha, I'm *perfectly* safe." *Liar, liar, pants on fire* . . .

"Okay, just checking. Now where's Tommy? I'm starved!"

I left Cat's bedside when Tommy returned, and headed back to my office to get ready for another long day. I had six clients on the agenda, and I needed some "me" time before the first one arrived.

Getting to the office, I checked my messages first. There were several, so I jotted down all the names and phone numbers, then went into my reading room and sat down for a little meditation.

While I was meditating the phone rang, and I thought about answering it, but decided to ignore it and let it go to voice mail. The thought about checking the message bugged me for several minutes, so finally I got up and played the message.

"Hey, Abby, it's Dutch. Sorry I missed you. I tried you at home and on your cell, so I thought maybe you were already at work. Listen, I just wanted to call and tell you that I've been thinking about you, and I miss you, and I'd like a chance to start over once I'm done with this assignment. I'll call you in the next couple days and we'll talk then."

My eyes got misty as I listened to the recording. *Damn!* I really did miss him. I wondered where he was, and what he was up to, and part of me worried for him because his new job was all about dealing with the worst of the worst. Just then there was a knock on my door, and I sighed heavily as I set the receiver down and got back to the business of the day.

Later that night I went back to the hospital and I grilled Cat about what she'd said to Milo when he'd interviewed her. Fortunately she backed up my version, but warned me that Milo didn't seem to believe her, and kept asking her if she'd seen anyone else come to her rescue.

"Crap," I said, annoyed that Milo wasn't backing off.

"Hey, come on now," my sister said encouragingly. "Maybe you can trust Milo. Maybe he'll know of a way to get your client's testimony without exposing him. I think you should talk to him."

"Cat, you're just going to have to trust me on this one. It's a can of worms that I really can't open right now, okay?"

"Okay," she said, holding up her arms in surrender. "If you say so. Listen, the hospital is discharging me tomorrow morning. Will you come see us off to the airport?"

"You're leaving already?" I asked, hiding a huge sigh of relief.

"Yes. Tommy's taking me to Aruba so that I can make a full recovery. The boys'll be in Disney for another week, so this works out perfectly. Our flight leaves at ten. Can you come see us off?"

"Wouldn't miss it," I said, privately thankful she was going someplace remote and out of harm's way.

The rest of the weekend was a flurry of activity. On Saturday I saw Tommy and Cat off at the airport, heaving a huge sigh of relief when I watched their plane take off for the tropics, then headed back to work for two more busy days until the moment of truth on Sunday night, when, at exactly seven o'clock, a silver sedan pulled to a stop at the foot of my driveway. I'd been watching out the window and immediately went outside to the car. Without a word I opened the door and got in. There was the familiar driver in the front seat, but no Goon to greet me in the back. I shrugged my shoulders at his absence; it was obvious Andros would want us separated until I'd helped him with his "project"— whatever that might be.

The driver nodded to me as I buckled my seat belt, and we set off, heading southeast. We got onto I-696, then to I-75, and exited at Mack Avenue. Twisting and winding our way through various neighborhoods in alternating states of decay, we finally got off of Mack and entered a completely different world. Mere blocks away the ravages of poverty and social inequity had decimated homes and neighborhoods as effectively as a bomb blast, but here . . . I looked upon opulence so overt it took my breath away.

Mansions of enormous size sat pregnant and bloated atop small ridges that overlooked immaculate lawns. My jaw dropped as I gazed upon real estate that kept escalating in size and scope in a display of overindulgence that I'd seen only on television.

Our car wound its way down to Lakeshore Drive, and here the party really began. To my right was Lake Michigan; to my left sat mansions tall as cathedrals, built to one purpose—a grand view of the lake. Our journey ended about a half mile down the road, as we turned into a driveway that wound its way through a colossal wrought-iron gate imprinted with a gigantic Old English *K,* and up to a mansion that made Cat's house look like an outhouse.

The "home" was enormous, at least fifteen thousand square feet. We passed a tennis court, pool and volleyball pit. The circular driveway ended around a large fountain, drained for the winter, and several other luxury cars parked neatly in parallel spaces along the west side. I got out of the sedan and craned my neck to look up at Kapordelis's home.

Three stories fanned out evenly across the face of the structure. The mansion was colored gray brick, with black shutters and a black slate roof. Three stairs led up to a large dais partially covered by a balcony jutting out from the second floor. The front door was at least eleven feet tall, and made of intricately carved wood. It looked far too heavy to open, but my driver seemed to have no trouble as he led me inside.

Once I crossed the threshold and into the front foyer, it was hard not to let my jaw dangle; the interior was like the Taj Mahal. Sparkling white marble floors, and eggshell-painted walls were offset by an abundance of trim in gilded relief. The furniture was dark walnut, shined to a brilliant sheen, and an enormous divided staircase sloped grandly up to the second floor.

I was told to wait in the foyer as my driver disappeared through a set of French doors to my right. I stood nervously looking around, unsure of what to do with my hands. I wanted to look poised and confident, but it just occurred to me that I'd entered the den of a very dangerous lion, so, nervously, I shoved my hands into my jeans pockets and waited.

After a short while the French doors opened and a gorgeous olive-skinned man with jet-black hair and ebony eyes greeted me with a warm smile. "Good evening, Miss Cooper. I'm Demetrius Kapordelis. My father is expecting you. If you'll please come this way?" he said, indicating that I should follow him.

Demetrius led me through the French doors and into a spacious sitting area that spun off onto three other rooms, one containing a dining area, another that seemed largely devoted to watching television, and yet another that was lined with shelf upon shelf of books. We turned a corner at some point, my head bobbing from side to side as I tried to take everything in, and finally we came to rest in front of two large wooden doors that faintly resembled the front door. Demetrius opened one of them and led me through, then closed the door behind us and stood with his back against the frame, effectively cutting off any escape I might be considering.

Even though I'd enjoyed giving him the lookie-loo I had to assume that he was as deeply involved with his father's business as Andros was, and the warning bells my intuition was giving off seemed to confirm that he was just as violent and deadly a man as his father, so, mentally, I kept my distance.

I looked quickly around the room, which appeared to be a study, getting a feel for the environment. The room was a good size, roughly fifteen by twenty, painted a deep burgundy, and offset by richly stained wood trim and chair railing. There was a seating area off to one side, with two comfortable brown leather sofas that sat facing each other, and a big-screen plasma TV hung on one wall.

My eyes wandered in a circular motion, taking in expensive sculptures, oil paintings, and knickknacks, and coming to rest—with a little gasp of surprise from me—on Andros, who was seated behind an enormous desk of carved wood. I recovered myself quickly as I looked at the desk he sat behind. A true craftsman had carved intricate designs into the base of the desk, and I imagined that it was probably worth more than my house.

My gaze drifted back to Andros, who looked pale and sweaty this evening, his breathing quite labored and his pupils tiny. He'd obviously been taking heavy doses of pain medication to deal with his condition. Waves of pain and sickness emanated from him, and it was all I could do to stop myself from assessing his energy. I satisfied myself by letting my eyes go out of focus and allowing his aura to appear to me. Andros was covered in a brown so dark it bordered on black. He had, I guessed, only a very short while left to live.

"Good evening, Miss Cooper," he said in greeting.

"Mr. Kapordelis." I nodded, meeting his gaze.

"That will be all for now, Demetrius," Andros said dismissively.

Reflexively I looked at Demetrius, and noticed his eyes narrow at his father for a split second, then return to their normal shape as he asked, "You don't want me to stay for the interview?"

Andros grew angry. "I said leave us, Demetrius!"

Quickly Andros's son withdrew from the room. I wondered at the tone Andros had been quick to use with his son, but figured it probably came with the territory.

"So what's this 'project' you need me to work on, Mr. Kapordelis?"

Andros regarded me thoughtfully for a moment, the way a crocodile might watch a deer dipping low to drink before he attacked. "First things first, Miss Cooper," he said without explanation.

"Okay . . ." I said after a long minute. "What's first?"

"A test."

My brow furrowed. I didn't think I was going to like this. "What kind of 'test' we talkin' about?"

"Well," said Andros matter-of-factly, splaying his hands for effect, "I can hardly trust you on your word, now, can I? After all, I could give you my project and you could make up all sorts of stories about it, and there'd be little I could do if you were lying, correct?"

"I have no idea," I said bluntly, "because you have yet to tell me what your little 'project' involves. But you do know my work. I've given you a reading before, and that was given under duress. If I were going to lie, don't you think I would have done so then?"

Andros chuckled. "Perhaps," he said, toying with me. "Perhaps not. The only way for me to be certain, how-

ever, is to give you a small test. You pass the test and
I'll give you the project and we move on with our bargain. You don't pass the test and I know that you're
lying, and we move on to other things. . . ."

I gulped in spite of myself. "That wasn't part of our
deal."

"It is now," he said, his voice quiet and menacing.

I sneered at Andros for a minute or two, coming to
the conclusion that I really didn't have much choice. If
he wanted to tack on a bunch of games, there really
wasn't anything I could do about it. He had a better
hand than I did. "Fine," I said, giving in, "but once I
pass this test we move forward. You got it? I'm not
going to jump through a lot of hoops for you, so give
me the test and let's get this over with." As I said this
I came around to one of the chairs in front of his desk
and took my seat with a huff. I refused to be intimidated.

"Wise choice." Andros chuckled, then leaned forward
to pick up his phone and dial two numbers. After a
moment he said, "Bring them in," and hung up.

We waited in silence for what, I didn't know; then
after a minute or two the double doors to the study
opened and I began to turn as I heard shuffling behind
me. I pivoted in the chair for a better look, and luckily
my reaction was hidden from Andros as my jaw dropped
clear down to my shoes. There, looking rumpled, disheveled and struggling against the four thugs who shoved
them through the door, were my boyfriend and his
partner.

Chapter Eleven

There was a moment when the world moved in slow motion. I looked at Dutch, he looked at me, and our eyes locked. I watched as his beautiful blues widened slightly, then in an instant narrowed with anger. His hands appeared to be bound behind him, but that didn't stop him from struggling with his captors.

Joe, on the other hand, gave nothing away. She glanced at me as if I were something distasteful, then focused on Andros. "Who's the whore?" she asked, motioning her head my way.

My back was still to Andros. I couldn't risk him noticing the surprise on my face, so I continued to stare at Dutch and Joe. I didn't know why they were here, or what Andros knew about whom they worked for. I figured I'd keep quiet until someone let me know what was going on, and until then I was going to try to blank up my expression.

"Who she is would not matter to you, Sylvia. It's what she can do that is of interest. Miss Cooper is a psychic," Andros explained with a small chuckle. "Tell me, Miss Cooper, what does your gift say about these two people?"

So this was my test. One wrong answer and Dutch and Joe would be taken out behind the woodshed.

Dutch had stopped looking at me and was focused now on Andros. "This is bullshit, Andros. What's she going to do, pull out a crystal ball and levitate a table?"

Andros laughed heartily. "Mr. Wilson, this is why you find yourself in the predicament you're in. It is your temper that has led to my suspicion and tells me you have something to hide."

My brain was working furiously to put the clues from their conversation together. Dutch and Joe obviously weren't using their real names. They were aliases. Also, they both looked different. Dutch's hair, typically neatly combed, had a more gelled look; he'd also grown a goatee that gave him a sinister cast. Joe was dressed for a night of clubbing. Much of her outfit consisted of leather and buckles, and I figured that she had a lot of nerve calling me a whore.

My guess was that Dutch and Joe were undercover, and Andros suspected foul play. Obviously Andros didn't know about our connection to one another, or I would have been accompanying Dutch and Joe out to the woodshed about now. That meant that if I was *very* careful I could confirm their story and buy them some time. It would be tricky, because I didn't know what Andros suspected, so I'd have to be cautious. "There's some sort of business deal these two want to make with you," I said abruptly.

Dutch's eyes pivoted back to me. The sneer on his face let me know exactly what he thought of my input.

"Go on," Andros encouraged from behind me.

"The feeling I get is that there's some sort of trust issue at work here. I'm getting that there's another party involved in this whom you don't necessarily trust. . . ."

"Yes, indeed," Andros confirmed.

I was now alternately looking from Dutch and Joe back to Andros, feeling my way carefully along. I had to be extra cautious to filter the messages coming to me and put them in a way that wouldn't incriminate Dutch or Joe. I closed my eyes, sifting through the assortment of messages. There was something about Florida, or a connection to Florida, and I didn't know if I could mention that or not. There was also a connection to a brother, or someone like a brother, and something about betrayal. A memory flickered in my head and I blurted out, "Oh! These guys are from your cousin!" The moment I said it I wanted to retrieve it. I hadn't followed the line of information long enough to weigh whether that was something I should say out loud or not. I prayed I hadn't just revealed something that would jeopardize Dutch, and breathed a huge sigh of relief as I saw a hint of relief in Joe's expression.

"Very good, Miss Cooper. What else do you see?" Andros prodded.

I shut my eyes again and sorted. I was getting the image of a badge, and lots of focus on a betrayal, but this had more to do with the present than the past. That part I definitely wasn't going to mention. And then in my mind's eye I saw a pyramid made out of rifles. I opened my eyes and said, "Guns. This is a business arrangement about guns."

Andros clapped his hands together and barked out a laugh. "You are exceptionally gifted, even better than Madame Jarosolov. Now, here is my concern. I had a dream last night that my cousin had sent me a gift, only this gift was a horse carved out of wood. I opened the gift and it exploded. Can you see where I'm going with this?"

"You're afraid your cousin has sent you a Trojan horse," I replied easily.

"Exactly. The thing I remember most from the dream, other than the bomb, is that I opened the present with a letter opener in the shape of a police badge. I think these two are not who they say they are. I think they are Feds."

My heart was beating fast and furious. I looked back at Dutch, who refused to meet my gaze. He wasn't going to give me anything to go on, and I understood that I now held his life in my hands. My mind whirred, and I pretended to close my eyes and concentrate, but what I was really looking for was an explanation that would fly with Andros. A memory drifted up to me. It was the day

Dutch had taken me out for lunch, and the memory was of him holding the ticket he'd gotten for parking illegally in front of my building. I snapped my eyes open and looked quickly at him. He was wearing the same suede coat he'd worn that day. My eyes drifted to his pocket, and I sent up a silent prayer as I took a huge chance. "Yeah, you're right, Andros. This one over here," I said, waving a finger at Dutch, "he's the one with the badge in his energy."

Dutch's eyes returned to me, and if looks could kill I'd'a been toast. I swallowed hard and continued, begging with my eyes for him to trust me. "Now, the weird thing is that I'm not picking up the badge in connection to what he does, 'cause they're showing me a no-parking sign, and then the badge . . . like, I don't know, like he's gotten a parking ticket recently or something like that."

Dutch's eyes relaxed a fraction, and he said, "Your whore's got talent, Andros. I've got the ticket in my jacket pocket."

I knew we were just putting on a good show, but the fact that Dutch had just called me a whore made me want to pop him one. I held my cool, however, while one of the thugs reached into Dutch's coat and pulled out the parking ticket, handing it over to Andros.

Andros took the ticket and inspected it carefully. "You should be more careful where you park your car, Mr. Wilson," he said, and tossed the ticket onto his desk. Turning back to me he said, "Now what about the dream, Miss Cooper? Do you think I can trust my cousin after such a dream?"

I had to step carefully here. "Well, the feeling that I get is that this is an opportunity for you to make some good coin. This gun deal . . . it's pretty lucrative, right?"

"Possibly," Andros said.

"My sense is that there's going to be a big payoff here, and you're going to have to trust your cousin a little bit to get the payoff. The dream, I think, represents more of your fears than your reality. Dreams can often be a reflection of what we fear, rather than a prophetic vision. You say you suspected your cousin of betraying you in the past, correct?"

Andros nodded slowly. "Yes. Yes, I believe he did."

"Then there you have it. The dream is just your subconscious working out your fear of being betrayed again. It simply means you'll need to keep your eyes open. My feeling is that these two are who they say they are." For effect I turned to Dutch and asked, "Wilson, right?"

Dutch nodded curtly at me, the scowl on his face deepening.

"You deal in heavy artillery, right?"

Another curt nod. *Liar, liar . . . pants on fire . . .*

I turned back to Andros and explained: "I'm good at knowing when people are lying, and this guy's not flagging my radar. So my advice to you is that you can trust them. Make your deal with your cousin and enjoy the profits."

Andros had reclaimed his seat in the chair, his elbows on the desk with his hands coming up into a steeple, which he rested against his lips, deep in thought. He was weighing everything I said, and I was praying he'd buy into it. Finally he waved to his thugs and said, "Untie them, and have them wait outside for me while I finish with Miss Cooper."

Dutch and Joe were untied and led outside. Joe's lip curled slightly at me, and she reached out to grab Dutch's arm as the two were escorted out of the room. I didn't care. For now Dutch was safe, and that was all that mattered to me.

"So have I passed your 'test'?" I asked smugly.

"For now," he answered, then reached into a drawer and pulled out a large manila folder bound by rubber bands and chock-full of paper. He looked at it thoughtfully for a moment, then pushed it toward me. "Here," he said.

I took the folder and looked at it curiously. It appeared to be old and weathered, and I didn't really know what to do with it. "What's this?" I asked.

"It is my wife, Dora's, missing-persons police file, or a copy of her file, plus a few of the leads Madame Jarosolov was able to produce. Over the years I've hired many private detectives, hoping to find her, and all of them met dead ends. Madame Jarosolov produced some of the best leads, but still nothing concrete. I want to know what happened to my wife, Miss Cooper. This is your project. Find her, or find out what happened to her, and we will see about your sister's attacker."

My heart sank. I picked up the folder and I realized the "bargain" I'd struck with Andros was no bargain at all. "You've got to be kidding!" I said as I dropped the heavy folder with a thud.

"You think I am trying to amuse you?" Andros said in a dangerous tone. "I assure you, there is no joke in my request. I want to find my wife, or find out what happened to her, and I'm a man with limited time left to wait for such things. You want information about your sister's attacker? You will find Dora."

I ground my teeth for a minute, wondering what I'd gotten myself into, when my intuition began buzzing. Distractedly I picked up the message, which basically said, *Take the file.* . . . I questioned this message, but got it again more urgently, so, shrugging my shoulders, I stood up and carried the folder with me. "Fine. I'll work on this, but I can't guarantee anything. . . ."

"Yes, that was Madame Jarosolov's excuse as well," he said so ominously that I got a chill all the way up my spine. Andros picked up his phone again and barked something Greek into it, and a moment later my driver reappeared. As I turned to leave Andros gave me a parting warning: "I trust your discretion about what you've seen here tonight, all right, Miss Cooper?"

I turned back to him and copped an attitude. "Yeah, I've gone this long without reporting any of the bullshit you've done to me over the last week, but this is going to push me right over the edge!" Andros's brow darkened, and I knew that I was playing with fire. "Listen," I said more calmly, "you Mafia boys want to kill each other? Fine by me. The last thing I want to do is get mixed up in it, so trust me, I'm not going to dial nine-one-one anytime soon."

"It would be a grave mistake," Andros threatened, his eyes forming small slits and his mouth in a hard, frightening frown. "I also know you have been helping the police in your town with their rapist investigation, and I will not tolerate any mention of me in connection to that case. Do you understand?"

"Perfectly," I said, and turned toward the door.

As the driver and I headed back through the house we walked right past Dutch and Joe, who were sulking in two wing chairs, surrounded by brutes and waiting to be summoned. I wanted to catch Dutch's eye, but figured I wouldn't be doing him any favors by visually checking in with him in front of so many witnesses. It was better to pretend I didn't care, so I only stole a glance his way out of the corner of my eye. He looked ready to kill me, but I assumed it was all part of the act.

In a moment we'd left them behind, and I privately crossed my fingers that he'd be safe tonight.

Thirty minutes later I was back home, where I warmed up in a hot bath, complete with bubbles. I needed a little pampering tonight. Cat called while I was in the tub, and we talked briefly about her trip to Aruba.

"So how was the flight?"

"It was long, but totally worth it. We checked into the most gorgeous hotel, and Tommy has been so sweet to me. He's been having the staff here wait on me hand and foot."

"I'll bet," I said, smirking. It was so good to hear my sister talking like her old self again.

"Hey, has that client of yours given you any clues about the guy who jumped me?"

"Uh . . . no . . . not yet. Actually, he's had to keep a really low profile lately, but we're supposed to meet in the next couple of days, and I'm sure he'll give me something to go on."

Cat sighed audibly and said, "I'm just worried for the next poor girl who might not be as lucky as me."

My face pinched in guilt. I hated lying to my sister. "Yeah, I know. I promise I'll do my best to get what I can out of my client, okay?"

"Will you please be careful while you're doing that? This Russian Mafia thing has me really worried about you."

"Oh, Cat, *please*," I scoffed. "I'm perfectly fine. Geez, you and the drama of it all . . ."

"I'm serious," she insisted. "What if this man pointed these guys in your direction? I mean, what if someone without the best of intentions wanted to take advantage of your abilities? It could be very dangerous, you know."

I gulped at how close she was to the truth and said with a forced laugh, "My God, Catherine, have you been watching too much Court TV lately, or what?"

"I'm just saying. . . ."

"Well, don't worry about it, sweetie. I'm fine, and I will remain fine. Listen, you guys get back to your vacation and I'll talk to you in a couple of days, okay?"

"Okay. Give Milo our number here for me, won't you? I promised I'd call him when I got in, but if you could pass it along it would save me another phone call."

"Not a problem. I'll take care of it pronto." *Liar, liar . . . pants on fire . . .*

There was no way I was going to make it easy for Milo to follow up with my sister. He was already too suspicious, and I didn't want him to press her until I had the rapist's description in hand. "Take care of yourself, Cat, and give Tommy my love."

We clicked off and I climbed out of the tub and got into my flannel jammies. The house seemed empty without Eggy, and I got a pang in my stomach from missing him. I missed Dave too, and as I trotted into my room and turned off the space heater before getting into bed, I wondered how soon before my life would get back to normal.

I sighed as I puffed up my pillows and pulled the police file Andros had given me off the nightstand. I peeled back the rubber bands and opened up the folder, looking at page one. The paper was old and abused. After I'd looked it over a few times it dawned on me that I was looking at a copy of the police report taken twenty years earlier on the day of Dora Kapordelis's disappearance.

The report indicated that there had been a call to the Perry Drugstore on Fourth Street to investigate a lost child. The officers on the scene soon discovered that a little boy had been found wandering the aisles of a drugstore, looking frantically for his mother. The store had paged her over the intercom, but no one had come forward to claim the little boy. The child's home number revealed a housekeeper, who said that the boy had gone off with his mother to run several errands, and had not returned home yet.

I read through the police report a couple of times, then allowed my intuition to chime in. My eye searched the top of the page, and I was shocked to discover that the Kapordelis family once lived in Royal Oak, mere blocks from my office, in fact. I read on and saw that the little boy's name was Demetrius, and remembered something about Andros telling me that Demetrius had had a rough time dealing with his mother's disappearance.

I flipped back through the folder and found a picture of Dora. I held it in my hand for a minute, looking at her picture. My first thought was that she'd probably been abducted and possibly murdered—I mean, Andros was bound to have enemies. But her picture didn't reveal the flat plastic image that I usually got when looking at a dead person. I had to assume then that Dora was still alive.

That was a pivotal revelation if it were true, because it meant that Dora had probably been responsible for her own disappearance.

But why would a woman leave her children behind? Her youngest had been only a toddler. How could she be that cold? I stared at the image, and something popped into my head. I saw a map of the United States, and the state of Texas rose up out of the image. *Hmmm.* So there was a connection to Texas here. I wondered what it was. I also had an urge to turn to the next page of the report, which simply documented how the police had canvassed the neighborhoods around the drugstore, and short statements from possible witnesses. My eye drifted to the upper left-hand corner, and curiously I noted that the page began with the digit 3. I flipped back to the first page, which was numbered with a 1, then back to page three. Where was page two?

I searched the rest of the file, thinking that perhaps page two had gotten rearranged within the folder, but it wasn't there. Curious.

I flipped back to Dora's picture again, wondering if I could focus in on her energy, but my eyelids were beginning to droop, and I gave in to a tremendous yawn. Tiredly, I closed the file and vowed that tomorrow I'd concentrate on this again, and see what I could come up with. Already I felt like I'd made some good progress. The pressure was on, however, if I wanted to get a physical description to the police before Thursday rolled around again.

Sluggishly, I put the folder back on the nightstand and turned off the light, drifting off to sleep almost immediately.

I don't know what initially woke me—a sound, perhaps, or just the presence of another person—but in an instant I was wide-awake . . . and terrified. I strained to hear what had woken me, and I was too scared to move, because I knew someone else was in my bedroom.

My heart raced with terror as I realized my alarm hadn't gone off. My intruder had managed to bypass it, which meant that he'd probably also cut the phone lines. My mind whirred as I began to run through a list of ways to escape, my heart thumping so hard in my chest I thought it would certainly give me away. I couldn't really hear above the pounding in my ears, and I was about to risk turning my head to look around the room when an arm snaked its way across my chest, and another covered my mouth to muffle my scream.

I was pulled off the bed and onto the floor, but I was not pulled willingly. Fighting like a rabid cat I scratched and flailed and kicked, throwing my attacker off balance and gaining a small purchase on the floor. With all the strength I could muster I pushed up from the floor and heaved backward as hard as I could with my right elbow, making contact with a rib cage and sending my attacker momentarily backward. I didn't waste any time clawing and scrambling my way out of the bedroom, my limbs working independently of each other in their effort to propel me away from danger.

I could hear nothing but my own heartbeat and cries of terror as I made it to the stairway, still not having made it fully to my feet. Not pausing to stand up I simply launched myself forward, trying to get to the bottom as fast as possible.

I rolled down the stairs, hitting my head, scraping my knee and banging my hand. I was oblivious to the pain, the terror of the man in my bedroom crowding out all else.

Somehow I made it to the front door. I reached up to the handle and pulled myself up, snatching at the lock and yanking before I'd unleashed the catch. I sobbed as I struggled, aware that my attacker was close behind; then the door gave and I had a nanosecond of relief until a tremendous weight crashed into it, and the door was slammed shut as the body of my attacker hit the door frame and squashed me in the middle.

"No!" I screamed, sandwiched between the great bulk of the intruder and the door. I wriggled and clawed and continued to pull at the door. A hand with a viselike grip grabbed my shoulder and spun me around; another hand grabbed my other shoulder, and I was shaken so hard my teeth rattled. Finally the shaking stopped and I was let go, but I was dizzy from the manhandling and fell to the floor. Shuffling backward I pushed myself into the small space behind the front door and blubbered like a baby, "P-p-please . . . d-d-don't hurt me!"

"I'm not going to hurt you, Abby; now calm the hell down!" came a deep baritone.

In the dark it was impossible to see the man in my house, but his voice marked him as distinctly as his face. "Dutch?" I said with a sniffle.

"Well, who the hell did you think it was?"

"Obviously *not* you!" I said, getting angry. "What the *hell* are you doing here, and why did you *attack* me?" I demanded.

"I didn't 'attack' you, and keep your voice down," Dutch said, sternly kneeling down in front of me. Faintly I saw him rub his rib cage. "I think you cracked a rib," he complained.

"Do you *know* how much you scared me? Have you

thought about . . . oh, I don't know . . . calling me on the *phone* or ringing the *doorbell* instead of breaking and entering into my house? What are they teaching you guys at Quantico, anyway?" I snapped at him, the overflow of my terror fueling my anger.

Dutch sat down next to me and said, "I couldn't call or knock on your door. Kapordelis has your phone bugged, and your house is being watched. I had to get in through the back."

"How'd you bypass my alarm?" I demanded.

"I'm not the only one who uses their birthday as a PIN," he answered smugly. "Hey," he said, looking around, "where's Eggy? I was surprised when the little guy didn't start barking."

"Kapordelis tried to poison him. He's fine, but I'm keeping him at Dave's until I can sort all this out."

"Which reminds me—what in God's name are you doing getting mixed up with a guy like Andros? Do you *know* who you're dealing with?"

I sighed heavily. "Of course I know, but it's complicated."

"So you're working for him willingly?"

"No! I mean, sort of, but not really. The truth is, my sister was attacked the other day by the Royal Oak rapist, and one of Kapordelis's men got a good look at him. I need to cooperate with Andros until I can get the information I need out of his goon, and then we're done with each other. The reason I got involved in your little operation is only because Kapordelis wanted to test me—and, I might add, you're damn lucky I did. That guy was going to kill the two of you."

Dutch smirked. "Joe and I had a backup plan, so don't you worry about it. But that's not why I'm here. You can't work for this guy; it's too dangerous. Milo's working on this rapist, and he'll get him. You don't need Kapordelis's help."

I couldn't explain why, but something told me that I had to stick close to Andros for some other reason. I pondered that as I looked at Dutch, and something flashed through my mind. "Hey, you really need to be careful around this guy. He's got cancer—bad—and he doesn't care if he lives to see another day, 'cause he knows he's only got a couple of them left. He's a man with nothing to live for, and if he feels like taking you down because you're wearing the wrong kind of aftershave, then that's what he'll do."

"He's got cancer?"

"Bad."

"You're sure?"

"Yes. I'd be surprised if he made it to Christmas. . . ."

"Then we'll have to move fast. In the meantime, I'm warning you, back off this case. I mean it. Joe thinks you're on the take, and I'm having a hard time convincing her otherwise. What's Kapordelis want from you, anyway?"

"He wants me to help him find out what happened to his wife."

There was a very long pause, and I squinted in the dark to see Dutch's face. Finally he said in a voice that suggested he meant business, "You cannot help him with that."

"Why not?"

"Just back off, Edgar. I mean it. Okay?"

I was confused by the ice that had materialized in his voice. He was waiting for me to agree to walk away. But I didn't think Dutch fully understood what I had to lose here. Not only did I feel I was very close to cracking the case of the rapist, but something was pushing me to find Dora. All of my intuition screamed for me to continue poking through the file on my nightstand.

I could tell, however, that Dutch would have none of that, so I put it all back on his plate. "And just how would you suggest I deal with Andros in the meantime? I mean, the guy's not going to take a 'no, thank you' from me, you know."

"Stall. Tell him nothing—and I do mean *nothing*—until we make our move. We're really close to nailing his entire organization, and if you go poking around in this you could blow the whole case for us. Andros may die before we can bring him to justice, but there are a lot of other members of the family willing to take his place at a moment's notice. You're way out of your league here, so you need to lie low. We clear?" he asked, standing up and holding his right side tenderly.

"Fine," I said getting to my feet. "Are you taking off now?"

"Got to. I'd stay and make a dishonest woman out of you, but I think you cracked a rib, and besides, your room is freezing! What's going on up there?"

"It's a long story. Listen, please, *please* be careful. This guy Andros is a lunatic, and I don't think he's totally convinced that you're not a Fed."

"I'll be fine," Dutch said, and kissed me lightly. "Walk me out the back?"

I walked him to my back porch, where he turned to me and held my chin, looking into my eyes for a long moment. Finally he said, "I really miss you, sweethot."

"So hurry home," I replied as he leaned in and kissed me senseless.

After Dutch had gone I locked up again, set the alarm and went back to bed. My hand hurt and my knee was swollen, so I popped an aspirin before crawling back under the covers. I took a look at the clock before shutting my eyes, and noticed it was after two. One of these days I was going to work off my sleep deficit and get a decent night's shut-eye. Little did I know as I closed my eyes and sank down into the covers then that I wouldn't get that particular opportunity for several more days.

Chapter Twelve

The next morning I'd barely woken when there was an insistent knock at my door. I came downstairs in my bathrobe and slippers, stopping to hike up the heat while the next round of knocking encouraged me to hurry.

I peeked through the peephole and saw a young officer there wearing a grim expression and about to raise his hand yet again against my door. I pulled the door open and said, "Can I help you?"

"Miss Cooper?"

"Yes?"

"I'm here to escort you to the police department. Detective Johnson would like to speak to you."

"And instead of calling me on the phone he sent you?"

"Yes, ma'am."

Uh-oh.

"Fine, give me a minute and I'll be right with you," I said as I waved him into my living room and beat a quick path up the stairs. I had an inkling why Milo would send an officer to fetch me—my guess was that he'd viewed the video from the parking garage and wanted some answers. Pronto.

I sighed my way into a pair of jeans and a thick sweater, skipping the stiletto boots and choosing a pair of comfortable loafers instead.

After I'd locked up the house the officer and I headed over to the department, and dutifully I followed behind him as we walked up the stairs and into the Detectives' Unit. We pushed through the double doors, and I noticed immediately that Milo wasn't in the large, open room. Instead of dropping me off to wait at Milo's desk, my escort motioned me down the hallway to one of the interrogation rooms. The officer stopped before one of the doors on the left and, after opening it, waited for me to enter. I walked in and heard the door close briskly behind me. I turned sharply at the sound and noticed that I was alone . . . or so it appeared.

I turned back to the room and sat down in one of the chairs behind a secondhand table. I folded my arms and waited. There was a clock on the wall that marked off the seconds, and I watched them tick-tock for a while, then grew impatient. Bored with Milo's little tactic, I concentrated for a moment sending out my intuitive feelers.

Milo was nearby; I could feel his energy. I made an exaggerated eye roll in the direction of the two-way mirror on one side of the wall. He was behind it, watching me. I was sure of it.

Finally, nearing the point of being royally pissed off, I closed my eyes and focused in the direction of the two-way mirror. The feeling I had was that another person was with Milo, older, male, and light-haired. I honed in on that energy for a minute, and started picking up details right away. Good, this would be fun.

"Milo, your buddy needs to be careful about his back," I said loudly in the direction of the mirror. "He's got some sort of alignment problem in his lower vertebrae, and his posture isn't helping matters any. Also, his daughter has been taking the family car without permission, and if she's not careful she's going to get a speeding ticket . . . and won't that be embarrassing?" I chuckled, slapping my knee. "Also, I'm sensing something about an addition on the back of his house, like where the deck is. There's this area for a hot tub or something . . . and there's going to be a discussion about what size to put in—he should go with the bigger one. Also there seems to be an issue again with the daughter. Like she's hanging out with the wrong crowd. She's also stealing money from him, and if he's not careful she could take a bite out of his savings account—"

That did it. The door opened briskly as Milo and a rather shocked, balding, white-haired second detective walked in.

"That's enough, Abby," Milo said sharply.

"My sentiments exactly," I replied coolly, opening my eyes and sitting up tall and straight. There was no way I was buying into any intimidation tactics.

"This is Detective Anderson," Milo said, waving to the man next to him, who, I happened to notice, had a bent, rather pitched posture.

"Charmed," I said, scrunching up my face in a mock grin.

Anderson merely nodded, although he continued to eye me warily.

"I suppose you know why you're here?" Milo asked coolly.

"None whatsoever," I answered dismissively.

Milo pulled out one of the chairs and brought it close to me. Turning it backward and straddling it, he rested his arms on the frame and eyed me critically. "I don't like being lied to."

"Who does?" I was the picture of innocence, staring back eyeball-to-eyeball.

Milo sighed and stood up again. Quickly he walked out of the room and shut the door, leaving me with Detective Anderson.

I eyed Anderson, who eyed me back nervously. I smiled wickedly and asked, "So, Anderson, how you like your new boat?"

Anderson's jaw dropped, and he scooted his chair back a tiny bit before catching himself. Then he said nervously, "Cut that out."

I ignored him and continued, "And your wife, what's her connection to Pittsburgh? Is there a sister in Pittsburgh who's got a birthday coming up? Tell her she should go—she'll have a blast. But you need to stay home—you're no fun at parties . . ." I taunted. Anderson began to fidget and squirm. Nothing delighted me more than spooking big, burly men who thought they were God's gift. In a minute I'd have this guy peeing his pants. "Oh, and while she's away you can hang out with your girlfriend without fear of getting caught. She's the blonde, right? Or is that your wife, and your girlfriend's the brunette?" Anderson squirmed in his chair, his face turning red and a vein popping up in his temple. "Oh . . ." I said, making a sudden connection. "That's why your daughter's acting out, isn't it? She knows about your little affair, doesn't she?"

Anderson's eyes nearly popped out of his head, and he stood up abruptly. I'd hit a nerve, and this guy was chicken. He made a motion to turn toward the door when it opened, and Milo came in pulling a TV/VCR into the room on a cart. He took one look at Anderson's ashen face and said, "Goddamn it, Abby! Cut that out!"

I worked my face into a "Who, me?" expression and batted my eyelashes at Milo as Anderson reluctantly took his seat again after moving it to the back of the room. Milo scowled at him but didn't say anything as he loaded a tape into the television's VCR unit and pressed play. "This is the videotape of the garage the day your sister was attacked."

I turned my attention to the monitor as it went from fuzzy to a grainy black and then a black-and-white image taken from the ceiling of the parking garage above the stairwell appeared. I watched as the top of my sister's head came into view. She walked around in a small circle as she searched for my car; then she took out her cell phone and began to dial. There was no sound, but in my ear I could hear her words echoing from my memory as she called me and began to speak.

Suddenly a tall figure dressed in a ski mask and a long trench coat appeared from the direction of the stairwell and shadowed my sister as she walked toward a row of cars. Cat paused for the briefest of seconds, and then, like a tiger, he pounced on her. The force of his attack caught me off guard. He swung his arm around her neck, yanking upward savagely. I watched in horror as my sister was pulled backward, her feet dangling off the ground and her arms flailing. The attacker raised his free hand, wielding a tire iron, and brought it down on Cat's head.

Horrified, I felt my hand come up to cover my mouth, and tears fell freely from my eyes. I'd seen only the aftermath of the attack, which had been bad enough. Somehow watching it unfold on the television screen was so very much worse.

Shaking, but unable to tear my eyes away, I saw another figure appear, this one much bigger than the man who'd attacked Cat. As Goon charged forward, the Royal Oak rapist scuttled backward, still holding on to my sister's nearly limp body. Goon rushed him with all the fury of an angry bear. The rapist hesitated for a moment; then, just as Goon was about to pounce, he threw my sister at Goon and turned to run.

With amazing agility Goon caught my sister in one hand and reached out to grab her attacker with the other. For a moment it looked as if Goon had caught the man, but his bulky frame blocked a clear image of what happened next. There was half a second of scuffling; then the attacker was running away, his head ducked low and his coat collar pulled up high as he ran to the other end of the garage. He appeared to have dark hair, but we already knew that; any other details about his appearance were obscured by the grainy image of the video.

Just as the assailant flew down another stairwell, I appeared on the monitor, rushing toward Goon, who carefully handed Cat to me as I sank to my knees in near hysteria. I watched the screen as Goon then bent down and retrieved something off the ground, clearly the ski mask, and I could see that he tucked it into his overcoat, then dashed away just before the police came up the garage ramp.

The video had gone on for no longer than two minutes, if that, and yet it felt elongated somehow. Like so much energy needed hours to expend itself rather than the minutes it had actually taken.

Once the police arrived, Milo flipped off the television and turned to me, his eyes dark and intent, his voice icy. "So who is he?"

"Who is who?" I asked, stalling.

"Don't play around; this is serious," Milo warned.

"If you're talking about the man in the video, I have no idea." *Liar, liar, pants on fire . . .*

"Bullshit." Apparently Milo had his own inboard lie detector.

"Listen," I began, my voice reasonable, "now that I've seen the video I will admit that I vaguely remember there being someone else in the parking garage, but you have to understand, my main focus was getting to Cat. I guess I was so traumatized by the event that I blocked out everything else."

Milo straddled the chair again, eyeing me with a dull expression. He didn't believe me for a second. I waited for him to say something, but long minutes ticked by as he continued to stare at me without changing his expression. It was hard, but I kept my mouth shut and waited him out. Finally he motioned to Anderson. "Can you give us a minute?"

Anderson barely hid his relief as he stood up quickly and exited the room. Milo turned back to me after he'd gone, and asked, "Why don't you want us to catch the guy who nearly killed your sister?"

"Oh, for God's sake, Milo! Of course I want you to catch him, but if I've got a trauma-induced memory-selection thing going on . . . well, then there's nothing I can do about it. I don't know who that guy was—just some Good Samaritan in the right place at the right time, thank God."

"The same Good Samaritan you were seen talking to in the hallway of your office building?"

Oh, crap. He had me. "I'm sorry?" I asked, doing my best to look shocked.

"In case you hadn't noticed, I'm damn good at my job. Two witnesses who first called nine-one-one swear they heard you talking to a man in the hallway of your office building, then saw you rushing down the stairwell with this guy in tow when your sister was attacked. It's pretty clear by the video that we now have an *eyewitness* who can not only help identify the rapist, but who also has the physical evidence of the ski mask in his possession. What *I* don't understand is why *you* would want to hide the identity of someone who could lead us right to the guy that tried to kill your own flesh and blood!"

"No," I said, shaking my head back and forth and easing into another lie. "No, that's wrong. Milo, I don't know the guy in the video. The man I was talking to in the hallway is a client, who may have *looked* a little like that guy on the videotape, but he didn't come with me across the street to the parking garage."

"So where'd your client go?" Milo pressed.

"Hell, I don't know! Maybe he was also trying to call for help. I mean, I know he ran down the stairs with me, but I swear to you he was not with me when I crossed the street to the parking garage." That, at least, was true. Goon had already made it across the street when I'd pushed through my lobby doors. "And I'm sure it's not my client on the video. I would have recognized him, and of course I would have told you about him if I'd known him."

"Okay, so what's your *client's* name?"

"Why do you need to know his name?" I asked, feeling like a mouse in front of a cat.

"Maybe he heard something, or saw something—you know, we'd want to talk to anyone in the vicinity near the time of the attack."

"Uh, I don't remember his name offhand—"

"But you keep records, don't you? You could look it up, couldn't you?"

Despite my efforts to appear nonchalant and trustworthy, I was beginning to turn red and fidget. "Uh, sure . . . I guess. Still, don't you think you need to be looking for the big guy in the video instead of harassing my clients?"

"Why are you getting so defensive?" Milo asked me, cocking his head in mock shock.

"I'm not getting defensive; I'm merely *suggesting* that you put your focus where the focus should go—namely on the guy who tried to murder my sister!" I was angry now, and quickly losing my cool.

"Okay, Abby, I'll make you a deal," Milo said softly as he leaned in close to me again. "You tell me who that other guy in the video is, and I promise you I'll focus my *full* attention on finding the son of a bitch who put Cat in the hospital, because the fact of the matter is, sweetheart, I *know* you can tell me who he is, and your 'selective memory' explanation is full of shit."

I sat there staring at Milo for a long moment. The truth was that I really did want to tell him about Goon. But doing so would only put him, me and everyone else I cared about in real danger. I had to go with the intuitive feeling that I needed to tread carefully here. If Andros suspected I had told the police about Goon, he would kill me. He'd as much promised me that in his study the night of my test. I shut my eyes for a brief moment and collected myself, then opened them again, looking him squarely in the eye as I quietly said, "Milo, I really can't help you."

The look Milo gave me made me want to cry. I'd known him only a short time, but I really genuinely liked him. His look made it clear that he'd formed a new and permanent opinion of me; in his mind I was now one notch below pond scum, and for some reason that really, really bothered me. "You understand that my butt is on the line for you where this investigation is concerned, don't you?"

"Come again?" I asked, not picking up the subtle turn in the conversation.

"I'm risking my *career* here by having you contribute your . . . uh . . . talents to this investigation, and instead of respecting the fact that I'm going out on a limb for you, and *helping* me, you're working hard to point me in the wrong direction. Why?"

I gulped before answering him. Milo really knew how to lay on the guilt. "I've already given you my impressions, Milo. I don't know what else you want from me."

"How about the truth?"

"I've told you everything I know. I can't make something up just to please you, now, can I?"

After a long, tense moment Milo took a deep breath and slowly let out his obvious disappointment in me. "Fine," he said after a moment. "Have it your way," he added dismissively and got up, turning his back to me.

The way Milo turned away bothered me the most, so in a last-ditch effort to appear cooperative I asked, "Milo? If you guys have this video of my sister's attack, isn't it possible that there's a video of Karen Millstone's attack? I mean, she was probably grabbed in the garage the same way Cat was. . . . Maybe there's a clue—"

"No," Milo said harshly, not turning around but cutting me off with the ice in his voice. "The video only records from Sunday through Saturday of every week, then loops back and starts over. Karen's attack has been recorded over. If we'd known she'd been attacked in the garage instead of the post office we could have gotten to the tape sooner."

"Oh," I said humbly. Long moments ticked by with neither of us saying a word, so finally I asked, "Can I go?"

"For now."

With downcast eyes I made my way out of the room, noticing that Milo never looked at me as I walked out the door.

I made my way downstairs and ran into Detective Steve Hurst. Steve was newly promoted to detective, having served on the Detroit police force for a couple of years before applying here to Royal Oak for the detective position. He was an extremely humorous young man who'd kept us all in stitches the night we'd gotten together to play poker. In fact, because he was so genuinely likable, I'd allowed him to count the change in his pocket as an article of clothing—otherwise he would have been wearing his birthday suit a whole lot sooner. "Hey, Abby!" he said jovially.

"Morning, Steve, how's it going?" I asked, turning to him and smiling broadly. Steve was cute in a boyish kind of way, with big green eyes, strawberry-blond hair and a quick smile. He had an energy that people just warmed to, and I imagined he was very good at gaining trust from people when it was necessary to do so quickly.

"Not bad . . . Hey, sorry to hear about your sister. How is she?"

"She'll be okay; thanks for asking," I said with a sigh.

"Give her my best, and you take care, you hear?" he said as he moved past me to head up the stairs.

I remembered something then, and before he'd gotten too far I called after him, "Hey, Steve, can I ask you a favor?"

"Sure, what's up?" he asked, pausing on the third stair from the top.

"If I needed to look at an old police file from a long time ago, how could I go about doing that?"

"Milo's got you helping out on some of our cold case files?" he asked, coming back down the stairs to stand next to me.

"Uh . . . yeah . . . that's right, some cold case files. He gave me a copy of one that I've been tuning in on, but when I was looking through it I noticed that the second page was missing."

"How old is the case?" he asked, scratching his short-cropped hair.

"About twenty years."

"Well, most of the files that old are kept on microfiche down in the basement. Didn't Milo drag you down there when he gave you a copy of the file?"

"Uh, no . . . he actually had me pick it up. See, it was sort of my idea to look into it; the case is a missing woman who was the mother of a friend of mine. I asked Milo about it and he got me a copy of the file, but someone forgot to make a copy of the second page. I'd ask Milo again," I said, looking nervously up the staircase to the double doors, "but he's so wrapped up in this serial-rapist case, and I don't want to keep bothering him about stuff. Do you think you can spare me just five minutes to help find the file?"

"Sure, come on with me," he said, and motioned for me to follow him.

We headed down the stairs to the basement and

through a long corridor that dead-ended, forcing us to make a sharp left; then we went through some double doors and came to a large storage space with a microfiche machine, several tables and chairs, a copy machine and row upon row of filing cabinets.

Toward the back wall and sitting behind a short counter was a pretty young woman with slim features, a perky nose and flyaway brown hair, who looked up as we entered. Steve walked over to where she sat sorting and organizing a gigantic stack of files. "Hey, Kristy, how are ya?" Steve said fondly to her.

"I'm fine, Detective Hurst. What brings you down to the dungeon this morning?"

"Well, this," he said, indicating me standing right behind him, "is Abigail Cooper. She's helping us with a case or two, and she wants to have a look at a cold case file. I'll vouch for her if you help her out, okay?"

"Sure," Kristy said. "No sweat."

With that Steve patted me good-naturedly on the shoulder and said, "Kristy'll take good care of you. Good luck, and I'll catch you babes later."

"Thanks, Steve, see ya," I said with a grateful smile as he walked back out the double doors.

After Steve had gone I turned back to Kristy and said, "Hi. I don't have a case number or file number, but I do have a first and last name—is that enough?"

Kristy swiveled in her chair to her computer and set her hands just above the keyboard. "Not a problem. What's the last name?"

"Kapordelis—that's spelled K-A-P-O-R-D-E-L-I-S."

"First name?"

"Dora."

Kristy typed in the information and hit the search key. We both waited while the computer thought through the request, then bleeped that it had found something. "Yeah, here it is. Missing persons, huh?"

"That's the one. All I need is a copy of the second page of the police report. Can you help me find it?"

"Sure, just give me a minute," Kristy said, and scribbled down a number onto a sticky note. She then tore off the sticky note and walked over to one of the rows of filing cabinets. She came back a moment later with a roll of microfiche in her hand, and stepped purposefully over to the microfiche machine. She threaded a roll of film through the machine and pressed the forward button. We both watched in silence as the machine whirred and the film zipped by the viewer in a dizzying display of motion. Kristy then pressed the stop button, and I smiled as she had only to tab the film forward slightly to reach Dora's police report.

"You've done this before," I kidded.

"Oh, once or twice," she said, smiling. "Okay, so you just need the second page, right?"

"Yep, I have the rest; this one was the only page that got left out."

"Cool," Kristy said, and hit a button on the right side of the microfiche. The copier behind us whirred into action, and we both turned to look at it as the moving ray of light whined underneath the cover, and in a moment a copy appeared in the tray.

I smiled at Kristy, who was already rewinding the film, and picked up the paper, folding it twice and shoving it into my purse. I'd look at it later tonight and see if there was anything there worth tuning in for. "Thanks so much, Kristy; you're the best!" I said as I headed for the door.

"No problem. It was nice meeting you," she sang as I waved good-bye through the double doors.

Quickly I headed back upstairs. I figured it was only a matter of time before Milo heard I was poking around in some old police file and came down here to investigate. On my way up I ran into the same officer who had picked me up that morning, and asked him for a ride back home. He looked a little annoyed to be playing taxi, but agreed after only two heavy sighs and an eye roll.

The officer dropped me at the curb, and I made my way to my front door. Reaching for the door handle, though, I caught myself, and felt icy panic run down my spine. My door was not only unlocked, but partially open. Someone was inside, waiting for me, and I had a feeling it wasn't the welcome wagon.

I pushed the door open and hesitated on the porch, waiting for something from inside to jump out at me. Nothing happened, but the distinct odor of cigar smoke wafted out to assault my nasal passages. I grimaced in distaste and peered into my vestibule. Two figures sat, fat and troll-like, on my suede couch, dripping cigar ashes onto my wool rug and smearing the air with puffs of acrid odor from the fat Cubans dangling from their mouths.

The first thing I noticed, other than their smelly cigars, was how ugly they were. One was short and incredibly fat; his face looked like it'd been squashed in an elevator and stayed permanently scrunched. His complexion was heavily pockmarked, and his eyes were small and sunken as they stared unblinking in my direction. He reminded me of a goblin, errant in his mission back to Hades after Halloween.

The other one was tall and rickety. His posture was bent forward, giving him a sinister cast. His face was narrow and pinched, his nose a little too long, and his lower lip fell away from his bottom teeth, giving the appearance of a snarl. All he needed was a pair of bat wings to protrude out his back and he could have been the model for one of the gargoyles atop Notre Dame.

"There's no smoking allowed here, boys," I said coolly as I stepped into my home. I was seriously hoping that my bravado would hide the fact that I was scared witless.

It was obvious Andros had sent his henchmen to fetch me, but the question was why. The men stood as one, and regarded me. Gargoyle smiled evilly at Goblin and said, "No problem; we'll put these out right away." And with that he dropped his cigar on my rug and ground his heel into the butt, smearing ash and tobacco on one of the colored squares. Damn it, I loved that rug.

"Nice," I said giving him my best "Jerk!" expression. Goblin watched the exchange, chuckling, the sound like coins rattling in the dryer. Then he too dropped his cigar, mimicking Gargoyle and smearing a separate spot of ash and tobacco, causing both men to cackle like witches.

Watching them I was seething with rage, but what

could I do? I had no choice but to wait the bastards out until finally they'd had enough at my expense.

When they'd finished laughing they turned as one in my direction, and without another word they walked to me and motioned toward the door.

I pivoted on my heel and stepped outside, walking just ahead of them, when I noticed a car just down the street suddenly come to life and meet us at the bottom of the walkway. Goblin held open the door, and obediently I got in. Gargoyle came around to the other side, and blocked my exit by getting in and sandwiching me in between both of them.

When all the doors were closed, we took off through my neighborhood, headed to the highway, then downtown.

This time I didn't look out the window; I was too busy worrying about what this impromptu visit was all about. I didn't know if Andros had tired of me, or if he'd decided I knew too much, or if perhaps he'd found out about my connection to Dutch. What I was terribly afraid of was that all of those things were distinct possibilities, and that perhaps it was my turn to be fitted for a pair of cement-soled shoes—size nine.

We reached the Kapordelis estate twenty minutes later, and I was allowed to exit the car without a great deal of manhandling. We walked through the enormous front door, down the same corridors and hallways I had previously been escorted through, and came to a rest in front of the closed double wooden doors leading to Andros's study. Goblin pointed to a chair set off to the right of one of the doors, and I took a seat as I waited to meet my doom.

Chapter Thirteen

Time ticked slowly by as I waited inside the Kapordelis household. I could hear muffled voices coming from inside Andros's study, but was unable to make out any words. Gargoyle and Goblin stood sentinel on both sides of the doorway, their vapid stares into space giving credence to my suspicion of their lack of intelligence. I scowled as I looked at them. The only thing worse than being kidnapped by dangerous mobsters was being kidnapped by *dumb* dangerous mobsters.

Finally the double doors opened, and a familiar figure walked out. I sucked in a breath of surprise and quickly looked at the floor, trying desperately to conceal my face. I hardly needed the effort; Officer Shawn Bennington strolled out of Andros's office with a sickening grin and a sweaty wad of money folded in his pudgy little hand. He was busy counting it as he absently followed Gargoyle out the way we'd come.

As I stared at Bennington's back, a cold chill tickled its way along my spine, and I remembered the parking ticket written by Bennington that I'd smugly handed over to Andros. In an instant I knew I'd made a big mistake, and Dutch was now in trouble. Big trouble.

And presently I was in no position to help him. In fact, I suddenly realized, I could very well be in the exact same predicament.

I looked to Goblin, whom I expected to wave me into Andros's study, but instead he poked his head inside briefly, then closed the doors again and waited with me outside the doors. Ten minutes or so ticked by as my knee began to jump and dance with my worry. I had to get a warning to Dutch, but how? How could I possibly do that now?

Movement to my left caught my attention, and I looked up to see a man of medium height with a forgettable face stroll into view. He paused outside the double doors and regarded me, and as I met his eyes I had the distinct impression we'd met before. He smiled slightly, inclining his head, then pulled open the doors and went inside. I blinked several times, wondering if I'd really seen what I thought I'd seen. The man seemed to know me, but I couldn't place his face.

As my knee bounced I worried over it, until a short time later, when the man appeared again, this time ignoring me as he walked quickly away. I watched his back as he disappeared down the hallway, and then I remembered something that sent a chill up my spine. I was sure I'd met him before, but I couldn't recall his face. The only thing that seemed even remotely familiar was the way he had looked at me; there was a way about his eyes that tickled my memory banks . . . and then I had it. The man who had just come out of Andros's study was the hit man I'd read for at the wedding.

I tried to swallow the lump that had just formed in the back of my throat, but I couldn't seem to manage any saliva. Just then Goblin opened one of the doors and motioned me inside. On shaking legs I walked forward into the den of the lion and faced Andros, fat and pungent in his big leather chair behind the monstrous desk.

"Miss Cooper, you disappoint me," he began, getting directly to the point.

"How's that?" I asked as I took a seat and met his stare.

"I had hoped you would keep the police out of the picture, and my staff informs me that you were downtown at the station for several hours this morning."

My heart was hammering in my chest. Oh, God, he thought I'd leaked information to the police. I had to think fast. "On the contrary, Mr. Kapordelis, it's you who disappoint me."

Andros regarded me with a dangerous look. I was pushing his buttons, and he was quickly losing patience. "Excuse me?" he asked in a voice that gave me the willies.

"You gave me an incomplete file on Dora."

Andros leaned forward, his beefy upper body resting on his elbows as he perched on the desk. "What do you mean?"

"The file you gave me on Dora—the police report in it was missing the second page. I was asked by Detective Johnson to come down to the police station to verify some facts on my sister's case, and while I was there I was able to go through the original police report on Dora's disappearance."

Andros tapped his fingers across his desk as he thought about what I'd said. I took the opportunity to offer a little proof of my story. "See, I've got a copy of the second page right here," I said as I leaned over and picked up my purse. Before I could fully lift it to my lap my arm was halted midmotion as a large, viselike hand gripped mine and painfully yanked the purse out of my grasp. Another henchman I hadn't even been aware of had come from somewhere in the room to protect Andros from any false moves.

The man who stood above me was tall like Gargoyle, but not nearly as thin. He was younger too, with jet-black hair and olive skin. He had broad shoulders, and would have been handsome were it not for the grim expression that turned his features angry and mean.

I watched helplessly as he ripped open my purse and began to rifle through it, no doubt looking for the Stealth Bomber I kept hidden in my small change pocket. Finally, after rooting through hair spray, lipstick, wallet, gum, keys and a few unmentionables, Grim pushed the purse back at me and stepped to the far side of the room. I sighed my irritation and pulled out the now-crumpled copy of the second page of Dora's police report, handing it over to Andros for observation.

"Now, if all I wanted to do was point the police in your direction, why would I take a copy of Dora's police report with me from the station? I mean, if I'd told the police about you, do you think I'd still be working on finding your wife?"

Andros looked from the crumpled paper to me, then back again. I noticed that his hand shook slightly as he held the paper, either from pain or too much medication. But I had a hard time feeling sorry for the bastard.

"I remember this page," he said slowly. "I think Madame Jarosolov took it from the file when she had it."

"Yeah, well, there may be something there that I can focus on to get a bead on Dora. I'm surprised you wouldn't have thought about getting me the complete file to begin with; after all, you do want to find her, don't you?"

Andros regarded me the way a lion regards a pesky mosquito, and tossed the paper back in my direction with irritation. "Take the paper, Miss Cooper, and find my wife. I'm giving you three days from today. If you're as good as you say you are, you should have no more trouble. Oh, and no more visits to the police department . . . you now have everything you need to find my wife. Are we clear?"

Relieved beyond measure that I'd pulled my escape off so easily, I stood quickly and tucked the copy of the report into my purse. Turning toward the door before Andros had a chance to change his mind, I said, "We are perfectly clear, Mr. Kapordelis. See you in a few days." Bravely I marched forward and put my hand on the door handle, pausing for the briefest of seconds to see if anyone would try to stop my progress. No one did, so I pulled open the door and stepped through quickly, walking down the hallway like I owned the place, hoping no one would notice and bar my exit.

To my immense relief I made it to the car without incident, and took my seat on the large leather cushion, waiting for someone to climb in with me. Instead, Goblin—who had followed briskly after me out of the house—shut the door behind me from the outside and then pounded on the side of the car, letting the driver know to leave.

Without further ado I was headed toward home, and as we pulled out of the driveway and onto Lakeshore Drive I wanted to sob with relief; somehow I had made it out alive. Now all I had to do was warn Dutch the moment I reached home. I tapped my foot anxiously on the carpeted floor of the car as I willed the driver to hurry, but as we got onto the highway all thoughts of making it home quickly evaporated.

There was a major traffic jam, and cars were bumper-to-bumper as far as the eye could see. My intuition was buzzing in the back of my head, and the only reccurring thought I seemed to be able to focus on was that I had to warn Dutch—now . . . there was no time to lose. I eyed my purse on the floor of the sedan, and with a racing heart reached into it and pulled out my cell phone. I had to be quick and clever, and I wondered if I'd get away with the conversation I was about to have. As I flipped open the phone and began to dial I happened to look up suddenly, and I noticed the driver of the car watching me intently from the front seat. I had to be careful here, very, *very* careful.

Plastering a relaxed, almost bored expression onto my face and ignoring the driver, I waited as the phone on the other end rang once, twice, then three times before it was finally picked up and I heard Milo announce, "Johnson," into the mouthpiece.

"Hey there," I said anxiously.

"Abby?" Milo asked while I watched the driver's eyes stare suspiciously at me in the rearview mirror.

"I have a message from Edgar," I said.

"Who?"

"Edgar," I enunciated. "He wants to warn you that you need to call his partner in Holland tonight. He said he knows it may be kind of tough to reach him, but that he thinks you've got the number, correct?"

There was a long pause while Milo tried to figure out

my coded message. Finally he asked in a hushed tone, "Abby, are you in trouble?"

"Nope," I said, "But Edgar thinks there's something really bad brewing in Holland and that's why you need to call. Got it?"

"Yeah, you want me to call Dutch, I got it, but you're going to fill me in on why later on, right?"

"Sounds good. Talk to you soon, buddy," I said and flipped the cell phone closed as I stared out the window, sighing heavily as if I were bored. Inside my stomach was in knots and my heart was beating so loudly that I thought I was going to pass out, but somehow I managed to hold it together.

It took us nearly an hour to make it back to my house, and after getting out of the car I practically bolted to the front door. Frantically I fished for my keys; then I remembered I hadn't had a chance to lock the door when Goblin and Gargoyle had kidnapped me. I turned the knob quickly and walked inside, slamming it shut behind me and throwing the bolt home.

I laid my head against the door for a moment, collecting myself, then pushed away from it and surveyed the room. The smell of burned carpet and pungent cigar smoke still hung heavily in the air. Deciding the smell was too much, I held my nose and went upstairs to my bedroom, which had been shut off from the rest of the house because of the cold. I opened my bedroom door and stepped inside, shivering a little at the coldness of the room and my own fear, and quickly closed the door behind me. Next I turned on the space heater, and after a few minutes the room became comfortable.

Not knowing what else to do, I sat on the bed for a long moment and thought about how to get myself out of the mess I was in. I felt like there was a way out, but I was a long way from it. I prayed that Milo had gotten a warning to Dutch, and that he was okay. I'd have to let Milo know about Bennington, but for now all I could do was hide away in my bedroom and wait . . . for what I didn't know, but something big was about to happen; I just knew it.

As the room heated up, I felt my eyelids begin to

droop. With all the adrenaline and stress from the past few weeks, I figured I could really use a power nap, so I reclined on my pillows and huddled underneath one of the thick afghans on my bed. In moments I was asleep.

I was aware that I was in a familiar place, but that didn't make me feel at ease. I looked around the large parking lot, nervous for reasons I couldn't remember. I saw a grocery store in the distance, and a post office next to that, and for some reason that alarmed me.

A figure appeared and began to walk toward me. I didn't like the figure, but I couldn't remember why. Before he got close enough to recognize, I turned and ran out of the parking lot as fast as I could. Suddenly a Krispy Kreme doughnut shop appeared in front of me, and I ran inside. The doughnut shop was bright and warm, and I felt safer here. I took in the surroundings. I appeared to be alone, but there was something odd about the place. All the doughnuts were displayed in a coffin, and I couldn't figure out why that didn't make sense. I approached the counter to get a closer look, and from out of the back walked J. R. Ewing sporting a ten-gallon hat, a flashy gold sheriff's star on his right lapel and a brilliant smile.

I was shocked by his appearance, but he seemed to know me, and for some reason that put me at ease. "Hello, little lady," he said winningly. "I bet you're here for the special of the day."

I nodded yes, even though I didn't know what the special of the day was. "Well, come around the counter, missy, and have a look!" J.R. said.

Without hesitation I rounded the corner and walked to where he pointed. "It's back there," he said, indicating an elaborately decorated doorway with beautiful stenciled vines and flowers snaking their way along the frame of a large wood door.

The door itself was bright yellow, and seemed so inviting I had to go in. "Uh, hold on there just a sec," J.R. said, making me wait a moment. "You almost forgot your tea." And he handed me a cup of tea that smelled divinely sweet. I took a sip, and it was delicious except for the little particles of tea leaves still floating in the liquid. I smiled politely at J.R. and moved again toward the door. Just as I reached for the door handle, someone from behind grabbed me and whirled me around, sending my tea smashing against the doughnut-filled coffin.

It was the masked postman, and his eyes told me he was furious. He raised his arm, and a tire iron caked in blood loomed over my head, ready to crash down on me. I screamed at the top of my lungs and sat straight up in bed, sweat soaking my clothes and my breath coming in short bursts of fright.

I looked around the room, for a moment confused by my surroundings. When it finally registered that I'd just had a simple nightmare and that I was okay, I was able to get my breathing under control. After a few minutes I rolled my feet over the edge of the bed, and got up to change out of my damp clothes.

I slipped on a pair of fresh undies, jeans and another woolly sweater; all the while the fragments of the dream buzzed around in my head. I was certain there were several clues my guides were trying to get to me, but I wasn't certain how they all fit together. As soon as I'd dressed I looked around for something to write on, and remembered I had a small notebook in my purse. I grabbed my purse, plopped back down onto the bed, got out the pad of paper and a pen and quickly jotted down the dream.

After I was finished, my eye kept coming back to the Krispy Kreme doughnut shop. What was the deal with J. R. Ewing? I thought about my childhood memories of the show *Dallas,* and smiled at how hooked I'd been on the show. I sighed and put the pad aside for a minute, letting my mind wander.

I thought more about the dream, but nothing was really coming together for me, so I flipped on the television, thinking I could change the subject for a while, then go back to it later.

After surfing through a couple of channels I landed on the news. There was a breaking story, and goose bumps lined my arms even before the news anchor turned quickly to a reporter on the scene outside of a Detroit police station.

"Thank you, Nancy. I'm at Detroit's East Precinct, where the body of a man pulled out of the Detroit River three days ago and riddled with bullets has been positively identified as Giolini Garzopolis. . . ." A mug shot appeared on the screen, and I felt my stomach drop to the floor. The mug shot was of Goon.

I stopped listening to the reporter for a moment, and focused on the face, shock and panic raising my heart rate. A moment later the mug shot disappeared, and I had no choice but to listen to the reporter again as she rattled off the details: ". . . suspected of being connected to the Greek Mafia. It is unknown when Mr. Garzopolis was murdered, but the coroner's report suggests that it was sometime late last week.

"Also, a few minutes ago I was able to interview Detective Milo Johnson of the Royal Oak Police Department, who has come down to Detroit's East Precinct looking for a possible connection between Mr. Garzopolis and the serial rapist who has been stalking that Detroit suburb. It is unclear at this time what that connection may be, but we will be following this story closely, and update you as details develop.

"Reporting live from Detroit's east side, this is Elizabeth Johansson for Fox Two News."

I clicked the television off and sat back against the pillows on the bed. My brow furrowed as I tried to make sense of Goon's murder. Intuitively I knew that Andros had ordered the hit, but why? Why would Kapordelis want Goon dead? Suddenly my intuition buzzed again, and the image of a canary popped into my head.

Goon was killed because Kapordelis thought he'd snitch about something? I asked mentally.

Right side, light airy feeling . . . My sign for yes.

Well, that explains why I haven't seen Goon since Cat's attack. He must have been killed right after I agreed to do the project with Andros. . . .

Just then I had a terrible thought, and I bolted up and

swiveled my feet to the floor, bracing myself with my hands as adrenaline coursed through my body.

If Kapordelis saw the newscast, he would now know that the Royal Oak PD had made a connection between Goon and the rapist; but what Andros *didn't* know was that Milo had gotten *that* particular link from a video surveillance tape—and not from me.

My mouth went dry as I realized that Andros would most definitely make the conclusion that I had lied to him, and I alone had tipped off Milo . . . which, of course, meant that I was now a sitting duck. A chill swept through me as I remembered Dutch saying that Kapordelis's goons were close by and watching my house.

Oh, no!

At the exact moment I had that thought I heard a tremendous *wham!* against my front door. Someone was breaking into my house. Startled, I jumped off the bed and grabbed the cordless. I clicked the on button and dialed 911, then put the phone to my ear and listened to silence. The phone was dead. I depressed the on button twice more, each time raising it to my ear, but no sound came on the line. My phone line had been cut. Panicking now, I searched the room trying to think. Spying my purse I grabbed it and snatched out my cell phone. Quickly I dialed 911 and before the operator even had a chance to speak I screamed my address into the receiver and begged the dispatcher to send the police.

Wham! . . . crack . . ."

My front door was giving way!" Please hurry!" I begged and clicked off the phone. I then turned in a circle. . . . What to do? Where to go? Quickly I shuffled into my loafers and grabbed my purse again, opening my bedroom door and looking toward the stairs.

Wham! . . . Wham! More wood splintering.

I was about to rush out of my room, down the stairs and out the back door, but quickly thought better of it— they were probably waiting for a move exactly like that and had someone at my back door just in case I decided to run out that way.

Wham! . . . Wham! . . . Wham!

"Damn!" I whined as I shut my bedroom door again and turned in a circle, searching the room for a hiding place. Just then my eye fell on the small door to my attic, and without further hesitation I ran to it, heaving it open, then ducking through into the cold, dark space of my attic as I quickly shut the door behind me.

I squinted into the fading light, searching for a place to hide, my vision obscured by the dimness. Suddenly I heard the front door give way, and instinct pushed me deeper into the room as I walked carefully over piles of old clothes and boxes of junk while my eyes darted around, looking for someplace to hide. Just then, through the darkness of the room, I saw to my immense relief a large black trunk that I'd had since college. It was an ancient relic I'd picked up at a flea market, and I knew from memory that it was also empty.

As quietly as I could I stepped over several more piles of clothes and lifted the lid of the trunk. I'd be cramped in here, but I could fit. Swiftly I wrapped my purse strap over my head and plunged inside, even as I heard thunderous footsteps on the stairs. Quickly I reached over my head and closed the lid as quietly as I could, trying not to quiver too much and make the trunk rattle. I knew that if Kapordelis's men found me, I was as dead as Goon.

From inside the trunk I heard my bedroom door open, and not a moment later the contents of my room began to crash against the walls as if they were being strewn around like so much trash. I kept as still as I could in the trunk, waiting . . . barely breathing, my heart hammering in my chest so forcefully it hurt. I could hear at least two men shouting and yelling in Greek. There was more furniture tossing, and what I gathered were several colorful descriptors of me and my mama in Greek.

After a few minutes I heard one of the men tramp his way back downstairs, while the other creaked the floorboards as he walked the hallway to my bathroom. After rooting around in my shower, he came back to my bedroom and tossed some more furniture around, cursing loud enough for me to hear. Finally he must have noticed the small door to the attic, because I heard it being tugged violently open.

I stopped breathing and closed my eyes in fear as I heard him come into the attic and kick aside boxes and clothing. I knew it was dark up here, and prayed that he wouldn't see the trunk, which was tucked into the far back corner of the attic. Because it was black, it wouldn't stand out unless you knew it was there—or so I hoped.

Even so, I heard my intruder's footsteps coming near, and I tried to make myself smaller. I could hear him approach, one step at a time, closer and closer. He was going to find me . . . I was done. The footsteps stopped right in front of the trunk; silent tears fell down my cheeks because I knew it was over. He was two seconds away from killing me, and I hadn't had a chance to say my good-byes to anyone I loved. Just then, however, through the leather of the trunk came a commotion from downstairs, and after a moment I clearly heard someone yelling, "Police! Police!" from the stairwell, even as the sound of sirens reached my ears, and I wanted to sob in relief.

The man hovering over my hiding space paused for only a moment; then to my disbelieving ears I heard him dart quickly back through the attic opening. I prayed he'd leave the house quickly with the other man, and bit my lip anxiously as I listened to his footsteps stop in my bedroom, where he lingered for a moment or two. Then, to my great relief, he finally barreled down the stairs, and I heard no more from anyone except the sound of approaching sirens.

Slowly, cautiously, I opened the lid to the trunk and sat up, shivering with adrenaline. I took just a moment as the sirens grew closer and closer to try to collect myself, breathing deeply and trying not to hyperventilate . . . and that was when I smelled the first hint of smoke as a foggy tendril snaked its way through the doorway to the attic and circled the room like a hungry serpent.

Chapter Fourteen

Alarm made my eyes bulge and my knuckles turn white against the sides of the trunk as I sniffed the air. My heart began to thud hard in my chest again even as the smoke alarm sounded, and with mounting terror I knew my house was on fire.

Without further hesitation I bolted out of the trunk and rushed to the attic door, which was still partially open. I looked through the opening to my bedroom, which was alight with red flames of fire growing larger by the nanosecond. Before my eyes my window treatments billowed and danced with flames, my bookcase smoked with acrid black fumes, and my bedspread was one giant red-orange ball, and all I could do was stand there, too stunned by the horror of it to move.

Something instinctual snapped me out of my shock, and I slammed the attic door closed, but the smoke was quickly growing in intensity. I looked around the attic, searching for a way out . . . but the door behind me was the only way in or out, and I realized with horror that I was now trapped!

In seconds the smoke became thicker and thicker, and suddenly I could no longer see. Remembering my fire-safety class from grade school, I dropped to my knees and began to crawl away from the bedroom toward the outer wall. The smoke was choking me, and I had to drop lower and lower to find any form of suitable air. I was so terrified I began to sob hysterically; I have a tremendous fear of fire, and it was all I could do not to faint from fright.

I reached the far end of the attic, coughing and choking now as I clawed at the wall, pleading out loud for someone to help me. There was a roaring sound behind me as the fire feasted itself on the contents of my bedroom, and I inched along the wall, pounding on it and screaming for help. I couldn't see; my eyes were forced closed by the biting sting of the smoke. I couldn't breathe either, and I knew I was losing consciousness. I put every ounce of effort into inching across the floor, pounding on the wall, screaming at the top of my lungs, when my hand pushed through a flimsy piece of plastic and my arm dangled out into the cool, crisp night air.

For a split second I didn't move, the sensation of my hand extending beyond the wall taking a moment to catch up with my panicked, oxygen-starved brain. Then I remembered.

Dave had told me about the small window he'd accidentally broken up here when he was trying to repair the rafters, and I remembered him telling me he'd replace it as soon as he was finished because he didn't want to risk breaking it again. He must have covered the opening with plastic to try to keep out the cold.

I shoved my face out of the window and gulped great gobs of air. My respite was short-lived, as the smoke now had a way out as well, and quickly took over the small window. With wobbly knees I stood up and pushed my body out of the opening. Behind me I could feel the heat of the smoke intensifying, beginning to burn my skin. I had seconds to live if I didn't get out now.

I pushed out of the window, still blind from the smoke, and something scratched at my arms and face. Synapses fired in my brain as I remembered that this window sat next to a huge evergreen that shaded my whole house on this side.

Coughing and choking, while trying to open my eyes a tiny fraction as they watered and stung, I felt around the prickly needles, and my hand connected with a thick branch. Without hesitation I grabbed the branch with one hand and swung out of the window, my grip barely holding me as I groped forward and got my legs around the trunk. I faced away from my house and clung to the tree, coughing and sputtering and trying not to pass out.

I had barely recovered myself when my back, which faced the house, started to feel hot, and I realized the room I'd just been in was completely ablaze by now, and flames were about to replace the smoke coming through the window. I had to get out of the tree before it too caught fire.

As quickly as I could I shimmied down the trunk, feeling my way because my eyes stung too much to open. My purse, still wrapped across my body, caught on a branch, and it took several panicky seconds to untangle myself before I finally got to the ground and crawled clear of the tree and the house.

Around the front I could hear sirens and shouting and someone screaming. Loudest of all, however, was the roar of the fire as it gorged on all of my treasures and memories. I sat there in the backyard for a long moment, staring through the small slits of my eyes as they watered out the toxins that still stung them, and a grief like I'd never known took hold deep in my heart.

It's a terrible thing to watch your world burn away before your eyes, and as long as I live I will never forget the misery of that moment.

Several minutes passed as my breathing, although still painful, slowly returned to normal. I was coughing only every third or fourth breath now, and I felt just about strong enough to stand again. I had to get some help, but everyone seemed to be at the front of the house. Dully, I stood up and swayed my way across the backyard, no longer looking at the house because it was gone and I knew it. I got to the back gate and peered through the opening, and what I saw stopped my heart cold.

Gargoyle and Goblin stood in my driveway with twisted little smirks on their ugly, dark faces. Around them were my neighbors, slack-jawed and terrified, some pointing to my house, others crying as if it were their own.

If I pushed through the gates I'd be met first by Gargoyle and Goon, but my neighbors, the police and fire department were also there, so how much danger could I still be in?

Just then my intuition buzzed loudly in my ear, and I turned my head out of sheer habit. *Don't . . .* circled around and around in my head. My hand rested on the gate as I debated what to do. *Don't!* my intuition screamed. Just then I was overcome by a succession of coughs, and I saw Gargoyle's head snap up in my direction. He couldn't see me through the gate, but I watched, horrified, as he slapped Goblin on the shoulder and the two quietly edged their way through the crowd in my direction.

Get away! my intuition screamed, and instinctively I backed away from the gate. As quickly as I could I darted into the shadows of the yard and around to the back shed. There was a bin where I stowed my compost back there, and without waiting I pulled myself up onto it and managed to swing my way over the back fence. I was rewarded with a couple of splinters, but with everything I'd been through in the last several minutes that was the least of my worries.

As quietly as I could I made my way across the yard of my neighbor, desperately trying not to make too much noise as dried leaves crunched softly under my shoes. I reached the driveway, eyeing the house nervously. Why, I didn't know, but I couldn't risk being seen right now. I knew that it was imperative that people presume I had died in that blaze, at least for the time being.

For the next hour I kept to the shadows, slowly making my way toward my office building, which was ten minutes by car or a half an hour on foot. Of course, if you're trying to be stealthy about it, you can add an extra twenty minutes.

Finally, nearly frozen by the cold of the November evening, I rounded the block my office was on, and walked quickly to the back of the building. It was now around eight thirty, and I figured just about everyone I had to worry about would be out of the building. Punching in my security code to the back door, I made my way quietly up the back stairs and cautiously down the hallway to my office. I let myself inside and avoided turning on the lights.

Instead I lit a candle from my reading room and walked around to my desk. Pulling out a key from my purse, I opened the bottom drawer and extracted a metal box with a lock. I inserted another key from my key chain and lifted the lid.

As I looked at the contents, a mixture of melancholy and relief flooded my numbed emotions. There was three thousand dollars in that box, and it was now that I remembered the last time I'd seen that money.

Three years earlier I'd had a vivid and powerful vision. I'd been meditating, and one of my guides had stepped forward with a very strong message. He had instructed me to gather three thousand dollars as quickly as I could and put it into a lockbox to be kept in the bottom drawer of my desk at the office. He told me point-blank that I was not to touch this money under any circumstances until such time as an absolute emergency required me to use it. I remember thinking that perhaps my imagination was playing tricks on me, but even as I had the thought something compelled me to comply.

It had taken me several months to gather the money, mostly because at the time I was also saving to buy a house—the very one that had now been reduced to ashes—but I'd managed it somehow. Over the years I'd forgotten about the box, but in my neighbor's backyard I'd suddenly remembered it, and I had a feeling that now was the time when it was safe to dip into the well.

I gathered up the money, tucking it into my purse, and then blew out the candle. I went back out into the hallway and made my way down the hall to the ladies' room, where I locked the door from the inside. I turned then and looked in the mirror and froze as I saw my reflection. I looked wretched.

Dark ash coated my skin, clothes and hair. My sweater

was torn, snagged and dirty; my face and arms were scratched and swollen. My eyes were puffy—slits, really—and a painful mask of remorse colored my expression. I quickly lowered my eyes, not wanting to look at the reflection any longer, and moved to the sink. I pulled off my sweater and turned on the faucet, letting the water warm my cold hands before I attempted to make myself presentable.

It took about twenty minutes, but eventually I was as clean as I could be. I'd wound my hair up into a tight bun, scrubbed the soot off the rest of me, and used just about every paper towel in the dispenser, but at least I looked somewhat passable. I eyed the sweater woefully—I hated to put that thing back on—when I remembered something that would be much better.

Quickly I gathered up the sweater and headed back down the hallway to my office, once again letting myself inside. I went to the spare office Theresa had once used and checked behind the door. There, to my great relief, was the bulging shopping bag from my sister, stuffed to the gills with clothes she'd purchased for me, and which I'd had every intention of returning. I lifted the bag, which was much heavier than I remembered, and smiled ruefully.

For once I was going to accept my sister's generosity without a fight. I fished around in the bag and retrieved a pair of black cotton pants and a beautiful cream-colored cashmere sweater. I decided not to look at the price tags as I got dressed; better to just assume they were expensive than to look at the price and remove all doubt. When I was dressed I went back to the shopping bag and fished around in it some more, smiling as my hand connected with a beautiful, thick, long black sweater coat that belted in the front. Thank God for Cat.

Quickly I wrapped myself in the sweater coat, then folded the other ruined sweater and my smelly jeans and looked around for something to put them in. I walked over to my garbage can and extracted the liner bag the cleaning crew supplied. I chucked the smelly clothes into the plastic bag, tucked them under my arm, grabbed the shopping bag and bolted out the door. Quickly I trotted down the hallway, taking the back stairwell, and exited the building.

I paused in the alley behind the building, looking around until I spied a large Dumpster, and without a thought I tossed in the ruined sweater and jeans and shut the lid. Then I headed across the street to the Greyhound bus station, where I intended to purchase a ticket for anything that would get me the hell out of Dodge. Pronto.

My options were reduced to Lansing, Milwaukee, or Toledo. I chose Toledo mostly for the fact that that bus was leaving in ten minutes. I took my ticket outside, got on the bus, found a seat all to myself in the back and bit my lip until we pulled out of the station.

Two hours later we arrived in Toledo, and I stepped off the bus and eyed the neighborhood. I saw a Motel 6 just down the block, and with a small sigh of relief I noticed a Wal-Mart about two blocks farther. I walked first to the motel and purchased a room for cash. Normally the nightly rate was forty bucks, but if you didn't want to present the clerk with ID it was an extra twenty. I wanted to remain incognito, so I gladly peeled off the extra bill.

I took the room key down to my room and unlocked the door, setting the shopping bag just inside without turning on the lights, then closed the door again and quickly headed back out into the crisp night air. It was chilly, about thirty-five degrees, and I wasn't dressed properly, but at least I had layers.

I hurried to Wal-Mart and walked into the brightly lit megastore, looking around for the section I wanted.

"Can I help you?" an elderly gentleman wearing a blue smock and a pin with a giant happy face asked me.

"Can you point me in the direction of women's underwear and the luggage department?"

"Women's lingerie is in aisle five, down this walkway to the left. Luggage is in aisle twenty-six, all the way to the back of the store, just past electronics."

"Thanks," I said, trying to smile but failing.

I grabbed a cart and hurried through the store,

snatching a six-pack of undies, two sports bras, socks, and, one aisle over, I grabbed a three-pack of men's white cotton T-shirts. Then I headed to the back of the building for a large duffel bag, and paused before checking out to soap, shampoo, conditioner, toothbrush, toothpaste, lotion and my usual mascara and blush. I also found a contact lens case and enough saline to wash out the soot still making my eyes sting.

Half an hour later I was back in my room, and I peeled off my clothes, carefully folding the new ones from Cat, and throwing my underwear and bra into the trash.

The shower felt wonderful and, exhausted as I was, I still stood there for nearly twenty minutes, shampooing and rinsing over and over until the smell of soot had been washed down the drain.

Pink from the hot shower I finally got out and wrapped myself in a towel. I walked back out to the room and snatched up two of the Wal-Mart bags. Bringing them into the bathroom I pulled out the pack of T-shirts, undies and cotton socks and put on a fresh pair of each. I then brushed my hair and paused for a moment to consider my image in the shadowy reflection of the still-steamed morror. It was my eyes that bugged me. They were flat and angry. I didn't like the thoughts that were swimming in them, so after a moment I looked away.

I dried my hair with the hotel's built-in dryer, but because I was so tired I left it slightly damp and headed back out into the room. The bed beckoned, but I had to come up with a game plan before I could even think about sleep. I sighed and rounded the bed, sitting down cross-legged on top of the covers. I put my head in my hands and closed my eyes. *What should I do now?* I asked in my mind.

Visit J.R., came the thought in answer.

I lifted my chin and cocked my head. *What?* I asked. *Visit J.R. . . .* came again.

My eye drifted to my purse just then, and I noticed the small notebook that I'd used when I'd written down the details of my dream tucked into the side pocket. I must have snatched it up when I'd been trying to hide from Goblin and Gargoyle. I got up from the bed and retrieved my purse. Pulling out the pad of paper, I went over the details of the dream again.

The message in my head was to visit J.R—so maybe I was supposed to go to Dallas?

Left side, heavy feeling . . . No.

Then where?

Krispy Kreme . . . drifted into my thoughts, and the image of the sheriff's star that J.R. had been wearing also appeared in my mind's eye.

My brow furrowed. The sheriff's star was easy enough—I was supposed to go to Texas. J.R. from my dream also confirmed that. What I couldn't figure out was where in Texas. I wasn't supposed to go to Dallas, but somewhere else, and if I took my guides literally, I was supposed to go to a doughnut shop.

I sighed heavily and looked back at my notes. I focused on the Krispy Kreme shop, and read the detail about all those Krispy Kremes laid out in the coffin, and that struck me as curious. Why would my guides want me to focus on the inside of a coffin? I worked through the metaphor out loud, "Doughnuts . . . coffin . . . Krispy Kremes . . . dead . . . corpse . . . Krispy Kreme . . . Oh, my God!" I gasped—I had it! "Corpus Christi, Texas!" I shouted out loud.

Right side, light, airy feeling . . . My sign for jackpot.

Quickly I grabbed the phone and dialed information. I got the number for Northwest Airlines reservations and dialed the number. An agent came on the line and I inquired about available flights out of Toledo to Corpus Christi, Texas. I'd have to switch planes in Houston, but if I made it onto the six thirty a.m. flight the next morning, I could be there by one thirty p.m. I eyed the bedside clock and moaned.

"Would you like for me to reserve your flight, ma'am?" the agent said.

I hesitated for a moment, about to say yes, then thought better of it and said, "No, thank you," and hung up. I'd have to show my ID tomorrow at the airport, which was bad enough. What I didn't want was for some-

Chapter Fifteen

When they talk about Texas being "big sky" country, they aren't kidding. I'd never been to Texas, so the wide-openness of the place took me by surprise. I'd watched from the plane as the topography changed beneath me, and long stretches of time passed where, below, there was only dry, baked earth.

After boarding a puddle jumper in Houston, I finally stepped off the plane onto terra firma in Corpus Christi without a clue as to what the hell to do next. I carried my duffel bag across the tarmac and into the airport, looking around with uncertainty. I noticed a group of people gathered by a sign that read, SHUTTLE, so I joined them, allowing fate to bring me to the next step.

My intuition had been unusually quiet since I'd purchased the ticket, which was either a sign of sleep deprivation, or my crew had no comment. At this point I was too tired to care.

The shuttle arrived and we all boarded. The driver asked each of us where we were headed, and I chose the same location as a young businesswoman with a pronounced Southern drawl who asked to be taken to the La Quinta inn.

one to run my credit report and find me too quickly. Yes, there would be a record of my taking a flight, but hopefully it would be at least a few days before someone thought to check with the airlines outside of Detroit. It was just safer right now to pay in cash.

I set the alarm for five, which was a mere four hours away, and turned out the light. In the dark I wept about the loss of my house and all my worldly possessions until exhaustion put me out of my misery.

She and I were the third stop, and I trailed behind her as we stepped off the shuttle and walked into the Spanish-style hotel with a gorgeous brick driveway, white stucco and a clay roof. The inn was large and homey, with a tasteful Southwestern feel and a welcoming attitude.

I waited behind the businesswoman while she checked in at the front desk; then, when she was safely out of earshot, I stepped up to the clerk and told him I didn't have a reservation but was in need of a room. He nodded and turned to his computer terminal, where, after clicking the keys in a brisk fashion, he located a room on the third floor.

"How long will you be staying, Ms. Masters?" I was using Cat's last name just in case.

"Two nights . . ." came out of my mouth before I even had a chance to consider it. I was a little surprised by my answer, but figured this was my guides' way of telling me I wasn't supposed to dawdle here.

I was also relieved when the clerk told me that it was sixty-five a night—the place looked a lot more expensive—and after forking over a thousand dollars for my plane ticket, I was trying to watch my p's and q's.

I paid the clerk, walked through the lobby to an elevator that took me up to the third floor without stopping, and found my room at the end of a long hallway. After turning on the lights, I dumped my duffel on the luggage rack and looked around the room with a blank stare, then moved to the bed and sat down. I hadn't slept on the plane, and I was so tired I could drop. I pulled off my shoes, and, after puffing up the pillows behind my head, I reclined with a heavy sigh against them. I closed my eyes with the intention of taking only a minute to think about what to do next, and a moment later I fell fast asleep.

I was on the tarmac after getting off the plane, and I was hungry. I wanted a snack before continuing my journey, and luckily there was a Krispy Kreme shop near the entrance to the terminal. I walked into the doughnut shop and looked around. The doughnuts were still in the coffin, which I found very funny, and J. R. Ewing beamed at me from behind the counter.

"Abigail!" he said brightly. "I'm so glad you made it. Listen, she's waiting for you right now. You don't want to be late. Here's your tea," he said as I looked at him with a puzzled expression. "She's right in through there," he said, pointing to a door I'd seen before but couldn't remember from where. The door frame was elaborately painted with a mixture of vines and flowers snaking their way in an arch over a brightly painted yellow door with the name "Cooper's Abby" across the top.

Weird, I thought, *that's my name—only backward.*

Curious about the door I began to step forward, when J.R. caught my arm and said, "Careful, missy; you don't want to get wet."

I looked down at my feet and noticed a large puddle just in front of the door, so I raised my foot to step over it and reached for the door handle. Before I could grasp it I was yanked violently from behind, and as I spun around I came face-to-face with Andros Kapordelis.

He gripped my arm tightly in his hand and pulled me close to him, spitting in my face as he shouted with rage, "Did you think you could get away with it too? Did you think I wouldn't find you? Did you think you could go to her and get away from me?"

I was terrified as I looked at him, his face bulging with sickness and gluttony, the smell of his cancer-ridden body putrid to my nostrils, and the spit from his mouth stinging like acid as he raged at me. I struggled in his grip, trying to pull away, but he held me tightly, his mouth turning into a vicious snarl as he refused to let go. I still had one hand free, and as I looked at it I was amazed that somehow I'd still managed to hold on to my tea. Without thinking I threw the scalding liquid into his face, and he howled in pain, letting go of me and clutching at his eyes, dragging the small bits of residue from the tea down his fat cheeks. I didn't waste a moment, but turned and ran . . . and fell right out of bed onto the floor.

I hovered there on all fours for a moment, my breathing rapid and my eyes wide, trying to process where I was and what was real from what was imagined. Finally I was able to calm down and sit back up on the bed. Quickly, while the dream was still fresh in my mind, I grabbed my notebook from my purse and began to scribble the details of the dream. I knew I was in the right town, but where I was supposed to go within the city I felt was hidden in the dream.

The door was significant; that I was sure of. In this most recent version, my name had been across the front of the door. Why?

Just then I had a sudden urge to look at a city map. I wasn't sure what I was looking for, but didn't pause long enough to ration it out. I got up and went over to the dresser, where a stack of Corpus Christi guide information lay for my perusal. I sifted through the flyers from tourist hot spots, restaurants, room service menus, etc., until I found a detailed map of the city. I brought it back over to the bed and began to read off the names of the streets: "Williams Street, Comanche Street, Lipan Street, Cooper's Alley . . ." I read aloud. "Holy cow!" I said as my eye zipped back to Cooper's Alley. "Cooper's Abby—Cooper's Alley!" That was it! I needed to go there. I darted a look at the clock. Three thirty. I had to hurry.

Quickly I shuffled into my shoes and grabbed my purse, then darted out of the room, down the elevator and out to the front drive. I asked the bellhop for a cab, and he picked up a small phone, dialed a number and told me to wait inside, that one would be by shortly.

I waited only ten minutes, tipped him a five and got into the cab.

"Where to, miss?" the cabbie asked.

"Downtown," I said, "to Cooper's Alley."

"What address on Cooper's, miss?"

"Doesn't matter. Just get me there—pronto."

Fifteen minutes later the cabbie dropped me at the corner of Cooper's and Mesquite Street in downtow Corpus Christi. My intuition had begun to ring no and it was hard for me to focus on anything b humming sound buzzing through my mind. I looked west first, and felt my left side grow heavy. I turned east and began walking in the direction of the water. I didn't know what I was looking for, so I just kept walking.

Around me the city bustled with energy. Corpus Christi is a beautiful place that hugs the warm waters of the Gulf Coast tightly in the southernmost tip of Texas. The streets are wide and warm; a gentle breeze continually blows off the water. The temperature was quite comfortable, hovering around seventy-four degrees. Cooper's Alley is in the heart of the shopping district, and all around me were clothing stores, boutiques and souvenir shops. None of them held my attention.

While I walked down the bustling sidewalk, I became conscious of the fact that I had tucked my ponytail into my shirt and that I was walking with my head swiveling from side to side as I took note of my surroundings and the people who passed me. Ever since Cat had been attacked I'd been more careful when I was out and about. It dawned on me that Milo was now going it alone without my input, and just two days remained before Thursday—the next time the rapist would attack. I shivered involuntarily as I thought about what poor woman would become his next victim, but pushed that thought aside because I couldn't do a thing right now to alter it. I reminded myself that if I didn't find a way out of the mess I was in, there wouldn't be much I could do to help the police find the rapist in time anyway.

After walking several blocks I came to a side street and crossed at the light. The moment I got across my left side began to feel heavy. I stopped midstride and thought for a moment, then turned around and crossed back across the street, heading west. Within seconds after reaching the corner my left side again felt heavy. I stopped again and looked back the way I'd come. *Okay . . . I'm supposed to stop somewhere around here,* I thought.

I walked back to the side street and looked up at the street sign, which read, WATER STREET. Something tickled my brain, and I reached into my purse and pulled out my notebook. I flipped through several pages and read the notes from the part of my dream when I'd been about to go through the door and J.R. had warned me about getting my feet wet. The puddle lay just in front of the door with my name. Yep, Water Street was where I was supposed to go. I turned the corner and began to head down the south side of Water Street, and suddenly I stopped dead in my tracks as I looked just up the street on the north side and saw a large painted sign hanging over a door that said, J.R.'s ANTIQUES.

Quickly I crossed over to the other side, intent on getting to J.R.'s. Just before I got there I stopped dead in my tracks again. Right next to the antique shop was an elaborately painted door frame, with stenciled vines and flowers snaking their way up the archway as they framed a brightly colored yellow door. I looked up at the sign above the doorway: BRISHKA'S TEAROOM scrawled its way in gold calligraphy just above my head.

I walked forward and opened the door, my sixth sense buzzing and snapping with excitement. Inside my nostrils were greeted by the most delicious scent. Something sweet and citrus was in the air. I looked around the room and took in the quaint scene.

The entire tearoom was painted a tranquil mint green that was soothing to the eye while two white ceiling fans spun from the ceiling, creating a gentle breeze and circulating the scent of citrus.

Within the main dining room to my left there were only four tables demurely set with wrought-iron chairs decorated in colorful pastel ribbons that zigzagged through the iron slots and matched the overstuffed cushions on each chair. The tabletops were white marble, and each held a tray of creamer, sugar and assorted sweeteners. Along one back wall was a bookcase lined with dozens of used books and a sign that read, TAKE ONE HOME; BRING ONE BACK, secured to the wall above it.

To my right a large display case filled with sumptuous-looking pastries tempted even the most hardened dieter. I moved over to the case and peered in. There were tarts, croissants, scones and cinnamon buns dripping in icing, and huge muffins of a dozen flavors. As I sniffed the air I could also smell a hint of yeast lingering on t' breeze of the ceiling fans, no doubt the scent coming from baking done earlier that day.

To the left of the display case sat a giant urn and a chalkboard that listed the prices for the delicacies in the case. As I scanned the chalkboard, my stomach rumbled. I hadn't eaten a thing in almost two days.

Just then a tall, thin woman with silver-blond hair emerged from behind a curtain, which led, I guessed, to the kitchen and baking ovens in the back. She was startled to see me, and her hand came up to her chest when she gasped and said, "Oh, my! I'm sorry; I didn't know anyone had come in. Have you been waiting long?"

I smiled at her, liking her energy. "No, not at all. I'm really hungry, though. Can I order something?"

"Of course," she said, and waved me closer to the display case. I ordered a cinnamon scone and a blueberry muffin. I figured I deserved a carbo load.

"Anything else?" she asked.

"Yeah, can you tell me what that amazing smell is?" I asked, taking an extra big whiff.

The woman smiled and laughed. "That's our special home-brewed tea. Would you like a cup?"

"Yes, please."

"And would you like that with a reading?"

I paused, cocking my head as my intuition went haywire. Had I just heard her ask me what I thought she'd asked me? *Right side, light, airy feeling!* my intuition urged. "Uh, sure, throw that in too."

"Okay. It's good you got here when you did. Brishka was just about to go home for the night. You can have a seat anywhere, and when you've finished your tea I'll send her out for your reading, okay?"

I nodded, just a little mystified, and took a cup of the steaming liquid and my pastries over to a table, where I quickly sat down. I took a sip of the slightly orange-brown liquid and rolled my eyes up into my head—it was that good.

The tea was sweet and citrusy, yet light and smooth. I drank it and tried not to make too much of a display as I wolfed down the scone and the muffin, wondering what this Brishka woman was all about.

I'd been read several times in my life by other psychics, but I didn't tend to seek them out. Typically other psychics would come to me and ask for a trade, and it was always fun to compare styles and information.

Kendal was by far the best psychic I'd ever come across, and because I'd encountered him early in my career, he'd been the bar against which I measured everyone else—including myself. I wondered where Brishka would fall, and at the same time I wondered why my guides had led me to her.

Conscious of the fact that Brishka was about to leave, I swallowed the rest of my tea and took the cup over to the woman at the counter, who smiled kindly and gave me a glass of water, instructing me to go back to the table while she got Brishka.

I waited only a few moments before the curtain parted and out stepped a plump woman about my height, with piles of long, curly hair and huge brown eyes. Her skin was dark and tanned, and her clothing slightly wild. She was purple from head to toe: Purple earrings dangled from her ears, purple lipstick covered her mouth, a purple cotton shirt gripped her round body like a second skin, and a long, flowing purple prairie skirt swished about her as she strode purposely over to me, holding my teacup in her hand.

I guessed her to be in her late fifties to early sixties, but she'd held herself together quite well. Her cheeks were soft but unlined, her jaw strong and square, her lips full and pensive. There was an energy about her that was powerful, and for a moment I let my eyes go unfocused and looked at the space just above her head. Her aura came quickly into view, and I knew immediately this woman was quite gifted.

She came to the table and thrust her hand forward. "Hello," she said in a thick Slavic accent, "I am Brishka."

"Abby," I said as I shook her hand, waiting for her to take the lead. Brishka sat down and nodded at me, then closed her eyes for the briefest moment, and snapped them open to peer into my teacup.

"So . . ." she began, "you also have da sight."

I let my eyebrows dance up twice in a conspiratorial fashion, which caused Brishka to smile back as she continued. "You are visiting us from far avay, no?"

I nodded.

"You come from da Nort, no?"

I nodded again.

Brishka closed her eyes, sorting through the messages. "Do you know Andrew?" she asked me, and I felt a chill go through my bones.

"Yes," I said. I knew she had picked up on Andros.

"He is very bad man," she said as she looked at me. "Is dis your boyfriend?"

"No," I answered.

"Vell, you need to stay avay from dis Andrew. He's a bad man."

I nodded.

"Besides, dere is anoter man you like. A blonde—he is from Europe, no?"

I smiled. Dutch wasn't from Europe, but his nickname definitely connected him.

"He has a dangerous job, dough; he is policeman, correct?"

"Yes."

"You need to tell dis man from Europe to be very careful. Dere is something between him and dis Andrew here, and it is not good. I tink dis Andrew is jealous of dis man from Europe, and he's up to no good."

Goose bumps lined my arms, and I involuntarily shivered. Brishka looked at me sternly and said, "You go to funeral soon. Very sad for you, but you vill remember life goes on."

I sat back in my chair and my eyes grew wide. "Whose funeral?" I asked urgently.

"Is a man you know. He took chance and lost. But life goes on . . ." Brishka said matter-of-factly.

I was still chewing on that when she continued as if she'd just informed me that there was a cold front moving in and I'd need a sweater. "You look for new house, no?" she asked me.

I wasn't prepared for that, and my expression became tight as I fought to control my emotions. I'd done my best not to think about the fire, and unexpectedly, here it was again. After a moment I said, "Yes. Yes, I think I might be."

"Good. Your last place was crap. Dis next home vill be good. Less vork, more fun. You vait; you see."

I nodded.

"So, vat questions you have for me?"

I looked at her and considered my question for a long, tense moment before I finally asked, "How is it, Madame Jarosolov, that you managed to get away from Andros Kapordelis without losing your life?"

Chapter Sixteen

Madame Jarosolov's reaction was not one I had anticipated. After the briefest stunned silence between us she
jumped up with such force that she knocked over the
chair and nearly toppled the table behind her. She reeled
away from me, spinning and scrambling her way backward toward the counter. From the back came the
woman who had worked the counter, who rushed out to
see what all the commotion was about. I had already
jumped up and now stood statue still, watching as Madame J's mouth opened and closed, and her hand
clutched at her chest, her breathing coming in great
gulps as she fought her way back to the counter.

"Brishka!" the first woman shouted as she reached
Madame J. "Brishka! What is it? Tell me! What has
happened?"

Madame J pointed to me, her eyes wide and horrified
as she said, "Her! She's come to kill us! Andros has
sent her!"

The first woman looked at me, and her complexion
went stark white as her eyes went blank with something
akin to acceptance. "Is that true?" she asked me
hoarsely.

I continued to stand very still; any sudden movement could alarm these women even more, and I didn't want to do any more damage. "Absolutely not," I said in a cool, measured tone.

Madame J clutched at the other woman, sobs now choking her throat as fear blocked her ability to be rational. "She's going to kill us!" she wailed.

"Did Andros send you?" the other woman asked, hugging Madame J protectively.

"No. He has no idea where I am. In fact, my gut tells me right about now he's celebrating the fact that I'm dead."

"Then how did you find us?" the woman demanded, fear gripping her features in a pale, pained mask.

"I'm psychic," I said simply. There was no other explanation I could give that would make these women believe me, so going with the truth seemed like a plan.

Both women blinked, neither really comprehending what I meant by that, so I continued: "The truth is," I said, sitting down again with my hands in plain sight, resting them on the table, "Andros wanted me to find you, Dora, but I refused."

The woman I'd called Dora seemed to sag a little at the mention of her real name. Madame J continued to quiver in Dora's arms, her lips moving while she crossed herself.

"How did you know it was me?" Dora asked.

"It's your eyes. Your face is different from your picture—I'm guessing plastic surgery?"

Dora's mouth set in a tense line. She was terrified, I could tell, but she was holding herself bravely in spite of her fear. She turned to Madame J and said, "Brishka, go in the back and lie down. I'm going to talk to her. . . ."

"No! No, no, no! You mustn't! Ve must get avay; he'll kill us . . . !"

"Brishka, go in the back and let me talk to her. Let me deal with this, all right? We knew it would come to this someday anyway, so go now into the back," she said as she guided the older woman around the counter and through the curtain leading to the back. Dora watched until Madame J was safely on her way; then she turned to look at me, assessing how to proceed, I guessed.

Finally she moved to the big urn and filled two cups with steaming tea. Bringing them around the counter she set them on the table where I was seated, picked up the chair that Madame J had overturned, and took her seat. Her hands were shaking despite her effort to remain calm. "How do you know my husband?" she asked, getting right to the point.

"I was part of the entertainment at your daughter's wedding."

"Ophelia's married?" Dora asked me, tears instantly springing to her eyes.

"Yes, about three weeks now. She was a beautiful bride," I said, trying to make small talk and calm her down.

Dora's eyes held a faraway stare; then she closed them and shook her head, tamping down the pain of having to distance herself from her children. "I wanted to take them with me, you know."

"Then why didn't you?"

"The person who helped me would help me and only one of my children. He wouldn't take on the responsibility of all of them. Besides, it was supposed to be for only a short time. They were going to put my husband away forever, and when that didn't happen . . . well, there wasn't anything I could do but hide."

"Who helped you escape from him?" I asked.

"Andros's cousin, Nico. His wife, Sophia, was my best friend," Dora said, sighing heavily and taking a long sip from her tea. "Andros wasn't always like this, you know. We dated in high school, and back then he was sweet and even charming. He had big dreams of owning a restaurant. He didn't really want to be a part of the family business, but his father and older brother were gunned down shortly after we were married, and it changed him.

"His father was the don back then, and Andros was so angry at his family's murder that he stepped up to fill his father's shoes. He was so bent on revenge he was blind to any other option.

"He used to come home at night and tell me every

horrible thing he'd ordered his men to do that day. I guess he liked to unload his conscience. Anyway, after a while, hearing about all the horrible things he'd done, I became too terrified to leave him. I simply knew too much. So I lived with my fear for nearly ten years; then he told me about an argument he'd had with Nico. . . ."

"His cousin?"

"Yes. Andros said that Nico had become a coward. He said that Nico came to him and wanted out. But 'out' isn't an option when you're related to the mob. The only way out is in a pine box, and that can come early or late in life, depending on the choices you make.

"So shortly after Nico told Andros that he wanted to sell out his share and retire, Andros came home and confessed to me that he was going to take care of Nico. I knew that if Andros could kill his own cousin, then he wouldn't have any qualms about killing me too, so secretly I contacted Nico and told him about the plan. He immediately took extra precautions, and in return arranged for me to disappear. The problem was that I couldn't convince him to help me and all of my children. He was too afraid of Andros, I guess, so he would agree only to help me and one other. I chose Demetrius because he seemed the most impressionable at the time, and I didn't want him to grow up like his father.

"So the day I disappeared I took Demetrius with me to run some errands, and I was so nervous about being seen that I didn't keep a close eye on him." Dora had lifted a paper napkin from the dispenser at the side of the table and was wringing it in both hands as she recalled the painful memory. "When Nico showed up I couldn't find Demetrius. He'd wandered off, and we had such a small window of opportunity. I had no choice but to leave him behind, and it just about killed me. . . ." Dora stopped and took a sip of tea, tears slipping down her cheeks as the emotion of that memory stirred up all kinds of demons. "Nico talked me into leaving my son behind. He said he would send someone to find Demetrius right away, and he reasoned that we were in a safe neighborhood, but we couldn't wait a moment longer."

"I don't understand why you just didn't postpone your

escape, Dora," I said gently. The thought of leaving behind my own children was just unfathomable to me.

Dora snapped a look at me. Defensively she said, "It's not that simple. I mean, you have to understand—I was *terrified* of the man I slept next to every night. He was definitely going to figure out who tipped off his cousin, and when he did my life wasn't worth squat. Besides, Nico promised me that once we made our escape he would go to the authorities and turn state's evidence against his cousin, and I could then be reunited with all my children. He promised me he wanted nothing more to do with the business, and I believed him."

"So what happened?"

"Well, once Nico had gotten me safely away and was making arrangements to move his own family, his best friend was murdered and left in the trunk of Nico's car. That really frightened him, and instead of going to the authorities as he'd promised, he simply moved his operation to Florida, as far away from Andros as possible. Sophia and I kept in touch for a little while—she wanted her husband to get out of the business too. But I guess in the end the greed just took over, and Nico couldn't let it go."

"So what's your connection to Madame J?"

"Brishka was my nanny when I was a child. She retired here years ago and opened up this tearoom. When I tracked her down she offered me a safe haven. I hoped that in time Andros would just give up on trying to find me, but when word got to us that he was still actively pursuing me, Brishka offered her talents to help throw him off the track. She's read cards and tea leaves for fifty years, and I knew how superstitious Andros was—his mother had the gift, and he's always been in awe of it.

"So against my better judgment Brishka went to Michigan and sought Andros out, offering her services to him. The plan worked for a short while. She was good enough to provide Andros with lots of detailed information that would make him believe her, so she was also able to suggest that I was in California, then Europe, then Greece. Andros sent people all over the world trying to track me down, and in the meantime he had a stroke of genius and decided to use Brishka to help his business along.

"He demanded more and more from her until one night he called her and told her to come to his house immediately. When she got there, he ordered her to read a man sitting in his study. Brishka picked up several things about the man, including that he'd recently cheated in a card game, and without hesitation Andros shot the man point-blank right in front of her. Apparently Andros had hosted a poker game earlier in the evening and had lost heavily to the unfortunate man in his study. Brishka barely made it back here with her own life, and her fear of him is nearly paralyzing. Since then we've managed to keep a very low profile. That is until you showed up."

I nodded gravely. "Yeah, I'm sorry about that."

"So how *did* you find us?" Dora asked me.

"Well, Dora, the truth really *is* that I'm psychic. My name is Abigail Cooper, and I'm a professional clairvoyant from Royal Oak, Michigan. The way I got here was through several visions that led me directly to your door, but at the time I wasn't really looking for you. Andros wanted me to find you, but you have my word," I said, holding up my palm in a solemn pledge, "I would never, ever reveal to him where you are."

Dora didn't look convinced. "Andros can be a very persuasive man, Abigail."

"Call me Abby, and yes, I know. Listen, my boyfriend is an FBI agent. He's been trying these past few weeks to bring Andros down. Why don't I get in touch with him and maybe we can come up with a plan to keep you and Brishka safe, okay?"

"No."

"Why not?"

"Because Andros will stop at nothing to get me back. He's been able to circumvent the law for thirty years. He's a very, very dangerous man."

"Well, he may not be so dangerous for much longer," I said cryptically.

"What do you mean?"

"He's dying. He's got cancer."

Dora's jaw dropped, and she stared at me in shock. "He's got cancer?"

"Yes. I picked up on it when I met with him, and he confirmed it. My intuition says he won't make it another month. With him gone you could reconnect with your children, Dora, your family. . . ."

Dora stood up and began to pace the floor. She was clearly agitated. "It's not that simple," she said sharply.

"Why not?"

She stopped her pacing and looked at me, "Because I don't know *who* the hell you are or *if* you're telling me the truth."

"That's fair," I said. "So let me prove it."

"How?" she demanded.

I reached over and grabbed the paper napkin sitting next to my cup of tea. I smoothed it out, took a pen out of my purse and wrote Dutch's name on the napkin. "Dora, this is my boyfriend, Agent Roland Rivers. He's with the Troy, Michigan, division of the FBI. You can call information, get the number and leave him a message," I explained as I scribbled my name and my cell phone number underneath. "This is my cell. Call me after you talk to Dutch—uh, Roland; he goes by the nickname Dutch. He's a good guy and he can help you and Madame J. I promise."

Dora looked skeptically at the napkin, and I had no idea what she was thinking. I decided to let her mull it over, and if she felt okay about it, then she would get help. If not, there was nothing more I could do. "I'm staying at the La Quinta inn if you want to meet with me again. Otherwise, thank you for the tea, and take care of yourself."

With that I walked out of the shop and down the street, waving my arm at an available taxi.

I got back to the hotel twenty minutes later and went straight to the dining room. I was famished; the scone and blueberry muffin had only whetted my appetite for something more substantial. The hostess escorted me to a seat at a corner table near the back of the restaurant, and after sitting down I picked up the menu immediately. The dining room was filling up quickly; dinner hour had arrived.

I looked through the menu and chose the Southwestern chicken, with a basket of chips and salsa as an appetizer while I waited for my food. As I looked around the restaurant I became suddenly self-conscious; I was the only one eating alone. To give myself something to do I got up and headed out to the lobby, where I bought a *USA Today* newspaper and brought it back to my table. Absently I scanned the paper while I munched on the chips and salsa.

I read the entertainment section first, and sifted through a few articles on the state of the economy and world affairs. My food arrived and I set the paper aside, focusing on cutting my meat and avoiding eye contact with other patrons at the restaurant. I was halfway through the meal when something in the upper left-hand corner of the newspaper caught my attention, and I dropped my fork as I read the headline.

It read: *Two undercover FBI agents gunned down execution style in their hotel room near Detroit—possible Mafia connection . . .* My hands shook as I snatched up the paper and tore through the pages, looking for the article. My heart beat faster and faster, and a cold chill spread across my back. I found the article and read the first three lines quickly.

Detroit, Michigan: Two undercover FBI agents were gunned down in their sleep while on assignment at the Dorchester Hotel yesterday morning. Police and FBI agents on the scene have confirmed that one male and one female agent were shot at point-blank range in the back of the head while sleeping. The FBI will not release the identity of the victims until family members have been notified, but they are confirming that the male agent was new to the FBI, and had just completed his training at Quantico.

My hands started to shake so violently that I could no longer hold the article still enough to read it. I dropped the paper, and suddenly found it very difficult to breathe. My lungs were pumping, but no air seemed to satisfy my need for oxygen. The world began to spin and whirl, and I wasn't able to stand, even though that was what I wanted to do. I wanted to run out of the restaurant, and go where, I didn't know . . . someplace where the world made sense . . . someplace where Dutch was still alive.

I felt someone next to me, and I became aware that I was on the floor now, on all fours, still gasping for air. The world was growing dim, and I was seconds away from passing out when someone shoved a paper bag over my mouth and nose and lifted me off my hands to sit against the wall. My head was lowered close to my knees, and the bag still covered my mouth as I breathed in and out, inflating and deflating the bag.

Slowly I could feel my senses return; my breathing became more normal and the world had stopped spinning. I was now also aware that a small, concerned crowd had gathered, and the man next to me was speaking in slow, measured tones.

"That's it, miss, just breathe as normally as you can. I'm a doctor, and you're just having a little attack, but it's almost over. That's it . . . just breathe."

I focused on the kind stranger still holding the bag over my mouth. My mind wanted to wander down dark paths, where the enormity of the loss I now knew about would take me down for the count. I fought that temptation with everything I had. I couldn't lose it . . . not here . . . not publicly . . . not yet.

Finally I moved my hand up to the bag and gently pushed it aside. "Thank you," I said gratefully.

"You're welcome, little lady. Would you like to go to the hospital?" the kind doctor asked. He was an older gentleman with silver hair and a white beard, and even though he smiled reassuringly at me, his eyes held concern.

"No, really, I'm fine," I said to him. "Just a little panic attack there. I just want to go to my room and lie down," I said.

To my left a heavyset man with a bad comb-over and a name tag that read JIM MURRAY, MANAGER said, "Absolutely, ma'am. We'll get you right up to your room. And don't worry about your meal; it's on us this evening, all right?"

"Thank you. That's very kind. . . ." And even as I said this tears welled in my eyes, because no matter how hard I pushed against that dam of grief, it was still stronger than I was. Quickly I got up and with the help of the kind doctor walked on shaking legs out of the restaurant and to the elevator. There I assured the man that I was well enough to get back to my room by myself, and after hesitating a moment as he looked into my pleading eyes, the doctor nodded with a small smile and let me go.

A moment later the doors of the elevator opened and I rushed in, hugging myself as if I were going to fall apart at the seams. When I reached my hotel door I had trouble inserting the key card as tears dribbled down my cheeks and obscured my vision. I finally made it inside and shut the door. Sliding down to the floor I collapsed into great wails of agony.

Chapter Seventeen

It was hours later, and I was still on the floor. I was exhausted, but sleep was impossible. I'd been lying there, my face against the carpet for nearly an hour, trying to recall every detail of Dutch's face, and for some reason I couldn't remember him the way I wanted to. I could recall only the small things. Like the color of his eyes, the small dimple in his chin, the way his hair came to a gentle widow's peak at the top of his forehead. But when I tried to back my mind away a little, to envision him whole, like a mental snapshot, his image grew fuzzy and blurred.

When I realized I didn't even have a single physical photo of him to remind me of the way he looked, the agony was somehow sharper and more painful, like I'd betrayed him somehow by not carrying around a picture of the man I'd come to love.

I'd never told him about my true feelings for him either; and why I hadn't done so eluded me. Was I so caught up in treading carefully and playing it cool that I'd missed the opportunity to let him know how much I'd fallen for him? Was I really that callous? That much of a goddamned coward?

I sighed into the carpet, these thoughts swirling in my head, and I just wanted them to stop. I lifted my chin and looked around the room, which was now completely dark. I sighed again and lifted myself to my knees, and then slowly, painfully as my cramped muscles protested, I stood up and loped over to the bed. I sat down and turned on the light, which caused me to squint and shield my eyes. After a time my eyes adjusted, and I looked blankly around the room. Just then my intuition buzzed. Angrily I turned my head to the side and mentally screamed at my crew. How *dared* they do this to me! How could they let someone I love *die*? What the hell good was being psychic if I couldn't stop someone I loved from being killed? I raged.

I told my guides that I hated them, that I never, ever wanted to hear from them again, that I was through with readings, and tuning in, and—

Look in your purse . . .

"Screw you!" I said out loud.

Look in your purse . . .

"Back *off*!" I practically shouted, holding my hands over my ears as if someone were in the room trying to talk to me.

Look in your purse. . . .

The thought wouldn't go away. It swirled around and around in my head, despite my best efforts to ignore it. Finally, irritated beyond measure, I stomped over to my purse and brought it back to the bed. I looked in it and saw nothing unusual. *See?* I said in my head. *There's nothing here!*

Look in your purse. . . .

I gritted my teeth and growled, turning my purse upside down and dumping the contents onto the bed. I stared at the objects dully, waiting for a hint as to what I was supposed to be looking for, when my eye fell on the folded piece of paper that was the second page of the police report from Dora's file. Curiously I picked it up and opened it, skimming quickly through the details. Something tickled my brain, and I slowed my reading down and began at the top again, taking my time to reread it slowly.

The report was mostly Demetrius's account of the events of that day. His mother had picked him up from school and told him they needed to run some errands. Demetrius had complained that he wanted to go home and watch *G.I. Joe,* but his mother had insisted that he come along for the errands.

The officer had taken great pains to document every detail of the little boy's statement, and that was when I noticed why Madame J had stolen this page. Dora had told Demetrius a story about when she was his age and her nanny had taken her on her first airplane ride to visit her nanny's family in Texas, and how excited she was about flying in an airplane. I wasn't sure what prompted the story, but Dora was probably preparing Demetrius for their escape. At the time Dora probably thought it was harmless to mention her nanny, but later when Dora ended up living with her, it became a crucial clue, and one Madame J needed to hide from Andros.

I read the page all the way to the bottom, and something compelled me to read it again. I was missing something . . . and then, with a small gasp, I had it, and for me it was the final straw.

It's hard to say what motivates a person to want to end another's life. Some people could never be pushed that far; others need no reason at all. I can only speak for myself, and for me it took an attempt on my life, the destruction and devastation of my home and business, the murder of the man I loved, and now . . . the realization that Andros's evil extended far beyond the borders of my own world, reaching deep into the hearts, homes and lives of others who were only innocent bystanders. That moment turned my heart black, my resolve to steel, and my mind to one purpose.

Without further ado I reached for the phone.

Despite the wind and rough weather our pilot gave us one hell of a smooth landing. As the plane taxied over to the gate I stared blankly out the window with a hollow feeling eating out my insides. I was numb, but resigned to the task at hand. The dichotomy of that mixture would normally have made me ponder the meaning of life. At the moment all I wanted to do was get on with it already.

I waited my turn and exited the plane with the others, avoiding eye contact and holding my duffel bag awkwardly in front of me so as not to catch it on the seats as I deplaned. The pilot thanked me for flying Northwest. I gave him a curt nod and moved on.

I got to the terminal and luckily had to walk only a short distance to the tram that would take me to baggage claim. I had no bags to claim, but that was where I needed to go. I glanced at my watch; we were early, which was neither good nor bad. The tram stopped and I followed a large crowd down the escalator across a long hallway and down another escalator. I went through a small door for exiting passengers and smiled when I saw that my escorts were already here, waiting. *Good.*

I walked forward, acknowledging them with only my eyes as Gargoyle took up my right, Goblin my left, and Grim fell in step from behind. We walked a short distance to the same silver sedan with smoked windows that had been my chariot on other occasions, and without hesitation I got in and made myself comfortable.

Grim got in front opposite the driver, Gargoyle and Goblin got in on either side of me and without a word the driver took off.

We headed east, cruising at just above the speed limit, and I smiled at the irony of these big, bad Mafia types wanting to avoid a speeding ticket. Forty-five minutes later we reached the Kapordelis mansion, and I was instructed to leave my duffel in the car. Nonchalantly I shrugged my shoulders, which made my three escorts just a teeny bit nervous, I could tell. It had to be bugging the crap out of them that I was so cavalier about my obviously precarious circumstances, and it didn't help matters that I continued to smile like the Cheshire cat.

Goblin held the door open for me as we entered the mansion, and I followed him as we wound our way through the house to Andros's study. As we approached I could see that his door was already open, and as we neared I could also see the hit man who'd probably been the one who killed Dutch waiting in one of the wing chairs. *The more the merrier,* I thought.

Goblin stepped to the side and waved me into the study, and as I entered only Grim followed, while Goblin closed the door and waited outside with Gargoyle. Without pause I walked over to one of the chairs in front of Andros's desk and plopped down, crossing my legs and arms and screwing up my face with the cockiest expression I could muster.

Andros was seated in his usual spot behind his enormous chair. He looked awful, as sweat soaked his white cotton shirt and dripped down his puffy face. His skin had a yellowish hue, indicating that jaundice had set in. I could feel the waves of intense pain flowing off of him, and I allowed myself not an ounce of pity. "Miss Cooper, it is so nice to see that you have escaped that unfortunate fire in your home," he began.

"Yeah, I'm lucky like that," I said, beaming a fake smile at him.

"It is unfortunate, however, that we must end this relationship. Sadly, you have not held up your end of the bargain, and I will be forced to dismiss you."

Andros was a funny guy. He said the word "dismiss" as if he were merely discharging someone's employment, rather than ordering their murder. "Hang on there, big guy," I said, holding up my hand in a stopping motion. "Who says I haven't held up my end of the bargain?"

"I beg your pardon?" Andros asked me, acknowledging me fully for the first time.

"Who says I haven't held up my end of the bargain?" I repeated, more insistent this time.

"Miss Cooper, I have no time for games. You are clearly not the talent I am looking for, and you have failed in your assignment. These men will escort you—"

"As I recall, *Andros,*" I said, using his first name for impact, "my assignment was to find your wife, which I have done, by the way. So it is *you* who must pay up or be discharged, in my opinion."

"You found Dora?" Andros said with a smile. He didn't believe me. *Good.*

"Yes."

"Then where *is* my beloved wife?" Andros asked, looking around the room mocking me. "After all, I would love to accept you at your word, Miss Cooper, but you see, I am a skeptical man. . . ."

"So you don't believe me?" I asked, leaning in and holding Andros's beady little stare.

"No."

"She flew back with me on the plane. If your henchmen had been a little more observant they would have seen her walk down the terminal with me," I said, laughing and pointing a wagging finger at Grim, who suddenly looked exceedingly nervous as Andros and his hit man both turned to look at him.

"I didn't see anyone with her, Mr. Kapordelis. She was alone," Grim said quickly.

"Well, of course you didn't see anyone with me, Grimmy-boy. You had eyes only for me. Too bad too— you could have saved Andros from having to take a car ride."

Andros looked back at me with a scowl that could freeze a polar bear. "Miss Cooper, I've had enough of this. Sal, dispose of her. . . ."

Grim jumped forward and jerked up my arm as he began lifting me out of the chair. I decided it might be best to get to the point. "If you don't believe me then call her!" I shouted.

Grim heaved me clear of the chair and began to pull me over to the door. "She's got my cell phone!" I shouted. "Call my cell phone! She wants to meet you, Andros, and she's got your son with her!"

Grim paused for a moment, the shock of my statement reverberating through the room. "What are you talking about?" Andros asked me as I stood on tiptoe, still gripped by Grim.

"Have him let go of me and I'll tell you the whole sorry story," I said. Andros waved at Grim, who released me like a hot potato, and after I had straightened out my clothing and walked back to the chair I sat down and again crossed my legs and arms and began. "Okay, I found Dora. She was down South. Remember how

I told you there was a fourth son? Well, when Dora disappeared she was pregnant. She left because she was afraid of you, but she feels terrible about it, and now that she knows about your condition she wants to see you, and she wants her son to know his father before it's too late. Now I've met this young man, and I gotta tell you, Andros, he's a perfect fit to carry on your legacy. I've looked into his future, and he's a shining star. . . ."

A small tic formed just above Andros's left eye, punching his eyebrow up and down as he looked at me and considered what I'd just told him.

"If you don't believe me then make a phone call," I urged. "I gave Dora my cell phone; just call the number and when she answers ask her a question only she could know the answer to," I prodded. He had to take the bait, but I couldn't appear too anxious, so I sat back and waited for him to decide what to do.

A moment passed, then another and another, until finally Andros hit the speaker button on his phone and said, "What's the number?"

"Two-four-eight, five-five-five, twenty-four, twenty-nine."

Andros punched in the numbers and we waited as the phone rang once, twice, then was picked up by a female voice saying a tentative, "Hello?" into the line.

"Yes, this is Andros Kapordelis; who is this, please?" Andros said. I could see the tension on his face as he waited to hear more of the voice I knew he recognized.

"Oh, Andros! Thank God. This is Dora, and I'd like to see you."

"How do I know it's you?" Andros said, leaning a little closer to the phone.

"Ask me a question about when we were together," she offered.

Andros thought for a moment, then said, "What did you give me on our first wedding anniversary?"

There was a silvery laugh on the other end, and the voice said, "Lollipops! I wanted you to give up those smelly cigars, and I thought as long as you had a substitute you might give it a try."

As she said the word "lollipops" I watched Andros's jaw drop, and involuntarily he brought his hand up to caress the phone. "Dora? Is it really you?" he asked, his voice choked with emotion.

"Yes, darling, it is. Can I see you so that I can explain everything?"

"Yes," Andros said, quickly leaning forward to speak directly into the speakerphone. "Yes, yes, of course. Where are you? I will come to you," he said excitedly.

"First, darling, you must promise me something," she said.

"What? What do you want me to promise you?"

"That you will bring Abby, and that she won't be harmed under any circumstances."

Andros looked quickly up at me, almost puzzled that I was still in the room; then he looked back at the phone and said, "Of course, of course. Where are you?"

"Well, I thought it would be appropriate to meet at the place where I disappeared from you twenty years ago. I know that sounds odd, but I just think that once I tell you what really happened, you'll be able to understand. I can take you through that day and show you exactly what happened. Will you come?"

"I'm on my way, Dora," he said, getting up.

"When will you be here?"

"It will take us a little time, about half an hour. Will you wait for me?"

"Yes, yes, of course, darling. Hurry." And she clicked off.

Andros walked with difficulty around his desk, his breathing coming rapidly as he forced his legs to support him. Grim moved quickly to his side and helped him into his coat, while the hit man kept a wary eye on me. He wasn't buying it, which was exactly what I was hoping for.

"Andros," he said softly.

Andros turned slightly and regarded him. "Yes?"

"I don't like it," the man said.

"It was her, Sal. I'd know that voice anywhere."

"Oh, I'm not saying it wasn't her, my friend. I'm just saying I don't like it."

Andros looked at Sal, a silent conversation passing between them; then he looked at me, and I met his stare with confidence. He looked back at his personal assassin and said, "You may be right. Bring the boys."

With that Sal walked over to the phone and picked it up. He spoke quickly in Greek, replaced the receiver, then came around to me and grabbed me by the shoulder. His grip was firm, but not hurtful, and we all exited the room, Andros walking slowly and carefully, Grim holding him by the arm.

In the hall we met Demetrius, who smiled at his father and hurried toward him. "You wanted to see me, Pop?"

Andros stopped and regarded his son. "Yes, Demetrius, I need you to go down to the casino tonight and help Fitz."

"Awww, Pop," Demetrius complained, "I had a date tonight. . . ."

"You will do as I say!" Andros thundered, and we all jumped a little at the cannon of his voice.

Demetrius glared at his father and sniffed stubbornly, then gave in and said with a winning smile, "Okay, okay, Pop. I'll go, but I'll have you to blame when there are no grandchildren." And he leaned in to kiss his father on the cheek.

As he did so he brushed into me, and I flinched a little. "Excuse me," I said automatically.

"No sweat, cutie," he said, and winked at me before trotting away.

We reached the car a short time later, and instead of being taken to the silver sedan, I was forced to ride in the limousine with Andros and Sal. Grim, Gargoyle and Goblin got into the sedan, each toting a semiautomatic. Another car came out of the garage, also with smoked windows and filled, no doubt, with another group of men. As the limo pulled forward, I could see the other cars tag along behind.

All the way over Andros was lost deep in thought, his memory probably replaying happier times with his wife. Sal looked only at me for most of the ride, waiting and watching as I stared straight ahead, my outward appearance one of calm neutrality.

We exited the highway a while later, and headed through a familiar neck of the woods. We passed my office building, and it took some effort on my part not to look at it. Just a few blocks farther and we pulled into a small market plaza, taking up a parking space toward the back left corner of a Rite Aid Pharmacy.

The two other cars pulled up to our left, and with all the engines running we watched and waited.

Andros was now so anxious that he leaned forward across me to stare out the window, his tic even more pronounced as he watched everyone who entered the parking lot. We waited close to thirty minutes when finally a woman came out of the building. She was tall, elegant, with blond hair and high heels. In her arms she carried a small plastic bundle, her purchase from the pharmacy.

"Dora . . ." Andros said into the quiet of the car. "That's her!" he said louder, growing excited as she neared our side of the lot. "That's her, I'm sure of it!" he said again.

Suddenly a figure appeared out of the shadows from behind Dora. He was tall, cloaked in a long black trench coat, and his face was obscured by a black ski mask. We all watched with astonishment as in one swift motion the masked man's arm snaked around Dora's neck, and he jerked her violently backward.

"No!" Andros shouted as he came out of his shock and desperately tried to climb over Sal and me to get out of the car.

"No! Dora!" he shouted even as the woman was being dragged backward toward the shadows. I sat back and watched, pinned beneath Andros's tremendous bulk and unable to move—not that I tried. Sal, however, was also pinned, but he was frantically struggling to get free of Andros so that he could open the car door. No one in the other cars moved as the henchmen all waited to take their cue from us, and because the windows in our car were smoked, they couldn't see Andros's frantic attempts to rescue his wife.

In the next moment, however, everything changed as the parking lot flooded with lights and the loud squeal of sirens drowned out all other noise. Andros and Sal stopped midmotion and watched with disbelieving eyes as from every direction police cars appeared and patrolmen lunged out of their cars with their weapons drawn. The masked man was instantly surrounded, and quickly he let go of Dora and put his hands in the air, dropping something long and metallic to the ground.

In the light of the spotlights, the woman Andros thought was Dora pulled off her blond wig, shaking out her dark hair even as she spun around, the bundle in her arms now a gun pointed directly at the masked man's face.

Andros and Sal watched in stunned disbelief from inside the car as the woman playing Dora reached forward and yanked off the mask of her attacker. Andros heaved a great sob as he recognized his son Demetrius standing menacingly in the pool of lights surrounded by police.

For a long, tense moment nobody inside the car moved; then Andros shouted "My son!" into the stunned silence, and again he did his best to try to scramble over me and Sal and get out of the car. This time he was successful, and when he opened the car door his momentum carried him forward to the pavement. From the ground Andros shouted, "Demetrius! Demetrius!" And quicker than a man that sick and that heavy should, he got up and pulled out his gun, waving it above his head and firing a shot.

"Fuck!" Sal said angrily, still next to me in the car. Quickly he turned his head from side to side, assessing the situation and trying to decide what to do, as his boss was now out in the open, waving a gun at police. He caught my eye suddenly, and despite myself I couldn't hide the satisfied smirk plastering itself onto my face. In that moment Sal knew I'd set the whole thing up. With an angry snarl he grabbed my arm and wrenched me from the car as he bolted toward Andros, who was now running toward his son, still waving his gun in the air.

Upon seeing Andros fall out of the car and run toward police, Goblin, Gargoyle, Grim and the other henchmen scrambled out of their cars, their own weapons drawn and pointed at the police, who had been prepared for just such a scenario and quickly moved behind their patrol cars, getting into position and taking aim.

While the police organized their defensive Demetrius wasted no time taking advantage of his father's distraction by grabbing the female police officer posing as Dora, wrenching the gun from her hand and pulling her body close again. Quickly he scuttled backward toward his father's car with his hostage in tow and the gun now pointed at her temple.

Meanwhile Sal caught up with Andros, still dragging me along, but before Sal could do anything more, Andros raised his gun, leveling it at police, and fired. It was the last thing he ever did.

In the next instant a bullet ripped a small hole right between his eyes, and a much larger one found its way out the back of his head. Before my eyes Andros fell backward like a giant side of beef, hitting the ground with a dull thud and splattering my shoes with his blood. I stared as a thick pool of the dark red stuff formed more quickly than I'd imagined it could, leaking out to soak the pavement by my feet.

Just then, to my right, Sal jumped behind me, using my shoulder to steady his gun, and fired off a shot, the sound sending a cannonlike shock wave through my eardrum as gunpowder burned my cheek. I ducked down from the sound, but Sal dragged me back up, pulling me to his chest and crossing his left arm over my shoulder and across my sternum to grip my right arm tightly in a binding embrace. Out of my peripheral vision I could see him raise his gun again, and it occurred to me that I was now a human shield.

For some reason I didn't seem to care, and a feeling of disconnectedness settled over me like a gentle blanket as my eyes drifted hypnotically back to the pool of blood growing bigger around Andros. As I gazed at the shocked expression frozen in place on his face and forming his death mask, all I could feel was an odd sense of relief. He was dead. "Good riddance," I muttered at his corpse even as gunfire exploded all around me. I couldn't hear most of it; my sense of hearing was oddly off balance as the ringing in my right ear became more intense and vibrated through my head.

Finally, when I'd had my fill, I looked away from Andros just in time to watch as, off to my left, Gargoyle went down in a wild display of bullets and blood, beating Goblin in death by mere seconds as I watched him fall too.

From behind me Sal continued to fire away at police as they ducked behind cars, but periodically I could see an officer peeking up to rifle off a few shots in our direction. Meanwhile, Demetrius continued to snake his way backward toward our three cars, dragging his hostage with him. Suddenly, a mere ten yards from us, his captive gave him a solid elbow jab to the ribs, which bent him double while she dove out of the way. In the next instant he took a bullet to the shoulder and one to the leg and was down for the count.

I continued to watch in my sort of hypnotic trance, held tightly by Sal as men on both sides dove for cover and fired off shots, comprehension of the imminent danger I was in slow to make its way to my brain. I seemed disconnected from everything—it was too surreal for me to grasp—and I kept asking myself if all this was really happening.

Then, out of nowhere, something huge and heavy barreled into me, knocking both Sal and me to the ground. As the force hit us I tried to break my fall, but Sal had hold of my arms and all I could do was squeeze my eyes shut and brace for the impact. A second later my head hit the pavement with a thud and I went out like a light.

Chapter Eighteen

The ringing wouldn't stop, and the world was spinning around and around like a top. I wanted to open my eyes, but it was really, really hard. I pushed my hand out to stop the spinning motion, and it met the warm flesh of another hand. One eyelid fluttered open, and the searing pain in my head intensified. "Owwwww," I moaned, quickly shutting the eye.

Someone stroked my cheek, and a moment later I felt a featherlight kiss on my forehead. I struggled again to open my eyes, and this time managed to peer through one eye long enough to see who was showering me with love.

Midnight blues looked worriedly down at me, and I fought to comprehend who they belonged to. "Hey, Edgar," came a husky baritone.

I blinked the one eye, and with great effort got the other to open as well. I stared at a face I thought was lost forever, and then it dawned on me how this could be. I must be dead.

"I didn't know there was pain on the other side," I mumbled.

"Yeah, sorry about that, babe, but you were just

standing there in the line of fire, and I had to do *some-thing* to get you out of the way."

I blinked at him; I had no idea what the hell he was talking about. "What?"

"You hit your head pretty hard. Just try to lie still. The ambulance is on its way."

"There are ambulances over here?" I asked. "God, this is just like earth!"

Dutch laughed at me and leaned forward again to kiss me lightly. "I think we may have scrambled your brain a little, honey. Just lie still, okay?"

"Why is everything spinning?" I asked. I didn't like the fact that I couldn't make the world stop whirling around and around like some sort of carnival ride.

"You've probably got a concussion. Just close your eyes and we'll get you to the hospital, okay?"

"Where are my grandparents?" I asked. I really wanted to see them. I'd missed them so much when I was alive.

"Your grandparents?"

"Yeah! They're supposed to be here," I insisted.

"Uh, I'm not sure, Abby. Do you want me to call them?"

"Dutch, you silly," I said poking at him, "all you have to do is think about them and they'll appear. See, watch," I said, pushing up to a sitting position so that I could concentrate better. But the moment I sat up the world went dark as night, and I went out like a light . . . again.

The sound of a siren pounded in rhythm with the ache in my head. Something was covering my mouth, and there was movement all around me. With great effort I opened my eyes and people in blue jackets came into view. "Wha's going on?" I said groggily.

Someone by my feet tugged on my shoe, and I looked down toward the feeling and saw Dutch sitting uncomfortably in the cramped space of the inside of an ambulance as we raced across town. "I'm here," he said.

Even prone, I was incredibly dizzy, and my eyes fluttered as the darkness threatened to overtake me. I closed my eyes again and tried to ride it out. Who knew heaven was so much like earth? And then it hit me— what if this weren't heaven? What if I'd ended up at the other end?

Certainly I deserved it; after all, I'd purposely led Andros to his death, and I was hardly remorseful. After I'd read the police report in my hotel room I realized that Demetrius was the rapist, and his father had known the truth and had let him continue. With no one else suitable enough to inherit the family business, Andros had kept silent about his son's extracurricular activities, and would have died allowing a serial rapist to prey on more innocent women just so his illicit businesses could continue.

That was why Goon had been killed; Andros was afraid he would reveal the truth about his son and ordered him shut up permanently especially given Goon's tragic childhood. It also explained all of the clues I'd gotten in the beginning of the investigation, like the connection to Vegas—it wasn't Las Vegas, the place; it was the casino connection that had been the clue.

There was also a skiing connection that I hadn't hit on until reading the police report. The family owned a ski lodge in Vail, and if I'd just connected the dots from my reading with Ophelia's new husband, I could have put that together much sooner too.

I remembered the expression on Dora's face when I'd talked to her yesterday morning. She'd been horrified that her son had turned into such a monster, but admitted that even as a child he'd seemed disturbed. With great remorse and guilt she'd agreed to help me bring them both to justice. I'd given her my cell phone and told her when the call would come through. I'd also told her that Andros believed he might have a fourth son, and that this could be useful in convincing him to meet with her. She'd stayed in Texas, and the ruse had worked.

I'd also called Milo from my hotel, and left him a rather cryptic message on his voice mail. I'd told him how the rapist was reliving a day twenty years ago when his mother had abandoned him after running her errands. His mother had taken him grocery shopping first, then to the post office and lastly to the drugstore, where she'd disappeared. I knew then that Demetrius would show up at the same place he'd been left some twenty years previously, looking to take out his twisted rage on his mother's look-alike just like he'd done to the other five women who'd reminded him of Dora. The Perry Drugstore had been bought out years later by the Rite Aid Corporation, but every other element was still exactly the same. I'd been a little nervous when Demetrius was ordered by his father to head over to the casino, but when he agreed with his father, my lie detector had gone haywire. Then, when he'd brushed up against me, I'd felt his barely controlled rage, and knew he'd completely ignore the order—leading him right to Milo, who was ready and waiting for the trap.

In all honesty I'd set Milo up as well. My last words on his voice mail had been, "Bring plenty of firepower, Milo; he may have some backup with him you'll have to be careful about."

I'd had a vision just before I'd made that phone call to him, and I'd seen very clearly the shot that would take Andros down permanently. It was my ambition all along.

And now I'd paid the price. I was here, in hell, with my equilibrium spinning and a horrible pain in my head—but at least I had Dutch beside me. This thought made me curious, and I opened my eyes back up. What had he done to deserve coming here?

Just then the ambulance stopped abruptly, and the back doors were pulled open. I was lowered by several helping hands, and my vitals were run off like an auctioneer rattling off bids. My head swayed from side to side as I was wheeled down a brightly lit corridor. I glanced to my right and saw several doctors hovering over a figure covered in blood; one of them was administering chest compressions. I caught a glimpse of the man and I realized it was Sal. Yes, out of everyone he definitely deserved to be here.

My gurney came to a stop behind a small curtained enclosure, and a doctor and nurse came over to assess my injuries. I could see Dutch hovering nearby, looking anxiously at me, and I gave him a small smile. God, he looked good. I had really missed him.

My eyes were pried wide open then, and a blinding white light was shone into both pupils, sending a shock wave of fresh pain through my head. It hurt so bad my arm came up reflexively and pushed the penlight away. "Pupils responsive," the doctor said.

"That hurts!" I grumbled, and squeezed my eyes shut, refusing to cooperate. I heard a voice order a CT scan—stat—and within moments I was on the move again.

Several hours and dozens of tests, scans and X-rays later I was back in my curtained area sucking on ice chips from a paper cup. By now it was sinking in that I wasn't actually dead, but the way my head was pounding I still felt like hell.

I hadn't seen Dutch since I'd been back, and worriedly I wondered if my concussion had caused my grieving brain to create him. As I waited to be admitted overnight for observation, the curtain parted and in stepped six feet, two inches of gorgeousness. "Hey, Edgar," he said.

Tears formed in my eyes, and a sob burbled in my throat. I was so relieved to see him it was all I could do not to leap off the bed. "Hey, yourself," I said hoarsely. "I thought you were dead," I continued, getting right to the point.

Dutch smiled sadly and answered, "You heard the news about Joe then?"

"I read in the newspaper two days ago that two agents were executed in their hotel room. I thought one of them was you."

"No, not this time, and actually I have you to thank for it," he said, coming close and sitting on the edge of the gurney.

"Tell me," I begged.

"Well, after you called Milo with some sort of weird message about "trouble in Holland," he got a hold of my office with an urgent message to contact him. I told Joe I had to meet someone, and I'd be back in a couple of hours. She took advantage of the time to call her boyfriend, Agent Donovan, also a new recruit to the Bureau, and have him over for a romp in the hay."

"I thought there were strict rules about dating a subordinate. . . ."

"There are. She was sloppy and took chances, and it cost her and Agent Donovan their lives. She and Donovan were in the middle of things when Andros's man walked in and shot them point-blank. We knew Andros had ordered it, but we didn't know who had tipped him off."

"It was Bennington," I said quickly. "I saw him leaving Andros's study the night before Joe was killed with a fat wad of money and a big smirk on his face."

Dutch's mouth fell open. "You're shittin' me," he said.

"No, really, Dutch, I saw him," I insisted.

Instantly Dutch pulled out his cell phone and got up to walk away, stabbing at the buttons in furious anger. He exited the area, but I could hear him just down the hall, speaking urgently. After a couple of minutes he came back to my bed and explained: "That was the captain. Turns out Bennington took an unexpected vacation. He's somewhere in the Florida keys and won't be back till Monday. The captain's already starting the paperwork to investigate his bank account, that son of a bitch!"

"I'm sorry about Joe," I said, reaching out to touch his arm.

Dutch patted my hand and answered, "It's okay, Abby. She wasn't a good agent, and somehow she got away with all kinds of crap. It sucks that it cost her her life, but that's the chance you take when you're in this line of work. Anyway, thank you for getting a warning to Milo. We figured you were trying to warn me about something, but we didn't know what until I got back to the hotel."

"So tell me how you got the meeting with Andros in the first place," I said curiously.

"Well, the Bureau's been after both Andros and his cousin Nico for years. Nico got sloppy on last year's tax returns, and that let us in the door. He practically begged us to let him set up Andros, so Joe and I went to Florida posing as arms dealers. At the time we didn't know Andros was so suspicious of his cousin; I mean, he'd mentioned there had been a small rift in the family when Andros's wife had disappeared, but he never let on that the rift was so close to hatred. He let us come back up here thinking that his cousin would greet us with open arms, and it caught us completely off guard when Andros hauled us into his study, smelling a trap.

"And I gotta admit, when I first saw you in Andros's study I thought I'd been set up," he said, looking at me sternly.

"That's the problem with you and me, Dutch—you just don't trust me," I said testily.

He smiled mischievously and replied, "Oh, and the fact that my partner happened to be a girl never brought you a second of doubt?"

He had me there. . . . "That was different," I insisted.

"I see," he said, still mocking me.

Being the grown-up that I am, I answered by sticking my tongue out at him and grumbled, "I should have stayed in Texas."

"Yeah, about that—how the hell did you get out of here without being seen?"

"After the fire I took a bus to Toledo and flew out from there."

Dutch nodded in an "aha" gesture and said, "I gotta tell you, Edgar, you really scared the crap out of us with that house fire. We thought you'd bought the farm."

"How'd you know I hadn't?"

"Well, for one thing firefighters couldn't find a body. We combed all over that place, and there was no evidence that anyone had been inside. Of course, we didn't tell that to the public—my feeling was that if you weren't there then you must be somewhere else hiding out, and I'd just have to wait to spank you until you popped up again."

"Spank me?" I said indignantly.

"Yeah, little lady, *spank* you," Dutch said sternly. "Didn't I tell you to stop dealing with the Kapordelis

family? Didn't I tell you not to chase after Andros's
wife? Didn't Milo tell you to take a long extended vacation?" he asked, his brow darkening like that of an angry
father reprimanding an errant child. "What the hell were
you thinking? This time you really could have been
killed!"

I had no defense that Dutch would listen to, so I
scowled up at him and lay back on the pillows. I didn't
have the energy to argue with him anymore anyway, and
I was suddenly exhausted.

"Listen," he said, softening as he saw my tired expression, "why don't you try to get some sleep now, okay?
They're going to admit you for the night, right?"

"Yeah," I said, sighing heavily.

"Okay, so I'll check in with you in the morning and
drive you home. . . ."

He let that last sentence fade to an uncomfortable
silence as I visibly blanched. Obviously I had no home
left to go to. With an expression that I knew meant he
was mentally punching himself, he leaned forward and
kissed me lightly on the lips. "I'll see you in the morning,
Abby, and don't worry—we'll work everything out."

Dutch left me just as an orderly came to wheel me to
my room somewhere upstairs, where the staff gave me
a two-hundred-dollar aspirin and advised me to try to
get some sleep. The advances in modern medicine are
simply astounding.

The next morning right before I was discharged there
was a knock on my hospital door, and then a welcome
face peeked in. "Abby?"

"Kendal!" I called excitedly from my bed. "I wondered when you'd show back up."

Kendal came in through the door holding a gigantic
bouquet of roses in one hand and a beautiful blond in
the other. "Hello, sugar," he said as he came to the head
of my bed and bent down to kiss me on the forehead.
"I heard you were in a fire, and rushed back up here to
make sure you were okay."

"Uh, okay . . ." I said. If that was the story that Kendal
heard, then I was okay with letting him believe it. I didn't

really want to go into all the gory details. "Who's this?" I asked, pointing to the blond bombshell in the corner.

"Abby, this is Steve. My mother introduced us down in Tampa, and we're talking about moving in together."

"Hi," Steve said shyly, coming over to shake my hand.

"Hi, Steve. Wow, Kendal, looks like you've had quite the couple of weeks. Tell me all about it."

Kendal and Steve pulled up two chairs and began to tell me about their love affair. I was so glad Kendal seemed to be over Rick that I didn't care how quickly these two seemed to be moving forward.

Finally Kendal got up and squeezed my hand. "Listen, you're probably tired, and we need to be going. Rick's moving his stuff out, and I want to make sure he doesn't take anything of mine."

"Good plan," I said as the two moved to the door. Kendal paused before opening it and turned back to me. Thinking of something, he said, "Oh! I almost forgot! I read in the paper today that the father of the bride at the wedding we did—you know, the Mafia boss? Well, he died last night in a shoot-out with police! Can you believe it?"

"You're kidding," I said, a sly look on my face.

"Yes! It's true! So you really were right. I guess now I don't have to mail back that check, huh?"

The check! "Uh, actually Kendal, I already took care of that, so *you* owe *me* for a change," I said smugly.

"Oh," Kendal said looking disappointed. "You mean you already paid for it?"

"In spades, my friend, in spades."

An hour later both Dutch and Milo came trotting into my room, another huge bouquet of flowers held firmly in Dutch's hand. "Hey, boys," I said happily. I couldn't wait to get the hell out of here.

"Ready to go?" Dutch asked.

"Been ready," I said. I was already dressed, and hastily got out of bed. I was still a little woozy, but managed to cross to the wheelchair an orderly was holding for me. We took the elevator down as Milo plagued me with questions.

"So how did you find Andros's wife?"

"It's a long story," I said, not wanting to go through the whole thing all over again.

"Well, I gotta tell you, Abby, you really came through for us . . . again. Demetrius Kapordelis is under police watch downstairs, until he's well enough to face a judge."

"I saw him get shot. I can't believe he's still alive," I said.

"Yeah, he took one in the shoulder and another in the leg, but he should pull through without too much effort. Too bad the same can't be said for his victims."

"So what happened to everyone else?" I asked, meaning all the other men Andros had brought to the party.

"The only two who made it through were Demetrius and some guy named Augustus Ferolinus."

Odd as that name was to me, it still clicked a trigger in my brain. "Holy cow!" I said.

"What?" Dutch and Milo said together.

"Augustus Ferolinus is the guy who rammed into me! Now I can prove that he hit me, and I won't have to pay my deductible to get my car fixed!" I said happily.

Dutch and Joe both shuffled their feet uncomfortably, not making eye contact. "What?" I asked, swiveling in the chair to look at one, then the other.

Just then the elevator doors opened and we all swung out into the hallway. Neither man spoke until we reached the front lobby, where I put both feet on the ground, stopping the forward momentum of the wheelchair and refusing to go any farther until one of them told me what was wrong with my being happy about not having to pay my deductible.

Biting the bullet, Dutch leaned down and said, "You don't have to worry about a deductible, Abby. Your car didn't make it."

"What?" I asked, not understanding.

"The fire at your house . . . it spread to the garage . . . and your car."

I looked at him with my mouth open. I'd had that car for seven years! I *loved* that car!

Finally I pulled my feet up off the floor, allowing the orderly to continue, and as we exited out the automatic doors I slammed my fist on the arm of the wheelchair and sputtered, "Son of a bitch!"

Two weeks later I was cleaning up the breakfast dishes in the small kitchenette hotel room I was boarding in when I heard a knock on the door. It was Monday, and I had the whole day off and wasn't expecting visitors, so I went to the door suspiciously. After calming Eggy, who was back guarding me day and night, I peeked through the peephole and smiled as I recognized my visitor. I opened the door and shouted, "Dave!" as I jumped forward and hugged him.

"Morning," he said, giving me a quick squeeze and ruffling my hair. Eggy jumped up and down by Dave's feet until he bent over and picked him up, letting my puppy shower him with kisses.

"We've missed you." I giggled as Eggy went to town.

"I can see that." Dave laughed back.

"So," I said, waving him inside out of the cold, "what brings you by?"

"I wanted to see if you were willing to go for a drive with me?" Dave asked.

"What?" I asked, cocking an eyebrow at him. "A drive? To where?"

"Just come with me and I'll show you," Dave said, a small smile tugging at his mustache.

I shrugged my shoulders and reached for my coat. I had nothing better to do. "Can Eggy come?" I asked.

"Most definitely," Dave said, leading the way back out of the motel.

We headed down the outside stairwell to the parking lot. "So which one is yours?" he asked me, looking around at the parked cars.

"That one," I said, indicating the brand-new silver Mazda SUV parked nearby.

"Cool," Dave said enviously.

"That it is," I said, lifting Eggy into Dave's truck. We both got in, and Dave headed off, being conspicuously quiet about our destination.

My motel was just three blocks from my office, and I'd chosen it because it was cheap and convenient. It'd taken almost ten days to straighten out the insurance on my car, and it was going to take at least another ten to figure out the insurance on my house. I'd been by my old home only once; since the structure had burned almost completely to the ground, and it cut me to the quick that absolutely nothing had been spared.

I'd been told that arson investigators had determined that the fire had been made to look like it had been caused by my space heater, when in fact they'd been able to trace several small fires begun all over my bedroom, staircase and living room. Either Gargoyle or Goblin had made sure the fire would spread quickly and do the maximum amount of damage.

It had taken a while, but I'd come to terms with my recent ordeal with Kapordelis and his henchmen, and with the decisions I'd made as a result. As an intuitive, I'd like to believe that I hold myself to a higher moral code—and it was startling to me to discover that I was human after all.

As for the Kapordelis family . . . Well, my prediction that the estate would be run by the fourth son actually came true. After his father's death and his brother's arrest, Dorian Kapordelis shot himself up with enough heroin to put himself in a coma, and was currently in the same hospital as his brother. As a result his brain was mush, and he was never expected to fully recover.

Andros's second son, Darius, moved to California almost immediately following his father's funeral. He took only his trust fund and wanted nothing more to do with the family ever again. That left everything else to Ophelia, who was less than capable, but her new husband—Andros's fourth son *by marriage*—was more than able to handle the responsibility. I had little doubt that Jimmy was going to do away with his former father-in-law's unscrupulous businesses, and keep only those that made money legally. The Kapordelis legacy would be rejuvenated under his careful, moral care.

Madame Jarosolov had also been correct about my attending a funeral that was very sad, although she'd been off about the gender. Dutch and I had attended Josephine La Bond's funeral just two days after Kapordelis's death. It was a heart-wrenching affair, as her mother, father and brother all gathered around the closed casket, holding hands and leaning on each other. My heart went out to them, and I held on to Dutch a little tighter that afternoon.

These thoughts swirled in my head as Dave and I drove in companionable silence, the sound of classic rock wafting from the truck's speakers, and I watched the scenery pass with a detached sort of perspective. I'd been feeling homeless and sad of late, wanting the familiarity of my belongings, and no longer able to have that luxury. Dutch had offered to have me stay at his place until I made a decision on where I'd be living, but I didn't want our relationship, so fragile of late, to have that kind of pressure.

Besides, he was busy wrapping up all the loose ends from the Kapordelis case, and currently he was back in Florida, meeting with Nico again. He'd asked me to tell him where Dora was, but I'd declined. If she wanted to come forward, then that was her responsibility. For now, I figured she just needed some time to make that first move to reach out to a family who hadn't seen her in twenty years. It was better if she didn't have the pressure of answering a lot of questions from law enforcement while she worked up the courage.

Since my release from the hospital, Dutch and I had spent very little time together, as we'd both gone our separate ways the week before for Thanksgiving, which I'd spent at my sister's house, and Dutch at his parents' home in New York.

Thinking back on that week, I had to admit that it had been wonderful to see Cat, rested, tanned, and the gash on her forehead healing nicely. She seemed good as new as she bustled around playing hostess, and happy that she'd talked her staff into coming back, albeit the crew still seemed a little resentful of her short career as a psychic, as I caught a few of them making faces at her when her back was turned.

As far as catching Cat up to speed . . . well, I'd been very selective in doling out the details of my ordeal. She'd been in Aruba throughout most of the exciting

parts, and when she came home it had all been over—
with her none the wiser, which was exactly how I
planned to keep it.

She knew, of course, that the rapist had been caught,
and couldn't wait to testify against him when the trial
came around. She also knew that my house had burned
to the ground, but I'd managed to persuade her that it
was the result of a space heater left unattended, and not
at the hands of the local Mafia.

She'd also asked me about Goon, and I'd told her
only that he'd left the country headed to parts unknown.
She seemed appropriately sad at that news, and for some
odd reason, I was too.

Dave's truck hit a pothole suddenly, jolting the cab
on its springs, and me out of the moody thoughts swirling around in my brain. I looked curiously out the window at the passing scenery as Dave pulled down a quaint
side street just ten minutes from downtown. My brow
furrowed as he drove; where was he taking me?

When the truck pulled into a driveway and stopped,
Dave turned to me and said, "Now, I just want you to
keep an open mind, okay?"

"About what?" I asked. "Dave, where are we?" I
said, looking at the home we were in front of. There
were no other cars in the driveway and I wondered
whom I was here to meet. The house was a ranch, with
white brick and black shutters. A long deck-style porch
with huge flowerpots decorated the front, and a giant
oak tree, still holding on to a few of its leaves, hovered
overhead like a protective mother.

"Come with me," he said tauntingly, and got out of
the car.

I carried Eggy and followed Dave as he took me up
a walkway and onto the front porch of the ranch-style
home. He opened up the storm door and inserted a key
into the keyhole, opening the door wide and motioning
me inside. I stepped through the entrance and into a
large, spacious room, in the middle of reconstruction.

I looked a question mark at Dave, and he finally explained: "I took a job from a guy who had to relocate
to Colorado. He'd been in the middle of gutting the

place when he learned he had to move, so he hired me to finish the job. When he's finished with it he needs to sell it—quickly."

"Uh-huh," I said doubtfully, setting Eggy down and looking around. As my gaze took it in, I had to admit I really liked the room. It was large, open and airy with beautiful brand-new beech-wood floors. I took a few tentative steps and crossed into the kitchen.

Gorgeous new cherry-wood cabinets and granite countertops greeted my hungry eyes. All the appliances appeared to be brand-new too, and there was even an island between the sink and the dining area that was perfect for cutting and chopping.

I opened one of the cabinets and peered inside, then went through the kitchen inspecting the plumbing and fixtures. There was a separate entrance at the far end of the kitchen, and I followed it to a short hallway, which led to three bedrooms.

The master suite was at the end of the hallway and poking my head in I could see it was large and comfortable. Two more bedrooms flanked the master bedroom on each side. I checked out the master bathroom and the shower, which had new fixtures and a gigantic showerhead. Back down the hall was a small dining room, and this led into the living room, where Dave crouched, playing with Eggy while I continued to check things out.

I passed by him without a word, my mounting excitement building as I continued my tour. I headed out to the attached garage. Pressing a button I watched as the garage door swung up. I pressed the button again and the door came back down.

Next I went back to the kitchen and opened up the sliding glass door along one wall of the dining area, stepping out into the backyard. The space was large and fenced in. A birdbath was nestled in the middle of the yard, with shapely bushes and a bed perfect for flowers flanking one side of the house. Toward the back of the yard were two trees growing close together that still held a hammock between their trunks. Just then Dave came out with Eggy and set him loose to sniff around.

"So what do you think?" he asked, coming to stand next to me.

"You're sure this is within my price range?" I asked.

"Yep, I'm sure," he answered, rocking confidently back and forth on his heels.

I took my time answering, torturing him for not fessing up sooner in the truck. Finally, I turned to face him and said, "Sold," while I beamed him the full grille.